A Measure of Wheat for a Penny

By the same author

Pancardi's Pride

A Measure of Wheat for a Penny

Ron Clooney

Matador
9 De Montfort Mews
Leicester LE1 7FW, UK
Tel: (+44) 116 255 9311 / 9312
Email: books@troubador.co.uk
Web: www.troubador.co.uk/matador

ISBN 978-1848761-704

A Cataloguing-in-Publication (CIP) catalogue record for this book is available from the British Library

Typeset in 11pt Stempel Garamond by Troubador Publishing Ltd, Leicester, UK
Printed and bound in Great Britain by TJ International Ltd, Padstow, Cornwall

Matador is an imprint of Troubador Publishing Ltd

For the one who knew
I could write more than the one

Chapter 1

"He's still alive sir," said the nameless voice. "I can hear him breathing."

"Well get him out then," came the returned command.

"Yeah, it's always us that have to sort the scum out; I bet he's soaked too," a second man whispered under his breath as he snatched a crowbar from the ground. Punching it into the joint between the lid and the body of the box, "They always piss themselves," he muttered, "always."

Light stung his eyes as the lid of the rough-sawn pine-box was levered with a grunt. The sound of squealing nails and the scent of sawn wood, were replaced by the scrape of iron – shod boots on concrete and the stink of stale sweat.

A smiling face appeared at the edge of the box, looking down, "Mr. Verechico? It is Mr. Verechico, Michelangelo Verechico A.K.A. Michael Vaughan, isn't it?" asked the face, with a toothy grin.

The smiling man spoke with a broad accent and was dressed in military uniform. His hair was blonde and his eyes a startling blue; he almost looked Nordic and Verechico wondered if they might be in Sweden. It was cold and the air felt dry, a crisp dryness, which accentuated his parched palate and throat. The olive green and black jacket was smart and the man clearly had authority over those with the crowbars; they were in shirt sleeves and sweating. Michelangelo Verechico was trying to place the nationality of the officer and lock together the colour of the uniform, with the strong undertow of his accent. The red flashes at the neck and pockets, which ran at a jaunty angle, gave the uniform style, but the dull green was not complementary. This man wore a peaked cap with silver insignia, whilst the other men were bare headed. This man's English was good, and he was freshly shaven too; he had taken time over his appearance whilst some of the other men seemed more uncouth, almost slovenly. His teeth were white and he seemed sympathetic toward Verechico's predicament; Verechico deduced he was the officer in charge.

"I am so sorry for this method of travel," the commander continued, "but we needed to use diplomatic immunity and a box seemed most appropriate for us, or you." He paused, as if in genuine thought, "But, dare I say it is, a most uncomfortable method of travel for you. We attempted to line it with some padding but I'm afraid that has not been totally satisfactory; personally I think we should have used a coffin. You know lots of people never get to know what it feels like. Pleasant that's the way I'd describe it; homely, which I suppose it ought to be if you intend to spend eternity in it? " He smiled another toothy grin, "A four foot box, a foot for every year," he concluded.

"I don't get it?" Verechico spat in reply.

"Poetry, Mr. Verechico, poetry. The long and languid word play which separates us from animals. The thing which makes me," he paused, smiling again, "and you of course, more than a mere naked baboon. The world is full of baboons you can see them swinging from tree to tree every day, just look around you. They fill the supermarket trolleys and schools with their worthless offspring; they make repetitious noises, grunt and copulate; a marvellous end to the process of natural selection, don't you think?" The man laughed now, a bitter tinny laugh – a cruel laugh. "What have we achieved, after two world wars, the industrial revolution and the silicone chip? Pink clad scum, badly tattooed breeding sows and their mindless gorilla men. The proletariat, ah, the endless proletariat," he sighed heavily, "all plastic tits and tasteless jewellery and not a brain cell between them. The scum of humanity – pond life. My oh my, the future looks safe does it not? Do you read Mr. Verechico?" he paused and smiled again, "do you read poetry?"

Michelangelo Verechico was finding it hard to understand the situation he was in. One minute he had been talking to people at his club and the next he was here. There was nothing in his memory between the two. The last thing he could remember, was entering the Country Club for a brandy and soda with Major Arnold Vardhemmeyer of the South African Army. Vardhemmeyer had been a mercenary and also a devout believer in total war; he had worked in the Congo and Rwanda and whilst Verechico had found him slightly to the right of Attila the Hun, politically, he had been totally loyal and trust worthy. Vardhemmeyer was the kind of man that made an excellent friend and a terrible adversary, consequently Verechico respected him, despite his twisted political logic. The two of them often had a drink together and today had been no exception, a swift drink and chat and then off to the course to play a quick nine holes together.

Now he was waking up here, in some sort of hanger; he could see the corrugated roof above him and Vardhemmeyer was no where to be seen. Verechico's mind was racing, mentally retracing his steps; his mouth was dry and he needed to urinate. Where was he? Who were these people? He had been going to the toilet at the club house when everything went black and then nothing, nothing came into his mind. There was a gap, a lost space in time, and he had no idea how long it was, it could have been minutes or months.

"Stand up please," ordered the man with the accent.

Verechico pulled himself into the sitting position – his head swam. They were in some kind of warehouse; the walls were bare concrete blocks and the roof was grey corrugated steel. A tall, square, wooden post stood upright, wedged into the concrete floor; it stood like a tall, square tree, a sentinel, a totem pole. Looking upward he noticed there was rust and he was disorientated, his head thumped and he thought he might faint. At a table ahead there were men sitting, playing cards, and some chairs and more men with weapons, pacing. Then in the distance more men who sat cooking at stoves, with what looked like the old compo rations which the British army had long since phased out. His mind was dull and his fingers were unable to grip the edges of the rough wood with sufficient force to lift himself. It wasn't cold but the place looked austere, with sharp and piercing overhead neon lights which lit up the space like searchlights. There were large Salamander heaters which were blowing warm air through red hot elements for heating. At the far end of the building two covered vehicles were at the door end of the structure. Verechico thought one might be a tank, though his eyes could not focus fully, and the other some form of half-track transport vehicle. To his left there were several jeeps, some with machine guns mounted in the rear; these where lined up facing toward the door.

"You look a little confused Mr. Verechico?"

Verechico nodded, "I need the toilet," he said.

A large man, with hands the size of a frying pans, hauled Verechico to his feet. His knees wobbled and buckled slightly but he remained upright.

"Meet Sergeant Kernov Mr. Verechico," the officer said. "Mikhail," he then ordered, "help Mr. Verechico to the toilet."

"I don't need any help I'm not a child," said Verechico.

"Oh we know that," said the commander, "we know precisely what you are."

"I just need to pee," Verechico felt a stabbing pain in his lower abdomen as he spoke. "Where the hell is the toilet?" he asked.

"Over there," the Nordic man pointed, "the large bath in the corner. "It's primitive I'm afraid, but there is a little problem with the plumbing here today. There has been a very sharp frost and this old plumbing was not really intended for modern habitation. The pipes and drains seem to be frozen, alright for the cold war and I mean cold." He laughed at his own joke, "Typical of the old regime."

"What?" asked Verechico, whilst loudly relieving himself into the bath.

"Happened?" interrupted the officer, "drugged, I'm afraid."

"What?"

"Drugged," he repeated, "we drugged you and put you in that box and well the rest you know."

Verechico zipped his fly and asked, "Where the hell am I?"

The Nordic man laughed and then continued, "Well actually you are in hell. Allow me to give you some detail." He turned to one of the men, "A chair for Mr. Verechico, Corporal Perchenko."

A small dark and swarthy man pushed a chair into the back of Verechico's knees and forced him to sit by pushing down on his shoulders. Verechico buckled and sat.

Drawing up a chair opposite Verechico the officer placed a pack of cigarettes on the desk to his left and casually drawing one out lit it, then flicking the pack at Verechico said, "Help yourself please, we are all friends here."

"I don't smoke," Verechico replied.

"We know, but I was merely being polite. Manners make...eth man, don't you agree?"

"Well where are the manners in this then?" asked Verechico looking around.

"Ah, yes, introductions first," he replied. "Please allow me to give you some detail.

My name is Alexei Vissarianovich Ulyanov – my rank is Colonel KGB."

"What do you mean KGB, this is the twenty first century and you, I mean the KGB, don't exist anymore," Verechico erupted. "The Berlin wall is down and ..."

"But we very much do exist, am I not here now?" The officer raised his arms as if in acclamation.

"If you are KGB then we must be in Russia?" Verechico stated.

"Mr. Verechico I will now tell you these things to be polite." He smiled, "You were abducted from your country and flown in a box to Leningrad, though you will know this place as St. Petersburg. You were drugged and deposited here for interrogation."

"For what?"

"Interrogation."

"So where the hell are we?" Verechico asked angrily.

"I thought I had already answered that one. I think I said you were in hell – in fact this is likely to be the worst of all your nightmares. Would you like some coffee?" He threw the remark in much as an actor makes a dramatic aside. "I expect you are rather dehydrated, synpolycarsulphidine can play havoc with human water retention."

"Synpoly what?"

"Synpolycarsulphidine, it's what you were drugged with," Ulyanov nonchalantly replied. "It's one of our new drugs, but it does have horrible side effects. Urine retention being one, but you already know about that," he laughed. "I expect you thought your bladder would explode. As to our precise location, we are between Pikalevo and Borisovo-Sudskoye."

Verechico was racking his brain for a location, just in case an escape might be possible. All he could think of, was the coast opposite Finland, while he tried to calculate the distance to Helsinki by water.

"We are in air force base 417 of the atomic weapons institute." Ulyanov spun around making a three hundred and sixty degree turn, "All this was once home to our bombers. A grand Cathedral of the United Soviet Socialist Republic." He raised his arm like someone giving a guided tour, "Isn't it wonderful?" he laughed raucously.

"So I'm in Russia?" Verechico questioned again, unable to quite believe the reply.

"Correct."

"Why Russia?" asked Verechico, his head clearing from the calculations.

"I think we both know the answer to that question don't we Mr. Verechico?"

Verechico shook his head.

"Oh please Mr. Verechico, there is absolutely no need to be so obtuse."

Verechico shook his head again.

"Then let me explain." Ulyanov smiled a toothy grin, "You are a thief? And you had the temerity to steal something that belongs to me and my colleagues. That was rather naughty of you." He paused, wagging a finger as if admonishing a small child, "Have I given you any clues yet?"

Verechico shock his head, but his brain was racing ahead to be ready.

"The Banko Rolo in Florence?" Ulyanov questioned. "A little matter of the Romanov jewels? The jewels which you and your colleagues spirited away in the night? A very clever plan – yours?"

Verechico gave no reaction in either his facial expression or his body language.

"I thought so," Ulyanov paused, "you are a very clever man, but not nearly clever enough. Having examined the robbery and questioned all of our contacts, we now realise that you could never have made that job work unless you had insider information. Paul

West and your man Drecht, they did not have that capability – the real brains that was you. So who was your contact on the inside? That question will be answered shortly, once and for all."

Again Verechico gave no reaction.

"A very clever plan I must say and it was executed with precision, what a shame about the German and the DNA match. I thought you would be clever enough only to use people who had no criminal record. That was your one silly mistake, apart from West." Ulyanov paused again, "You see he was the weak link, he was too greedy and you should have foreseen that much."

Verechico smiled, but he knew that the information which Ulyanov had collected was precise. It was probably the same information which Interpol now held and these Russians might have even more from that wretched Italian detective Pancardi.

"We know that Paul West and his comrades made it to Canada. We know all about the plane crash and the fact that all of them were killed, all of them except this woman, Parsotti." Ulyanov paused thoughtfully, "And we shall find her too, just as we did you," he reflected. "But that still leaves the matter of the jewels which you sold and the missing emeralds which have not yet gone on to the market. Am I getting warm here?" He drew a pistol and placed it on the table before him.

"So now you're going to try to intimidate me with that?" Verechico asked.

"Oh no," Ulyanov replied, "we don't do threats. If we were going to intimidate you, you would know, and besides," he smiled, "we are all friends here."

"If you know so much, then you must know that all of that team are dead," Verechico proffered. "There were absolutely no survivors from the plane that crashed."

"You are being slippery now Michelangelo, please do call me Alexei, by the way. We are all friends now," smirked Ulyanov. "You know as well as I do that the woman got away. Also that she got a way with some of the jewels, some of the very best Russian emeralds. Do you think that killing Drecht would throw us off the scent? If they are all dead why are you waiting for some of these special," he drooled the word, special, "jewels to come onto the open market? Why?" He smiled broadly, "Because you know she is alive and if she starts to sell you can trace her. Revenge, and the need of it, is a terrible curse is it not?"

"They are all dead – all of them. They found two of the bodies, and the others were probably spread all over the mountains like raspberry jam," Verechico blurted.

"Really?" Ulyanov's voice was rasping and sarcastic, "So why is the case still an open file for Interpol then? And more importantly why are you still waiting for those lost emeralds to appear? Perhaps you believe in ghosts? You are a greedy little thief and now you have been found out – your greed is how we found you. You should have taken your share and run, crawled into a deep hole in the ground, but you had to have those emeralds. You know someone got away, someone special and clever – the girl did didn't she?"

Verechico said nothing.

"The girl is alive," Ulyanov snapped, "she is still alive. The others are all dead except the girl."

"She was just a fuck bunny for Paul West and he's dead," Verechico barked in sudden reply. "Besides Drecht stole those special emeralds, not her, she was just an amusement and he squirreled them away somewhere, somewhere so secret they might not come to light for a thousand years."

"A fuck bunny," Ulyanov paused grinning, "what an interesting turn of phrase."

"Well she was," said Verechico defensively. "She was very attractive, and she looked like the sort of girl who could get milk out of a crow-bar, that was her contribution to the world."

"And you like all the rest, were seduced by this simple fact?" asked Ulyanov.

"No, I never slept with her, if that's what you mean," replied Verechico.

"But you would have done?" asked Ulyanov, "if you had had the chance."

"Perhaps?"

"I'm sure you didn't," said the Russian. "If you had done then you would be dead by now."

"Don't be so ridiculous, she was just a bit of tail like I said."

"That is the trouble with you westerners," Ulyanov was cutting now, "you underestimate your women. During my father's time a woman could be as deadly as any man. You need neither strength nor stamina to pull a trigger, he used to say. All you need is a calm hand and a cold heart. Look to the Israelis if you want proof. Look at Vietnam and you will have countless examples of the female warrior. Michelangelo your male arrogance and testosterone ignorance are astounding, you are thinking with your balls. "

"Ok then, why have none of those emeralds, which I know Drecht had," he qualified quickly, "come on to the market?" Verechico asked.

"But they have," Ulyanov replied. "And you know they have, because you like many others have been looking for this Parsotti woman or whatever her name is, too. The Alsetti family gave some of the jewels provenance, but others have started to appear, just one or two at a time. "

Verechico remained silent, his decoy ploy had not been taken as bait, the Russian was far cleverer than he had anticipated.

Ulyanov's voice was cold now, passionless, remote, "If Drecht had them he could not have sold them unless like Lazarus he has risen from the grave. You shot him, did you not and rolled his body into a carpet to hide it, or was that West's idea?" He raised his voice, and spittle landed on the Italian's facc as hc spoke, "No Mr. Verechico you stole my jewels, my inheritance and you expect me now to roll over and simply let you walk away?" He paused. "That is rather foolish of you don't you think? Surely you must have expected the owners to come after them. Unless of course your naivety extended into believing the Romanov family themselves put them there, long after their deaths?"

Verechico tilted his head to the side, "Your inheritance?"

"Precisely! My grandfather wanted us to have something and how right he was. Look at the mess my country is in now. You capitalista and carpet baggers are bleeding it dry. The people need something to inspire them, there has to be more than greed and lust to human existence, would you not agree?" He paused and smiled widely, "But," he said, "I would hardly expect you to understand, after all you are a thief and murderer." His eyes met Verechico's and their stare was intense, "I want the money and all of my jewels back," he said coldly. "You are just a thief, a worthless piece of scum."

"Oh spare me the anti-capitalist drivel, you are just like all the rest, as greedy as hell," Verechico retaliated.

"You are very fond of the word hell are you not?" asked Ulyanov. "It is not a word we use so readily here in Russia – we have Siberia after all."

"Balls," replied Verechico.

"So now you are angry?" Ulyanov smiled broadly, "I like the fighting spirit it reminds me of my..."

"I don't have your bloody diamonds or emeralds."

"I know," Ulyanov replied, "I want information, the names of all the members of the gang and I want to know everything you can tell me? Did you honestly think we would take this lying down? That is our money – money set aside for our re-taking of power."

"What another Bolshevik revolution, or is it the Mensheviks this time? No doubt your grandfather will be turning in his cement filled cadaver."

"You are a very clever little man," Ulyanov sneered, "but not quite clever enough, or you would not be here now, would you?"

"Well it did not take too much thought. Leningrad and your age gave it away. I suppose like some would-be fictional, Bond novel, megalomaniac, you are going to take over Russia and then eventually the world."

"That Mr. Verechico is quite, quite, absurd," replied Ulyanov. "We just want our money, our nest egg. Am I looking to create another revolution, that could be an interesting idea, but at present I simply have bills to pay. "

"What capitalist heaven, your own private little Red Army, just like Uncle Joe." Verechico sneered, "I mean you got the Vissarianovich, from him did you not?"

"You are indeed a very clever and highly observant man Mr. Verechico, but let us not be too hasty shall we? You are after all just a petty thief first and foremost and that is not so noble a profession is it? And you are not that careful; if we could find you so can others."

"Well, grandson of the illustrious Vladimir Ilyich Ulyanov, or should I say Lenin. I am shaken but really not stirred," Verechico replied.

Ulyanov roared with laughter, he was almost unable to

respond, "But you will be I'm sure, when our next guest arrives." He was chuckling now, the laughter subsiding, "I think then, it will all make perfect sense. I just hope that your Bond-like bravado continues when you are faced with choices. It will make the whole thing far more entertaining for me. You see that was always the problem in the east the neon lights of Berlin faced outward, toward us; many nights I saw them when I was just a young border guard, and Russia can be so dull and grey."

"So now you want some of the bright lights and big city?" Verechico sneered in disgust.

"That," said Ulyanov, "you see, was always the problem with communism, even Mao made the same mistake. Everything grey, everything uniform, no spark, next time it will all be different. There can be individuals," Ulyanov paused, "how do you say – I do not need to blow your candle out to make mine glow brighter?"

"Oh please," sighed Verechico, "spare me the political indoctrination and shallow platitudes, you are just a capitalist by another name."

"Believe what you will thief," Ulyanov ejaculated. "There is a way to have the bright lights and to share common goals without the usurpation of others. Is it not possible to look after the sick and the elderly? Is that not the civilised thing to do? Why must everything be money? "

Verechico scoffed, "Oh please."

"Yes really," Ulyanov, replied. "You see your capitalism doesn't work does it? It's fine for those with money and power and for those without it, well," he paused, "they can steal it, or they can die."

"What like you did the Romanov jewels?"

"That was a revolution," Ulyanov snapped. "A revolution!"

"It was murder, nothing less," Verechico stated blandly. "And was it your wonderful grandfather, the saviour of Russia, who ordered the executions?"

"Spoken like a true capitalist. Every man for himself and the devil take the hind most?" Ulyanov paused as if in thought, "Mmm, an interesting notion, bearing in mind that at this present time you are the hind most." He laughed, "So how does that make you feel? About to sup with devils and you seem to have forgotten your long spoon." He tut-tutted and shook his head, smirking, "Rather silly of you don't you think?"

A large guard dressed in green appeared behind Ulyanov and spoke quietly into his ear. Verechico could not make out what was being said, but Ulyanov's facial reaction suddenly became serious.

"This has all been rather interesting," he said, "but all good things come to an end."

Verechico watched him rise from his seat, light a cigarette and walk over to some uniformed men. There was a discussion in Russian and he wished that he had studied the language a little more. He could make out one or two words, cloth being one and prisoner being the other. Then casually Ulyanov returned, crushing the cigarette under his heel as he approached.

"And as if on cue," the cruel Russian chuckled, "it seems our second guest has just arrived, wonderful," he snorted, "absolutely wonderful."

Chapter 2

Alice Parsotti walked down the length of Dubai airport lounge thankful that the air conditioning was working. Her legs had always been her best asset and they sparkled with femininity, as they crossed foot before foot in her hip swinging roll of the catwalk. The Italian passport she carried was in the name of Claudette Cicello with an occupation listed as a model and she was looking the part.

All of her planning had been carefully executed and now she just needed to get back to Europe.

Every man that saw her pass wanted her, except for the thin wizened Arab who was greedily checking the price of sovereigns at the gold counter. For many travellers a drink of alcohol had the same calming affect, for him it was the lustrous glint of gold. Staring at the bars and blocks of yellow metal his heart began to race; he could buy as many Parsotti as he needed; they were as plentiful as camels, and a quick glance told him that the young Romanian girl he had recently purchased, to slake his carnal thirst, was far better looking. He did not like this fake blonde, but could not rationalise his repulsion, she just looked hard-bitten, cold and self–confident, whereas, his new young mare had red hair and was extremely compliant and subservient to his wants. As Alice passed he caught her scent but gave it no more than a cursory thought-it was the gold bars that really caught his eye.

The flight from Male had been tedious but Emirate airlines had been a fine method of anonymous travel, anonymous enough to partially disappear. She binned the vile milkshake she had just bought and wondered how strawberries had become so synthetic. The pink gloop tasted of additives, e numbers and factory produced plastic and not of fresh fruit and freedom. She had travelled economy class to avoid the possibility of detection but men had noticed her despite that. Men who sat next to nagging wives, wives that drove them to build sheds in their gardens for escape and play golf at every opportunity. Men who had long since lost the heart for their relationship; men who drank too much and fantasized about having their own porn princess-she despised them all.

The seats were too small and she had been squashed between too fat Americans who constantly complained. The woman had been talking across her and eventually she had offered to exchange seats so the fat bores could sit together. Once that had happened her new seat offered the seedy middle-aged mummy's boy a chance to talk at her. She wondered if he was on the way back from a ball-draining holiday for sad emotionally inadequate men. She considered Pattaya to Colombo and then gave up the notion in favour of feigned sleep.

Now, in the airport lounge, she studied them, the assorted travellers; she sat waiting for the call on the connection to Heathrow and ate the chocolate covered dates which she had purchased to ease the cool of the milkshake. The replacement cold coke was welcome and at least that gave her a sense of normality.

"Hi little lady," said a voice behind her. "We were on the same flight. I noticed you but, hell I bet you didn't me?"

She smiled at the man who was wearing an Arab head dress, chewing gum and leering at her with bulbous eyes and a lolling tongue. In a strange way she was reminded of Duane Rightman and she fantasized about shooting this insidious bore there and then. Just like she had Rightman in Canada. She had a brief vision of him flying backward clutching at his testes, which she had just blown from his body. Instead she smiled, but thought, why on earth would I notice you, you nondescript moron.

"Mind if I join ya?" He made some motion with his head toward the seat next to her.

She shrugged and replied, "There's no one sitting there."

Having sat down he launched into the clumsiest of interrogation lines and tried to find out precisely where she was going, whether she was single, on holiday, or, in transit. It was as if the confines of the plane had stifled his approach and having gained more space and privacy he could now launch his purposeful full frontal attack.

She noticed his hair and the laughter-lines around his eyes. Once, perhaps twenty years before, he could have sparkled but now after years of throwing his wares against the rocks of beauty he was broken. Hunting out of his league and desperate to the point of hilarity, he stood there trying so hard to be interesting, funny and a charmer. Alice wanted to get him by the ears and twist his head and tell him to find some desperate divorcee who needed an honest father for her children and not be a man trying to pretend he was still in his prime. She estimated his age at forty, but the thinning hair and the growing gut made any guess closer than ten years impossible. She imagined him naked, naked and advancing, fully erect and menacing.

"London," she shuddered, almost unable to control her laughter.

She could sense that his sexual desperation would make him climax quickly.

"I bet you are a model," he said to complement her.

"Well actually I am a model," she said in reply.

His eyebrows raised and he knew now he had seen her somewhere before but he couldn't quite place her. The images in his mind were spinning through the various adverts, but her face appeared in all of them now; he wondered if he should ask more, but thought he might appear cooler if he didn't. He felt it was his lucky day. He wondered if she shaped her pubic hair into heart, a Brazilian, or settled for the full Hollywood. He knew her skin would be smooth and his eyes strayed to the pert nipples pushing against the fabric of her top. He wanted to reach out and squeeze them and, in consequence, his eyes stayed too long; he cursed his inability to hide his lust. Inwardly Alice chuckled at his discomfort and wondered if he were sporting a growing erection right now.

She listened carefully to his chat about himself, and like all men he would have bored her rigid had he not been able to serve a purpose. Had he been handsome and lithe, no doubt they would have rolled around in a hotel bed together until either one or both were exhausted. But this man was overweight, over confident and over reaching, and the combination of the three made him vulnerable to suggestion. Her voice grew soft and her eyes widened and the moist backdrop gave them a truly seductive appeal. The more she looked at him the more he wanted her; the more he showed interest, the more enticing she became. The circle of seduction begun, Alice knew that by the time they reached England he would have to relieve the tension somehow. She thought him a pathetic loser – a man destined to remain single. A man locked inside the mind of an eternal teenager, but she smiled broadly as he continued to waffle.

He on the other hand was amazed by his success and was having fantasies of her sitting astride him as they spoke. He could imagine her bucking in the reverse cowgirl and the mere thought of it made small beads of sweat appear at his temples. He could smell her perfume and trying to place it, pondered, should he ask, should he not? His mind dashed back and forth across that divide; he was clutching at every straw now and yet he still felt himself drowning. He continued to talk and Alice laughed at the banal jokes and listened intently to his boring stories of friends. She was finding it hard to stay awake, and resorted to memory recall as an aid. First a Shakespeare sonnet about roses, and then alteration in love, finally she was onto Richard Church and then Auden. The rhythm of the man's voice was lulling her to sleep, she imagined stapling his tongue to a notice board and leaving him there to miss the flight. She hoped they weren't seated next to each other on the way to London, she could so easily kill again.

"This is such a long flight isn't it?" she said, turning the conversation. "Sixteen hours and then I have to travel to Birmingham by train, that's after I get to London."

"Yeah travel is tiring," he replied sympathetically.

"And my flat will be all dark and lonely," she added.

"I have a place in London," he blurted.

"Oh lucky you," she giggled.

"You are welcome to stay there tonight and then you could go on in the morning. I have nothing to do. I'm not due back in the office for three more days and ..."

"Are you sure?" she giggled coquettishly.

He could see her now stepping out of his shower her hair wet and the small pearls of moisture forming on the floor as he stroked her legs and back. He wondered what it would be like to lick the moisture from her skin – to taste her.

"I've got spare rooms," he said defensively.

"Lovely, that's very kind of you," she said, fully aware of his kindness and masculine intentions. "I just need a little space to curl up in."

She continued to entice him by holding eye contact and playing upon his ulterior motives.

His mind was racing through fantasies and he could not believe his luck – a model no less.

"Where precisely is your place?" she asked almost casually.

"Oh not far ," he replied, "a short taxi ride to Stamford Street near Waterloo, close to the Elephant and Castle," he paused, "well on the corner virtually, just over Blackfriars bridge and you're into central London."

"It sounds charming," she said, thinking of the possible police surveillance at the airport.

She needed cover, perhaps they would not have identified the body yet. They were slow but she felt certain that Blondell would be on his way. He simply would not give up and as a result she had made that stupid immigration mistake. One silly miscalculation and Interpol had been alerted – she would not make that mistake again. She cursed the man and knew that she would have to be more serious about a deterrent. She had the perfect solution planned for him, it would give him the dichotomy of purpose that he was lacking and it would certainly get him off her back.

It was then some two hundred yards distant she spotted a face she knew, a face close to her immediate thoughts – Blondell's face. She watched him over the shoulder of her now almost salivating companion. She saw him standing near gate 14, he seemed to be waiting – waiting for a colleague. Her mind was playing and re-playing with a stuck needle, the single expletive, fuck; while her eyes searched the crowds, scanning the faces.

"This is so," she drooled the so, as if she were whispering encouragements into his ear during his frenzied climax, "very kind of you," she said.

She checked the flight board it clearly read gate 14 a flight to Male. She checked the flight gate for Heathrow it read 12.

"Perhaps we could have dinner when we get back," the man

was talking nonsense now, his voice was cracking and, to her, he was becoming an irritation.

She studied Blondell and knew that if he even glimpsed her she would be recognised. She wished she had flown via Oman instead of taking a rest stop in Dubai. Better still, a non – stop flight would have been quicker, but she wanted this stop to see how things were progressing. If there had been a problem, she would have received an early warning and she could have slipped off into the desert and worked her way back overland. She was beginning not to fully trust her own judgement and that made her jittery and that, made her make mistakes. Blondell was never going to give up, just like her father, she could see that now.

She watched him, he was older than when last they crossed swords. She wanted to go over to him and ask about her mother and father, about their relationship and why Pancardi had deserted her when he had found out she had been pregnant. Perhaps Pancardi had discussed it with him during the hunt for her? They were colleagues after all. Blondell certainly had an amazing amount of detail which he could only have gleaned from her father. Part of her wanted to walk over to the man and punch the truth out of him; another part wanted to listen and evaluate and understand. It would be so nice if she could walk over and they could just talk like human beings, but he was the enemy, the person coming to take her down. She noted he was alone and calm, but she scanned every corner cautiously; he was reading the paper now and sitting with his head down and his mind absorbed. He was off-duty and on low alert, she thought, he would not expect her to be there, he wasn't looking for her – if he was he would have found her right now. She scanned the area for other officers who might be attached and yet distant. There were no observers except the armed security guards who constantly swept the corridors as casually as road sweepers, she watched them intently.

"I know this nice little place," said a male voice.

"Lovely," she replied distractedly.

Her eyes continued to scan for observers, casual high-alert tourists. She knew how Interpol worked, maybe Blondell was just the bait and she was now the wild animal about to have the cage closed around her. She scanned for possible exit points – her heart was racing.

"I like Italian," she said almost listlessly.

"Oh in that case Guido's is the palace for us. A palace for a princess," he laughed at his own joke.

"Charming," she replied, wishing she could staple his tongue to his forehead to shut him up, or better still chop it out with scissors. Perhaps when they were back at his rat-hole flat she'd do that for him. Anything would be an improvement on the current state of affairs. The man was irritating and bordering on the lunatic. His desperation was so apparent it could be viewed in the aura which surrounded him. She had no intention of dining with this idiot at some Mr. Dolmio restaurant and then going back to his pokey little flat and screwing his brains out. She looked at him, his broad inane grin was in the left of frame and Blondell was clearly visible in the right over his shoulder. He had not moved, he was still reading the paper.

"You'll have to excuse me," she suddenly said, "just need to pop to the little girls' room before we get airborne. I hate those little cubicles on the plane."

"I know I hate those toilets too," said the man, "so confined but great if you're part of the mile high club."

She didn't reply but rose and walked quickly toward the toilets. She guessed he would be lucky to get sex at all with that clumsy joke, let alone in the public cubicles of an aircraft. Luckily the toilets lay in the opposite direction to Blondell. She was up now, up and walking, not looking back – she hoped he was still reading the paper.

The man who had been attempting the chat-up was lost, he thought that his banter had put her off, that she was trying to get away. Perhaps he had ruined his own chances; he was cursing and then rose to call after Alice.

"Hey we haven't introduced ourselves," he called, "Miles, I'm in 12 F."

She knew that turning around was impossible, her blood froze and she hoped Blondell was far enough away not to have noticed her movement and this chump's sudden desperation. She turned into the vast area of sinks and cubicles and slipped into one – the place seemed empty.

Inside the cubicle she removed her knickers and sat with her handbag between her feet. If Blondell had seen her it would only be a matter of seconds before they arrived. She checked her watch. She sat and waited. Five minutes passed .She thought of the idiot outside who was probably waiting, scanning the door for her to reappear. Her ticket read 68 B, so she was near the back of the plane and he was up front. She thanked the anonymous check in clerk.

She wondered why he thought that a woman in an airport might find him attractive -attractive enough to sleep with. Was he mad? Had he never heard himself nor looked in a mirror? He was a repulsive little worm of a man who should have been drowned in a bucket at birth, though he saw himself as the proud possessor of the gift for womankind. She smiled, checked her watch – seven minutes.

She could hear foot steps approaching, voices, and the hand dryer working. She checked her watch and wished she had noted the departure time for Blondell's flight. Nine minutes.

On the Tannoy her flight was being called, "Would passengers for flight 5482 to London, please go to gate 12 as the flight is now ready for boarding."

She checked her watch – twelve minutes.

She calculated she had twenty minutes max and then she would have to leave anyway or miss the flight. She'd go now, take the risk while the gates were busy; she'd walk down casually and simply pass, far easier than being the last name called, that might cause suspicion. Blondell would not be expecting to see her so he might not even notice her. It was a big gamble but there was no alternative.

She put her knickers in her bag, took a deep breath, flushed and stepped out of the cubicle.

Chapter 3

The sight which greeted Michelangelo Verechico was the one he least expected. After carrying in a pine box, identical to the one in which he had arrived, the uniformed men placed it near the table under Ulyanov's direction. The same crow bars were then applied and the squeaking whine as the nails were drawn from the wood echoed around the empty hanger. Like a gift whore in a birthday cake he half expected Alice Parsotti to leap out of the box and burst into song. The reality was quite different.

"Well," asked Ulyanov of his men, "is it dead?"

"It looks like it's breathing sir," piped Perchenko.

"Well what are you waiting for?" asked Ulyanov.

Verechico was straining to see past the mass of uniforms which were now crowding around the coffin-like box. He thought he could see glimpses of red and black material and he was half expecting Alice Parsotti to be standing upright and partially naked, with a group of leering men around her. Instead a lump rose in his throat as the crowd of Russian soldiers cleared.

"May I introduce Monsignor Cardinal Marco Cigannini," laughed Ulyanov. "Cardinal allow me to introduce, Michelangelo Verechico, professional thief." He paused, "But you already know each other don't you, how foolish of me?"

Verechico shook his head, but said nothing.

The Cardinal simply replied, "I do not know this man. Why am I here?"

"You are here Monsignor because you are the worst kind of clergyman that money can buy. You are the scum which sells its opiate to the masses and looks to the collection plate to feed your excesses," Ulyanov replied. "You are everything I despise in a man of faith and now you and this mindless imbecile," he nodded at Verechico, "have conspired to steal from me that which is rightfully mine."

"It was never yours," hissed Verechico under his breath.

Ulyanov spun on his heel and his voice was loaded with venom and hatred of the church, "Never mine? It was more mine than yours, you pair of broken down old crooks." He turned to the priest, "And how many Hail Mary did you say as you fed information on the Banko Rolo to this man? The bank run by your church for the beatification of God. Was God instructing you through your prayers to steal from the Catholics?"

"I think there has been some confusion," said the Cardinal, as he regained his composure.

Verechico marvelled at the man's bladder control after being drugged. Then he noticed the dark damp stain against the black robes and he knew the reason.

"And why my son would..." the Cardinal began, before he was interrupted.

"Do not, do not, never, call me your son," Ulyanov shrieked, "you sanctimonious, hypocritical thief. We'll have none of your pathetic religious tricks here. My men and I don't have time for games. You can keep your false understanding and your sympathetic whine for those who will listen. Don't try to sell me your opiate, you deranged drug dealer."

Verechico caught the eye of the priest and the recognition was instantaneous. So was the immediate mutual communication to say nothing .Though they had only met briefly once in a coffee shop in Rome the meeting had meant that the seeds of an idea on the Banko Rolo had been germinated. Cardinal Cigannini had provided the photographs of the viewing area inside the vaults and Verechico had passed these to Drecht who had, in turn, passed them to Paul West and his team of cracksmen.

Ulyanov's voice held all of the cruelty and anti-religious sentiment of the first Russian revolution. His use of the word opiate had been a direct reference to his grandfather Lenin and he knew it would both incense and unnerve the priest. Verechico however, was more concerned with what precisely this Russian really knew.

"Sit Monsignor," Ulyanov barked, as the same small man who had made Verechico sit appeared behind the priest with a chair and pushed him to his seat.

"I don't have time for games," he continued, "I want to know where the woman Parsotti is? Where my money is and the whereabouts of those residual jewels which Mr. Verechico's thieves left behind? But most of all I want to know where those priceless missing gems are now? Actually I want more than that I want them back. There are several emeralds and diamonds unaccounted for, where are they now?"

The priest shrugged, "Many things are not known to me."

"And you seriously expect me to believe that? That you, who knew so much, now know so little?"

"There is nothing to say," replied the priest, "I simply know nothing."

"Then we will find out from both of you, who precisely knows what," said Ulyanov, his calm self assurance restored.

"This much I do know," proffered the Cardinal, in an attempt to placate, "the jewels that were left were impounded as artefacts of history and I believe they are going to become part of a state exhibition on Tsarist Russia."

"You mean a museum?"

"I think so," said the Cardinal in reply. "I believe that some of your government are involved in the process."

"That," Ulyanov replied, "would be most appropriate." He paused thoughtfully, "Are they not charlatans, thieves and crooks? Just like the Romanovs they would bleed the nation dry. They are the sickeningly weak voice of corruption. Rags to rags in three generations."

"So would you have the rule of Stalin return?" asked the priest.

Ulyanov erupted, "What I would have," he roared, "is the sense of the masses. The sense to know that those who are now in charge of my country are nothing more than crooks." He looked at Verechico, "And do you think the rulers of Europe are any better? Are the Italians less corrupt, are the French, the British?" He paused in thought, "The truth is we are ruled by lesser men. The sons of men who did not go to war, but the residual scum which was left behind to breed. We, like no other animal, have managed to slaughter and bury our future greatness and allow the rubbish to procreate."

"You are beginning to sound like someone from the opposite end of the political spectrum," Verechico remarked. "Perhaps you are really nothing more than a simple fascist?"

Verechico was beginning to wonder whether the Russian was mentally unbalanced. His logic seemed skewed at times and, in consequence, he was likely to be unpredictable and dangerous.

"There is no point in continuing in this manner," Ulyanov smirked, his calm regained. "You have your beliefs and I have mine; the real issue is the information which I seek."

"And there my son," said the Cardinal, "is where only God can help."

Ulyanov roared with laughter. His eyes streamed with tears, "Spoken like a true Catholic," he said. "Petrov, cutters!" he shouted.

Within seconds the left hand of the priest had been nailed to the table through the centre of his palm. There had been a struggle and the large Sergeant Kernov and Corporal Perchenko had to subdue the priest as the nail was driven home. Verechico had watched as the blood spurted up the nail and ran over the Cardinal's fingers. The large man had held his wrist in place, while the younger swarthy man, who had seated Verechico, drove the nail home. There had been a sickening crunch as the hammer drove the nail through the flesh and bone and the priest had screamed as the pain bit.

Verechico sat in his chair transfixed by the sheer cruelty of the action.

"So shall we start again?" asked Ulyanov.

The Cardinal was studying his hand which was now fixed to the table.

"I am going to ask you some simple questions Monsignor. If you give me the answers I wish to hear then there will be no problem. If you lie, then Petrov here, will remove each one of your finger tips," he nervously licked his lips, "one by one. Do you understand?"

The priest seemed unable to muster an answer and Ulyanov's reaction was swift in response, "Water Petrov!" he barked.

The grinning man threw a bucket of water over the priest.

Verechico thought he looked like Peter Lorre in some bizarre technicolor pastiche of a Humphrey Bogart movie; he had the feeling that the man liked this kind of work a little too much.

"Listen carefully Monsignor," said Ulyanov. "Petrov the cutters."

The priest raised his head to see a man place the tip of his thumb into the jaws of a set of bolt cutters. Petrov, the man working the cutters, was grinning like a mad child at a zoo outing. Clearly he had done this kind of work before and the priest could see the naked enjoyment glistening in his eyes.

"Wonderful things thumbs," Ulyanov remarked, "are they not? Now I shall ask you a question and you will answer. The right answer and you keep your thumb – wrong and you lose it."

Petrov closed the jaws of the cutter at the joint and the priest froze.

"A simple one first?" Ulyanov asked.

Monsignor Cigannini nodded.

"Did you pass to this man plans of the inside of the Banko Rolo?" He nodded toward Verechico.

The priest shook his head and Ulyanov nodded to Petrov. There was a quick click which was followed by a deafening scream. Verechico saw the tip of the Cardinal's thumb fly across the table.

"Wrong answer," said Ulyanov with a cold and clinical calm. He turned to Verechico, "Perhaps I should ask you in the same manner?"

"No need," Verechico replied, "I would like to keep my thumbs. The plans did come from the Cardinal here."

"Good, good," laughed Ulyanov, "you are a quick learner." He turned to the man with the cutter, "index," was all he said.

The second question was short, "Do you know Alice Parsotti?"

The priest shook his head and Ulyanov nodded for a second time. There was a click once again and the tip of the Cardinal's finger fell to the table.

"You don't seem to have got the hang of this do you?" the Russian sneered. "Let's try again shall we? How about two fingers together next time?"

The Cardinal was shaking his head.

"All you have to do Monsignor is give me the correct answers. All too simple really. Then we all get to go home? And you still have some fingers left to claw money from the collection plate."

The priest was nodding now.

"So we'll try again shall we? And if you get it wrong this time you lose all but the little finger on that hand. Then we start on the other, then the toes." He paused, "And when the pain gets too much we'll give you a pain killer and then we'll carry on." He grabbed the priest by the chin and forced him to make eye contact, "You see I am a reasonable man," he said. "So did you ever meet the man Drecht?"

The priest shook his head.

"Never? Are you sure?"

The priest shook his head.

"Have you now got some of my jewels?"

The priest shook his head.

The bolt cutters clicked and the Cardinal screamed as if red hot pokers had been driven into his eyes.

"My fingers!" he screamed.

"What price fingers indeed?" laughed the Russian. "You see some of my jewels are missing and either they were taken by Mr. Verechico's team here or they were spirited away under someones hassock. Now if that robe happened to be black and red. Well it might have belonged to you. Water!" he yelled.

The priest began to burble, "I did not take the jewels, all the jewels were taken by the robbers. How could I take the jewels?" he spluttered, as water was thrown over his face. "There were so many people there that I could not take them."

"Is that the truth?" asked Ulyanov turning to Verechico.

Verechico nodded, "Absolutely," he said.

"So let me re-cap then," said Ulyanov. "The jewels were not kept by the bank?"

The priest nodded.

"No one had a chance to take any from the vault?"

The priest was looking at his hand and nodding. He studied the bloody pulp where his fingers had been and the pool of blood which was spreading across the table top and dripping onto the floor.

"There is an awful lot of blood Cardinal," Ulyanov laughed.

"An awful lot of blood. I think we shall have to stop that if we are going to continue, don't you?"

The Cardinal was looking at Verechico and suddenly screamed, "Why don't you ask him? He was there!"

"How very sacrificial of you," the Russian laughed. "It is so wonderful to see the indoctrinations of humility and sacrifice being preached with such virtue. And so the priest too comes to realise that it is in fact all about survival," he paused reflectively, "very Darwinian I must say. What about turning the other," he snorted, "hand?"

The Russian then produced some metal objects which he threw onto the table in front of the priest.

"Hand made ones," he said, "fashioned here in this forgotten outpost of the past." He picked one of the objects up and examined it, his finger-tip pricked by the spiked end. "They are very sharp," he continued, sucking his finger as if he had pricked it on a needle. "These could cause an awful injury, in the wrong hands."

The priest was burbling unable to come to terms with the details of what was happening to him. Ulyanov picked up his gun from the table and in one swift sweeping motion aimed and fired. Verechico screamed as the bullet smashed into his knee cap.

"You see Monsignor," said Ulyanov, "I intend to ask Mr. Verechico as many searching questions as you."

He fired again and Verechico's left ear disintegrated as the bullet tore along his cheek and ripped the flesh from his head and deposited it against the concrete wall behind him. The bullet ricocheted into the dull steel of the roof, ripping a clean hole as it went.

"So gentlemen," said Ulyanov calmly. "I will ask all the questions and you will blub out the answers. Wrong answer equals intense pain, correct answer equals pain relief." He placed two vials on the table and a hypodermic needle. "Two vials of morphine, one each, or two for one and none for all," he laughed. "Just a little joke among friends."

Verechico was clutching the bloody mass of pulp where his knee should have been. He was on his back now, the chair some ten yards away; a wound at the side of his head was pumping blood at a steady rate and the warm fluid was soaking into his shirt. He was hoping he might become unconscious and then the pain might vanish but a bucket of water hit his chest. He could feel himself being dragged as his leg hung limp and useless behind him.

His face hit the tub of urine, a mixture of fluid from all the men in the hanger and his own. His head wound burst into intense pain as the ammonia carved a path of agony into his nervous system. He wanted to yell, push back against the weight which was holding his head under, but his legs could get not purchase on the floor and he was slipping in his own blood. He could feel the fluid entering his nose, burning his throat. Then suddenly he was upright gasping for breath and the Russian was there asking him questions about Parsotti.

He tried to vary the answers, tried to stay alert but a club of some kind hit his wound and then he was back, face down, into the tub of urine. Then he was up again, more questions; down, up, down, up, his breath coming in gasps and deep intrusive inhalations of liquid. Eventually he was thrown to the ground his mind a mass of intense pain and unbridled relief.

Ulyanov returned to the Cardinal, "I have some interesting answers which I now want you to verify, Monsignor," he said. "Petrov get the Cardinal free," he ordered.

The grinning man pulled a claw hammer across the back of the Monsignor's hand in the direction of his wrist and the bones could be heard cracking as he levered against them.

"The block," Ulyanov ordered.

Two muscular men pulled the Cardinal toward a large brown lump. As he got closer he could see it was in fact a wooden railway sleeper.

"This," said Ulyanov, "is perfectly apt for a man of God."

The Cardinal was then unceremoniously kicked until he lay on his back exhausted, breathing through cracked and broken ribs with his arms outstretched.

"Your hand Monsignor," said the Russian, "is a mess but we have no further need of that now. I am simply going to ask you the same questions I asked Mr. Verechico there. If I get the right answers then we shall simply leave you and go on our merry way."

He lit a cigarette.

"Petrov here is now going to nail you to this beam. Rather apt I thought."

The grinning man had collected the square metal spikes from the table, and the priest now realised the significance of the earlier toying by Ulyanov with the objects.

"However, he is not going to nail your hands, instead, he'll go between the radius and the ulna, careful of course not to puncture the artery. You see the metacarpals would simply separate and you would fall. There another one of your failures in biblical fiction."

The Cardinal felt the nail driven home at the wrist of the injured hand with as little pain as a pin prick, on the other arm he tried to fight against Kernov who was now standing on his forearm. He bit a calf muscle as it passed too close to his mouth. The blows of retaliation were swift and decisive; Petrov's hammer removed two of his lower teeth and his jaw bone cracked, then a nail was being driven through his second wrist and the pain became intense. One of the other soldiers urinated on his face and the warm fluid caused vomit to rise to his throat, and burning at his gums.

"I must apologise," laughed Ulyanov, "but we have no thorns for you to wear."

Then he was being lifted, hauled up by pulleys and ropes, up to the pole in the centre of the hanger. His feet left the ground and were unsupported – the pain was excruciatingly intense across his chest as his sternum bore his total body weight. He was finding it difficult to breathe.

"We are giving you a block to rest your feet upon,"said the Russian as his men slotted the crossbeam into the upright. "The Romans were such barbaric people and yet they gave us so much more. I am going to ask you a few more questions now."

The Cardinal said nothing, he simply could not comprehend what was happening.

"Let me explain," said Ulyanov reassuringly, "it's all very simple really. I will ask you some questions and if the answers are the same as Mr. Verechico over there then the block stays. Wrong answer and the block goes. Now you may well ask about the purpose of the block – let me explain that too. When it is there you can push up against it and relieve that horrible pain in your chest. If I take it away, like this."

He kicked it away, and the Cardinal's body dropped, his chest cracked and he found it virtually impossible to breathe.

"Your sternum will crack," he laughed, "and your lungs will begin to fill with blood; eventually you'll drown in it." He turned to two of his men, "Get the Italian," he said.

The Cardinal hung suspended two feet from the floor as the block was replaced against the upright to give his feet support. Marco Cigannini hung crucified, his toes pushing up against the block to lift his weight and relieve the intense pain in his sternum. He breathed heavily and his voice now contained the huskiness of pain-induced truth.

Michelangelo Verechico was dragged by his remaining one good leg to the base of the crucifix and the questioning began once again in earnest.

Chapter 4

Alice Parsotti stood at the sink washing her hands. She had waited and not heard any calls for a flight to Male. She presumed that Blondell would be reading his paper. Toying briefly with the idea of walking out of the airport altogether she examined her face in the mirror.

"Will he recognise me?" she asked out loud, before splashing cold water on her forehead. "All I have to do is walk. He won't be expecting me, he'll be off-guard," she paused tilting her head in the mirror, "unless all my luck has finally run out."

She examined the image looking back at her. Thought logically about the situation, surmising, that if Blondell had the slightest inclination she was at the airport, the place would already be swarming with police and special agents. The hair colour, the emerald green eyes, the bronzed skin, all stared back at her and she knew that if he saw her, then she would be recognized in the instant. She cursed her tardiness in leaving Male.

"In for a penny," she mumbled to her reflection as an old lady entered.

"Yes dear," the older woman replied as she passed behind Parsotti. "It's all those hours sitting I'm afraid. As soon as I get up I have to spend a penny."

Alice smiled and realised that her verbalised thoughts had caused confusion in the old woman. She pondered briefly on what she thought might happen in her life when she was that age. Wondered if the woman had children, grandchildren, whether her pelvic floor muscles had collapsed after childbirth or whether, when she reached that age herself, what her own ailments might be.

"These airports are so cold aren't they?" the old woman continued.

"Oh yes," Alice confirmed, "air-conditioning."

"I always," said the woman, producing a shawl from her bag, "I always, keep some warm clothes in my hand luggage. That's what my husband used to say to do – bless him. When you get to my age then things make you cold very easily; I expect it's my circulation. Jack used to say circulation was the key and he was right."

Alice watched as the woman drew a bright tartan shawl around her shoulders before entering a cubicle. She pondered on whether the clothes the old lady wore would afford a disguise. At least she had no husband waiting outside, but there might be a companion, another friendly little widow who was guarding their cases. If she was alone, the opportunity was there, all Alice had to do was grasp it. Alice thought of strangling the woman and leaving her body in the toilets. She looked at the "last checked," sign left by the cleaner, it had been signed twenty minutes ago and the next detailed clean was scheduled for forty minutes hence. Her mind calculated quickly, they would not be airborne before the body was discovered. She decided to let the woman wee in peace. Besides, she concluded, she was smaller than useful and the clothes would look all wrong. She decided to take her chances with the walk.

When Alice Parsotti turned out of the toilets she walked quickly, with her head up, toward her departure gate. She had made the choice not to cross a causeway which passed a virtually disserted coffee bar, nor try to skulk past the departure gate unnoticed. Her walk was confident, controlled and purposeful. There were other people milling around and some were walking alongside her, she hoped that no one shouted or dropped something which might make Blondell look up. She studied the group of seated passengers waiting for their transfer flight to Male – to her horror she could not see her pursuer. The place where she had last seen him was empty, but the newspaper was on the chair. Her eyes rapidly scanned the crowd – she couldn't see him. Her heart was racing – where the hell was he? She studied the book shop – he was not there; studied the enquiry desks – he was not there either. For a brief second she contemplated turning on her heel and walking down to the exit doors and out into the heat of Arabia.

Suddenly without warning the man, who had offered her an overnight in London and who had watched her go into the toilets, re-appeared. In a gesture of over familiarity he linked his arm within hers as they passed gate 14. She was trapped, past the point of no return.

"I wondered if you'd got lost," he said in triumph, as if capturing a prize.

"No, I just thought I'd," she lowered her voice to a husky drawl, "freshen up, you know shower, before the long flight."

She continued looking for Blondell, first to her left and then to her right – he was nowhere to be seen. Her eyes were rapidly scanning the faces now. They had passed gate 13 and she could not see him in the departure lounge.

"I know it's nice to be fresh," the man replied, mistaking her lowered voice as a hint of sexual possibility.

"I haven't got any knickers on," she suddenly whispered, hiding her face against the man's shoulder.

"Wow, I mean crikey," he half snorted in reply, "why?" He didn't know what else to say.

"All my cleanies are in my case," whispered Alice, as they continued to walk further away from Blondell's gate. "So I hope they don't want to search me," she continued, "I mean that could be very embarrassing; being searched and someone finding I have no knickers on, they'll think I'm some kind of slapper."

She could sense the raw excitement of the man next to her. She could feel the tremble transmitted up her arm as his grip tightened – he was intoxicated. She knew his imagination would be running riot and that was precisely what she wanted. Just a few more strides she was thinking and then I won't need to try and hide my face against this animal any longer. She was counting them now 5, 6, 7 and then they were in, handing over tickets, through the gate and out onto the tarmac. She was waiting for a touch on her shoulder, a pull back against her forward movement – none came.

They were on the aircraft steps in clear visible daylight. If Blondell was watching he would see her clearly. Alice stopped and lifted her shoe as if to remove a small stone which troubled. Her companion stopped to make himself a leaning post and studied the balance between her thigh and her calf and wondered how she would look naked. Standing upright once again she moved sides to keep the man between her and the departure lounge window. She was scanning the window and the seating area; she was looking for the newspaper on the chair – now she couldn't see it. Either Blondell had removed the paper or someone else had. She studied the mass of glass but could not see the man anywhere.

Inside the plane Alice finally managed to extricate herself from the boorish man and began to walk ahead. She knew now she'd have to lure him into bed once they had landed in England and kill him. She walked down the length of the fuselage, thankful he was at the other end – it would give her some time to plan and relax, but he followed. Her mind was already planning, evaluating and deducing. She needed his flat, needed to vanish for a while, and not into a hotel; she needed to check precisely what these detectives now knew. Blondell was the awkward one, constantly sifting, checking, tracing and following her movements from place to place. She almost felt at times that he was just a few steps behind her; making her look back over her shoulder – she had to put an end to the charade. Obviously her letter to his home had not had the desired effect; he was like a Pinkerton, never knew when to give up. Perhaps they knew about her house in Venice or the penthouse in Brindley Place, or even the little cottage in Whitby. She needed to take stock and cover her movements.

Then there were the bank accounts, surely they would not have been able to discover those, the Swiss were far too cagey. She smiled to herself in the realisation of the emeralds and jewels, which she had not liquidated, being placed back inside a safe deposit box. Verechico had been true to his word with Paul West and the money for their share of the robbery had been deposited before they left Amsterdam. Drecht had taken the bullet for all of them and Paul, like all men, had believed her romantic post-coital drivel and she had seduced all the necessary codes out of him. She had said it was in case they got separated in the airports, or that Rightman might try a double-cross and for both their sakes she needed to know. She told had him she loved him, wanted his baby and like a typical arrogant man he had believed her. She had screamed his name when he exploded inside her, had sunk her nails into his back as she locked her legs about him and he, dumb schmuck, had taken the bait. But this Blondell was a different proposition – he could not be seduced, so she'd have to use some good old fashioned fear and get the bastard off her case.

The obnoxious man was following her, "I thought you were down there?" she questioned, pointing.

"I was," he replied, "but I managed to find the person in the seat next to you," he smiled a broad grin, "and we did a swap and hey presto, bob's your uncle we're sitting next to one another now."

She smiled back at him, "Lovely," she lied.

"A bit of luck I thought," he said, smiling. "I came down to the gate and got," he paused in a thoughtful re-phrase, "and spoke to lots of people. It'll give us a chance to get to know one another, have a chat and such."

It was the, "and such," which worried her. She wanted to stick a plastic knife in his eye and twist it while he screamed, the thought so consumed her that she spoke out loud. "Arseholes and bollocks," she cursed.

A woman in the row behind them gave her a piercing look which spoke of children and manners and women with sewer mouths.

"What's wrong?" Miles asked in earnest reply.

"Oh nothing really," she said regaining her composure, "I think I left my wet wipes in the bathroom of the airport and I hate those complimentary towel things they give you."

"What those lemony things, all scolding hot and yet slightly grubby before you start?"

"Got it in one!" she exclaimed, as she moved in toward the window seat. "You don't mind if I take the window do you?" she asked.

She continued to study the departure lounge, there seemed to be no security movement behind the glass nor on the tarmac.

"Be my guest, whatever the lady wants the lady gets." He sat down. "The name's Miles," he repeated, "Miles Bolton." He clipped his seat belt into place and offered his hand.

She took it, turning toward him, "Claudette Cicello, pleased to meet you Miles," she replied.

"What a beautiful name," he blurted in an unchecked reply.

"I blame my mother," said Alice.

"Or your father?" he laughed, nervously.

"I never really knew my father," she replied, and then paused thoughtfully, "he died."

She turned her face back toward the terminal building and watched for Blondell and any security activity through the window – there was none.

Bolton thought he had offended her but all he could think to say in reparation was, "I'm sorry."

"Oh that's alright," she said, "I never knew him. He died when I was very young but there was always Granny," and she laughed, but did not turn her head back away from the porthole.

She counted the security guards as Miles Bolton launched into a stream of apologetic ramblings which seemed incoherent and burbling. She could hear the undercurrent in his tone, an undercurrent which would ask her to open her legs wider or arch her back more fully. Alice knew the game, was a champion contender and he, Miles Bolton, was not a player, he was a piece to be played.

Alice turned to face the man, "So your little place," she said, "are you sure that you don't mind putting little ol' me up? It's terribly kind of you."

"Absolutely no bother," replied Bolton. "In fact it will be great to have a pretty face around the place."

"So what do you do Miles?"

He started to talk and as all men who are obsessed with themselves, talked about himself. She wanted to give him the tip of listening; tell him that if he listened to the woman or at least conversed by reacting to her conversation, his chances of getting laid would increase fifty fold. As he droned she wanted to grab him by the ears and head-butt his nose shattering the bone. Wanted to watch the blood drain down his shirt and hear him whimpering like a school-boy as she smashed his ribs with her heel. She wanted to tell him that he was possibly the most boring man alive and he would be lucky if anyone ever fucked him, but instead she smiled, cajoled and flashed her eyelids at the appropriate times.

After the food had been served she said she wanted to sleep and he said that he'd watch a movie. He almost went into top five movies of all time mode, waxing lyrical about the state of the modern movie industry, but she thanked providence that he didn't.

Inside the airport lounge Alexander Blondell heard a giant airbus leave the runway and bank left to turn back toward London and the grime of a wet winter. His forefinger and thumb fastened on the handle of a small cup which he lifted with one flowing movement to his lips. It was his third coffee, Pancardi style, and he knew that the airline would not have anything near a worthwhile substitute once they were airborne. He took a deep draft of sparkling water to slake his thirst. He was not reading the paper now, he had gone cover to cover twice on the flight from London and now he needed to clear his mind.

Hypnotised by the bar maid's hips rushing too and fro his mind drifted into recalled memories and precisely what he might say to Alice when he got to her island. He missed his wife Magdalene and daughter Charlotte and wondered what they would be doing right now. He could visualise Charlotte holding her little white "Mostro" dog or colouring at the dining room table with her mother. Both would be chattering and enjoying the company of the other and he knew in that instant that he loved them both more than anything in the world.

His back to the thronging departure lounge traffic he could see the departures listed on the muted T.V. screen which hung above the bar like a giant eye.

He ordered a fourth coffee and pondered on what Alice might be doing right now. Smiling he imagined her bathing in the sun, oblivious to his sudden arrival. This time it had to be absolutely right, there could be nowhere for her to run. The island was sealed as tight as a drum he'd seen to that – they had her this time.

The mobile cell-phone rang in his pocket, "Blondell," he replied, "what do you mean a fire? A fire in a cabin? What do you mean you're not sure? For God's sake man you must have some idea," he blurted. "I'm a few hours away and now you tell me. You just better be bloody right or your arse is going to be blowing in the wind like a ragged flag."

He snapped the phone shut in exasperation, downed the coffee in one and headed for his departure gate.

Chapter 5

Inside the hanger between Pikalevo and Borisovo-Sudskoye vehicle engines roared into life; a small amount of snow was falling on the ground outside. The entrance doors had been thrown open wide and the regiment of Russian men were ready to move. They worked quickly and with the minimum of fuss; most wore heavy coats and hats and some were pulling gloves over their hands. The Salamander heaters had been removed and stored in the troop carriers. The bath of urine lay upturned, a rancid pool spreading across the concrete floor. The cooking fires were doused and kicked into oblivion and the whole building now looked abandoned.

Cardinal Marco Cigannini, hung like a deer after a summer cull, his robes were soaked in sweat and splattered in blood, both Verechico's and his own. A small trickle of crimson ran from his left nostril and his chest felt as if it might explode. He lifted himself to his toe tips once again and the stinging pain of cramp hit the back of his calf muscles; he was torn between lowering his heels and the resultant pain in his chest and the imminent collapse of his legs.

Michelangelo Verechico lay on the ground before the block which supported the Cardinal's feet; his eyes stared up at the Cardinal's robe much as a lusty schoolboy might seek to view up a girl's skirt on a stairwell. His second knee cap had been smashed with a pick-axe handle and a steadily growing pool of blood was expanding behind his legs and soaking into the concrete. He knew his ribs had been broken by the repeated beating and kicking and he suspected that one rib had punctured his right lung. He could feel the fluid, which would eventually kill him, building in his chest.

The sound of heavy footfalls approached across the concrete, "I would like to say thank you gentlemen," said Ulyanov, as he pulled a leather glove over his fingers. "You could have told me more sooner and saved yourselves this whole nasty business. I do so abhor violence it is so unnecessary, but I think we understand each other now."

Verechico coughed.

"There's no need to speak," Ulyanov remarked, "there's not much more to say is there?"

The Cardinal slowly opened his eyes.

"You can scream all you like," Ulyanov continued, "nobody will hear you out here, except the scavengers. And Cardinal I don't think you can rely on your marvellous God to free you, he seems unable to help. Now might be a good time to ask for forgiveness and perhaps ask why you have been so forsaken," he laughed.

"You will never get those jewels back, you know," Cigannini taunted. "The woman is far cleverer than you and the Englishman will get there first." His breath was short and sharp.

"First things first Cardinal," Ulyanov replied. "First we shall reclaim those museum pieces. Then I will personally find this Parsotti and I can assure you we shall not be so gentle with her as we have been on you." He felt a sudden draught and drew his great coat about him, "The weather is turning cold, I do not think it will be long before the curtain is torn," he concluded.

The Cardinal's breath was short, as he pushed himself higher to relieve the pain in his sternum, he was fighting with the pain to be able to speak. "And do you think killing us will serve any purpose?" he asked, his voice husky in its dryness.

"Maybe not," Ulyanov laughed, "but there is a strange irony don't you think? You have to look at it like the Romans crucifying Spartans along the Apian Way. It didn't really do anything but it did send out some clear warnings and messages of intent. And this," he paused, "well this is my Apian warning and the message is simple; do not fuck with the KGB; do not fuck with Alexei Vissarianovich Ulyanov."

"Plucking stime, Vardhemmeyer," Verechico bubbled through broken lips and blood, "will fin..."

Ulyanov placed a well aimed kick to the side of Verechico's head and his whole body jolted and spasmed. His jaw broke with a loud snap and a tooth flew out through the pulp that once served as a mouth.

"What will he do?" Ulyanov teased. "Your friend Vardhemmeyer died with his head down a toilet, he drowned in his own blood. Sergeant Kernov has little time for mercenaries and he slit his throat like the pig he was. You really are the most obnoxious little thief," he snapped, "and you want to threaten me with some friend, some fat indolent mercenary? We are KGB, we are professionals, not some broken down ex-army scum which fights against a few badly armed natives in grass skirts. There is no cavalry which might appear on the horizon to rescue you, from the nasty Indians. This is not a movie, this I'm afraid is real life, or in your case death; you are alone, totally alone, and you are going to die – that is a certainty. I am going to leave you both here like the carrion you are. It will be interesting to see which one of you dies first. I would like to see which one of you cries like an abandoned bastard child left on a doorstep. Mr. Verechico, I suggest that you crawl like the slug you are to some corner to die and you Cardinal had best call as loudly as you can, to your God for assistance."

Corporal Perchenko swung a jeep out of the line and Ulyanov hopped into the passenger seat. He stood leaning against the roll bar, raised his left arm above his head and the vehicles began to stream out of the entrance way and disappear into the blanket of snow. Sergeant Mikhail Kernov, in the last jeep, pulled the release mechanism on the roll door at the entrance as he passed and the heavy clang of metal on concrete resounded as the roar of diesel engines subsided.

Cardinal Marco Cigannini twisted sideways and the block supporting his feet gave way; there was a resounding crack as his sternum snapped, his feet kicked rapidly for a few seconds and then became still as he gave up on life.

Michelangelo Verechico turned onto his left side and as he did so a pool of blood was coughed from his mouth. In the distance he could see a pile of old bags and paper and he began to crawl; one last desperate attempt to remain alive.

Chapter 6

"Dead? What a ridiculous assumption Alex, ridiculous."

"Well you could have told me." Blondell admonished.

"Of course I'm not dead, there, consider yourself told."

"Well you should have told other people where you were," repeated Alex Blondell.

"Mostro knows."

"Not the dog, and anyway is he here?" Blondell looked around for the familiar wagging white tail.

"No, hc is in Italy; agc has finally caught up with him it would seem."

"Who is he with then?"

"A friend of a friend."

"Oh this is so ridiculous, all this secrecy I thought we were friends?" Blondell replied.

"But we are Alex, we are."

"Then why not tell me."

"What like you told me?" Pancardi was questioning now.

"That's different," replied Blondell, "and anyway you are fully retired, so this job is out of your hands. Perhaps you ought to take a leaf out of Mostro's book?"

"Out of my hands?" Pancardi seemed injured by the notion. "This is my case, my daughter, my mess, and you want me to walk away? The Questura may wish to see this old Inspector gone but I have pride. Giancarlo Pancardi is no fool – this has to be finished once and for all. Remember? I had to stand by and watch Roberto, my oldest friend, bleed to death. You were there too remember?"

"I know, I hardly knew the man but I liked him. Calvetti's wife's got the dog then, to keep her company? That's rather kind."

"Si," he chirped in reply. "She too loves Mostro, like all the women he makes of the sad eyes and they melt. He is clever no?"

"You should have said something," Blondell snapped again.

"Why you are clever enough to be here?" Pancardi was smiling now.

"That's not the bloody point," Blondell was exasperated, "other people were getting worried."

"But life is short Alex, sometimes we must act on instinct no?"

"Instinct and curiosity nearly got you killed last time. Next time it might do. This is bollocks and you know it Carlo." Blondell attempted to terminate their altercation with harsh language.

"You should deduce and not assume," Pancardi was smirking now, "didn't you learn anything from me? And as you can see I am clearly not dead, am I?" Pancardi was grinning widely.

"That might be the case," Blondell replied, affectionately returning the infectious smile, "but you could have told people before you went gallivanting off – especially Alaina."

"Ah Alaina."

"Yes Alaina – she loves you you know."

"This may be so Alex Blondell, but I do not need a wife and babies and a house in Chelsea and Alaina she has her career and it is a good one too." He became reflective, "Besides she has a new man and they will be making of the bambini soon, her time it is running out."

"Well Giancarlo Pancardi, if you were a little less self absorbed and a tad more thoughtful she might have told you that they split up over a year ago now." He paused for a reaction in Pancardi's face – he could see the shock. "She doesn't want anyone else, though God only knows why. So when you went gallivanting off she phoned me. Wanted to know if I was in on some mad-cap caper of yours?" He paused, "You made me look a right fool, and she cares for you much more than you would care to imagine, otherwise why would she always ask of you?"

"Alaina could phone me," Pancardi snapped, "and only your pride was wounded?"

"Can't you see you're too old to go gallivanting around like this? One day you'll be going back to Italy in a box; you should go home and grow olives or tomatoes or whatever you Italians do in your dotage?"

"Gallivanting indeed and why then are you in Dhangethi, are you on holiday? I don't see your young wife and family with you," Pancardi said with loaded sarcasm.

"I think we are here for the same reason Carlo," he looked straight into Pancardi's eyes, "you know where she is don't you?"

"Was Alex, was."

"You mean this shell is all that's left?" Blondell asked, scuffing the blackened sand with the point of his shoe. "This is it?"

The small grains of sand had fused into black glass in the heat, while the white of the crushed coral shone as a stark contrast in the glare of the sun. It gave the effect of a molten zebra, liquidised and then scattered under the scorched palms. Here and there stood blackened roof beams which still smouldered, issuing thin wisps of smoke into the clear air. There was a bathroom which had collapsed upon itself. The bath was now encased in a pupa of cracked tiles; a kitchen sink, a freezer, and washing machine all scorched black and useless, stood like sentinels at the gates of Hell. All that really remained was an outbuilding housing a chest freezer and some storage rooms of canned food, bottled water and linen.

"They found her body, so we are both too late," replied Pancardi. "It's a mess isn't it? The whole place burnt down. Fire investigators say there was a freak electrical fault on a ceiling fan and the place went up like a tinder box. No boats left the island and no planes have taken off with a person answering her description – I've checked."

Alex Blondell began to walk into the wreckage.

"Not too far Alex," Pancardi warned. "The electrical current is still on in the mains and there are some exposed cables buried in the sand."

"So she was on to the fact that I had found her?" questioned Blondell. "How in God's name did she know? She sent me a letter from Argentina threatening me to keep away, I knew then I was close, and suddenly she dies in a fire. I don't believe it. It's all too simple, too neat, too contrived. Why would this happen to her?

"Coincidence Alex, bad luck and poor judgement, or a mixture of all three?" Pancardi's voice was sharp, "There's no where to go, we're on an island in the Indian Ocean. Everybody knows everybody and she was a bit of a celebrity on this one. All the locals knew her, she was the rich lady in the house by the beach. She kept away from most of the island life and some of the locals couldn't even recognise her if she walked down the street."

"Precisely," replied Blondell, "she could have slipped out and many people would not even know. Your deductions don't take account of her tenacity, your judgement is poor because she is your daughter."

"What do you mean poor judgement?" Pancardi snapped in reply.

"Shot at by my own daughter," mocked Blondell.

"And why would Charlotte want to shoot you, she's only five?"

"Don't try to be amusing, we know each other too well to be flippant, you know perfectly well what I mean." Blondell's voice raised an octave, "Alice fired at you as I recall, tried to kill you?"

"Ah the graveyard," Pancardi reminisced, "that was rather foolish of me I know. To suppose that she would not."

"What try to kill you?"

"No," he hesitated, "want to get away." Pancardi again paused thoughtfully, "If she had wanted to kill me she could have done so easily, we were only feet apart. Less distance than that security guard in Amsterdam and she blew his head apart without a second thought. No she only chose to dissuade me from trying to capture her. She would not kill her own father, now would she?"

Blondell's face broadened into a smile, "Dissuade?" he mocked, "I think a bullet was more or less an attempt at your life don't you? It would dissuade me, I certainly wouldn't be here on this island right now."

"Actually no I don't, if she had wanted to kill me she could have done so easily, a second shot would have done it. She killed Rightman, and West too and then there was Dalvin, she can be lethal when she wants to be. She did nothing more than try to get away. All she did to Mostro, the poor little chap, was make me put him on a leash, and me, well it was cold, but eventually Mostro got the grave diggers attention with all his barking. All that was really wounded was my pride. Sitting trussed like a turkey ready for

Christmas; she was just playing for time – time to escape. No, she had no intention of killing me she just valued her freedom more than…"

"Than what?" asked Blondell.

"Anything else. She left as she came, in the flower van and vanished. They found that abandoned less than a mile away, so she had a getaway planned just in case. She covers all eventualities and that makes her impossible to trace. I should have told you about the DNA match but I wanted so much to talk with her. I loved her mother and Alice was never known to me as a girl. That was why I flew out here."

"This being the woman who tied you up in a graveyard, wounded, and left for dead? You wanted to have a, chat?" Blondell accentuated the word chat. "What did you want to talk about, old times? You never had a relationship with her; she may be your daughter but she has no regard for you."

"I disagree," replied Pancardi, "had she wished to, she could have killed me."

"And on the basis of that you thought that she might what ?"

"Listen?" said Pancardi, "just listen."

"You told her you were coming here didn't you?"

"Of course not, but she knew – she sensed I was coming. She's a Pancardi after all."

"Jesus Christ she was warned, and you gave her a chance to set up an escape," Blondell hissed.

Blondell removed the Panama hat from his head and wiped the sweat band with a handkerchief. His eyes strained and half closed against the reflected light from the white sand. He took a pair of dark glasses from his pocket and placed them on his nose.

"So now that you know she is your daughter does that change things?" he asked.

"That was why I was here," Pancardi's replied, "to tell her that it couldn't. I wanted to offer her help."

"Don't be so guarded. She may be your daughter but she is also a cold blooded killer. She is as cold as ice – an ice maiden, she is beyond help."

"Do you really think she was born like this Alex? Something made her like this. The Alsetti family were, as I recall, ruthless, self–centred and scheming. Money and status were the only things her grandmother really valued. She turned Margarite against me and made Alice a monster."

A short and very dark skinned official came toward the two men and directed them toward the local hospital.

Less than four hundred yards away, down the sandy street a single storey building, made up of three rooms, stood white and tiled – offering cool sanctuary to all that might enter. Within, there were three stark white rooms, but the local official was immensely proud of the fact that his group of islands on the North Ari Atoll had a doctor. One room was an operating theatre, and here the local doctor was turned into a celebrity by performing appendectomies, or the spearing of boils and the administering of antibiotics. Blondell wondered what medical provision had been in place prior to the arrival of the doctor. Larger operations were dealt with in Male the capital or Colombo in Sri Lanka and both the western men knew in an instant the luck of being born into a first world nation.

The second room was a consultation area and the third a ward. Adjacent to the main block was a small morgue and it was here the body of Alice Parsotti had been brought. Pancardi noted the strain in the generator which was housed on a flat concrete pad to the rear of the building. It was spitting forth a great fume of diesel as it provided the hospital with air conditioning. This was a circuit separate from the main grid and used primarily to give emergency power to the most modern resource on the island. Blondell noticed the bare foot children and Pancardi the men who sat avoiding the sun, drinking and waiting. The old men seemed to have the patience of people in any third world country; the patience to wait for death or destruction with quiet resolve, whilst the children followed the new arrivals as if they were great Hollywood celebrities.

At the morgue the charred and twisted body of a woman was inside a bare, unlined coffin. The corpse was so badly burned that fingerprint identification was not possible, DNA or dental records were the only real certainty.

"Bloody hell," said Blondell, "how did she pull this one off?"

His eyes strained in the poor light of the storage facility. He noted the cooler air and was thankful lest the smell of decomposition were too strong for his stomach.

Pancardi studied the body. It was roughly the right height. The build however, was, he felt, more thickly set. The hips seemed too wide and the feet too large; bones protruded from the rough knee and he could see a curve in the lower left leg, a break, long healed, but sufficient to cause a thickening of the bone. This woman would have had a slight limp he deduced; Alice walked with a swaggering leggy gait. She was elegant, this corpse would have lumbered and avoided high heels which drew attention to the legs. The other issue which troubled him was the ankles. Alice he remembered had fine slim ankles, this woman had ankles like a runner, sturdy thick ankles built to withstand punishment. He looked at the hands with their flesh burned down to the bone and he felt, rather than knew, that this was not the body of his daughter. The doctor was explaining how the Maldivian Islands had no facilities to undertake a DNA test except at Male in the capital. He had arranged for the body to be flown there by sea plane the following morning and that it would be three days at least before the results were back. Pancardi had begun to leave and Blondell followed, mindful of the older man's anguish created by the sight of the corpse.

"It's not her Alex," he blurted as they stepped into the sunlight. "She has done it again, she has somehow fixed a fabrication. I do not need to see the results of a DNA match."

"I know this must be hard for you to believe," Blondell was trying to sound sympathetic, but he began to play the devil's advocate nonetheless, "but if no boats have left the island she couldn't simply just swim away could she?"

"Why not?" asked Pancardi sharply.

It was working, Pancardi had taken the lure, "Well the nearest resort," Blondell continued, "is half an hour away by boat," he paused, "and you know how sceptical I am, but even I think you may be clutching at straws. We'll need to wait for the DNA to be absolutely sure."

"So?" Pancardi was becoming monosyllabic.

"No boats left the island," Blondell confirmed, secretly noting the success of his reverse psychology , "I know you want her to be alive," Blondell continued, "but it is most likely that she was in the fire and that the corpse is her. Even I can begin to accept that; maybe there really was an accident."

"So certain aren't you Alex?" Pancardi was thinking quickly now.

"No this time I'm being realistic."

"So am I," Pancardi replied, "so am I."

Blondell was falsely adamant, "Well all I can say is that Interpol have been watching this island for days. She made the mistake of returning for too long and immigration is very bureaucratic and strict here. I mean what is all that spraying the air inside the aircraft before you land stuff. Some sort of air disinfectant?"

Pancardi did not speak.

Blondell continued, "So Alice is tracked here by her simple error, an error which records her stay. She stays one day too long on her last visit and we have an alert for her when she passes through immigration again, that was five days ago. Interpol picked her scent up and then alerted me."

Pancardi nodded wistfully.

"She comes here on holiday," Blondell's foot was scuffing the sand, "and swans around like lady muck. There are locals who look after her place and then suddenly the place goes up in smoke – a freak accident. She got wind of us and besides why did Interpol tell you as well as me – this stinks?" He stared straight into Pancardi's eyes, "You used your connections at the Carabineri didn't you?" he asked.

"Your theory is rubbish Alex and you know it, that is precisely what she wants everyone to think – she's alive. How come nobody else was in the house? No servant or local and the body is found in the bed, all curled up and smoked like a kipper. It's rubbish, there is something we have missed, think it through. And yes of course I pulled a few favours in, there were others who wanted to get those jewels recovered. You forget the influence of the Holy Father in Rome and there, connections are long. Would you not use a favour or two to get the matter solved? Do not patronise me with some righteous virtue, or reverse psychology, we are too well versed in each others cunning to be so puerile."

Blondell knew Pancardi's mind, "Always so sure aren't you," he chided, "but what if just this once the great Giancarlo Pancardi, pride of the Italian Questura, is wrong?" He placed a fist to his mouth in a stance of mock horror. "How could this be?" he continued, "the great Pancardi wrong. If you are so sure start then, thinking like her, you are her father, what would you do?"

Pancardi looked at Blondell, "I'd swim, use diving equipment and travel to a nearby island," he said calmly.

"And then?" asked Blondell.

"Well I would have to find someone who looked like me to place in the house, a false corpse."

"Ok let's start with that premise then shall we?" Blondell stopped himself, "So how come we don't have anybody missing yet?" he asked. "No hapless tourist who stumbled into her path. Or a person on holiday on another island ripe to be plucked, slaughtered and cooked."

"Very culinary Alex," Pancardi joked.

"Oh come on Carlo," Blondell scoffed. "What she just arrived back from a shopping trip with a body? I suppose she had it rolled up in a carpet?"

"Why not, they did it before?" Pancardi replied.

"This is becoming more absurd by the minute, and you know it, the fact is she is probably dead, but you so much want her to be alive you can almost taste it. She could not have swum from island to island dragging a body through shark infested waters, much less hauled it up the beach, placed it in a bed, and then set the building on fire." Blondell paused, "Oh and then swim off the island, where to Sri Lanka I suppose?"

Pancardi's voice was serious now, "I know she is alive and she had this planned. She must have had a contingency, Paul West did and she knew that would be the safe thing to do. The essence of the problem is that we need to find out what the contingency was."

"But she knows we have a DNA match, you told her."

"Absolutely," Pancardi was reasoning now, "but she also knows it will take time to verify. Time is what she needs to run away. She will have bolt holes all over the world and she knows that we cannot find them all. She is long gone."

"So how, when?"

"This we will have to guess no?"

Blondell nodded.

"This letter from Argentina?"

"International mailbox facility." Blondell was detailed, "It was mailed on and the company have no record of where it was originally posted. I've had investigators check it out, they drew a complete blank – nothing."

"Funny no?" Pancardi questioned.

"Why so?"

"Magentosa, the people who owned the safe deposit box which housed the Romanov jewels, they were based in Argentina, no?"

"There is no connection with her," Blondell scoffed. "You're barking up the wrong tree there."

"Maybe, maybe not," Pancardi smiled, "I think she is playing with us no?"

"To hell with it, I think a cold drink would be in order now," Blondell suddenly barked, "dehydration and all this thinking don't mix."

"Agreed," Pancardi replied. "And I think we need to go over the fire site with a fine tooth comb. Is there a hotel or something?"

"That doesn't mean I think you are right you know," said Blondell. "In fact I think the body we have is more likely to be Alice Parsotti, Pancardi, Alsetti, or whatever you want to call her." He grimaced at his inability to find the correct name.

"Let's just call her Alice shall we?" Pancardi interjected. "Her mother was an Alsetti, she was never named Pancardi and I do not know where Parsotti came from as a name. But we will soon know if this is Alice – I will give a cheek swab to accompany the corpse. The Official said the corpse is going in the morning?"

"Yes."

In the main street smooth skinned children tried to get the two men into their shops to buy the native wood carvings and necklaces made from local shell. They did not succeed.

"If, and I say if reservedly, she has fabricated her own death," said Blondell, "that body must be someone, who."

"Precisely, who?" Pancardi agreed.

Blondell flipped his mobile cell phone open and spoke rapidly issuing instructions, "Every island within a five mile radius. I don't care how, get every available man on it, every one needs to be checked." He snapped the phone shut. "How far could you swim dragging a body?" he asked Pancardi.

"This even Pancardi does not know, but if we start with five miles then we should soon know or drown."

"I think it's too risky – sharks. She must have had a boat of some kind."

Inside a street café, Alex Blondell took a deep swig of his coke and continued,

"Funny isn't it?" he remarked, "you can travel all around the world and even in the most remote corners of the world you can get this stuff. Lipsmackin, thirst quenchin ever givin cool fizzin."

"That's Pepsi, wrong advert," said Pancardi, as he drank a draught of bitter lemon, the only other soft drink available.

"The place reeks of poverty," said Blondell, as he nodded at the children waiting for them to reappear in the street.

The local official returned to join them after completing the transit papers on the transfer of the body.

"See bureaucrats all," Blondell quipped. "You'll need to get a cheek swab of the Inspector here," he said to the man. "To check the DNA. The corpse may be his daughter."

The man started to speak and Pancardi raised his hand to silence him, "I do not think that the woman in the coffin is my daughter. In fact I think it is someone else and that you may have a murder investigation on your hands. I would recommend that you contact your superior and then interview every boat owner on the island."

The man was spluttering to reply, his mind still attempting to grasp the title Inspector.

"Don't worry you have done nothing wrong, but you are dealing with someone who is beyond your capabilities. Have a drink and join us and we'll attempt to explain."

Pancardi then launched into the story of the jewel robbery in Florence while the local official realised that he had stumbled into the middle of an international film, just like the American ones that were beamed across the international airwaves. He was excited, enthralled and scared all at the same time.

"Ah, Coke, it's the real thing," Pancardi concluded, as he drifted in and out of thoughts on Alice, "but what is real and what is illusion?"

"Not everything is an illusion you know," Blondell returned.

The local official was like a child listening to an adult dinner conversation. Most of it was flying way beyond his personal experience or belief, but it had to be listened to nonetheless.

“But mis-direction is also an illusion no?” Pancardi mocked.

Blondell tried to turn the conversation, “It must cost more to cool it than to produce it.”

“Produce what?” asked Pancardi almost abstractly, his mind absorbed by the case.

“This stuff,” said Blondell lifting his bottle, “this brown sugar water. Generators for every island, power cuts galore, candles in the dark. But this stuff is ice-cold, nice cold, just for the tourists.”

Suddenly Pancardi jumped to his feet, “That’s it, my God, so simple, so very simple and yet so very cunning. A candle – a simple candle, check power cuts, freezers and time, nice cold, ice cold,” he spluttered, “and time delays.”

“I don’t understand,” replied Blondell, looking bemused.

“I don’t expect you to, just follow the logic. Come on we must go back to the fire site. I think we shall find some interesting things.”

As they walked back to the Parsotti house Pancardi was asking a series of detailed questions on sharks, power cuts and missing persons. The local official was making call after call on his mobile cell-phone and a small dory carrying more police was arriving at the jetty. A seaplane passed low overhead and the drone of the engines cut through their conversation like a knife. For a retired Inspector, thought Blondell, his eyes were alive and Blondell knew now that the pursuit of Alice had begun again in earnest.

Chapter 7

"There is something not right here," said Pancardi, as he scanned the site and the remains of the Parsotti house.

"Strange that someone who is now so wealthy should choose to live in a rather modest place like this," replied Blondell, "I expected a place with servants and such."

"I didn't," Pancardi snorted.

"And why?" asked Blondell, sarcastically.

"Simple, ostentation draws the eye, and the eye she observe, and the mouth she then talk about what the eye see and she needs to melt into the background."

Pancardi was being cryptic and Blondell hated this about him. He seemed to like to play games, at first he had thought it was arrogance and then he realised that Pancardi's methodology needed something upon which to feed.

"She's probably," Pancardi paused, "got lots of little hideaways, just like this. Like Count Dracula she must have fifty boxes of earth in which to hide and we have just found one of them." He laughed, "Countess Dracula, now there's a thought."

"So uh," Blondell fumbled for words, "you think she has places like this scattered all over the world and she moves between them?" Blondell quizzed.

"Why not?"

"That sounds bloody awful, that's why not. No place to call home, no roots, that's awful," he repeated.

"To you maybe," Pancardi paused, "but she has no child like you, she has no one to love and no one can love her back, for she is not the same person for all of the year.

She has the ultimate freedom, but for that she must make the ultimate sacrifice."

"Like Dracula," replied Blondell, smiling at Pancardi's cunning, before turning the analogy back at him. "She can party all night but must shun the light." He continued in the same tone, "Do what she wants but she is destined to be forever in the dark, all the people she knows are not vampires and they must die." He paused reflectively, "I almost feel sorry for her."

"But it is worse than that, like Dracula she is constantly hunted," said Pancardi.

"This is far too Gothic an analogy for me for me," Blondell snorted, "and anyway you don't find Goths hiding in the sunny Maldives now do you? I haven't seen a sunburnt Dracula yet."

"I have," Pancardi quipped laughing, "Frank Langella played the part complete with Hollywood tan."

"Yes, but that was the movies," laughed Blondell. "Jesus though, what a way to live your life?"

"Better than working no?"

Blondell nodded.

"Most people are in a job they hate, working with people they despise, and having to take orders, to pay their bills, from people they consider to be idiots. Look at us and our superiors? So many sycophants I have seen, climbing the greasy pole to success." Pancardi paused philosophically, "And for what? Money? Sex? Freedom?" His mind strayed and he began to feel rather than think, "We are all clay, carbon and water; we start as nothing and leave the same, but Alice, my Alice, she has her own prison, only she cannot see the bars."

"It's not much like a prison though is it?" Blondell corrected, "all this."

"But once inside she cannot escape no?" asked Pancardi. "She must stay in the trap, make no mistakes or she will die."

"I don't think either of us is likely to kill her do you?"

"That would depend," Pancardi replied abstractly.

"Oh please," Blondell chided, "that one I don't believe. You follow her out here, for a," he paused, "a chat? Then in the next breath you tell me that she may end up dead." He paused and looked directly into Pancardi's eyes, "That is just ridiculous, no it's absurd – a fantasy. You would no more kill her than I would Charlotte."

Pancardi was on his knees now sifting the sand through his fingers, "You miss the point," he said nonchalantly. "Charlotte is only a little girl and she may yet grow into another Alice, she is after all a product of you."

"I don't think it's that simple," asserted Blondell.

"But I do," Pancardi repeated.

"Oh so please enlighten me, oh wise and wonderful sage?"

"There really is no need to be so sarcastic Alex."

Pancardi was striding toward the scorched storage room now.

"Come on then?" said Blondell, "what have I missed?"

Pancardi's tone changed, "Her real problem is not us, but the owners of the jewels – she stole them from someone. It is these she must run from. And though we do not yet know who they are, they know who we are. That much must be certain, they could be watching us right now."

Blondell paused, "I hadn't seen it like that." Blondell considered his mistake, "So she must be ready to take off at any moment, therefore she cannot have all the money in one place either."

"Correct," Pancardi affirmed.

"My God this thing is like a spider web of deceit."

"Yes, but any web can be untangled no?"

"So who is the so-called owner of the jewels?"

"Now that is the million dollar question," Pancardi replied.

"And I suppose we need to consider the Cardinals and the Pope in all of this especially as they have controlling interest in the Banko Rolo. My God are we being watched now?" Blondell spun on his heel.

"There are eyes everywhere and you forget," Pancardi paused, "mm this is strange."

"Just what have I forgotten now?" asked an exasperated Blondell.

"Your beloved Mafioso." Pancardi was examining a lock as he spoke.

"They are not my beloved Mafia."

"And why not, you married into them no? That lovely wife of yours she is a beauty but she is Mafioso no?"

Pancardi was examining the lock on the large chest freezer which now lay open and empty. The inner of beaten aluminium was blackened. The hasp lock flipped back but the heavy duty pad–lock was snapped shut around the hasp.

"Here is her mistake Alex," he crowed in triumph, "now I know!"

"I'm lost," said Blondell.

"Follow the logic now, I may ask questions – there may be a test."

"Ha bloody ha, let's hear this so clever theory of yours then Batman!"

"If I am Batman then you are the Robin no?" he laughed. "First do you not find it strange that someone who came for only parts of the year should have two freezers?" asked Pancardi.

Blondell shrugged, "Maybe," he said, "but food needs to be stored here. Just look at all these cans?"

"Would you freeze so much?" Pancardi was being rhetorical, "no you would not." He answered his own question, "That is precisely why there are so many cans. Cans are safe, cans do not need a reliable source of power, but a freezer does." He paused thoughtfully, "Just think of the German and the small amount of food he had."

"Yeah," Blondell reasoned, "but he could phone out for a Pizza or nip to the local shop. You can't do that here."

"Alex my dear boy you are not working the problem." Pancardi was grinning as he continued, "First this Island has power cuts so the food might go off in this heat. Then it freezes and re-freezes. Think about the German – his common sense no? The food he is poison."

"Where is this going?" Blondell asked.

"Patience Alex."

"Don't toy with me Carlo, just give me your ideas please, we are friends and there is no need to play-up for an audience – there isn't one."

"Very well then, Mr. Impatient I will tell you," said Pancardi. He stopped and felt the sand at his feet. "The apex would have been here," he said, "there candle wax." He proffered his fingertips to Alex who continued to be bemused.

"So how was it done?" asked Blondell. "You seem to have some clear idea on the matter so let me hear it. Let's stop with the games."

"First," said Pancardi, almost automatically, "first she must have a body, and then this body must be kept ready for use. Then when she is needed the body can replace her in the bed.

"Christ, the body, it was curled up," Blondell was reasoning, "she kept it in the freezer."

"Precisely," answered Pancardi.

"Oh my God she had this escape planned in case she needed it," said Blondell. "She killed someone and got the body into the chest freezer. That's why the lock, not to stop food being stolen but to keep nosey intruders out. If the power went down the body would stay cold for a while and then re-freeze. If the power went on the whole island then she would simply not return. The little freezer was for essentials like cold drinks." He paused to clear his throat, "That's why the freezer is empty and the lid up with the lock still there. She couldn't even be bothered to shut it."

"And that would make all the DNA traces harder to find," Pancardi affirmed. "What with all the ash and smoke and water the surfaces would yield no traces." He pondered, "The other freezer she is closed no?"

"Yes," Blondell replied.

"And there is no lock?"

"No."

"Then," said Pancardi, "who was the body in the freezer?"

Blondell was on his cell phone and as he spoke to the Interpol agents at Male his eyes followed Pancardi who was examining a seemingly innocuous group of electrical wires which lay as a tangled mass in the sand.

"I want every missing person file for the last four, no make that five years. I want them flown over to Dhangethi and I want them within two hours," he barked.

There was a complaining voice on the line but Pancardi could not make out the words.

"I don't give a tinker's cuss," yelled Blondell, "get the bloody things on a plane as fast as possible and get the locals in on it. Check near Dhangethi and work outwards."

"Look at this," said Pancardi, as he lifted the wires from the sand. "See these wires they have been cut. How can a fan cut its own wires? No she did this and then the people think that the blown fuse in the fuse box causes a short, but in reality something else happens."

"The candle wax – a time delay which has simply melted away," said Blondell.

"I think so," Pancardi confirmed. He thought a little more, "What if," he said, "what if she cuts the wires, which blow the fuse and then on the fan she places a candle. She could pack the area with very dry palm leaves and then when the candle reaches them the fire starts?"

"Risky very risky," replied Blondell. "What if the candle blew out, or it went up early? It's not very scientific is it?"

"But somehow it worked, no?"

"Ok, agreed," said Blondell, "that would account for the wax but there is one major flaw," he said triumphantly. "How did she leave the island unseen?"

"Diving," replied Pancardi. "One more diver here and there would make no difference in the throng of tourists."

"How would she know what to do?" asked Blondell.

"Don't be so naive, she must have listened and studied when they practised for the Banko Rolo," Pancardi paused, "maybe she was the back up and so she too had to learn how to use the equipment? Maybe she learnt out here? Either way we should check the diving schools," he paused again, "just in case."

"It's a hell of a long way to the nearest island though," Blondell evaluated, "at least four miles."

"But the water is not cold," laughed Pancardi, "more like four miles in a warm bath."

"A warm bath full to bursting with live and deadly sharks – nice," quipped Blondell, "very," he paused searching for the appropriate word, "pleasant"

"Maybe, she had a boat then?" Pancardi reasoned.

Blondell was adamant, "But no boats left the island," he said.

"But what if one was moored off shore? Out beyond the reef?"

"But it would have to be there virtually all year round?"

"So?"

"So the locals would know who or if the reclusive lady had one."

"Have you checked? Pancardi asked.

Blondell shook his head.

"Have the locals?"

Blondell shrugged.

At this point a dark haired man, wearing a blue military style tunic, who had been listening intently to the pair's conversation, appeared from behind one of the nearby palms. Simultaneously the official who had accompanied them both to the morgue also reappeared. It was clear from the interaction between the two who had the greater authority. They conversed swiftly and then the military official approached the two Europeans and spoke.

"Faaia, tells me that you have a theory on the woman and the fire?"

"Yes," replied Blondell, "Inspector Pancardi here of Interpol has some serious concerns about the investigation."

The military official heard the words Inspector and Interpol and instantly his attention antennae were raised.

"I am sure that he will ask you for some requirements," Blondell continued, and turning to Pancardi asked him to explain the situation.

As Pancardi reiterated his theory, Blondell moved to the local man who had already heard the full explanation.

" How many servants did the woman have?" he asked.

The man was swift in his reply, " Just the one, the one I've interviewed."

" I want to speak to her," Blondell requested.

"She is being re-questioned at the official residence right now. By the government officers you saw coming ashore," he added.

"So what is your title?" Blondell asked.

"I am the assistant to the official on the island," the man replied.

" So you would know if the woman had a boat."

" She did," he said, he had issued the mooring permit. He turned and pointed to the plush power boat moored off shore, "That's hers, was hers" he said. " That boat is cursed."

Blondell's ears pricked up.

"The last couple that owned the boat died in an accident while diving," he said, "then the boat remained for a while because no one wanted to buy it. People said it was unlucky, and now this and another owner of that boat dead."

"So how come the dead woman got the boat?" asked Blondell.

"I think she bought it from the insurance company in the end. It was one of the worst incidents of shark attack we have ever had, before or since. The tourists were frightened to go into the water and there was a government cull on tiger sharks. That was until the conservationists got involved. She only ever used the boat for diving though, and she didn't seem scared at all." He paused and then added, "Your friend is wrong."

" Why?" asked Blondell.

"Because the boat is there and the dingy which the dead woman used to get out to it is still at the shoreline, see," he pointed, "she could not have done what he said, no woman could."

Blondell smiled at the man and tried to estimate his age – he guessed mid twenties.

He imagined how the ideas of Pancardi might seem too incredible for contemplation. How murder, intrigue and a sheer, callous, devotion to freedom at all cost, might seem too far fetched to comprehend. Blondell considered the worst crime such a small village community could experience and then realised that Pancardi was indeed a character whose experience and pathology must seem alarming.

" This woman," said Blondell, " has already killed four men, one woman and a boy that we know of."

The jaw of the assistant dropped, " But she was so gentle and feminine," he said incredulously.

" Ah the female of the species being more deadly than the male and all that," replied Blondell. "She has no issue with killing," he paused smiling, "in fact she'd have thought it rather amusing, a bit of fun." Blondell paused again, "In fact with the boy she killed, she gutted him to hide the proceeds of a robbery inside his corpse. Oh and she strangled a nurse with her bare hands."

The Assistant was trying to come to terms with the woman he had known; the charming ,well presented, and often rather helpless female he had known and the description of the deeds she had undertaken – the two did not equate.

"If you were of use to her," Blondell continued, "she would have seemed lovely."

"My God," interrupted the man, now slightly green at the gills.

Blondell continued, " But if you had got in her way she would have killed you with as much ease and lack of compassion as you swat a fly."

Blondell could see the man gulp, "Carlo," he called to Pancardi, "there is a boat it seems." He turned back to the now unnerved assistant, "I want the file on the shark attack and any details on that boat," he said.

Chapter 8

"It is almost too incredible to believe," said the dark skinned official, "she was so polite and very nice to me."

They were walking now, back toward the air-conditioned office and the cool of the tiled walls and ceiling fans of the official residence. The air was heavy and the sand hot on Blondell's sandals. He could have done with dipping his feet into the sea, washing his face in the cool of clear water. His imagination ran to the idea of a long cold drink, something made from fresh fruit, freshly squeezed. He wiped the sweat from his face and the white handkerchief was now a grubby shade of grey. He noted the looks on the faces of the local populace as the young man passed them. The look was a look known to policemen throughout the world. A look which was thrown in the direction of men, who were seen as an intrusion for most of the time, until their presence, defence, or solace, was needed. There were the traffic cops who rode around giving people speeding tickets and pulling them over to check cars for defects. The same men who at other times would be calmly lifting bodies out of cars and covering corpses with the red blankets they carried in their boots. Blondell knew the terminology, "pig," he had used it himself during the anti-war demonstrations in London, and yet here he was one of the "sic-em" team. He was now, "the man," he was one of them. One of those to be distrusted, abused and finally used when convenience became expedient. The young official walking ahead of him had not noticed it yet, but Blondell could see and smell it in the wind, his faculties were attuned to it – it was so strong here he could almost taste it.

Blondell pondered on a death in paradise and knew that Pancardi was probably right. Pancardi had learned to accept the failure of the human race over the years; learned to accept that people were inherently greedy, cowardly and stupid. Blondell questioned whether he would also be able to make the quantum leap of realising that his own daughter was in fact a monster. He pondered on the freezer, had she been devious enough to store a corpse there and wait, wait for the right time to use it. She was probably one of the most cruel and hard adversaries he had worked against. He reflected, no she was the hardest – her heart was a stone.

A stone caught in his sandal and he bent to twist it loose from under his toe. Then it struck him in a simple blinding flash; the correct answer was nearly always the simple one.

"She would be nice to you," Blondell scoffed, as they entered the official residence, which doubled as a police station, "because," he continued cruelly, "you were useful."

"But why I have no official status."

"Really? What you could not warn her if the police were on their way? You might even go to her house yourself and try to solve things. After all she was, nice," he accentuated the term with a sneer and a lilt to his voice. "You might even have warned her, inadvertently of course, but it would have been a warning nonetheless."

"If I had a suspicion of wrong doing," said the official, in the most indignant of tones, "I would have no reason to warn any one – especially Mrs. Alice."

"That isn't her name, even that is false."

The young official was opening filing cabinets now and apologising for the way information was stored. He lifted a large plastic wallet out of the grey metal drawer and placed it on the large desk in the centre of the room. Then he reached up to turn on an overhead light which hung like the illumination over a snooker table in the gloom.

The whole room looked like a throw back to the nineteen seventies. There was no computer, no link to the outside world, except by telephone, and the one on the table was the old dial fronted black bakelite model. The cord was a plaid of brown and black which gave the room the sombre look of a cold-war interrogation room. Little wonder thought Blondell that the locals greeted the man with suspicion as he passed. He pondered on how many had been interviewed under the snooker light and how many had been cowered into submission by the stark austerity of the room.

"This was a big case," said the official leaning under the light.

"Really?" replied Blondell, pulling up a chair.

"Since I have been here there have only ever been two shark attacks and this was by far the worst we have ever seen."

Blondell was spreading the papers before him on the table. A small ceiling fan was struggling to circulate the air and the generator outside was fighting a gasping battle with life. As he flicked the pages he asked casually, "So what is your title exactly?" he paused, "and I don't even know your name," he paused again as he flicked the pages of the file. He did not make eye contact.

The official's stature grew visibly as he said, "Faaia Zakariyaa, and I am Assistant Island Administrator."

"So you're the assistant, where is the official?"

"He," replied Faaia, "he is at the President's residence organizing the tour for next year. It is the independence celebrations and the President he will come to Dhangethi." He paused thoughtfully, "The President's residence is on another island in the South Atoll so the official is not able to meet with you."

"That's rather lucky for my colleague and me then?"

The younger man was bemused by the European stranger and the things he said which seemed to make little or no sense. He would have thought that seeing the official would have been an asset. There would have been more fuss and then an official meal at the residence. The only other person who had behaved in the same humble style had been Mrs. Alice and she was now being classified as some kind of monster; he was confused and doubting his own evaluations. In the last twenty four hours the whole of reality had been turned upon its head and he simply didn't like it.

"So you're in charge?" asked Blondell.

"Yes I suppose that is so."

"Good, excellent in fact," laughed Blondell. "Then you can get us out to this boat which was the property of..."

"Mrs. Alice," chirped Faaia.

"The details in here say a frenzied shark attack on two divers," quoted Blondell, looking at the papers before him.

Faaia nodded.

"And how often do these happen?"

"Never," Faaia replied, "not in my lifetime anyway. He paused thoughtfully, "But the old men of the island tell of the legend of the Tiger Ghost."

Blondell's ears pricked up, "The Tiger Ghost?" he asked.

"The legend says that once when food was scarce, because the men had hunted all the tuna and marlin the tiger sharks set siege to the islands of the North Atoll. Any man that went into a boat to fish was attacked and killed. The people of the villages got so scared that fishing ceased and they thought of offering up their old, sick and dying to the sharks in payment for all the tuna they had taken. It was said that the leader of the sharks was a ghost tiger. A virtually white shark with just the bare minimum of stripes along his flanks," Faaia paused, "when all the old and sick had been thrown into the sea the sharks were still not happy, and their leader came to the shore to speak with the village elders. He walked onto the sand on his fins and spoke with a cruel sharp tongue; an agreement was struck that all the human dead were to be thrown into the sea from that day onward and the sharks would leave."

"And would Alice have known this legend?"

"Oh yes," said the young official, "she loved to talk with the old men in the coffee houses and they were flattered by her beauty. No," he corrected himself, "she seduced them with her looks. Sat with them and talked even when their English was not too good. One or two of them did work at her house, some on the walls others on a garden of sorts. They did her decorating even if they were not that good she paid them." He reflected again, "She just managed to charm everyone that she met," he smiled as if recollecting, "everyone liked her. She kept herself to herself but the old men she liked. Perhaps she saw them as father figures," he paused again, "those were the men she liked."

"And this charm was like the Devil himself," Blondell added. "She was a woman of wealth and taste?"

Faaia was nodding, "She was," he said.

Blondell was flicking through the papers, "It says here that nothing of Mrs Halspen was found? Not a thing."

"Well that's not totally true," Faaia replied, "they found her tank scored by the teeth of tiger sharks. Parts of her wetsuit were also found."

Blondell was studying the reports in front of him, "But no body parts, nothing."

"The Tiger Ghost he leaves nothing, the old men said," Faaia was grinning.

"But you don't believe that do you?" asked Blondell.

"No I don't!" the younger man exclaimed.

"Why?" asked Blondell.

"Because the white shark is a legend, an old wives tale."

"And?" added Blondell.

"And there were bits of the man found."

"So what did happen?" asked Blondell.

Faaia's voice lowered, "There was a real problem for our official here because the word got out. The divers they stopped visiting and so a national cull was organized to get the shark numbers down. Look at all the shops they have shark teeth and jaws still in the windows. It was all a panic and a knee-jerk reaction." His face distorted, "It was all a mess," he continued. "Mrs Alice she was good, she still went diving and used her boat, and some others too were not afraid."

"So what do you think happened?"asked Blondell, closing the file. "There's not much more here than complete panic," he reflected, "and not many answers."

Faaia considered, "Well I believe they were attacked by sharks. Tiger sharks are the most aggressive and they will attack until everything is gone." He paused, "I have seen them when they do this and they can destroy totally." His voice lowered, "I think the woman she got into trouble on the dive, in water they did not know. Maybe she cut herself and then she was in trouble and the husband is in the water and he goes to help and they both end up dead."

"He must have been very brave?" Blondell questioned.

"No he was very stupid," replied Faaia. "No local would get into the water when there was an attack going on. There would have been nothing he could do."

"So he is attacked too and only parts of him are eaten in the confusion."

"Yes."

"But the woman was the first attack so they ripped her apart in a feeding frenzy?"

"Maybe?" Faaia seemed unsure, "but it did seem strange to me, at the time."

"Why, you know about sharks?" asked Blondell.

"Yes I do, but it just did not feel right. Like it was some kind of elaborate fraud."

"And the island official?"

"Well he and the President wanted everything back to normal as quickly as possible."

"And the boat stayed where it was?"

"Yes, until Mrs. Alice bought it."

"And you didn't say anything about how you felt."

"On what?" asked Faaia.

"The murder," Blondell was emphatic.

"What murder?" asked Faaia totally bemused by the word.

Alex Blondell pushed the file back across the desk, "This murder," he said, "Alice Parsotti staged this and because the authorities were either too lazy or too inept to do a clear investigation the whole thing was quickly hushed up. There is a massive shark cull and I expect a few albino sharks also got exterminated in the process, so the local legend could stay alive. The islands get the all clear for divers again and the tourism isn't interrupted too much. All those dollars coming in, all that necessity and Mrs. Alice has her corpse."

"Precisely," said a voice from the shadows, "Alice has her corpse." Pancardi stepped into the room, "I think we have found the identity of the corpse don't you Alex? And I think she kept the body in that freezer. No – I know she kept that body in that freezer. She had her escape planned just in case."

"She reminds me of you," replied Blondell turning as he heard the Italian's voice behind him.

"Really!" exclaimed Pancardi, "she reminds you of me?"

"You know what I mean," Blondell defensively replied. "She is your daughter after all said."

Faaia Zakariyaa's jaw dropped as his eyes moved from man to man. He was having difficulty understanding how Mrs. Alice and the Italian detective could be father and daughter, but he could see a family resemblance around the chin and ears.

Chapter 9

Miles Bolton sat next to Alice Parsotti engrossed by the individual screen which was before him; his headphones were placed over his head.

The drone of the aircraft engines and the surprisingly pleasant meal, following the adrenaline rush of seeing Blondell, made Alice feel sleepy. Her head was propped against the fuselage and the airline standard brown chenille blanket was wrapped around her shoulders and draped over her lap. Since the crash in Canada she had been less happy with flying, but in the end her head had won over her heart and she had taken a short flight to get her back into normality. Her reasoning had been very simple: Air flight is more safe than driving a car, statistically, therefore if she was on one of those flights that did go down, how likely was it to happen to her a second time? Her mind started to meander through statistics and the surreal jokes of Vic Reeves and Bob Mortimer and their statement that 88.2% of all statistics were made up on the spot. She snorted and Bolton stirred in his seat. Her half-awake mind wandered through the statistics on women over the age forty being more likely to be run over by a bus than receive a marriage proposal. She thought of her own, Paul West, on a warm April day in Florence. Her mind drifted through the ancient cafes and walkways and she then was at the door of the house in Venice. Paul was gone, and she was alone but there were people watching her and despite having a key she could not get in. She examined the lock and there was some substance jamming it and then an eagle flew above her making her look up and then she saw a marksman in the square. Now she was running and bullets were whizzing by, there was screaming and Alex Blondell was blocking the exit – she couldn't get out and she fumbled and dropped her .38 calibre and Pancardi…She turned to her side and the dream changed.

Miles Bolton didn't even notice her, his mind was engrossed in the images set before his grinning face.

The stewardesses in matching brown uniforms and bright red headgear were moving up and down the length of the plane as Alice began to enter a whole new arena of sleep.

"Wow a whacking great turtle," said the man, as he pulled his diving mask from his face. "Must have been nearly four feet across if it was an inch."

The man was dark haired but no longer young. His stomach was paunchy and the wet-suit he wore, in consequence, looked too tight. He was hauling himself out of the water up a set of chrome steps and threw his flippers onto the deck, before turning to offer his hand to the woman in the water behind him.

"Fantastic Alice," he said to her as he grabbed her arm. He called to a second woman who had been in the shade of an awning reading, "You should have seen it Sheila," he said, "it was a monster." He laughed, "Sheila, it had a beak like a parrot."

"I'm glad dear," the woman replied totally disinterested.

"Alice you're a marvel, that's one of the best dives I've been out on. How do you know about these places?"

Alice Parsotti smiled and removed the single oxygen tank from her back as she spoke, "A lot of the locals know this place but they don't take the tourists. Dhangethi is their place and they don't like to share it." She paused, as if she was recalling something, "But the local official showed me some fantastic spots."

"How did you get him to reveal such a treasure?"

"Trade secret I'm afraid," Alice replied.

"And now you've shown us," said Sheila, as she handed them both a cold beer. She shot a knowing look at the man as if to say, don't ask personal questions.

"You know I can't drink, Sheila," said the man, "not if I'm diving again."

"Well if you do go again John," chirped Alice, "I'm afraid it will be on your own. I am bushed. And with the location I don't think it's a good idea to go alone. There are quite a few tiger sharks off this reef."

He took the beer.

"Anyway I have to get back ashore," said Alice, "I'm cooking tonight remember?"

Sheila nodded, obviously pleased that she had the opportunity to get off the boat for a little while. Diving had not really been her idea of a holiday. The water was too dangerous and she simply didn't feel safe with sharks. The sun was too hot and there was not enough to do – no shops to visit. In fact she had asked John not to buy the boat but to rent it for a year or two, just to, "See how they got on." He however, as always, had jumped in with both feet and now they had it for life. She would have liked to cruise the fashion outlets of Rome, rather than huff and puff around the reefs of the Maldives. She could see all the fish she needed on her television screen and she blamed David Attenborough and the false notion that everyone had to experience certain things before they died. They were still on her husband John's list, she wanted glamour, a casino, a fast car, and runs through the Dolomites with wind in her hair, not this roughing it on a boat moored off a desert island.

Alice was climbing into the small dingy tied up alongside, "About seven Sheila?" she called.

"Lovely," Sheila replied, "and we'll bring the wine. John keeps the odd bottle here for special occasions. I think he's got some Rothschild, some wonderful Chateau or other," she called more loudly as the dingy began to move away on the current.

"It won't be that special you know," Alice shouted in reply. "I'm not that good a cook."

"That's what you said last time," John yelled, waving as Alice Parsotti disappeared behind an outboard toward the shore and her preparations for that, special, dinner.

Miles Bolton was absorbed by the film and when the stewardess passed to ask if either of them wanted coffee he turned to see Alice asleep. He thought about disturbing her but saw that her eyelids were moving rapidly and that she was dreaming. He thought about sliding his hand under the blanket to see if she really had no knickers on, and then changed his mind; he could do that later when they were back at his home.

Alice was in the kitchen now and the preparations were nearly complete. The freezer had been chilling down and she was pleased that the shell fish were properly laced. She knew her two guests would relish them, whilst she could absolve eating them on the grounds of an allergy and go for melon. Last time they had eaten their fill of shell fish and she had avoided them. If she did so again then nothing would seem suspicious. They had a long discussion on how certain foods tended to disagree with some people and how she could eat fish quite happily but nothing in a shell.

Her eyes were moving rapidly now as the adrenaline in her system began to kick into her dream.

She calculated the body weight of the man and knew that getting his corpse to the boat would be hard work but if she wrapped him in a blanket she could drag the body, rather than lift it, to the dingy under the cover of darkness. If things went wrong and the poison didn't work she could always smash his skull with a claw hammer. She thought of Rasputin and the poison and the bullets and the river and how even then he had fought for life, she couldn't afford that mistake – she doubled the dose of strychnine, before leaving the kitchen.

The real problem was the woman, she had to collapse first and there could not be any broken bones or there would be immediate suspicion. She knew that the DNA test would take time and that the strychnine would be found even if the body was burnt, and if they found the body in the freezer she would at least have a few hours head start.

She shifted in her seat and arched her back against the stiff posture. Miles Bolton looked at her and asked if she was ok – she gave a nonsense reply and he went back to his film.

"Mrs. Alice?" called Marjarla from the table near the shore line.

The girl was young and only too pleased to have the work of looking after the house when Mrs. Alice was not there – Alice knew that much. She was paid twenty five American dollars a day and the money went into her bank account as regularly as day followed night. She was the envy of the other island girls. Soon she would have enough for herself and her boyfriend to have their own place and she could still keep house for Mrs. Alice. That much she had told Alice when they had their – girlie chats.

Alice turned from her completed cooking, "Coming Marjarla," she called.

Outside the young Maldivian had set a table under the coconut palms. The table cloth was bright red cotton with napkins of a dark copper colour next to fine silver.

A Venetian cut glass decanter holding iced water sat in the centre next to a cork screw, though she knew John Halspen was pretentious enough to uncork the wine before they arrived. Last time he, and his wife with no taste in clothes, had lectured her on the merits of wine and how to prepare it for the table.

"Take the night off and go and see that boyfriend of yours Marjarla," said Alice, "this looks wonderful, wonderful."

In each wine glass stood an angel fish made from folded and trimmed Palm frond.

"It looks lovely," continued Alice. "Oh and there is no need to be here for breakfast, I don't expect either I or my guests will get up early." She reflected, "Tell you what, take the day off. I can throw this lot into the dishwasher myself in the morning and the clearing up can be done the next day. There'll only be a bed to make." She paused again, "Yes," she reflected, "you go off and enjoy yourself; you've worked hard enough looking after this place this year."

After several profuse thank you, thank you, thank you exchanges, Marjarla Jungarilly left the house and began to walk toward her boyfriend's parent's home. Alice knew she would stay there and they would make love, though neither her parents, who would think she was at Mrs. Alice's, nor his, who would assume the same, would know about it. Alice had given her condoms before and shown her how to use them and had told her that she could use the spare room from time to time. Marjarla had been careful on both counts, but her boyfriend wanted to come to the house more often. Marjarla knew when to take the chance and Alice liked her for that and despite her young age she was learning very fast.

Alice always left plenty of free condoms but she still had the new chest freezer fitted with a large hasp lock. Marjarla had wondered why when the thing was empty; when it was full she would never steal from Mrs. Alice, she did not want to lose her job. She had told her that too, but Alice still had the lock fitted.

Alice visualised Marjarla turning into the main street, she saw one of the local gossips ahead and melted into the semi-darkness of bushes, before turning onto the beach to approach her boyfriend's house silently from the shoreline. In the morning she would slip out after his parents had gone to work and his little sister had left the house for the school; but in the night she would make love. Despite only being fifteen Alice had told her what to do. She had told the girl things about men and what to do to excite them, she had laughed nervously when Alice told her to use her mouth, hands and fingers in a certain way. At first the girl had thought it strange, but when she tried certain techniques on her boyfriend she reported back how he had moaned and writhed. Marjarla had evaluated the situation after that and if Alice wanted to lock her freezer – she could.

John Halspen was clutching his chest, "What's the matter?" Alice was asking, "Where does it hurt? Do you need a doctor?"

He was trying to speak as Sheila began to vomit into the bowl of shellfish she had before her.

"The shell fish, food poisoning," he said, trying to struggle to his feet.

His body was swaying now and he couldn't breathe and he was grabbing at Alice.

"There's something wrong with the food," he struggled, sweat oozing from his face.

"Oh?" said Alice calmly as she helped him to the ground, "there's nothing wrong, you've just been poisoned." She smiled, "In about two minutes you'll be dead, just like your wife there."

John Halspen was trying to get up, trying to see Sheila. He wanted to call her name but all the muscles in his body were convulsing and his throat didn't work. He wanted her to help him. Alice was pushing a tea towel into his mouth and he wanted to pull it away but his hands wouldn't work.

"I am sorry about this John," said Alice aloud, though she was still asleep.

"Sorry about what?" asked Bolton, pulling one of the earphones away from his ear.

Alice gave no reply and Bolton knew she was talking incoherently in her sleep. He wondered if John was an ex-lover who she was re-dumping in a dream.

"Do you want some coffee?" Miles Bolton asked her nonchalantly, as she turned and moved again.

She said, "No thanks," and pushed the tea towel into the bastard.

She could see his eyes going wide and they hadn't even started the main course, never mind the coffee. She'd have coffee later, after she had sorted the mess out.

"After dinner," Alice spoke in her sleep again.

"Ok," Bolton said, glad he could return to his second movie; it took up where the first one left off. She could sleep on the plane now, as long as she was lively later, or in the morning. Whoever John was he was very unlucky. Bolton could see the ratio of Parsotti's waist to hips and he liked the fullness of the inverted strawberry which stared back at him. She could mumble all she liked as far as he was concerned.

The crack of gunfire spat out of the screen and the woman driver was hit and the car was over a bridge and now the agent was trying to revive the woman under water. He replaced the earpiece and left Parsotti to her uncomfortable dreams.

Shelia Halspen had died as she had lived, in obscurity. She was face down in a bowl of mixed clams and her own vomit. Her fat husband had lasted longer than Alice expected. His complexion was blue and there seemed to be a glazed and startled look on his face as he lay in the sand looking up at the stars with the tea-towel in his mouth. The rigidity of his muscles brought on by the strychnine would soon pass and then she'd move him out to their dingy and onto the bigger boat.

Alice worked quickly. She lifted the woman under the arms and walking backward dragged the corpse into the utility area of the house. Two large rail tracks were left in the sand as she pulled the body toward the chest freezer. Sheila was roughly the same build as herself, perhaps a little stockier and certainly a little heavier. But they were the same height give or take an inch. Her hands and feet were larger and less dainty than Alice, but that was a small detail. Once a good fire had taken hold of the corpse those little details would be insignificant. She wiped the vomit from the woman's face and pushed her headlong into the freezer. With the corpse on its back she arranged the legs and arms into a sleeping posture, and then shut the lid and snapped the lock shut.

With a counterpane from the spare bed she made a travois with which she could pull the lump of a man to the dingy. To her surprise it was easier than she thought, and no locals were walking on the beach. Moonlit walks were the preserve of tourists, the city dealers and dwellers who relished the natural beauty of the Maldives, whilst the locals sat in front of their flat screen televisions wishing they were somewhere else.

Lifting the body was more difficult than Alice had envisioned. The man was heavy and the body lolled and rolled in the tide until eventually she pushed it into the bottom of the small boat. She sat in the water and realised that the Gucci dress she wore was now ruined.

At the table she removed the vomit stained table cloth, emptied the plates of strychnine and clams into the sea, rinsing the plates and removing evidence as she did so. All the while she was scanning the darkness for shapes and movement – there was nothing. She had chosen her night well, making sure there was plenty of family entertainment on the local television station.

The immediate panic over and the crime scene cleared , her mind turned to the complexities of the night ahead as she sat calmly eating her main course and staring out toward the dingy with the body under the counterpane. Fish she concluded were marvellous creatures; they would devour the evidence for her and leave nothing. She considered the strychnine. No one would find anything remiss about the odd fish corpse on the shore, the early morning wading birds would probably clear those away.

Now she had the body she needed, her plan was so simple it was virtually fool-proof. First she would lash her dingy to Halspen's and then she would take the both and the body out to the Halspen's power boat, after that, take all three out beyond the reef. She would then put Halspen's fat corpse into his diving gear and chum the water with the blood and fish heads she had in the dingy, that would attract the sharks. She would put some of the chum into Sheila's wet-suit and then lower that into the water too. By the time the tigers had finished the authorities would find some bits and pieces of diving gear and they'd think shark attack. By morning the deed would be done and she could take her own dingy back to shore. Marjarla would not be back until at least late afternoon, and about now she'd be more concerned about not making a noise when her orgasm came in her boyfriend's bed. Perfect, she poured some more wine and noted the fruity flavour;

she turned the bottle to look at the label. She'd try to get some of this when she was in Europe it would be worth the effort.

She spoke, "And don't forget the oars."

Bolton lifted his earpiece, in case she might be talking to him. Satisfied she wasn't, he returned to the movie which was now reaching a bloody car-crash climax.

"Need the oars to get back to shore, without the outboard," she muttered.

Now she needed to keep her strength up for the night ahead. She looked at her watch it read 9.41. Alice was particularly pleased with the Pork which had a crisp crackling and was complemented perfectly by the rich red wine which the Halspens had brought along. The smell of the garlic within the meat and the lemon balm sauce over it drifted into the night air.

Now she had her escape ready if she needed it. She wondered what would happen if there was a power cut. Marjarla was loyal but the thing would stink if it went on too long, perhaps she thought, a generator, get a generator. She lifted her glass and gave a toast to the night, "to success" she laughed out loud, "mine."

"What?" asked Bolton.

She woke from her dream state and stretched.

"You were talking in your sleep," he commented, removing the headphones as the credits began.

"Nothing too incriminating I hope?" she giggled.

"Well it sounded to me like you were giving a toast at a do or something."

"Really?" she yawned, "how strange. How was your film?"

"Films," he corrected.

She yawned again, "How long have I been asleep then?" she asked.

Bolton looked at his watch, "I'd say about four hours give or take."

"That long," she stretched and Bolton noticed her ample breasts, they were firm with erect nipples and he knew he was going to enjoy them.

"Do you want some coffee?" he asked.

"Actually," she paused, "I could do with the loo first."

Chapter 10

When Miles Bolton and Claudette Cicello stepped out of the London cab at the end of Stamford Street, Alice was suitably unimpressed as he unexpectedly led them both across the street to a set of heavy mahogany doors which looked like the entrance to a factory.

The cabbie placed their suitcases at the kerb and rang a large bell and immediately a concierge in a smart uniform appeared as the doors opened inward. He lifted the cases inside and Bolton gave him a handsome tip.

"Mr. Bolton," said the concierge, "nice holiday?"

"Wonderful Fred, thank you," Bolton replied walking into the large entrance hall.

Alice noted the large Victorian glass dome in the ceiling and the ornate tiling on the floor which the developers had left in tact during the conversion.

"This is Miss Cicello, she is an old friend and she'll be staying for a while," Bolton added.

Alice Parsotti noted the, "for a while reference," and the overly friendly smile of the concierge, which gave an air of acceptance and supplication to Bolton.

"Shall I get a key done sir?" Fred asked nonchalantly.

Bolton looked at Cicello, the concierge looked from one to the other; Alice then studied Bolton, who grinned and shrugged, "Good idea Fred, excellent in fact," he replied.

"I'll bring the cases up sir, or get young John to," said Fred, as both Cicello and Bolton stepped into the lift.

"Fine Fred," Bolton acknowledged.

Alice felt the whole begin to move upward slowly and wondered on what floor his little flat was located.

"This whole building used to be some sort of printing works," Bolton informed, "IPC I think, you know those that did Woman's Own and other glossy magazines. Then when Murdoch moved his papers out of Fleet Street down to Canary Wharf well the flood gates opened and IPC sold up. I got in early and had a bit of an investment opportunity and well here we are."

The lift stopped, the indicator light was illuminated against the top floor.

"Top floor, nice," Alice Parsotti remarked. She certainly had not been expecting this.

"It is." Bolton smiled, "I got in very early through some connections and got the penthouse." He paused, "There's a lovely roof-top garden as well and a fine view of the river."

Alice Parsotti was beginning to re-evaluate the man, "So what precisely do you do Miles?" she asked.

"What now?" he replied, turning the key in the lock to the Penthouse. "Well I deal in works of art, it's a bit of a hobby of mine."

As the door opened her eyes were greeted by fine marble sculpture, paintings, and porcelain. She had expected an old woman world of chintz and lace, and a mother waiting, holding his slippers, or a minimalist bloke-pad – what she saw astounded her.

"All this from a hobby?" she asked.

"Well I used to be an investment banker, and when mother died I inherited a little."

Alice sighed; inwardly thankful her radar and character assessment had not totally deserted her. That was why he was a boor – he was a mother's boy, a social loser, a man who was inept with women; and yet he had something which made him interesting, he had confidence and a kind of self-assurance. It was a strange mix within one personality.

"This is lovely," she said, passing a picture which hung next to the telephone table in the expansive entrance hall.

The painting in predominantly blues and green depicted a group of female nudes bathing. Alongside it were sketches in pastels and chalk which looked like they might be copies of Degas.

"Cezanne," he said with an almost casual distain. "I don't like it much, but mother and father did – I'll probably sell it on some time."

As they turned into the lounge she wondered if the Degas drawings were originals too.

"Coffee?" he asked. "That," he said, "is my favourite," he nodded toward the bedroom.

How cheesy she thought. He hasn't even been inside the place for more than a few minutes and already he expects me to perform like some whore.

"Go see," he said, "I'll fix us a drink, would you like some champagne?"

Immediately she thought of Richard Dalvin, the sex-pest Professor she had garrotted in Florence. The remembered scent of his body odour came back to her nostrils and briefly she thought she might use the same technique on this man.

"No thanks," she replied, "just a coffee would be nice, and a shower."

She walked into the master bedroom which had a warm atmosphere. In a display cabinet stood three figurines. Three white porcelain figures of young girls, each with their wrists or ankles bound with golden chains; one standing, one sitting and one kneeling. The cabinet was well lit and the mirrored back gave an unusual perspective to the figures. Below those, on a lower shelf, stood Mephistopheles holding a girl by the hips and hair, her buttocks up against his loins while she supported herself against his pelvic thrusts, on an antique chest; he was leering as he entered her.

At the far end of the room and covering a whole wall hung a canvass of red and maroon. A canvass which spread from wall to wall and drew the eyes deep into the shades.

"Seductive, isn't it?" Bolton asked entering the room.

"It's beautiful," replied Alice with sincere honesty.

"The coffee will be brewed in a moment or two; is Viennese style ok? It's got a hint of fig?"

"Lovely."

"The canvass is a Rothkowitz. Father bought that in New York in 1951. I even got to meet the artist when I was a boy. Father knew him quite well; there was some sort of connection with the Kennedy family, Joe the father and not the two boys. I always found Roth rather remote, with his Russian accent and intense eyes. I think he frightened me a little bit."

"Mark Rothko?"

"That's the one. Father sold a few of his pieces but mother couldn't bear to part with this one, she said it was Rothko's portrait of him," he paused, "especially after he killed himself."

"Who your father?"

"No Rothko. And I have come to love it, she was right it is my father, emotionally not physically."

Alice Parsotti was stunned.

"I only have a few nice things left now; some of the smaller ones, done after he had his heart attacks." Bolton continued, "Like these figurines, father had these made. A special commission for mother's birthday, the slave market he named them. Made by Peggy Davies Ceramics in Stoke on Trent. My father always liked German porcelain especially the stuff from Selb in Bavaria and after they went out of business he had these made. Peggy Davies worked for Royal Doulton years ago, all those hideous crinoline ladies and she knew Clarice Cliff. Well she trained this young modeller and he did these."

Bolton opened the cabinet case and handed one piece to Alice.

"They're beautiful," she said, "the models are beautiful."

"I only collect the most beautiful of pieces," he replied.

"And these are beautiful," she returned.

"And so too are you Claudette," he blurted.

It was at that point she realised how totally inept he could be. A cultured man who could or would not be able to really understand his own failings. She found it hard to evaluate the dichotomy of his character.

"Coffee?" she said, "I am whacked and I think I need to sleep."

"Of course," he said apologetically, and led her across the open-plan living space toward a terracotta and blue room.

"I call this the Florence room," he laughed as they entered. "It reminds me of Florence in the spring, the terracotta of the tiles and the blue of the Wisteria."

Alice noticed the large white double bed which was flanked by two small ornately inlaid mahogany cabinets. She wondered if they were original – she evaluated they would be. On either side of the bed above each of the cabinets hung some fine pencil studies – they looked like the early work of Renoir.

"I hope you like it here?" he blurted.

The door bell rang.

"That'll be our luggage," he chirped, "en suite is through that door," he pointed, "there are towels and everything you need in there."

The door bell rang again and he scuttled away.

Alice Parsotti looked at the works of art and estimated that the man must be a millionaire. She wondered what his father had done to be able to appreciate the beauty and investment of the works of art and what had been passed on to Miles.

"Miss Cicello's case in here John, if you please," he said as the cases arrived. And then handing Alice her coffee, said, "I'll leave you to your ablutions and rustle up a little something for us as a snack. You'll find a robe in the bathroom," and closed the door behind him.

Alice Parsotti lay naked on the bed her whole being refreshed by the pummelling massage of the shower. Her body glistened with the moisturiser which she had found and applied in the bathroom.

There was a soft knock at the door, "Can I interest you in a little food?" asked Bolton.

Alice drew a towel about her and stood, "Depends on what it is," she replied coquettishly.

"Just some smoked Salmon, Olives, Asparagus, and some fresh bread," Bolton replied.

Alice Parsotti wrapped in a huge bath towel opened the door and walked into the main living area. She was greeted by a smiling Bolton and a table set out with a small buffet and a bottle of Laura Pazzi Chianti opened and breathing.

"Did you find everything you needed," asked Bolton. He was showered himself and wrapped in a large robe.

"Yes, thank you," replied Alice.

"I expect you are tired?"

"I am."

"Well," said Bolton, "the bed is very comfortable, so you'll get a good nights sleep."

"I don't know London very well," Alice piped while they were eating, "how far is Chelsea from here?"

"It's not very far, just over the bridge and then you could walk to it, why?"

"Oh, I know someone who lives there, or did live there," Alice replied.

"There is a phone book if you want to look them up. Or I could get Fred to find out for you."

"Oh, it's not urgent," she nonchalantly replied. "This is a lovely wine," she added, though she thought she could detect a slight bitter edge at the back of her palate. "So what did your father do to be so interested in art?"

"Well that's rather a long story, are you sure you want to hear it?"

"I find all this sort of stuff fascinating." She quaffed another huge gulp of wine and Bolton watched her swallow. "Families and their history, mine is all screwed up with the Alsetti and the Pancardi, and then my mother and my grandmother and my father, well he was a right bastard by all accounts."

"Well," said Bolton, "we are the product of these people, but we don't have to be like them." He paused, "My father met my mother when on a visit to New York. He was in the civil service and had some sort of attachment to the Kennedy family and the Democrats. I don't really remember I was a small boy. Are you bored yet?"

Alice shook her head.

"Well," Bolton continued, "on a visit to the States in 19, something or other, he met my mother."

"So your mother was American?"

Bolton nodded, "She was ebrea."

"Meaning?" asked Alice.

"Jewish American."

"Oh, I see."

"I don't think you see at all. A bit like the blind man who says, I see, but doesn't really see at all, because he's blind. You see," he smirked, "mother worked with Dorothy Miller at the Museum of Modern Art."

"In New York?"

"Yes. She had in her turn worked with Peggy Guggenheim and Howard Putzel and when Jack the Dripper knocked my mother off her feet during one of his stupendous rages at a show, my rather gallant father, being an Englishman, stepped in. Mark Rothko was there and the whole thing became a bit of a riot. My father, fists raised to a drunk who could hardly see across the room let alone fight. Then Rothko paints my father for my mother, well paints his emotions at the time and the rest is history."

"Now I am lost," said Alice, "Jack the Dripper? And the canvas in your bedroom that is Rothko's portrait of your father?"

"The infamous Jackson Pollock, drunken bum." He was nodding in reply to her arm which was raised and pointing in the direction of his bedroom.

"So your mother is rescued from Jackson Pollack no less, by her knight in shining armour and then along comes you?"

"Well they did get married first," said Bolton smiling.

"So now they are both gone you are the sole inheritor of this fortune in modern art?" Alice asked.

"I had an older sister," the volume of his voice lowered, "but she died – heroin, about ten years ago," he paused as if recalling an event, "after that things were never really the same anymore. I gave up the banking and sold some of the artworks and houses and now I live here."

"Have you never been married?" asked Alice, her head feeling woozy and her vision blurring from the wine.

"Married?" laughed Bolton, "good lord no. I'm hardly an oil painting am I?"

Alice stood up, "I think I need to lie down,"she said, "I'm ..."

Bolton caught her as she swooned and lifted her into the cradle of his arms, as he did so the bath towel fell to the floor and she was naked in his arms. He carried Alice into his bedroom and laid her gently on the bed. Then he casually removed his robe and lay down beside her. She was aware of his presence and yet she was unable to resist him, it was as if the command wires between her brain and her muscles had been severed.

He touched her breast cupping it in the palm of his hand and her nipple sprang to attention. His mouth clamped upon it and she felt him suck and chew lightly as he ran his fingertips down her spine; she wanted to tell him to stop but her mouth would not work. Now he was behind her kissing her buttocks and then she was being turned over and her thighs parted; he was searching through all her intimate places with his tongue. She tried to stop him wanted to push him away but now her legs were over his shoulders and he was thrusting, pushing, driving and she simply could not move from under him.

He was talking to her throughout her ordeal telling her what he was going to do to her. Telling her that she was beautiful, telling her he was going to, "Fuck her senseless, lick her clitoris until her head exploded, and then come inside her." She could feel him deep inside her, and hear every word and grunt of encouragement he uttered, as the wine continued to make her limbs useless.

The wine, she remembered the bitter taste; his searching tongue and head was back between her legs now and she was beginning to feel the onset of sexual abandon. She wanted to bite his face, to fight, as he lifted her legs again, pushing her ankles against the mattress behind her head – then he was inside her again. This time he was deeper than ever and his urgency increased; she could feel his pace quicken and his body suddenly become rigid as he sought to drive himself ever deeper into her – and then it began to happen. Against her better judgement and her will she could feel the inner walls of her sex begin to clamp around him and her own muscular shudders and pulsations began.

Chapter 11

When Alice Parsotti woke her bladder felt as if it might explode, her inner thighs felt bruised and she lifted herself from the soft white bed and stumbled into the bathroom. She sat relieving the tension in her abdominal muscles and noticed the light streaming in through the yellow regency style chintz curtains; it gave the whole room a warm, light atmosphere. Her mouth was dry and there was a distinctive bitter taste at the back of her palate.

She flushed and stood up. Her muscles were stiff and the backs of her calves felt as if she had run a marathon. She tried to recall the events of the night before but they seemed lost in a mist of uncertainty. Something had happened but she couldn't quite be sure precisely what had been reality and what imagined or dreamt.

In the mirror a pale face with sunken eyes stared at her and she stuck out her tongue like Einstein for the intrusive camera. She felt exhausted, drained of her will and unconsciously her hand strayed to her sex – there was no sticky residue from a night of passion. She thought that she had slept in another room but she was awake here now.

She unwrapped a fresh toothbrush which Bolton had placed in the tumbler and began the ritual of cleaning away the fur from her tongue. Suddenly she turned to the bed to see if Bolton was in it; only one side showed the signs of use.

Alice sat on the edge of the bed and a sharp stinging sensation shot along her groin. It was the same feeling she remembered from when as a teenager she had danced for a hobby and persistent attempts at spreading her legs for the finale splits, had strained her groin. Things didn't make sense. She was always guarded, careful not to drink too much, why could she not remember how she got into bed? Her mind was struggling to find some images to replay but the recordings were blurred and all she could remember was the vague recollection of Bolton whispering obscenities into her ear. She felt rather than knew something was wrong.

She found her watch on the bedside table and next to it a brief note.

"Sorry about this but I've had to pop out for an hour or two – Miles."

She looked at the watch it read 12.41.The noted was timed 8.30. There was a knock at the door.

"May I come in?" asked a voice she recalled. She jumped back into the bed to cover her nudity.

"Please do," she called in reply.

It was Bolton with a tray.

"Scrambled eggs, fruit juice and coffee. I heard you flush so I thought you were up." He smiled, "I hope you slept well?" he enquired.

"I'm shattered," she said, "Actually, I feel like I've been run over by a train. How did I get to here?" she asked.

"Ah a little too much wine I'm afraid, you got a bit tipsy and went to bed. It might be a bit of jet lag too. There's no need to hurry off anyhow, stay as long as you like."

"So did you undress me?" she asked.

"Certainly not," Bolton replied indignantly, "I remembered what you said at the airport in Dubai."

Alice was having difficulty remembering, fine detail seemed to be eluding her.

"You know," Bolton whispered, "the knickers?"

"Oh," replied Alice, taking a forkful of eggs, they had a strange nutty taste. "Nice," she commented, "unusual aftertaste."

"That's the nutmeg. I know some people think it's a queer mix but mother said it works and it does. What's that one, eggs Benedict, with Worcester sauce? Now that is seriously strong," he replied.

"This is quite strong though?"

"An acquired Bolton taste, a bit like the porcelain?" he laughed.

"How did I get to bed then?" asked Alice.

"You stumbled," he smirked in reply.

"Oh dear how embarrassing," she took a deep draft of coffee.

"So I got you in here to sort yourself out, and toddled off to bed myself. Though to be frank I think I would have liked to undress you," he grinned.

"But you didn't?"

"Absolutely not."

"Mmm, what a gentleman," she said, taking another forkful of eggs.

"I fact, I would like to sketch you," he suddenly said.

She almost choked and reached for the freshly squeezed juice.

"You are incredibly beautiful and I think you would make an excellent model. You see I'm rather fond of the female form and being a bit of an amateur artist myself, I think I can do you justice. Would you let me sketch you sometime?"

Alice was so taken a back by the sincerity and originality of the request all she could muster was an open mouthed nod.

"Right that's settled then," he chirped. "Now I'm off to get some more coffee before the cha lady arrives.

"What?"

"Oh she comes in and tidies up and does my ironing and has a flick around with the duster."

"And she's not here yet is she?"

"Nope she's due at two. I'm a night owl so she never comes in the mornings, you've got plenty of time for a shower," he said, as he pulled the door closed behind him.

It was then that she noticed the clothes – her clothes, folded neatly across the back of a dressing table chair. It was like the dressing table itself, like the bathroom, everything was neat, tidy, and straight, with an almost military precision. Things didn't seem to fit with his character in the airport. The porcelain, the paintings, things were all wrong and she was feeling very sleepy again–she thought it was the jet-lag.

When Miles Bolton reappeared he was carrying an easel papers and pencils; Alice wanted to ask him what he was doing but for some reason her jaw would not work and her throat refused to obey any commands.

"First I'll get rid of the tray shall I?" he said, as he approached.

Alice sat propped against the headboard unable to move.

"Don't want a mess now do we?" He was talking to himself.

Alice could hear what he was saying but somehow it was not registering, it was deep in a chasm somewhere in a dream.

"In a few days you'll get used to it," he was saying, "Rohypnol, marvellous what it can do isn't it?"

He was pulling the duvet cover away now and posing her as if she were an artist's mannequin.

"You really are quite, quite, beautiful Claudette Cicello," his hands gently squeezed her breasts, "these are marvellous," he said.

He parted her thighs to expose her, there was no resistance and then stroked her intimately to make her moist and inviting; then finally he set up his easel like a serious artist.

"First I am going to draw you, then I'm going to fuck you, and when you wake up you won't remember a thing." He was speaking directly to her now. "After a few days you'll be totally unable to exist without it. That's the draw back I'm afraid. And people call it a date rape drug. Now that is absurd, Rohypnol is far more sophisticated than that." He began to sketch her, "No this is no rape drug, this my dear is far better than that crude stuff they developed some years ago. You see you can hear me, and when I fuck you, you'll feel me. You'll act like you would normally and then you'll forget everything." He chuckled as he worked, "I mean last night your orgasm was deafening."

❧

"I'm sick of all of this," said Blondell. "I sometimes think that we'll never catch her; she always seems one stage ahead."

"What we need to do is think like her?" Pancardi replied.

"Right! Well I've tried that and look where it has taken me – up another dead end. Besides she is your daughter and even you don't seem able to do that magical thing."

"No that is true," said Pancardi. "Look, she has tried to sell some of the jewels which disappeared from the main haul."

"And?"

"Well, if we think, then maybe we can be ahead of her." Pancardi was stern now, "We must think motive, motive, motive."

"I don't understand," Blondell yawned.

Pancardi's voice was cold, "Precisely!" he exclaimed. "Neither do I, but you must be having an effect – reason it out."

"Red wine," he ordered and the smiling girl poured him another.

The hotel was geared for tourists, and alcohol permitted. The local officials had returned to their meagre homes on Dhangethi and Blondell and Pancardi sat like large western potentates on pillows, perched at the bar on Vakaru, a neighbouring island.

"Think!" exclaimed Pancardi. "First why would she need to sell one of the jewels, or any of them? She has all of the money from Drecht and his backers, she would have made sure of that much. So why try to sell something which could be traced back to her?"

Blondell shrugged.

"Because," said Pancardi, "something has gone wrong for her. Maybe the money from the robbery is stashed away and she cannot get to it because someone is close to her, someone is watching her and she knows it."

"This is absurd," Blondell ejaculated, "so who is after her then and frightening her into making these mistakes."

"Isn't it obvious?" asked Pancardi.

"If it was would I be asking? It's not those lovely people at the Catholic Church is it?"

"It's you, you bloody fool." Pancardi wanted to grab his lapels and shake him a little. "You dog her wherever she goes. Do you have all the banks in Switzerland on red alert and Interpol at each, she knows you are waiting. Then there are those who placed the jewels in the vault, do you not think they are looking for her too."

"Yes," replied Blondell.

"So you have blocked off her cash supply – cut the supply lines and the army cannot survive; it must change course and she is changing course, this is making her do of the mistakes, no?"

"Oh really Carlo, she has money in other places, surely."

"But how does she know that you do not have these covered. Can she risk the chance of an appearance to collect money? She must sell something to fill the gap, to give her the one thing she needs, space, and that is her biggest mistake – she has over rated you as a pursuer."

"Charming acclamation," Blondell snorted.

"I do not wish to be cruel," said Pancardi, "but she fears you and thinks you know more than you do. She is wary of you and her threat letter to you proves this."

"So you think because of her fear of me she has not been to Switzerland to collect cash."

"Why did you say Switzerland?" asked Pancardi thoughtfully.

"Because that is one of the places I would use."

"Precisely it's so obvious," Pancardi replied with sincerity, "that is how she thinks. She needs money, being there is the only way she can get it, no?" Pancardi was grinning from ear to ear. "It must be in safe deposit boxes and not accounts, rather ironic. You have one or all of her Banks, how do you say, staked out. But you do not know which one is right and the banks won't help you."

"Christ we have the bitch."

"But we also do not," Pancardi corrected him.

"When she sells we can trace her through the sales."

"So where would you go now?" Pancardi asked.

"Somewhere safe, another bolt hole," Blondell replied. "And I'd try to do something to break up the surveillance and information gathering."

"Yes?" said Pancardi, slowly.

"So I'd get the investigators off my back."

"Yes," said Pancardi, "and?"

"I'm lost," replied Blondell quizzically.

"She thinks you know the bank, so if you know others do too. What else do these pursuers know? All the time she is thinking, maybe they know where she has her bolt holes, so she cannot use them either, just in case." He paused, "Hotels will be checked that you have seen to, so she must move in silence but where? And she must get you off her back – you are getting too close."

"All this is very good," replied Blondell, "but she is still out there free as a bird."

"So what would you do now?" asked Pancardi.

Miles Bolton entered Alice Parsotti. He was gripping one hip and like his Satanic figurine was pulling her hair to make her arch her back. She was on all fours on the bed and he was standing behind her, taking the pleasure he knew he deserved. His desire had been heightened as he drew her, until finally, he had been unable to restrain himself and had to take her. His sketch pad and pencils lay on the bed next to Alice and the pumping of his loins scattered them around his victim.

Alice was struggling with the Rohypnol, her loins were telling her to enjoy the moment and brace herself as the rhythm of his movements increased, but her strong mind was searching to rationalise the situation, to establish some connection with the here and now.

Miles Bolton made his mistake. He pulled savagely at her hair, jerking her head back, and clicking her vertebrae in a wild and uncontrolled attempt to reach his moment of bliss. The pain in her lower spine and scalp was so intense and so sharp that for brief fleeting seconds Alice was conscious and in control. A sharpened pencil rolled close to her fingers and she grabbed it and punched it like a dagger behind her.

Miles Bolton let out a yell of terror as the pencil penetrated his right thigh at the groin, instantly he released his grip and dropped to his knees at the end of the bed. Alice could see him between her spread thighs as he fell, he was pulling the pencil from the wound and blood was spurting from his groin. He was hissing through his teeth and holding the wound, trying to clamp it shut to stop the flow, but the blood was pumping into the air through his slipping fingers. Blood was hitting her back and legs as his artery sprayed a warm, sticky, masterpiece across the carpet and bed. Bolton's eyes were rolling in sheer terror as he tried to stem the flow of crimson which bubbled like a fountain. Alice collapsed onto her face and saw nothing more.

"I would find somewhere safe to lie low for a bit," said Blondell, "and you?"

"That doesn't really matter does it?" Pancardi replied. "What we need to ask is what would Alice do?"

"Right, so you've posed the question, what's the answer?" asked Blondell.

Pancardi's reply was swift, "A diversion," he said.

"A what?" asked Blondell.

"A diversion," Pancardi reiterated.

"And what would you suggest?"

"She has already told you in the letter she sent," Pancardi took a deep gulp of wine.

"Charlotte and Magdalene and the little one," Blondell blurted, "and we're sitting here in a damn hotel waiting for some DNA results that we already know the answer to and they are in danger. Fuck!" Blondell flipped open his phone.

Pancardi clasped his hand over Blondell's, "There is absolutely no need," he said, "Angelo Massimo and Pietro Grillva are at your home right now. This I have arranged personally today."

"Who the hell are they?" Blondell asked.

"They," Pancardi replied, "are the very best the Questura can supply. They are personal friends of Roberto Calvetti and me. They would not let any harm come to your little girl."

Blondell was sceptical, "Just how good?"

"Angelo," replied Pancardi "would lay down his life if he had to. Twice he has been wounded and once he fought off a group in a witness protection programme. He is from Italy and loyalty is his middle name – Magdalene will like him. If any man can be trusted he can; he is just like Roberto was, a man of honour and he will not let anything happen to your little girl." He paused thoughtfully, "Of this I am certain."

"How can you be so sure?" Blondell asked opening his phone once again.

"Because his daughter was killed."

"Shit!" exclaimed Blondell; his fingers froze on the key pad. "Who?"

"That is of no consequence," Pancardi lowered his voice, "we took care of those responsible."

Blondell knew precisely what that meant in Italian terms, but his fingers hit the home button on the key pad nonetheless and his phone called home. There was a brief interlude before a small laughing voice answered.

"Buongiorno," said Charlotte

Chapter 12

Angelo Massimo was a careful man who had been doing surveillance and witness protection work for years. Hair which was once lustrous and a deep black was now a pale grey; his moustache, still thick, was pure silver white. When Giancarlo Pancardi had called him and told him that he needed a personal favour, he had not objected, nor made excuses, nor had he told his old boss that he had been having chemotherapy for cancer. Instead he had packed and left Rome on the next available plane for London. He had no close family now and his divorce was some fifteen years in his past; Pancardi's call had been the stimulus he needed to push him back into the land of the living.

At the Blondell home in Chelsea a little white dog called Noodle greeted Pietro Grillva with exuberance, as he rang the bell at the large metal gates which sealed the entrance to the drive. The small dog was yapping loudly and Grillva, a lover of animals, petted it through the bars. His appearance was haggard and wiry and his face had the quality of looking perpetually as if he needed a shave. Clothes were never his friend and his choices often made him look underweight; he had the knack of always looking slightly scruffy despite paying for quality items.

A chirpy voice boomed through the intercom and he looked squarely at the newly installed surveillance camera on the high steel pole, which was some twenty metres inside the entrance. He gave his name and there was a click which opened the tubular steel gate. He picked up the dog, which then tried to lick his face, read the name on the collar tag and smiled.

As he walked up the short driveway he could see a man installing a new camera on the roof and a further two men seated in a small shed. They looked as if they were simply smoking a cigarette, but their eyes followed him closely as he walked toward the front door.

Suddenly a shrill, human, two note whistle pierced the air and Grillva stopped in his tracks. Angelo Massimo appeared from the side of the building and motioned Grillva toward him.

The two men greeted each other, first with a handshake and then with an embrace. They conversed in Italian.

"So you miserable old fool!" said Massimo, "Carlo calls and we both come running?"

Grillva smiled, "So this is the fortress we must defend," he said in a businesslike manner.

"Just like the old days," Massimo replied. He noticed Grillva carried only a small suitcase. "Is this all you brought?" he asked, grabbing the case to take it.

"No you don't Angelo," snapped Grillva, "I'm not having a man in your condition carry my bag."

"Always the same," he replied.

"They have shops in London and you my friend have cancer. I can shop for a shirt, but can you get treatment here?"

Massimo raised his left index finger to his lips in a ssshing motion in mute reply.

A little girl came bounding out of the house and ran toward the two men. The dog leapt from Grillva's arm and ran toward her, barking as he went. He jumped and she caught him and he repaid her catch by smothering her giggling face with sloppy licks.

"That," said Massimo, "is Noodle."

"I know," Grillva replied, "I read."

The dark haired girl was wearing a school uniform; a dark green blazer with a pocket badge of red and gold, long white socks and patent leather shoes; on her head she wore a straw boater.

"So there's another entrance?" said Grillva.

"Yes under a covered arch which the car comes through."

"So the house is between two roads?"

Massimo nodded, "And I drive the girl to school," he said.

"Well that makes things nice and easy then," returned Grillva.

"Charlotte, put him down!" a woman's voice called from a distance.

Grillva noted the accent as southern, maybe Naples, but definitely Italian.

The woman walked across the lawn toward the two men and before she was within hearing distance Grillva asked quietly, "Who is she?"

"A friend's wife, that is all I know but she is very important to Carlo. It is like we are protecting a daughter," Massimo added.

"Maybe she is," Grillva chuckled, "you know how secretive he can be. His past is a dark place where only he goes. She might even be his mistress."

The conversation was cut short as Magdalene Blondell reached the two men. She was a little worn about the eyes from lack of sleep and the constant vigils she was keeping on her children. Charlotte ran around the group as the information exchange was swift and controlled. Grillva explained that he had been sent by Pancardi to aid Massimo and that the two younger men in the shed, were assigned to cover by MI5. The two younger men would cover the grounds while the two Italians would ostensibly be based in the house and car, when it left the premises.

"My husband Alex says that Pancardi speaks very highly of you both," said Magdalene.

Massimo smiled and nodded but Grillva was more controlled in the face of flattery.

"He is a fat old fool," he laughed. "Too much pasta and wine has addled his brain." Grillva continued with a wry smile, "We have been in a tight scrape or two over the years, the four musketeers they used to call us."

"So who was the fourth?" Magdalene asked.

"That was Roberto Calvetti, but sadly he is no longer with us," Massimo added.

"He was the fat one!" Grillva exclaimed.

"So if he was Porthos, which one are you?" chirped Magdalene, taking up the challenge.

"Well," laughed Massimo, "he is not Aramis that's for sure," he replied, pointing at Grillva.

Magdalene Blondell led the men into the house. Angelo Massimo had chosen a guest room at the head of the stairs. A room which gave a clear advantage in two areas, one, that he could be near the stairs and two, be close to a bathroom which lay across the hall – ideal if bouts of vomiting occurred. He hoped it was a short term assignment – no more than three weeks Pancardi had said. There were his painkillers but with only enough for four weeks, timings would be crucial. He had made a pact with himself, that if the surveillance went on longer than that he would tell Pancardi that he would be no good. Time was limited, that much he knew but he would hold his tongue until he was no longer able to be useful or the pain too debilitating – that much at least he owed Pancardi.

Pietro Grillva was offered the room next to Massimo but instead chose a room at the far end of the hall. He had noticed a short fire escape as he approached the house; noticed that it dropped onto a large expanse of flat roof to the side and back of the property and the one single window which would make an excellent quiet entry point was accessible from that roof. If he had wanted to get inside the building that would be where he would try. He noted that Charlotte slept next door to his and her room had that window. The younger sibling was in a room through an adjoining door to his parent's bedroom.

Grillva threw his bag onto the bed.

"It's a very small room," said Magdalene.

"This is perfect," he replied.

"It only has a velux roof window I'm afraid but it does tilt and you can stand up in it."

Grillva stood at the loft style window and had an excellent vantage point and vision across the expanse of flat roof and adjacent gardens and down both sides of the street to the rear.

Magdalene apologised yet again, "It used to be a young nannies room, when the previous owner had it." She opened a door to the side of the room, "But it has a bathroom and a shower and a sort of kitchenette through here. There's a coffee maker too."

Massimo had wondered about using that room but had settled for the best internal vantage point. Grillva had done exactly what he would have done had he been the second of the musketeers to arrive.

"Noodle?" asked Grillva, "where does he sleep?"

"Oh he sleeps in Charlotte's room," Magdalene replied, "but not on her bed he has his own bed," she added defensively.

"Good," replied Grillva, with approval. "The best burglar alarm money can buy is a dog, more sensitive and alert than any machine. I was going to ask if you could bring him up here; his ears will hear far more than ours."

"He sleeps downstairs during the day, in the kitchen. Well he has the run of the place," she added, "and the garden, there's a kennel out there too."

"Good," replied Grillva, "he is another set of eyes and ears. Better the small mobile watchman than the lumbering brute of a policeman."

"He is the son of Mostro," Magdalene offered, but without knowing why she had.

"What Carlo's little wretch? Well I never, detective, lover and dog breeder all in one person. Let us hope he is smart like his father eh?"

Magdalene Blondell did not understand the reference to lover but offered a quick tour of the house and grounds.

As they passed the bathroom at the head of the stairs Pietro Grillva gave a quick double tap at the door and Massimo appeared. Magdalene had not seen him go, not even missed him while she had been occupied with Grillva. He was carrying a small package which Magdalene thought looked like a diabetic's syringe case. He slipped it into his jacket pocket and joined them as they began to descend the stairs.

Alice Parsotti opened her eyes and began to regain consciousness. She tried to remember her name and then the name of the person she was supposed to be – neither was registering. Some parts of her memory worked, others didn't, and she knew that something had happened, but could not recall exactly what.

She was on her face on a bed, naked and cold and the room was pitch dark, save for the pale light which came in through the gaps in the curtains. She could see light under a door but could not remember where the door led to or whether she was alone. Her hand reached behind her to touch the backs of her thighs and she could feel sticky, tacky and encrusted substances there. She checked her vagina and the same tackiness met her fingertips, there was too much to be the residue from one man – she wondered if she had been gang raped. She rolled onto her back and lay looking at the ceiling, her head was swimming and she was listening for voices. There was silence and darkness and she was thankful not to have to fight off would be attackers. Her scalp was sore as if her hair had been tugged and her back ached mercilessly.

She was standing now, next to the bed in the darkness her legs almost unable to propel her across the carpet. Ears alert and poised like a cat she was listening, waiting. Her objective was the door – escape, before who ever it was who had her here returned. Gingerly she stepped forward trying to recall how to walk, her limbs ached and her whole being felt bruised and battered. One step and then a second and then a third, a floor board creaked and she froze listening to the pounding of her own heartbeat; on the fourth stride her foot met the water. A damp marsh which lay like a lake before her and the encouraging strip of escape light under the door. Another step and then another, each more damp than the last, until she felt for the handle, it was slippery, she pulled at the door. It was locked – she couldn't get out.

Something was in front of it, the top was opening but the base remained shut fast, she reached down to what looked like a large sack and finding hair knew that it was someone rather than something. She recoiled, hoping the guard had not noticed her touch. He didn't move, nor speak and she could not hear him breathing; after a few seconds she felt at his throat for a pulse – there was none. Fear and panic pushed her survival instinct into overdrive and she heaved the corpse away from the door to open it enough for her to pass through.

She stepped into the bright and well lit kitchen area. Padded to the sink and turned on the tap. Water cascaded over her fingers and she splashed copious amounts of it over her face in an attempt to revive her senses. Then she listened – listened to see if there were voices or movement in the building. There was silence.

On the unit there was a kettle – she flicked the switch to on and the translucent front showed the bubble of heated water as it began to rise. Coffee, she needed something to make her sane, needed to escape before they came back. Then at the window she spotted the note. It was in a plain white envelope addressed to "Mr. Boltin."

"Fucking Bolton," she said, and remembered how he had talked to her on the plane. She wondered if that was where she was – his place.

Alice opened the note. It was written on scrap paper in a child like script, badly spelt, with all lower case i's having a small circle drawn for the dot. It was clearly a woman and a poorly educated one at that – she began to read.

Dear Mr. Boltin

I done the house cleanin but as you was not up I sispects you and you new lady was havin a sleep after you long trip the door was locked so I done no hooverin their is shopping I done I could of done some more but I d'nt know what to by anyway I am on holidays all next week as you knows so I will see you a week on Friday when I gets back.

Lots of Luv
Danielle.

PS – thanks for them extra wages that is nice

Alice read it for a second time. There were no sentences and the spelling was terrible, but there had been no gang, there was no gang, she was there alone. A fuckwit cleaner had come and gone and left a note thinking that Bolton was in bed asleep.

The kettle boiled and switched off automatically. She splashed more water over her face. Her memory was returning, Miles Bolton had given her something and she had passed out and he had raped her. She grabbed a mug from the stacking tree and tossing in an unmeasured amount of coffee from a jar next to the kettle she topped up the mug with cold water, to cool it, and took a deep swig. The strong taste hit her throat, increased her adrenaline and brought her back to life.

She turned around and looked into the room behind her, it was then that she noticed her footprints of crimson running from the door to the sink. Her mind buzzed and then she remembered.

Miles Bolton lay slumped at the doorframe as Alice Parsotti pushed the door open and felt for the light switch. The sight which greeted her was almost overwhelming as the room was bathed in light; a great pool of blood in a mixture of browns, reds and crimson lay at the foot of the bed and a trail like the slime of a poisoned slug ran from that to the door. The door handle and the door itself were covered in hand prints as Bolton had frantically clawed at the exit point before slumping like a sack of drained potatoes beneath the handle. His eyes were open and his mouth looked as if he were underwater gasping for air. One hand was at his crotch and the other stretched out as if pleading for mercy. She wondered at what point in her drugged sleep he had died.

The copious blood clearly showed the lucky success of her attack in puncturing an artery; she took another deep swig of coffee and wiped the soles of her feet on a dry area of carpet. She contemplated urinating on his corpse but then thought that the stench would eventually overwhelm her. Instead she walked to the bathroom used the toilet and rinsed her feet clean in the bidet.

Back in the kitchen she began to make lucid sense of the last twenty four hours.

Bolton had drugged her and used her sexually with the aid of Rohypnol. Her first impression of him had been totally correct, he was a loser, a man who did not understand women, but she had not seen him as dangerous. She also recalled their sexual encounter and his prowess had been matched by his dominating technique; in another scenario, with the right female, he could have wealth, security and sexual fulfilment. His big thing had been control – she recalled the obscene language as he encouraged her to thrust back at him and his deep penetrations. She looked at his corpse and felt a little remorse for him. With the right woman he could have been deliriously content, she thought, the problem was he could not find his submissive – so he resorted to drugs.

She spoke directly to his corpse, “Perhaps you should have bought yourself a Russian bride or a third world fuck bunny, you perverted sack of shit. At least that way you’d still be alive. You just had a bad day sunshine.”

She wondered how many other victims had fallen under his drug induced spell and then she kicked his corpse as she passed back into the kitchen, pulling the door closed behind her.

She went to the fridge and pulled out a bottle of cold milk and flipping open the foil top placed the opening to her mouth and drank. She was thirsty and needed to get rid of the stale taste at the back of her throat. It felt like a hangover, but her leg muscles ached and her spine felt slightly twisted too and she wondered precisely what Bolton had done to her while she was drugged.

Alice Parsotti knew she needed to eat and then sleep again to fully clear her mind. She began scrambling eggs and grilling bacon. The toaster popped and she buttered and sank her teeth into a piece as she watched the eggs microwave. She gave them a stir and flipped the bacon under the grill.

Perhaps she had been luckier than she at first thought. Bolton was dead and there would be no cleaning lady for a week, because of her stupid holiday. That was a total stroke of luck. Perhaps she could get the bank in Switzerland to wire some money to London, then she re-evaluated, too risky. The door man knew her now as Claudette Cicello and she was close to Chelsea that was also another clear piece of luck. She wondered if Bolton had an A-Z of the city kicking about. Alice Parsotti could come and go as she pleased, it was perfect. No Interpol, no suspicion, she stopped eating and stood up to stretch her stiffening back; eight days and then the cleaning lady would return. How far could a body decompose in that time? She would lay it on the bed and wrap the sheets around it, turn the air-conditioning on full and if necessary order some ice.

Suddenly for no logical reason she remembered the weird tale of Jim Morrison's death in 1971; how his body had been packed in ice in Paris to preserve it after he had died. Then how the Lizard King could do anything, but even he couldn't cheat death. Pamela Courson couldn't cheat it either; Alice's mind went into overdrive as her blood sugar increased; all of her memory being replayed in flashed seconds; everyone shit on Courson until she ended up working as a prostitute. Strains of a Doors tune hit her recall and she was humming Moonlight Drive. Then came Riders on the Storm as the four horsemen of the apocalypse chased across her vision, interlocking tangents racing through her brain. She thought of Rothko's suicide and the finding of his body and the Menil Chapel and Gabriel's Fourteen Black Paintings. Then as suddenly as if a shutter had come down in a Glasgow bar at closing time, the mind chaos stopped and she spoke aloud with stone cold clarity, "I could make it look like a suicide when I go, it's so fucking simple, so simple," she said.

Walking around the room, her head was clearing; she was trying to recall where London Zoo was and whether they had an amphibian section. Perhaps she could get what she needed from a pet shop, there must be a specialist one somewhere – her mind was working again. Some form of rapid de-tox was happening, her mind was recalling, sharpening, she was back. She stretched up to touch the ceiling and then bent to touch the floor, her palms were fully flat on the wooden surface. Money, she needed working cash, maybe Blondell had a trace on her credit cards – she thought about using Bolton's. Deciding she needed a shower to wash the blood off and a sleep, a proper sleep, one that would clear the jet lag and her heavy head at the same time, she checked the time, it was just after 3 am.

After a refreshing shower Alice Parsotti strolled into Bolton's other bedroom and lay on the bed staring at the window, pondering on whether she could sell some of his portable antiques over the next few days, to give her some working capital. The porcelain could make something in the right quarters, enough to pay for those little green hoppers – they would sort out her pursuers once and for all. She would go to sleep now as Alice and wake up as Claudette.

Suddenly she burped and laughing said, "Oh pardon me."

Chapter 13

"I knew it," said Pancardi, "the DNA does not match. I knew I was right on this, that body is someone else. Halspen, it must be her. "

"The scales of pitiless justice, always balance in the end," laughed Blondell. "Isn't that what it says in the King James Bible? The book of revelations, the bit about the four horsemen of the apocalypse? Luck and numbers and being in the right place at the wrong time. Even Alice cannot escape indefinitely – we shall find her yet."

Faaia Zakariyaa had collected the test results himself and when the Italian detective had seen them, a full twenty four hours early, he had been delighted. The same was said of the flight bookings and the speed with which the young Maldivian operated had impressed the older man.

"I knew that you would wish to return," Faaia had said, "so I booked some flights for you. We used the internet and have you pre-booked first class to Heathrow. Your flight leaves in the late morning and a special Ambassador's plane will fly you straight to the capital. This has been done in the name of the island official who wishes us to co-operate as much as possible."

"I like your style," Pancardi had said, after he had thanked him.

Faaia's confidence had increased and he knew that he would be noticed for a promotion when the time came. He liked the Italian, he was bleak but honest, hard but fair and he wished that his political master exhibited just a little of the same.

As he boarded the sea plane Pancardi had been on the phone to the central Presidential office to make a specific note of the young Maldivian's efforts. Blondell had been on the phone to Magdalene to tell her they were on the way back.

Faaia had waved them a fond farewell as the small dory ploughed back through the calm sea to the idyllic island which, though warm and wonderful for tourists was impoverished and existing on the edge for the locals. Pancardi could see the catamaran which had run aground on the southern edge of Dhangethi. A structure which had once been a luxury millionaire's plaything was now covered in sheets of corrugated iron which had rusted under the salt of the sea. He wondered just how many people lived in the structure now, a structure that had once been a palace for one.

The small dory carrying the young official was carving a white wake as the plane turned east and climbed into the clouds.

"Magdalene says that you have two men at the house," Blondell shouted over the droning engine, "thank you."

"These are not two of my men," Pancardi replied, leaning in and cupping Blondell's ear, "they are my friends, Pietro and Angelo."

"It's a bit like that poem," Blondell shouted again, "you know about the famous people how does it go? Oh yeah, Roberto, Pietro, Angelo and Pan-car-dee, all sitting down for afternoon tea."

"Are you trying to be funny when you talk of poetry?" Pancardi asked. "Harrison," he said, "it's Tony Harrison, something about, Byron, Moliere, Descartes and me?"

"Well whatever," Blondell replied, "I don't want to leave my family at the mercy of some psychopath, even if she is your daughter."

"And well you should not, but Alice is no psychopath, she is merely someone who is scared. There are far darker forces out there. She was not born like this, it is the Alsetti and the protection of their wealth which has made all the difference. As I said before you have drawn all those monsters out into the daylight. Money Alex, like sex, will make people do strange things, let us hope that the strange things they do, do not get us all killed."

"Well I hope these two friends of yours are as good as you say they are," Blondell replied.

"Once we were the very best," laughed Pancardi, "then Roberto he becomes fat and goes to work for the Cardinals. Pietro is a private detective, following rich young wives – he hates it. All the hiding in alleys and bars and then finding out that which even a novice could see, he is bored," he paused, "but he never misses a thing. He is the most observant of all those I have worked with, he can smell danger like a shark can smell blood. And me well I must hobble like a cripple until they give me a plastic knee. What a fine mess we have gotten into now we are old," he was laughing loudly now, "like the Hardy and Laurel jokers we continue."

"It's Laurel and Hardy," Blondell corrected. "Another fine mess you have gotten me into Stanley."

Pancardi's face scrunched up.

"Stanley Laurel, Stan, and Oliver Hardy. Oliver Hardy was the fat one Carlo."

Blondell looked directly at the older man's stomach.

"Then Stanley was you, no?" Pancardi retaliated, "rather stupid?"

It was Blondell's turn to distort his face.

"And as they say," Pancardi continued, "I may be fat," he patted his midriff, "but you are stupid, and I can always go on a diet." He paused with indignation, "And besides Roberto, he was the fat one. I am not fat," he considered, "I'm just heavily built."

"What about Angelo Massimo?" asked Blondell, suddenly changing the conversation back to business.

"Now he is mad," Pancardi replied, raising his voice. "Once we were on an assignment together and the fool gets shot in the foot. Blew his own toes off in the hurry to get his weapon out, how crazy is that? His daughter died some years ago, she was very young and that whole thing broke his marriage, which was not happy at the best of times; he has been very unlucky in love. Secretly I think his wife, she blamed him for their little girl's death. They wanted to throw him out of the Questura because his performance was poor for a while – he drank, and who can blame him after that. You know now what it would be like to lose a child, think of Charlotte." Pancardi levelled his voice, "The best logistician we ever had and because of the trouble at home the bureaucrats wanted to get him out. He was never a sycophant and they hated that. First his daughter dies, then his wife leaves and then they want to destroy his career. He came and worked the murder squad with me." He laughed over the engines, "He has a great sense of humour and he will defend your daughter with his life, if he has to. I expect she has already taken him to her heart, and he, her to him."

"I'm glad to hear it," shouted Blondell, "especially as he is mad enough to shoot his own toes off. This plane is so bloody noisy I can't hear you."

"Earplugs," Pancardi replied, "put them in and we talk later no?"

Blondell nodded.

Alexei Ulyanov was sitting in the back of a large telephone repair truck as Mikhail Kernov casually climbed the telegraph pole which conveyed the overhead phone cable to the Blondell home. In the road in front of the truck the smaller man, Petrov, was placing cones around a man hole and Perchenko was starting to lift some of the paving slabs with a pick axe. The men at work signs were already out and they looked the part, dressed in overalls and hard hats.

Ulyanov knew that Blondell would return to the house eventually and his best hope of finding his jewels was to let the police do the donkey work and he could step in at the last minute and lift both the girl and the emeralds – his emeralds.

There was a tap on the side of the truck and a police officer was leaning in. His face was jovial and he smiled as his radio crackled.

"Hello lads," he said convivially, and then realised there was only one man inside the van. "Just doing a routine check," he continued.

Ulyanov's voice was hesitant, and he realised that not only was the house covered internally the exterior also had patrol cars and beat officers keeping a watchful eye.

"Is there a problem officer?" Ulyanov asked, as he stepped into the street and saw a squad car parked on the opposite side of the road, with a man on a radio.

"No," replied the police officer, "no problem at all. It's just that there have been some burglaries in the area of late and we're checking out everyone's credentials."

Kernov descended from the pole and tucked the .44 automatic under his yellow high visibility jacket at the small of his back. If there were any trouble he knew he could drop the man in the car. Perchenko had the pick axe over his shoulder now and was also walking to join the conversation.

As the three converged a blonde woman dressed in a headscarf and dark glasses appeared from around the corner of a side road and walked past the men almost unnoticed. Her stride was confident and leggy and she could have been a celebrity of some kind judging by the quality of her clothes. The dog she was walking was lithe and leggy too, a red setter which promptly urinated against one of the cones which Petrov had placed around the manhole.

"Sorry boys," she said. "And Gerald you are a very naughty boy to wee wee on the man's cones like that." She was wagging a finger and had her ankles and high heels together as she leaned over the now sitting dog. It could so easily have been a forces pin-up pose from the Second World War, and had the men not otherwise been engaged, they would have noticed the length of her legs leading to the hour glass of her figure and the red rouge of her slightly pouting and inviting lips. This woman was beautiful.

Petrov noticed her legs first which were fine and elegant and the blonde hair reminded him of Marilyn Monroe and as she passed he thought he recognised her, but the face wouldn't come. The waist was slim and the hips pronounced; then she was gone, crossing the road and walking past the gates to the Blondell house. Nice he thought and then his attention was diverted back to the policemen as the second officer exited the squad car and crossed to join the other.

At the Blondells' rear gate the young woman slowed, allowed her dog to relieve himself against the wall. She studied the security cameras and wondered at the two men who seemed to be stationed in the garden, and then quietly moved on, before turning into a small side street and vanishing into the parallel road which ran at the front of the residence.

A large dark car approached and she caught a glimpse of two men as the security entrance opened and the vehicle turned into the driveway. She crossed to the opposite side of the street and heard the voice of Giancarlo Pancardi. He was doing introductions.

"Pietro," he said, "meet Alex Blondell."

She wanted to turn her head, look into the face of Blondell but instead she walked the dog into a driveway to allow the men to enter the building without them noticing her. As she did so, a man who had been gardening unnoticed in the house opposite, stood up.

"Hey lady, don't bring that bleedin' animal in here," he said, "I don't want to have to clear dog crap up, this ain't a public park."

She didn't reply and merely moved off quickly so that attention would not be drawn to her. The gardener resumed his work of weeding and muttered to himself about bloody cheek and dogs shitting everywhere.

"Yeah, I think we will be here for two days," said Ulyanov.

The policemen nodded.

"Looks like the whole system's fucked," added Kernov. "We're gonna have to take the cables up in the road and renew 'em. Nobody's gettin' broadband in this area for a while. Some desperado cowboys have been in there and the whole thing is buggered."

"What's the problem?" asked Perchenko, addressing the policeman, as he lowered the pick axe.

"There have been some burglaries," replied the policeman for the second time.

"And I suppose because we're foreigners you thought that you would check us out?" Perchenko questioned.

"Now, now lads," said the second policeman, who had been checking the licence plate of the Open Reach van on the radio. "We're just doing our job, and anyway you all check out," he laughed. "It's OK Stan, these boys are Polish right?"

Ulyanov nodded.

"What part of Poland you boys from then?" he continued.

"Gdansk," Ulyanov answered.

"And I bet you guys are all engineers?"

Ulyanov nodded, "Well Josef there," he nodded at Perchenko, "he just digs the holes. But in Poland he was a welder on the ships and we were electricians. Here in England we work putting in phone cables and cable TV."

"Well that's great." The policeman named Stan was moving

now, back toward the car, "we'll leave you blokes to get on with it," he concluded. And the two crossed the street.

Once inside the car as they pulled away Stan voiced his true thoughts, "Bloody Poles," he said, "coming here and taking the work from us."

"But they're not are they Stan?" the driver replied.

"Listen, my bother-in-law is constantly being undercut by these unskilled blokes."

"But they're not unskilled are they Stan?"

"Well the fuckers are here and they should be in Poland."

The driver was turning now, "Well I think it takes bollocks to do what a lot of these guys do. Come over to another country and work. And you should know how lazy some of the natives round here are. They are lazy bastards and we have to feel their collars enough. Anyway those blokes are just trying to earn some corn and wouldn't you do that, you're not some lazy sod are you?"

"Neither is my sister's bloke," Stan replied.

"Ok, but those guys are just doing jobs that need doing and some of the natives here are so thick they can't find their arses with both hands."

"That's not the point though is it?" Stan was beginning to move into new territory, "First it's the blacks then it's the Poles; it'll be the bloody Romanians next."

The driver remained silent, he knew when not to get into a logical argument with an illogical man.

"Anyway some of those Romanian girls," the driver remarked, "by Christ have you seen them? Bloody lovely they are and they know how to work their little arses off."

Stan was laughing in reply, "Yep, that'll do you with your special breathalyzer kit in your pants. I'm sure some of those would be only too happy to oblige." And he laughed heartily as the car continued to cruise the narrow streets, checking number plates and parking permits as they passed.

❧

"That was close," said Kernov. "Two surveillance cameras, two guards outside and sealed iron gates, front and back. This one is not going to be easy to get into."

"We're not going to try and get in," Ulyanov replied, "we sit and wait, if they find her or there is a flurry of activity we'll soon know. We must be patient, take our time."

"But surely they'll find the men who should be in this truck?" Perchenko questioned, "and when they do they find us."

"They will never find them," Petrov confirmed, "that is a certainty, I took care of it, they have vanished."

"So, two here and two at the front," said Ulyanov. "Kernov and Perchenko you take the front. You'll have to find another vantage point. Petrov stays here with me. All we have to do is be patient." He was calm and methodical and knew that eventually all would work in his favour. "Remember," he said to his men, "we are KGB and that makes us the very best. Kernov I want that line bugged, any calls in or out of that house I want to know. I want to be able to listen to them in the van and get a trace."

Chapter 14

"How was Gerald?" asked the young kennel maid. She turned to the dog and placing her face close to his, continued, "Who's a clever boy then? It's Miss Cicello isn't?" she said, taking a card from a panel of cards which lay behind the main reception area. "We get so many dogs in here it's hard to keep track of what they are like, but Gerald, he's lovely, so friendly. He didn't pull did he, when you went for a walk?" Alice began to be annoyed by the constant rhetorical questioning and her inability to get an answer in.

"No, he was absolutely fine," Alice replied, "he's an absolute sweetie," she patted his head as she spoke.

"So would you like to keep him for a few days, on a sort of trial basis?" the kennel maid asked with a real essence of pleading in her voice. She had noticed how the young woman had given away acceptance in her body language.

"Mmm, well I'm not really sure," Alice replied, feigning reluctance.

"I'm sure Gerald would love to stay with you to show you how well trained he is," she stroked the top of the dog's head and he gave a solitary bark. "He is only here because his owner died suddenly and there was no one else to care for him. The old man loved that dog but his son claimed that he could not look after him because of business commitments and his girlfriend hated him; apparently she was frightened by him." The girl bent once again to stoke the dog. "I'm sure he would love to stay with you though, he really has taken to you, just look at his cute face." She cupped his muzzle and gave it a slight shake, "Yes you are a pretty boy aren't you?"

The red setter sat and looked at the kennel maid who passed him a snack treat as a reward and then gave another solitary bark.

"He doesn't bark all the time does he?" asked Alice. "I mean if he barks a lot then I could have problems where I live." She smiled broadly, "He is lovely though and his coat is so glossy and smooth."

"No, no, he just likes to let us know he's here."

"Loud though isn't it? You see I live in the city – Stamford Street."

"Oh he'll like that, there's the park nearby so he would be able to do his business there." The girl's voice was persuasive now, "Why don't you take him for just three days and then see, a sort of sale and return?" She was smiling broadly and passing the pen as if to sign a contract.

Alice looked at the girl, she did not want to look too keen to take the dog, "Well I suppose there's the roof top garden if he has an emergency," she said.

"That's even better," the girl persuaded again, "he always has a chance to get outside then, that's lovely." She could sense the closing of a deal. "So shall I put you down for three days?" She was nodding at Alice.

Very clever thought Alice as she replied, "Go on then, three days; but I can bring him back if he is totally out of control?"

"Absolutely, what was the address again?"

Less than thirty minutes later Alice Parsotti had returned to the flat of Miles Bolton and the dog lay panting in the back of a hired Bentley, which was parked in a side road below. The car gave the dog space and also put off those who might decide to pry. Gerald liked the opulence and the plush interior and settled onto a snug blanket on the back seat.

Alice had greeted the concierge Fred with a smile and he had made some joke about Mr. Bolton being in bed, again, exhausted. Alice had replied that he was not feeling too well after the trip abroad, a, "Rummy tummy, or something," she had said. Fred had given a wry smile thinking he knew the real reason – this new Italian girl was too much for Bolton. They were probably fucking like rabbits and Bolton had finally bitten off more than he could chew. Fred wondered what tricks this blonde Claudette could do, the things that would make her a dream lover but also every mans nightmare. He tried to imagine her naked, the size and length of her nipples when erect, the softness of her pubic hair and then quickly he pondered if she had pubic hair, whether she waxed or shaved. Briefly he fantasized on lathering her womanhood and then running a razor over it; he wondered what she tasted liked and whether she was a screamer.

Then she was inside the lift and gone and all the concierge could muster was a breathless, "Lucky fucking bastard," under his breath. He knew he could have fucked her to death and yet here he was poncing about in the foyer while that wealthy over-privileged prick Bolton had her sitting on his face.

"Four," said Alice, "for Cicello and just one of the others."

"Listen lady," said the man on the phone, his voice was loaded with a London twang which reminded her of Paul West. Her memory flashed a brief picture of snow and blood and his death and then as the man continued talking it vanished. "These Fuuuuckin'," he drooled the word like a slobbering dog, "babies are deadly and I don't want them hangin' about," he paused, "know what I mean? It's all a bit fuuuckin' QT, but as you are coughin' up top dollar we'll say nuffink, right?"

"Right," Alice replied, "I'll be over in about two hours." Her English became impeccable as she subconsciously reacted to his, "You're on the Tottenham Court road correct?" she confirmed.

"That'll do for this," he replied. "Harry Chopin's pets, number 132. And cash only got it? If I even gets a whiff of the plod I'm fuckin' gone – got it?"

Alice Parsotti sat on the bed and counted out the twenty pound notes she had received for the porcelain sales from earlier in the morning. It had been so easy to sell Bolton's figures claiming she had inherited them when her mother died and that she did not know their worth. The dealers had salivated in an attempt to get her to part with them cheaply. The Hutschenreuther, Selb, Royal Doulton, all snapped up for cash by the greedy monsters of capitalism. Alice had marvelled at the porcelain dealers, who without scruples would have taken items for a song as long as there was a heavy profit in it for them. Once again she had increased the prices by simply flashing her eyelids. She would have liked to sell the Rothko too but that would be impossible, she vowed to take it with her instead. Then she realised that the sheer size would preclude this and she could never sell it on the open market. She thought about the destruction of evidence knowing what Interpol would find once Bolton's body had been discovered.

On the bed she lay out, stacked in neat piles, nearly nine thousand pounds in twenties and fifties and thought that might keep her pursuers at bay for a little longer. Bolton's credit cards had paid for the hire of the car and she had stripped his bank account by taking the maximum limit from the hole in the wall. She had searched the flat for jewellery which she could take with her and sell, but the truth was that most of his money was in art not gold. Bolton had been very astute to hold onto works of art and lucky to anticipate fashion. She thought briefly of Rothko and his love for a woman half his age; marvelled at the way men could be manipulated so easily by the softness of a tight, moist, female and then she laughed out loud. She had remembered a postcard she had once seen of two children showing their private parts to each other. The small boy's caption read, "I have one of these." The girl's reply said it all, as she pulled the waistband of her knickers away from her flat stomach, "Ah," she said, "but with one of these I can get as many of those as I want."

Alice was laughing now taking deep gulps of air through her nostrils. The pungent aroma of the blood on the carpet was creeping under the door from Bolton's bedroom and she wondered about throwing ice on the corpse to stave off the putrefaction. He was probably rotting under the bed sheets. In the end she dampened two towels and rolling them into sausage shapes, placed them at the bottom of the bedroom door. She reckoned on one more night and then she would move on.

In the house opposite the Blondell's front entrance two Russians sat behind net curtains watching the road. Mikhail Kernov was a large, patient and methodical man who had chosen the house well. It seemed unoccupied and the gardener, when he left had not even come inside. Gregorian Perchenko had stretched a piece of cheese wire between his swarthy gloved hands and waited for the click of the latch and the opening of the door – the gardener had not entered, clear proof that he did not have a key. The simple fact that the owners of the house, an older and untrusting couple, had not given the gardener a key had, by this simple act, saved his life, his possible decapitation and in turn their need to redecorate.

The men had heard him clattering around outside the property for some time, whistling, and then all went silent. Inside they sat in the growing gloom. Perchenko lit a cigarette and Kernov admonished him for the brief flash of light which lit up their faces.

"Put the damn thing out," he had hissed.

"It's only a single cigarette," Perchenko had replied.

"Enough for a sniper though," Kernov had remarked in reply. "One aim and fire and the back of your head comes off like the top of a breakfast egg. Where is your training? KGB do not make mistakes. Don't make mistakes with me; I want to live to spend this money."

"Oh stop the whining," Perchenko replied, "we are all on the samc sidc." Hc took a large deep toke on the cigarette and, in consequence, the tip glowed a bright scarlet.

Kernov grabbed wildly into the dark and made contact with Perchenko's testes; he gripped hard and twisted slightly.

"We take shifts," he said. "One sleeps and the other watches. But if you give us away I will gut you like a pig and leave your carcass for the vultures to pick over. The cigarettes stop now." His grip tightened and Perchenko dropped the cigarette on the carpet.

"Put the damn thing out," Kernov ordered.

"But in the early hours do we need to keep watching?" asked Perchenko meekly. "They will all be asleep and this Alice woman she would not risk being seen on the streets."

"When would you come then?" asked Kernov in a relaxed manner, his grip released.

"Whenever I thought it most safe," Perchenko replied, crushing the cigarette into the carpet.

"You see Gregori that is why you are the Corporal and I am the Sergeant."

Perchenko found the answer rather cryptic and reminiscent of the sarcasm of Ulyanov, but his temper did not flair, his commitment did not falter – he simply bit his tongue and thought of the money. Kernov was a man who could kill easily and his loyalty to Ulyanov was absolute. Perchenko had seen him gut a man as if he were a fish and from another he casually removed an eye as if it were some Sushi delicacy worth special treatment. Kernov was a firm friend and a deadly adversary; of all Ulyanov's men he was both the best and the worst; cunning, deadly, loyal, trustworthy and sadistic – a lethal combination. Perchenko knew when to back down.

"Then who takes the first shift?" he asked.

"I can," Kernov replied. "I have turned the water on but we cannot have any lights in case someone is checking the house. No cigarettes at the front either." He continued to stare through the curtains for any movement at the house opposite. "The people here must be on holiday or something? We must use the moonlight."

"This will be just like being at home in Siberia," Perchenko mocked, trying to lighten the mood.

"But at least the water will be hot and you can take a bath," Kernov's voice rang from the hollow darkened silhouette he had become by the window. "And that will be better for both of us."

Alice Parsotti had made the afternoon trip to the Chopin's Pet shop by taxi and left Gerald in the hired car. The weather was mild for winter, but she wondered if some busy body would report her to the RSPCA anyway. She decided to take the gamble. When she got back she would have to take him upstairs.

She was trying to calculate the break, when Fred might not be there and the younger boy John had taken his place. It would be easier to get the dog in with him on duty, primarily due to the laziness of his youth. He would watch television, any television, be drawn into the stupefying morass of reality TV which numbed the brain and dulled the imagination. She imagined him being a dullard, a person for whom life held little in the way of chances – in a way she pitied him.

In Tottenham Court Road, she had stopped to buy a few essentials at a grocery come general store and studied the pet shop from the coffee bar across the street. To the untrained eye it seemed like any other small trader on the edge of the city. But Alice knew how to be cautious. People came and went, some carrying boxes with ventilation holes, others with bags of cat litter or dog biscuits. Alice had sat and observed, the frothy cappuccino making her senses come alive, her nerves jangling like Indian bells in a soft, sensual, summer breeze. What she saw made her believe the coast was clear, but she wanted to avoid the possibility of being picked up by a local investigation into illegal animal trading.

She had studied the care of Dendrobates and the Bufo Marinus, commonly known as the Cane Toad and had the basic facts committed to memory, just in case the seller had more interest in animal welfare than she had imagined. Her summation was one of a small time profiteer who cared little for humanity and even less for animal welfare – a man whose primary function was to make money by any means possible.

Once inside the transaction had been swift with the seller making absolutely no eye contact .The money had changed hands swiftly and within what seemed like seconds, she was in a taxi to Euston. From there she took a train to Holborn, stopped twice, crossed a maze of underground tunnels, changed platforms and lines, took two more trains and was back in Stamford Street in under an hour.

She placed the cartons containing the frogs in the boot of the hired car and let Gerald out into the road. Immediately he urinated against a fence.

Gregori Perchenko explored the upstairs bathroom. It was typically English with the over powering scent of lavender. Even in the gloom he could see the large floral patterns on the wallpaper and the chintz curtains which when drawn would plunge the room into total darkness. It was English, old fashioned and yet strangely comforting. He looked for the shower and being unable to locate it began to draw the bath. One thing he was thankful for was the horse chestnut smell of the Badedas which he poured into the water in copious amounts.

He sought out a room in which to sleep – choosing the one at the front of the house which overlooked Blondell's on the other side of the street. He lit a cigarette and paused looking across at the house which seemed so quiet and …The bed was large and deeply comfortable, though light from the street lamps gave the dark mahogany cupboards and wardrobes a ghostly feel – a feeling that some past owner might come along and demand their wardrobe or its contents back. He threw back the covers and returning to the bath immersed himself complete with underwear, and vest.

He inhaled deeply from his cigarette as he lay immersed in the warm blood heat and exhaled a plume of pure blue smoke into the night air. Kernov would be dealt with in due course, he would see to that, and Ulyanov too the arrogant cock-sucking prick. He spat the cigarette across the carpeted floor and submerged below the water line.

Alice Parsotti had studied the life cycle and habits of the Amazonian tree frog and she had to agree with the illegal dealer who had told her, "They look fuuuckin' 'armless don't vey? But these sticky bastards are more deadly than one of those spade crack 'eads wiv a shooter on a Brixton drive by. Like a fuuuckin' rattle snake on fuuuckin' speed they are… really fuuuckin' deadly."

"Like all poisonous things," Alice had replied, "they come in small packages."

"Yeah like women," he had snapped.

Alice did not reply and the transaction had been completed at hyper-speed. She wondered what his wife was like. Certainly not black or Asian, but he was chauvinistic enough to keep her down trodden, that she had seen very clearly, along with his racism.

The translucent green with the bright patches of red made them instantly conspicuous and yet the other animals of the Amazon forest had learned to leave them alone. It was natures perfect defence and allowed them to make themselves colourful to attract that elusive mate, but deadly to any predator. Like all things they needed to mate, to procreate, to continue to make another generation. Yellow ringed eyes stared at her and the sticky pads of their feet stuck to the leaves inside the carton. They looked so helpless and yet she knew precisely how deadly they were.

She hadn't understood all of the inferences as the seller spoke but she had agreed that the animals needed to be handled carefully. He had lifted them one by one into the darkened carton; he had worn surgical gloves and muttered about The Endangered Species Act and how he could have, "His balls kicked up to the back of his throat if the filth found out."

Alice placed a wad of cash into his hand and his trepidation evaporated as his fingers clenched around the twenty pound notes. His smile was broad and his whole being seemed excited by the prospect of profit.

"When they gets stressed they starts to spit and then the oozin' fuuuuckin' starts. That's the poison. Don't get any of that shit in a cut or under your nails or you'll be fuuuuckin' stone dead by mornin'." He had casually remarked, his heavy cockney accent overpowering all he said. "No need to go to Athelhampton to see the monkey. You'll fuuuuuckin' hear the wail of the Banshee alright, Irish or fuuuckin' not." He drooled his words and slurred his speech like a drunkard.

Alice was lost in his riddles and had simply smiled politely to avoid getting involved in a conversation which she could not understand. The only concern she had was that the frogs could kill – they needed to kill. Her whole future depended upon it.

❧

Mikhail Kernov sat in the dark, his hands laid palm down on the flat of the armrests. He sat like a statue waiting for the sun to rise like some wise holy man on the edge of an ancient civilisation. His breathing was shallow and his eyes barely flickered as they carried out intensive sweeps of the area. His KGB training had taught him how to stay awake even when faced with total boredom.

His nostrils picked up the scent of Perchenko's bath additives and he smiled. He flipped open a mobile phone and using the speed dialler was connected almost instantly.

"Nothing," he said, quietly.

The reply was short and Ulyanov confirmed that the same was happening at the other side of the building.

"Perchenko is in the bath," he mocked, in reply, "like some fashion model he pampers himself. Our enemy will smell him approaching like one of those whores in the street, smothered in cheap perfume."

The remainder of the conversation was a factual exchange – short and swift.

Chapter 15

Charlotte Blondell threw her arms around her father's neck and planted a large kiss on his cheek. As he picked her up she squealed, "Papa," and a small white dog jumped first at his legs and then at his companion Pancardi; who picked the animal up and as a reward – it tried to lick his face.

"Uncle Carlo," Charlotte squealed, "Mamma Uncle Carlo he is here too." She was beside herself with excitement now.

"Let us get in," chided Blondell, as he and Pancardi stepped through the rear entrance of the house and into the brightly lit kitchen. The place was modern chrome and Beech and decorated in hues of green mixed with a counterpoint of pale lilac and purple. It was a woman's space, designed to be both functional and homely. In the far corner of the room was a family breakfast table and Pancardi imagined the Blondells all eating in domestic bliss, perhaps breakfast at the start of the day before Charlotte went off to school.

"Have you been a good girl whilst I've been away?" asked Blondell of his daughter.

"Depends what you call goooood," Magdalene's voice oozed into Blondell's ear like molasses and he remembered in the instant why he had been captivated by her.

"Just like Mostro when he was younger," Pancardi joked setting the dog down. "Lively as a cricket; you see he was an excellent gift Alex, excellent Magdalene."

She nodded and moved forward from the doorway an infant boy balanced on her left hip. She kissed her husband and smiled.

He knew in the instant that they would be making love that night despite his fatigue and despite his possible protestations – her eyes told him.

Charlotte began to rummage through her father's jacket pockets to see if he had sweets and Magdalene was tut-tut-ing at the way he spoilt their child. As soon as she had discovered two chocolate bars she wanted down and ran to Pancardi and stood before him, her hands behind her back, while he delved into his briefcase. Like a magician at a birthday party he produced a large bumper pack of assorted candies. This was followed by a doll and a girls' comic.

Blondell's jaw dropped, he had not seen the old Italian buy any gifts, nor had he seen him purchase sweets. He tried to consider how he had done it when they had spent all of their time together.

"Thank you Uncle Carlo," she said with perfect sweetness.

"And for Robby," Pancardi laughed, advancing toward the younger boy child, now reaching to be carried by his father, "a," he placed it on his head, "cap, and tee shirt."

The boy looked disappointed until, from Pancardi's seemingly infinitely expandable briefcase a large box of soft fudge appeared. He pulled the cap from his head and threw it to the floor as only a distracted infant can and reached for and grasped the box which went straight to his mouth. The corner of a fudge box in Roberto's mouth and Noodle now shaking the cap at his feet, Pancardi let out a singular infectious laugh which set the others off to join in.

"Ah this is what life is truly made of Alex," he snorted. "You my friend are a very lucky man. To have such a beautiful wife," Magdalene blushed, "and two wonderful offspring."

"You left out the adjective spoilt," Magdalene chirped, "and spoil them he does more and more every day."

Pancardi rested his cane against a kitchen unit and made for a chair at the table. He hated being cramped in cars and virtually everyday his knees were getting worse. Once ensconced Charlotte was on his lap and Noodle jumping at the side of his leg. Roberto had managed by use of sharp milk teeth and his father's fingers to open the fudge and his mouth was being stretched by a large piece which he was half chewing and half sucking. Blondell was trying to put the box down but the infant was securing his next piece and would not release it.

"I expect you could do with a coffee?" Magdalene asked. "I know I could and I expect we all could."

Pietro Grillva stood in the doorway leading into the heart of the house; he said nothing, merely nodded at Pancardi as if to say we will talk in depth later and melted back into the shadows. Something was taking his attention and Pancardi knew that he had to trust him. His gaunt face and keen eyes missed nothing, even if his heart missed the scene he had witnessed in the room.

Outside Angelo Massimo spoke to the driver of the car before it pulled away and giving the family some personal time to greet each other waited. The pain was returning and his medication was inside the house. That he now knew was a mistake he would not make a second time. He reached into his pocket and finding his wallet he flicked two small Voltarol tablets into his palm from the foil-wrapped emergency supply he carried and placed them on his tongue. They were bitter and they needed to be washed down, Massimo settled for a swig of water in his cupped hand from the outside tap. His experience had shown that there would be time enough to talk shop with Pancardi, when the niceties and introductions had been accomplished. His eyes scanned as he waited for the pills to bite into the pain and he thought he saw, though he was not certain, a light in the house opposite. A house which was known to be unoccupied, as the owners were on an extensive European cruise. He wondered if the pain were playing tricks with his vision and he waited peering into the gloom, hoping his head would clear. There the light was again, brief, dancing and definitely a torch upstairs. He stepped forward into the driveway and Mikhail Kernov saw him peering across the street. His spine became rigid and he gripped the arms of the chair behind the net curtains. Kernov was counting and wondering when the flash of light, signalling a cigarette being lit, would alleviate his tension – it never came.

Massimo waited and then nonchalantly stepped back into the shadows lest he alert any person in the house. Kernov saw him go but knew he had noticed something – knew he would still be watching.

Kernov pulled his revolver from his jacket and fitted a silencer. He could see the back door across the street had not opened and that whoever the man opposite was, he had not yet re-entered the property. He was not smoking and Kernov knew he was watching. If he was still outside he had chosen a spot where he could observe without being observed. Kernov liked his style and he knew in that simple action that he was not a novice guard but a highly skilled professional. Laying the pistol on the arm of the chair he jumped the few steps up to the first floor and gave a low whistle to Perchenko who immediately came alive.

"There's somebody watching this place," Kernov hissed, "have you had a flashlight on?"

"No, of course not, why would I?" Perchenko lied.

"Well you had better get dressed," he snarled as a terse reply, "we are likely to have visitors shortly."

With that he bounded down stairs and retrieved his revolver and then quickly opened the back door to the property so he could scan the garden for movement. He could see trees, bushes quite close and beyond that a stretch of lawn which disappeared into the shadows. He watched diligently and even though the trees and bushes looked human his KGB training told him to fix upon a shape and wait for it to move to confirm it had life. There was no movement save Perchenko now panting down the stairs.

Catching the draught from the open door Perchenko moved to join Kernov but said nothing. Kernov noticed his hair was wet.

Gerald lay panting in the corner of Bolton's penthouse flat. His legs had buckled less than a minute after the venom had been administered. The vomiting had stopped quite quickly and his eyes had rolled showing the white of his eyeballs. Now he was on his side panting as he fought with the dizziness which was overtaking his whole being. The dog's head was forced against the carpet as he sought to regain his equilibrium, his balance, his control. Cramps had started in his legs which were extended from his body as if he were stretching. To any observer it might look like he was stretching, trying to make his limbs extend, but the motion was forced, accompanied by violent shaking and Alice knew that the poison was working. She was timing the whole thing.

On the table lay the air pistol which had delivered the lethal dart; alongside it lay three further darts which matched the one protruding from the dog's shoulder; a simple needle fastened with twine and gauged to pass down the barrel, propelled by a puff of air which had been trapped in the nylon fibres trimmed as flights. It was simple, effective, and lethal. A small purple dart which looked like the bud of a chrysanthemum about to burst into bloom.

Gerald had been useful in many ways. He had scared the frogs so much that they excreted the deadly venom from their pores in copious amounts and then, despite his repeated and annoying attempts to get into Bolton's room, he had proved an excellent Guinea Pig.

She checked the clock above the door; Gerald had been dying for almost two minutes and now his lungs were bubbling and the frothy residue of death was exploding into the carpet a foot away from his mouth. The froth was turning red and the dog's lungs were pumping in his chest, gasping for air. He gave one final lurch and then a large patch of urine appeared behind and underneath him, signalling his death. The heaving stopped and silence reigned. Alice checked the clock – two minutes and twenty one seconds.

"We have your room ready for you Uncle Carlo, because you are staying here with us," Charlotte proudly announced. "It is near mine and that other man who arrived."

"The other man?"

"Well there are two of them, a fat one and a thin one."

"Really," laughed Pancardi. "How fat exactly?"

Charlotte Blondell puffed out her cheeks and made herself round with her arms to emulate Massimo's bulk.

"Charlotte," her mother chastised, "that young lady is extremely rude."

"Si Mama," Charlotte replied, and cast her eyes down.

"Is he really that fat?" asked Pancardi. "As fat as Father Christmas?"

The little girl smiled and nodded, a beaming smile on her face. She raised her hand to her mouth to stifle a growing giggle at her beloved uncle Carlo who understood her sense of humour – that was why she loved him so. She had her arm around his neck now and her mother shot her a look which said, just you dare Charlotte Blondell, just you dare.

"But he is fat," Pancardi offered in the little girl's defence.

"Si," Charlotte said.

"Fatter than a very fat thing?" Pancardi confirmed, watching as Massimo silently entered the room behind the now unaware girl, who once again had blown her cheeks out and made a round shape with her arms.

"My goodness," Pancardi continued, "he must eat lots of pasta?"

"Big platefuls," Charlotte laughed. "Giant platefuls!"

"Charlotte Blondell," her mother chastised, "you are so very rude. I don't know what your father will think of me if you carry on like this." She looked at her husband holding the younger Robert, his face beaming with fudge. "And what will Mr. Massimo think, especially as he is right behind you."

Charlotte Blondell froze unable to extricate herself.

"I don't mind," said Massimo as he entered through the door from the garden, his vigil on the house opposite complete. "Pietro he is the slim one and the little girl she is like all children, she speaks the truth. Out of the mouths of babes and beggars as we Italians say."

"Ah, a valuable lesson learned young Charlotte," Pancardi chirped. "Do not be led into saying things about others for the sake of popularity or a joke."

"I'm so sorry Angelo," said Magdalene, obviously embarrassed by her daughter, "perhaps we should all have coffee? Charlotte go and ask Signore Grillva to join us please." Her nervousness and embarrassment at her daughter's behaviour had made her slip back into Italian.

In the typical exuberance of youth, Charlotte rushed from the room and sped up the stairs seeking Pietro Grillva. Noodle was close behind her, whilst Robert Blondell was now being held in his father's arms completely oblivious to the growing nervous tension. A second piece of fudge in one hand and a drooled stain on the front of his clothing, life, for him, was completely satisfying.

"There's a flashlight being used on the other side of the street, chief," Massimo remarked to Pancardi.

"But the place is empty, I think the people are away on holiday or so the police said," Magdalene replied.

"Well there's definitely someone in there," Pietro Grillva remarked from the doorway where he suddenly re-appeared. "I've been studying the place for the last ten minutes. It looks like a burglary to me."

"Well the police can deal with that then," Pancardi snorted. "Unless maybe this house is under surveillance."

"Who the hell is observing my family?" asked Blondell. "It's certainly not part of any organisation we know of," his temper was rising, "just who the hell is it?"

"It is probably just an opportunist thief," Massimo replied, in an attempt to reduce the tension in the room. "We could take a look if you like?" He looked toward Pancardi for confirmation.

The Inspector who had been their inspirational leader during their time at the Questura was shaking his head. The four musketeers were one down already and he wasn't about to lose another to some young opportunist who might be nothing more than a drug fuelled reprobate.

"Let the police handle it," he said, fully aware of precisely how jumpy people had become.

"It could be Alice," Blondell remarked.

"Now that is totally unlikely," Pancardi smirked, "it is probably nothing of the sort. This is London after all and all big cities have coincidences – this is just that. Why would your family be…?"

"A target?" Blondell snorted. "That I thought was most apparent in her letter," Blondell snapped.

"What letter is this?" asked Magdalene.

And silence fell as the smell of freshly ground coffee permeated into the thick atmosphere of the room. Eventually Pancardi broke the temporary silence with an explanation.

"A letter to Alex," he said. "A letter with a veiled threat."

Magdalene's eyes were now welling with tears, as she turned to her husband, "And you did nothing?" she choked.

"But that is not true," Pancardi's reply was forthright and protective. "He has used contacts in MI5 and in the police to protect you and he asked me to put the best men here to make absolutely certain," he paused, "when we had a clue on the

Maldives." He was exaggerating for effect now, "So at no time were you vulnerable. In fact you have two of the very best Italy can offer."

"Charlotte? Where's Charlotte?" Magdalene suddenly asked, a mild tinge of panic in her voice when she noticed the young girl was not among them.

Alexei Ulyanov took a deep draw on his cigarette as the police patrol vehicle passed the repair truck for the third time. Something was happening and he knew it. He jabbed the ribs of the sleeping Petrov, whose turn it had been to sleep. This had been the fourth time now that a police car had passed and this one had suddenly drawn into the kerb and doused its lights. The two officers inside were wearing protective flak jackets and Ulyanov glimpsed a handgun raised above the line of the window. As an armed response team arrived he placed a text to Kernov warning of the sudden higher police presence.

Mikhail Kernov sat like a statue in the large arm chair behind the net curtains. His silent phone vibrated on the arm of the chair. He read the message and quickly snapped it shut before pushing it into his pocket. He checked the clip on his weapon and released the safety catch. The back door was open and he could feel the cool night air driving up the hall. His heart was racing and he felt, rather than knew, that they had been spotted. He would need to act quickly, if he were to get away.

"What's all the fuss about?" asked Perchenko as he entered the room. "There's nobody out there at the back."

"The fuss," Kernov replied, "is just that you used a light."

"No way," he lied in reply.

"You greedy little Siberian," Kernov mocked. "What were you looking for up in those rooms, some cheap Jewish jewellery, or were you looking in the underwear drawers? You knew what my orders were. And you still wish to steal some little thing from which you can make some Rooouuuubles. " Kernov stretched the word to accentuate its meaning. “Just as you did in Siberia. Stealing wedding rings and taking anything just to give promises, and still those people went into the mines.” He paused, “You will never change, never listen,” he paused again, “you are not KGB you are an opportunist. How will you help us to regain the Republic?”

“I had no flashlight,” Perchenko lied yet again.

“Then why was there a man looking up at the windows?”

“Cigarette, perhaps he came outside for a cigarette,” Perchenko was nervous now.

“But he didn’t light one, and he kept on looking up at the windows. A fat man with…

“I just thought there might be a thing or two worth taking.”

“What like, some girl’s virginity in exchange for her freedom. You did that too – only you wouldn’t give them that either would you?”

“That was Siberia and a long time ago,” Perchenko was being defensive.

“You are a fucking piece of slime,” Kernov hissed in Russian, “Siberian slime that will get us all killed. A wasteful, stupid, ignorant, petty thief whose cruelty let him advance in the KGB. A worthless maggot ridden, grave robbing…..”

“Hold on,” said Perchenko, “don’t you get so fucking holier than thou with me, you’re just as bad.”

“Really?” Kernov was being sarcastic. “What? I held virgins face down over my desk and promised them freedom in exchange for their willingness. Did you like to hear then cry, call for their mother whilst you forced them? You Gregori are a first class bastard, a pig, and now, now you have put us both in danger and dishonoured our cause.

“I was jus…”

His voice was cut short by the first bullet which punctured his throat. The second took the back of his head off and spread his brain across the wall immediately behind him like a can of emulsion paint kicked into the air. The muffled puff from Kernov’s recoil was the only reply that he was prepared to give. He had no intention of a fire fight with the London police force, nor a protracted discussion when he only had seconds with which to work. A shell casing ejected from the chamber of his weapon and landed silently on the carpet and then rolled away under the heavy chair. His fingers tips strove to locate it but he decided to leave it and move instead.

He was running now, through the back garden, and hearing voices he turned and slid like a rugby player scoring a try under the cover of some bushes. Sharp brambles caught his face as he saw shadows pass him just metres away.

His eyes and ears tuned like a cat, he waited concealed in the tangled undergrowth, before slipping silently to a rear fence which he vaulted and then passed into another garden. Four times all in all he passed from garden to garden before exiting into a small street in total silence. His face was lacerated and his back sweaty from the exertion of the escape – but he was clear.

Under a street lamp he sent a short text in Russian before disappearing into a maze of alley ways.

Chapter 16

The body was rigid and his eyes were closed as if in peaceful sleep. The heavy heaving of his rasping chest had ceased and the gurgling frothy residue on his muzzle was seeping into the carpet; at last his tenuous grip on life was passing. Alice tapped Gerald with her toe. She was satisfied with the result and knew that any mammal receiving such an infusion of venom must die – this included her prey the human. If someone in the Blondell household could be stricken with the poisonous dart she would have achieved precisely what she wanted; a warning, a deadly and precise warning to leave her in peace and stop this relentless pursuit. She would then simply melt away and Alexander Blondell would have to back off, or she would really attack his family. Perhaps the little girl would present herself an easy target – if not she would simply take out one or even two of the security men. A walk past, a quick dart to somewhere, anywhere on the body and then away and into hiding for a while. A chance to take stock, to read, go to the theatre, listen to music and perhaps even travel less; put down some roots – it was very appealing.

She pulled the home-made dart from Gerald's shoulder and lifted it to the light. The tip was smooth without a single blemish. No blood, no vile little animal with teeth, a tick, signifying the presence of an interloper. No fat bodied flea crushed between fingernails and popping blood onto the varnish like a crimson stained surrender flag. It was smooth like polished chrome – she sealed it inside an envelope.

She had checked the banking transfers – everything was ready;

she could lie low at her Brindley Place flat for a few days – maybe even a month. See Christmas out and let the world go by. Perhaps she would even cook a bird, a fat choice goose, or a ham smothered in orange and lime, baked slowly Italian style. She could almost smell the cinnamon and the apples and taste the gingerbread on her tongue; it would be a good time of year to lie low. There she could feed the pigeons and watch as they crapped on the business suits below. The more they ate the more they crapped and she had a perverse pleasure in watching that, as the new young executives below, drove themselves toward oblivion like so many lemmings. They passed the fountains, always in a hurry, always late, all the bite of rebellion driven out of them by the enormous debt of their education. She liked to see them covered in pigeon shit, it fed her sense of justice and inevitability. She had all she needed there, clothes, shoes, a complete wardrobe and no one would suspect Birmingham as her hiding place. The month of November was always cold in England but Christmas was something worth seeing in the now modernised Birmingham.

What once had been a concrete jungle of roads and tower blocks was a silent city of pedestrian walkways and long disused canals. Canals which had been dredged, cleared and now were the basis for afternoon strolls and picnics or pub lunches for real ale enthusiasts. The concert hall was just around the corner, she might even take in a performance or two to lift her spirits. Tesco delivered now so she could shop on-line and not move outside the door, if she chose not to. Inside that flat there was a further identity – Joan Black, a dark haired bespectacled girl and some emergency disappearing money too; a few hundred dollars in a safe and one solitary jewel – just in case. Nothing too large, just a small diamond, one that could easily be sold if needs be. When the coast was clear again she would move back to Italy, melt into the crowds, maybe have a little plastic surgery in Los Angeles and then, she paused in her thought processes, and then enjoy some of the money. Her face stared back at her from the mirror in the hall. Collagen in a few strategic places and a little change to the jaw line and she would look very different. Age was making her gain a little weight now and that too would alter her shape. She chuckled at the thought of being a little tubby and wondered briefly how men might perceive her.

She clasped her breasts through her blouse, "And these," she spoke aloud, "will these get bigger? Maybe Alice my love," she twisted her reflection to accentuate her rear and bent forward, "you'll have a cleavage like the Grand Canyon, or an arse the size of Texas." She laughed and put on a deeper male voice, "There's plenty of men that like a big booty." She laughed again, "As long as I don't get saddlebag hips and bingo wings, now that would be awful. Thighs, I could get those tree-trunk ones," she shuddered and turned away from the mirror. "Still most men don't mind a little bit of grabbing material, but who wants one of them anyway. It's not like I'm going to get married, settle down and have kids."

She pondered her simple mistake which had led the detectives to her Maldives hideaway – she would not make that mistake a second time. A new identity meant a new start, a bit fatter, a bit darker and much, much wiser.

The frogs, now useless, she flushed away and the Cane Toad was boiling in a saucepan, the body bloated and oozing a brown liquor which once ingested would render the consumer helpless – much as if they had a stroke. She gave it a stir and turned down the gas to a gentle simmer and thought about what she was going to say. They had probably seen women leave before. Then the precise reasoning came to her – it would be the perfect excuse, anyone would fall for that. It was too perfect and would cover her tracks precisely, she just needed to reduce the toad matter down to a thick stock. She gave the item one final stir and then turned off the gas to allow the liquor to cool and switched on Bolton's laptop.

At the table she studied the screen as the train times appeared. It should all run like clockwork. And just in case there was always the Bentley.

The house opposite the Blondell's home was bathed in light and police officers were moving to and fro. Alex Blondell crossed the street, followed by Pietro Grillva. Massimo and Pancardi remained inside the kitchen lest the whole incident were a diversion. Massimo was quiet as if deep in thought and Pancardi spotted it; he made a mental note to seek some answers to his questions once this initial panic was over.

"A corpse sir. Just like that slumped against the wall," said the officer, as Blondell approached.

Grillva was studying the windows of adjacent properties in the darkness, his eyes straining to see any movement behind drawn curtains – there was none. Blondell was already inside the front room when he finally entered.

"It's a bloody mess sir," one of the plain clothes MI5 men remarked at Blondell. "There must have been two of them. I don't think his own mother would be able to recognise him now though. God only knows why they quarrelled and why he. "

"Why was he shot?" Blondell interrupted.

"That's the point," the police officer replied, "he was not shot by us. Nor any of the other plain clothes guys here."

"So he was shot by his own colleague?" Pancardi asked, as he stood behind Grillva.

"I thought you were staying at the house?" Blondell noted.

"I was, but some of your men arrived and I do not think I am needed, besides Angelo he is there. He will not let your family out of his sight, of that I am absolutely certain and I can be of more use here."

Pietro Grillva now realising he was surplus to requirement moved out into the garden and taking a flashlight from one of the officers began to scan the lawn. The depressed grass and the overhanging bushes drew him toward the far end fencing. He was using his logic and experience and placing himself in the position of what he would do. This would be the natural exit point he reasoned, but this was also the entry point for the special services. They must have almost tripped over each other in the darkness. Two men, one dead, the other in need of a quick exit. Out over the back of the gardens, across the backs of several if need be, and if there were an alarm or a guard dog, deal with it precisely as he had done with man inside. He could leave a trail of corpses, none of them would identify him and by the time the police had found the exit point he could be on the other side of the world. Grillva was reasoning, this man was no amateur burglar, no drug taking opportunist, he was a professional, and a dangerous one at that.

"He is not one of yours then?" Pancardi sighed.

Blondell shook his head.

"This is indeed interesting," Pancardi continued.

"It's more than interesting," said Blondell, "it's horrifying. Who the hell are they and what are they doing at my home?" He pondered, "They aren't anything to do with the bankers are they. The Pope's men?"

Pancardi shrugged.

"Oh come on," Blondell continued, "you know all of these people."

Pietro Grillva stood thinking, assessing the situation and then took several strides toward the spot where Kernov had slid. Making a mental note and stooping to examine the ground, he passed his palm over the soft earth. Suddenly he stood fully erect and walked casually back into the house – he had seen enough.

"Mafia?" Blondell questioned Pancardi again as the pathologist arrived.

"I don't think so."

Pancardi was looking at Perchenko's footwear now and reading a label stitched into the seam. They were heavy boots, utility boots, not the sort of footwear used in town. They were black leather, good quality and not the sort of light-weight trainer which a real thief might wear, they were too cumbersome, not the shoes of a runner. These were the shoes of a man used to marching, trudging; heavy leather boots of habit. He said nothing.

"He's not been dead long," said the pathologist, "not long at all. He's a bit of a mess though. One bullet to the throat, looks like that killed him instantly and the second, to the head, just to be absolutely certain. The shot came from over there," he indicated toward the armchair. "I presume that is his brain spread all over the carpet and wall?" He indicated with a sweep of his arm.

The police officer nodded.

The pathologist was looking into the bloody mouth, "Mm interesting," he remarked. "He's not British, might not even be European."

"How can you know?" Blondell asked.

"I can't say for certain," the professional replied, "but a best guess, call it a hunch."

"So give us your guess as to his origin then," requested Blondell.

"Perhaps eastern block," was the clipped reply. "That would seem to be consistent with the dentistry here."

Pancardi was evaluating; that he thought would make sense – perfect sense.

Pietro Grillva re-entered the room and spoke clearly, "He went over the back fence," he said.

"I find that hard to believe," the police officer in charge replied with indignation.

"Well I don't," snapped Grillva in a terse reply. "This man was a professional. You probably walked right over the top of him as he lay in the grass at your feet. After you came in here he leapt a fence and disappeared into the maze of gardens. I expect in the daylight his footprints will easily be seen."

"I rather resent that evaluation," the policeman replied.

Grillva's reply was delivered in a flat monotone of disinterest, "Resent all you like," he said. "But ask this, why did you not leave a back stop unit to keep the rear exit covered? He was a professional and if you had been, one or two of your men would now be corpses near that fence." His voice lowered, but other officers still heard his sarcastic tone which was cold and clinical, "A lucky escape I'd say for the men under your command."

The room fell into stunned silence as Grillva spoke Italian to Pancardi.

Inside the Blondell home the smell of fresh coffee did little to calm the nerves of Magdalene Blondell. Charlotte had returned to the kitchen to eat some of her candies and Angelo Massimo was deeply immersed in thought. She wondered why his loyalty to Pancardi was so strong and so unflinching. Something had happened in their combined pasts which had given them a bond which was almost intangible. Massimo had been the first to arrive, and now here he was the last to leave. Like a great mastiff he sat guarding, his eyes down but his ears alert to any minor sound, ready to tear apart anyone or anything that entered the building – their keeper. She studied him, he looked the loyal type, broad of shoulder, clear of conscience and with deep set eyes; he had a humility which spoke of kindness and humanity. Pietro Grillva was more removed, remote, steely. He looked the more dangerous of the two but Massimo looked like a loyal dog that would protect the family to the point of death – his own. She could see the butt of an automatic protruding from a gap in his jacket just below his right armpit, and his left hand was flat against the table. To her he looked like a professional gunslinger in a 1960's John Wayne movie. If the wrong person came through the door in front of him she knew he would not hesitate to kill instantly. Her blood ran cold at the thought, but inwardly she thanked Pancardi for placing this man there with them.

His eyes still cast down he said softly, "You and the children have nothing to fear."

She took a deep breath of air as if to reply, but was cut short.

"I will not let any harm come to any of you," he said. "I had a daughter once, a fine girl, beautiful like her mother, but she is dead. There is no love greater than that of a father for his daughter and your man, he understands this." He switched to Italian, "Il suo compleanno e il dodici febbraio."

Magdalene noted the co-incidence and something deep inside her reached out to understand the deep pain this man had experienced. His head was down as if he were in contemplative recollection, but his words echoed into the room. She tried to imagine the circumstances regarding his daughter's death, and then it dawned.

"I know how precious Charlotte is to you and I swear," he had returned to English, "on the memory of my Juliette that I would die rather than let any harm come to Charlotte or the boy. He is named after Rober..."

The back door opened slightly and Massimo's reflexes were instant, the gun was out pointed and cocked.

"Chi e?" he called loudly.

"Siamo noi !" Pancardi chirped.

As quickly as the gun had been drawn and aimed, the safety catch was off and the cartridge chamber primed for use, with the hammer back. This time there would be no hesitation, no opportunity to let the others get a shot off first. If there was one other face near them this time he would fire first and not make the same mistake again.

"Angelo? Sono io! Capisce?" Pancardi called.

"Si,"

"Juliette."

"Si," Massimo repeated.

"Do," Pancardi hesitated, "dodici, put the gun down this is us." Pancardi's voice rang with crystal clarity, as he reverted to English.

Massimo's reaction was instant, he lowered the pistol as if an agreed password had been uttered but kept the safety catch off – just in case.

As Alex Blondell entered he caught a glimpse of Angelo's face and having heard Pancardi's account of the Juliette incident, was relieved that firstly Massimo was guarding his family and secondly that there was an agreed password. An agreement which only Pancardi and Grillva seemed to be aware of. He stepped into the room and Massimo flicked the safety catch into place with his thumb and holstered the gun.

The tension in the room was defused as the small party re-entered the kitchen.

"It's a mess over there," Blondell said, in an attempt to lighten the mood. "Someone has been watching this house," he continued. "There is a guy dead and another has gone. It looks like there were two of them doing some sort of surveillance of us." He looked directly at his wife, "It could be your Sicilian mob or their friends protecting you without your knowledge?" He smiled at Magdalene.

She shook her head in reply, "No they would have told me," she said. "And by the way you go on you'd think I was related to the Corleone family. I don't know where you get this notion from. My father was a respectable business man."

"But he has many connections no?" Pancardi asked.

"What in Olive Oil?" Blondell laughed.

Magdalene was clearly upset by the remarks and Grillva had no inclination to witness a heated domestic argument.

"This is not the Mafioso," he said calmly, killing the tension stone dead. "If it was them there would have been a huge fire fight."

Pancardi was nodding in agreement.

"So who was it then?" Blondell asked.

"I think that is most apparent Alex don't you?" Pancardi confirmed.

Blondell looked bemused.

"The owners of the jewels," Grillva hissed, "the owners."

"Who the hell are they?" Blondell quizzed. "What do they expect me to do?"

"Perhaps they think you know where they are, after your trip to the Maldives. Now they will come for them?" Massimo added. "And if your family get in the way God help them."

"No I do not think this is so," Pancardi interjected. "They are hoping that you will give them a vital clue. Or that you will do the work for them, find the persons who have the whereabouts," he paused, looking directly at Massimo. "They are after my daughter, they are after Alice."

"I need a drink," said Blondell, "and something a little stronger than coffee." Turning to Angelo Massimo he asked, "Posso offrirle qualcosa da bere?"

Massimo started to laugh.

"Perche ride?" Blondell questioned.

"You're not Italian?" he replied in English.

Blondell stuck with the Italian, "Parlo cosi male l'italiano?" he asked.

"No, your Italian is very good," Massimo replied. "I'd like a brandy if you have any?"

"I think we could all do with a stiff brandy after this, I think there's a bottle of Courvoisier Cognac in the drawing room I'll go and fetch it," Magdalene said.

Pietro Grillva was quick to react, "I'll get it," he offered. He wanted to do a quick sweep, just to make sure that no one had entered while he had been out. Satisfied that all was well, he returned to the kitchen to see the tension somewhat diffused and the grim faces he had witnessed when he left, now replaced with smiles.

"I am glad to see that we have some quality here," he chuckled. "Courvoisier, the nectar of the Gods."

"More like the elixir of the Devil," Magdalene replied, "and I need a large one."

Chapter 17

Alice Parsotti had packed all of her clothes, those that she considered worth taking anyway, the rest, including the soiled ones, lay in a heap over the body of Gerald. They were unimportant and could be replaced – she needed to travel light. Speed was her companion of need now, the smaller the bag the better.

On the kitchen table lay her passport in the name of Claudette Cicello and few of Bolton's valuables and also the keys for the Bentley, parked on the street below.

A pocket watch, a few gold sovereigns and a diamond ring sat waiting to be pocketed.

These she reasoned could be sold on the way, perhaps even in Birmingham; that would give her some travelling money. The paintings, which she could carry, had been stripped from their frames and rolled carefully. Degas, and Renoir alone could net her a small fortune and it would be sacrilege to destroy such items of beauty. She thought of Bolton and his corpse in the bedroom, she wondered if it might be worth rummaging through underwear drawers to see if other trinkets might be available; but in the end decided that the smell of decomposition would be better contained – she had to sleep there that night. Perhaps she would look prior to departure.

The extract of Cane Toad had now cooled and she was using a hypodermic needle to inject the brown fluid into the centre of some cream cakes which she had on a plate. The liquor was seeping into the pastry bases giving them a deadly and lethal lacing. This she knew would be her final swansong and ensure that there were no witnesses who could identify her. A meal of these cakes and then the consumer's next meal would be taken either with demons or angels, which ever laid the greatest claim.

That task completed she took two packs of lighter fluid from her jacket, four boxes of non safety matches and a cheap electrical plug-in timer. She listened to the radio as she was working and stripped the wiring on a kitchen blender. Disconnecting it from the power supply she made certain that the bare neutral and live wires were not touching but close enough to arc when the power came on. The gap would act like the ignition spark plug in a car and then bang, the whole place would go up like a giant bomb. Bolton, the dog and the top of the building would either burn like tinder or be blown half way across the city in pieces the size of a postage stamp. She thought of the Rothko, sighed, but knew her trail would be covered. The arc would ignite the gas, and if unsuccessful on that count, the fail-safe of the papers and clothes placed around it; and in turn the cupboards above it, the doors of which she left open to help the combustion process.

"So who are these people and the dead guy over the road what happened there?" Blondell asked.

"Tell him Pietro," Pancardi replied.

"You were under surveillance. Angelo saw a torch and so did I," Grillva said.

"So?" Blondell snorted, "what does that prove?"

Grillva did not rise to the bait, instead his voice flattened into a monotone, "So they had been spotted and we too had been spotted watching them. One man was in the chair watching us and he took the logical step. He killed the man he was partnering, very quickly," he waited, "so he could get away."

"And Pietro found some items upstairs which looked like they were going to be taken," Pancardi added.

"So the thieves argued and then one killed the other." Blondell stated.

"It might look like that," added Grillva, "but these men had silencers. Why would burglary need a silencer? No these men were professionals." He paused, "And then there are the boots."

"Boots? You've lost me," said Blondell.

"Russian army issue – Red Army to be precise," said Pancardi. "In the seam of the boot CCCP a tag almost polished out."

"Well they could be ex-army boots; you know bankrupt stock or something?" Blondell was clutching at straws and he knew it, "Russian?"

"At least now we know what we are dealing with," Pancardi replied.

"So the ..." Blondell stopped himself.

"Precisely," said Pancardi, "those jewels were being held by Russians in Florence. The plot it thickens. Maybe these are the original people who took the jewels from Yekaterinburg during the revolution."

"That's impossible," Blondell snorted in reply, "they would be over a hundred years old now."

"And," added Grillva, "these are no ordinary Russians they are combat trained and the boots are not standard Red Army." He looked from man to man and then to Magdalene before he laid his final card upon the table. "They are professionals," he paused, "I think they are KGB."

"Oh bloody hell!" exclaimed Blondell, "and one of them is dead in that house over the road. We could have a full scale international incident here. I had best get on to the Foreign Minister and alert the office. Christ alive that's all we sodding well need."

"Language Alex," Magdalene snapped.

"Sorry," he replied, casting a sly look at Charlotte, who seemed oblivious of what was happening. She was too busy attacking a rather irksome sweet wrapper which had the temerity to be stuck around her next choice morsel.

"Maybe that was why the one man killed the other," Massimo interjected, "so that he could cover his tracks."

Blondell's mind was racing now, "We need to get in contact with the Russians to see if this is covert or what."

"And what would they say?" Pancardi sighed, "Yes we have had operatives watching your every move and when we have the location of the Romanov jewels we will file an international law suit for their repatriation." His sarcasm was thick, "Of course they will deny any such operation." He was considering carefully now, "But let us just suppose that the men here are acting on behalf of someone else, someone with power and influence, someone inside the Red Army, but outside the mainstream of Government."

"Oh Jesus!" Blondell exclaimed, "it could be a group within a group. This is rapidly going from bad to worse."

"Or," said Pancardi, "it could be a small group who were privy to the information on the Romanov jewels. I think I need another brandy."

"I think I need more than one," agreed Blondell.

His wife shot him a look of, don't you dare.

Nobody had noticed Angelo Massimo leave and take a single injection into his arm. He had worked quickly, and taken no more time than going to the toilet. His pupils were dilated and his cheeks flushed, but the gnawing, nagging pain in his side was being subdued and he could concentrate again.

"We must eat!" Pancardi chirped.

"Well I have prepared for a siege laughed Magdalene, but first the youngsters must go to bed, and their father," she looked at her husband, "must do the honours."

It would be simple: In the morning she would plug the timer into the wall and set it for 1pm. If the doors were left open, the windows closed and the gas turned on full, with the pilot light out, and no switches on, the whole space would fill up nicely. If that did not work the lighter fluid would give the necessary back-up for a full fire. That way the cakes might have been consumed either as a mid-morning break or a lunchtime snack. The confusion of an explosion or a fire would make a nice news item. It might be classified as a terrorist attack and the whole of London's lawmen be tied up.

In the meantime she would have left the capital and be at New Street. The following day she would have collected the money and then she could lie low. A diversion, a warning and a covering of tracks all encapsulated in the one action.

In the spare bedroom of Bolton's unique flat she lay watching the television and eating Pizza which the delivery boy had brought up to the door. The greasy feel on her fingertips was comforting and the melted cheese combined with the rich tang of ripe tomato gave her senses a lift. She could enjoy the act of getting fatter she reasoned. She regretted, once again, the impending destruction of the Rothko painting but it could not be avoided. Watching the news it showed nothing eventful and eventually she switched off and drifted into sleep – she had set the alarm for 6 am.

Charlotte Blondell had managed to encourage her favourite Italian uncle to read to her, and had promptly fallen asleep as he did so. Pancardi had tucked her in and planted a small kiss upon her forehead. It was at times like these that he regretted the fact that his life had been so insular. He wondered if, had things been different, he could have been a father like this to Alice. There was no real envy left now, just deep regret. His mind flashed to Alaina and he wondered what she might be doing at that moment. She was still young enough to produce children.

"Silly old fool," he said, "she is far too young for you."

This was accentuated to his satisfaction when he stood erect next to the young girl's bed and a pain of precise stiletto intensity shot from his knee to his lower spine.

"See," he said, to himself, "there is no fool like an old fool and you are both."

He looked once more at the young Charlotte Blondell and then turned down the light and backed into the corridor, closing the door quietly behind him. As he did so Massimo appeared at the far end of the corridor, glanced at Pancardi, evaluated the situation and then disappeared again.

Roberto had been bathed and changed for the night. The whole party had eaten Italian style; olives, bread, pasta, meats and a sauce which Magdalene had produced, washed down with wine and water.

Pietro Grillva had showered and taken his automatic Berretta to pieces on the bed for cleaning. Angelo Massimo found that sleep would not come and had given himself another shot of morphine and set an alarm for 5.am. Then he would take over from Grillva, who had chosen the mid-shift after Pancardi, who was now sitting alone at the kitchen table listening to the purring hum of the dishwasher. He was flicking through the pages of a text which Blondell had provided on the history of the Romanov jewels. He was studying two or three passages on their disappearance during the revolution. He was trying to determine why the KGB would now be involved. It was late, he was tired, and his logic was not working. Also his mind for some unknown reason kept flicking to Alaina in Rome.

"So what happened to Angelo Massimo's daughter?" Magdalene asked as she climbed into the bed next to her husband – she was naked.

"Why?"

"Because when he said that he wouldn't let anything happen to Charlotte, he seemed so sincere and he was being otherworldly," she replied. "I don't think I've seen anyone quite so sad."

"That's a bit of an exaggeration isn't it? But I did get Pancardi to spill some of the beans." He lowered his voice as he lay next to his wife and felt her nipples touch his side as she reached into him. "Well there was some sort of witness protection programme, and Massimo was assigned to be the protection officer. Everything went well until the case was nearly at court. It was those Sicilian judges, Falconi and Borsoloni? Well to cut a long story short, Pancardi was outside his home and some hit men or something came to the place. There was some gun fire." He stopped suddenly.

"Go on," Magdalene requested, as her hand encased his manhood in her feminine grip.

Blondell's concentration was failing, "Well there was a fire fight and in the exchange his daughter was killed. But there's a bit I don't understand; why was this happening at Massimo's home and Pancardi was vague about that bit too; I seem to get the notion that the bullet went through Pancardi and then into young Juliette. The whole thing was a mess; Roberto Calvetti was injured and that guy Grillva shot and killed two men. I had to sort of get the story in bits and pieces."

"I want you," she said.

He didn't react.

"Then there was this thing about the four of them getting even.

I don't think it was legal. I think they may have done something to those on the case."

Her hand was working now and he was responding.

"I can imagine that," she said, "they are old colleagues and I would think they make loyal friends, but terrible adversaries. They may be old men but I would not wish to be hunted by them, KGB or no."

Magdalene kissed her husband, thankful in the knowledge that those protecting her daughter were ruthless enough to kill if they had to. In the morning the world would seem a brighter place. For now she wanted to make love.

Chapter 18

Alice Parsotti woke early, before the alarm, and drifted into the bathroom. She had slept well and she felt refreshed. She didn't shower and as she cleaned her teeth the alarm buzzed in the bedroom – 6am. The smell of putrefaction in the apartment was beginning to become offensive and she knew that there was absolutely no time to waste in vacating the place.

The plan was simple, first she would take her bag down to the Bentley and with it the box of re-sealed cream cakes for the concierge and his young apprentice. The men that had constantly undressed her with their eyes were about to get one of the biggest surprises of their lives. She imagined the older man Fred, frothing at the mouth and his eyeballs rolling in their sockets much as Gerald's had done, only this time it would not be out of lust, this would be absolute terror. She wondered if he would vomit, feel his insides rising to pass out through his throat.

The excuse she would use for the cakes, Mr. Bolton's birthday. She paused and looked at herself in the over-sink mirror, what if they knew it was not his birthday. She spat the residual toothpaste into the sink. There was blood from her gums and she examined them in the mirror running her tongue over the crisp fresh whiteness of her tooth enamel. She lowered her head and rinsed.

"No way," she said, her head rising to the over-sink mirror once again. "He was too mean, too self absorbed. They might not eat them though. What if one of them has a dairy allergy?" She cursed, then thanked providence that they were both men. Men she reasoned always seemed to have a healthier relationship with food. When hungry they ate, and they would eat junk food and not then go into paroxysms of guilt on the calorific count, or the spot inducing qualities of the content. It was a strange quirk of civilisation that women should not eat, why? Why they would tell each other that they had been good; why half a tomato and a lettuce leaf had filed them. Why couldn't she eat bacon sandwiches, fry ups, crisps and chocolate? The invention of the new man had changed that somewhat, some had become pumpkin seed eating health addicts, but in the main they too always succumbed to a pretty face and a good fuck. Even the vague possibility of sex made most men pliable and compliant. She smiled at herself and licked her lips, pouting in the mirror; then wondered how many men would not surrender to a good meal with wine; especially if they thought it might be followed by a willing fuck or easier still, a real semen ingesting, she pouted at herself again, blow job. Men were so easy to understand and so stupid – they'd eat the cakes.

In the kitchen she made a coffee, at the first gulp her senses rose as the insulin levels doubled in her body. She loved the pleasure of that first rush of caffeine, especially if there was an intense sugar hit to accompany it. She bit into the pastry and the icing stuck to the roof of her mouth as the soft custard filling oozed onto her tongue – it was morning.

She was thinking. First she would take the car to Arnold Street and there she'd slip into the uniform on the back seat. Then walk the few alleyways to the Blondell residence. She had a bag which was half full of old letters, it gave the image of a post-woman going about her early morning routine. Inside the bag she'd have the air pistol and with that take the one shot at a security guard. As a back up she had the envelope with the coated staples – just in case.

She also had the packet to post. If the person opening it was lazy she could get lucky, if not it might be a wasted effort but the terrorising effect would be the same either way. The warning would be loud and clear. Then she'd disappear back to the Bentley and take a leisurely drive up to Coventry, dump the car and get the train up to Birmingham. In the meantime the whole of London would be on red alert and the police tied up with possible terrorism threats. The flat would have exploded and the Blondells would be in turmoil. Her plan, she evaluated, was excellent, and even though they might have expected something they simply would not have expected this.

Alexei Ulyanov was tired and his back ached. He and Petrov had been sharing the small space of the repair truck for too long and the stench of the man had begun to hurt his nostrils. The space for sleeping they had manufactured behind the seats was cramped and narrow; there was no mattress and as a result the cold of the metal made true sleep virtually impossible.

They had taken turns to doze while the other had pretended to work outside. It had been a miserable way to spend the night but they had been able to keep tabs on the increased activity, which had taken place after Kernov had been discovered. Kernov was no longer situated at the front, Perchenko had been shot and MI5 were now crawling all over the area. It was less than satisfactory but at least they had the phone tapped and from where they were now the property could be partially seen.

They had seen the curtains open and the house come alive. One of the guards was patrolling and the place looked under siege. It was not ideal. The worst part of it was that they were now trapped in this vehicle. If they left too early their cover would be blown and they would risk having no chance at further information. So they had to stay put, despite the lack of creature comforts.

A large red car approached and the police surveillance teams came alive, Ulyanov saw the driver's face and recognised Kernov instantly. The car passed and made a single pass in front of the house; two minutes later Ulyanov's phone rang.

"It's all quiet out here," his Sergeant's familiar soft voice said. "The activity has died down but there are still very many police about. Surely this woman will not come to the house?"

"We stay put for another twenty four hours," Ulyanov replied. "If after that there is no show we go."

"I'll go again in three hours," Kernov announced, "but I'll have to get another car first." The phone connection died.

Links at the Foreign Office had given Ulyanov some information on the woman but if they lost her, the whole thing might evaporate under his gaze. He lit a cigarette, his mind was churning over possibilities. Kernov was contactable and available and the fact that he was less than a mile away gave him reassurance. He could pick them up if they needed a fast get away.

The phone text alert bleeped – the message was simple:

Parked up, walking on foot .

Past the front. Round the side toward the back and past you.

Ulyanov snapped the phone shut and stepped outside to speak to Petrov whose head appeared for the twentieth time from the man hole.

Inside the Blondell home, Pietro Grillva was laying on his bed unable to sleep. Having given the watch over to Angelo Massimo, dawn had broken and he could hear birdsong along with garbage trucks and early morning deliveries. He could hear the Blondells in their room with the infant boy, while Charlotte was in her own room watching TV and talking to someone. Someone who was laughing, he recognized the voice as Pancardi; Pancardi the favourite uncle. His thoughts drifted freely and he tried to imagine what, if anything, might happen, what if anything Parsotti might try.

Then he saw Massimo's daughter, a picture of horror. The recollection was total and clear, Angelo cradling his lifeless child, his hands covered in her blood. There was a bullet wound and his wife was screaming and Pancardi was slumped against the kitchen unit his eyes white in his head. There was blood running down his arm too, a bullet wound in his chest and the floor was covered in debris. Roberto was yelling down the phone and pointing a gun at him as he burst through the door – the whole thing was a mess. Confusion and corpses and mess, like some mad picture of Hell painted by Hieronymus Bosch. Pancardi was shot and dying, the girl was dead and he, he had arrived too late, foolishly he'd been distracted by inexperience and the diversion. True he had personally shot two of the assassins, but the important one, the trigger man had still got through, right up to the back door and fired straight through Pancardi's lung. The girl had been inside and the same bullet that almost killed Pancardi had killed Massimo's daughter outright. Grillva's eyes opened and then closed once again, he could not afford to make that mistake this time. This time he would not be distracted, this time Blondell's little laughing girl was not going to die because of his mistakes. He had to stay calm and alert, needed to regroup, to sleep – his eyes began to close and he dosed.

Angelo Massimo had taken his first shot of morphine for the day and was dressed. He wore jeans and a dark blue casual shirt. The official suit was gone and his hard leather shoes had been replaced by comfortable running ones. Not that he intended to run anywhere, but he needed to be comfortable, alert and vigilant.

The cancer he carried in his abdomen was growing like some implanted alien and he knew that eventually he would not be able to fight it, that it would consume him. For now the pain was controllable but the dosage needed to be bigger; the night he had passed had been fitful and a walk into the gardens to check on the outside surveillance teams and the CCTV had cleared his head, but the pain stayed. Stuck in his midriff like a forty pound boulder, a great lump weighing him down.

He was drinking coffee when Charlotte walked in.

"Good morning," she said, as if she were the lady of the house.

Pancardi was close behind.

"Uncle Carlo would like some coffee?" she asked as if she were fifteen and not six.

"Yes please," he replied, "does mamma let you make coffee?"

"No, she gets cross," the little girl replied, "but I can make it anyway. I know what to do, it's easy," she added.

"I'll do it," said Massimo.

"And I think you, young lady, ought to get dressed and stop eating all that candy," Pancardi remarked.

Charlotte had attacked the bag which Pancardi had bought for her and was busy sorting out the bits and pieces she wanted to have first.

"But you bought them for me," Charlotte protested.

Pancardi reached over and confiscated the bag, "After breakfast," he said; as he did so, she pulled a face. He gave in immediately and handed over a small chocolate bar.

"Now go and get dressed," he said, "and take that with you , and don't tell your mother."

She chuckled in triumph and left the room running.

"She is beautiful, is she not?" Pancardi asked.

Massimo nodded.

"She reminds me of Juliette," Pancardi continued, " a small woman, full of life. I am so sorry for you Angelo this assignment must be hard for you no?"

Massimo's reply was remote almost cold, "That was such a long time ago, she would have been a woman by now Carlo."

"Yes but it was my fault," Pancardi sighed. "If I had been a little quicker, a little sharper, then Juliette would still be alive."

"It was all our faults, and it was no fault," Massimo replied. "Pietro he blames himself for being held back by those two goons. Roberto he was late in the room, and you, what do you wish? That the bullet had not passed through you and into her. That you should have died and not her." His voice became thin, "Fate Carlo, it was just a simple twist of luck, or bad luck, or fate. There was no reason, no divine purpose, we both know there is no such thing." His voice lowered to a whisper, "And in the great scheme of humanity it does not matter."

"How long have you got?" Pancardi asked with a forthrightness which shocked Massimo into an instant honest reaction.

"A month of lucidity, maybe," he replied, "then another six weeks of hospice."

"Cancer?"

"Si ."

"What can I do to help?" asked Pancardi.

"Nothing, there is nothing to be done." He paused, "Except one thing."

"Name it."

"Do not take me off this duty. Put me in the front line, I am expendable and I see my Juliette in that little girl of your friend the Englishman and nothing must happen to her."

"I don't know how long this will go on for," Pancardi was being honest.

"I can survive I have the morphine." Massimo was being pragmatic.

"But would you not like to spend time with your family and friends?" Pancardi asked.

"And who are they? Marietta? She has long since abandoned me and her family? They no longer seek my company; I am a stranger to them now. An alien with another alien inside. They did not care for me then, why should they care for me now? No we musketeers are the only ones left."

The kitchen door opened and Magdalene walked in carrying the young Roberto.

"Good morning," she said, "Alex will be in a minute, apparently he wants to make a fry up for everybody." She smiled, "This should be interesting."

Pancardi clapped his hands together in delight, "With sausages," he chirped, "wonderful good quality English sausages. This is a perfect start to Pancardi's day."

" I am glad you're so happy," Magdalene returned. "The way to your heart is directly through your stomach."

Pancardi patted his stomach, "Love is expansive though," he laughed.

Magdalene filled the kettle and clattered some pans.

"I shall take another sweep of the grounds," said Massimo. He looked at Pancardi and both men made eye contact, nothing was said but both understood the other.

Pancardi simply nodded.

"Don't shoot the messenger," said Alice. "Miles, err, Mr. Bolton asked me to give them to you." She paused, " To celebrate his birthday. Something to have with your morning coffee?"

" Cream cakes, lovely. Me and the young boy we'll have these for our elevenses. Go down a real treat these will," said the concierge. " Can you thank Mr. Bolton for us Miss Cicello?" asked Fred. "And wish him happy birthday too," he added.

"You can thank him yourself later," Alice replied, "I think he's recovered and he should be out and about later."

Alice Parsotti slipped into the lift and rose to Bolton's flat for the last time. Closing the windows and setting the timer on the primed blender for 1pm she grabbed her hand bag, threw in the trinkets from the kitchen table and the passport, turned on all the gas appliances and re-entered the lift.

Downstairs she saw both Fred and John in the lobby and walked over to them to chat for a moment or two.

"Tell mister Bolton ffanks," said John, before he was nudged by the older man, "oh and can ya say happy birffday too."

"You can tell him yourself later," she replied. "He's having a sleep at the moment and as he feels a bit better. I think, when I get back, we'll go for a stroll in the park, or perhaps down by the river."

" We haven't seen him for a few days," said Fred, trying hard not to smirk.

" No he's been very tired," Alice replied. " So I've left him sleeping and I'll wake him up when I get back."

Fred wanted to ask how? By pulling on his cock? But instead smiled and wished she would pull his cock to wake him up. She was a most distinctive woman, the sort a man could easily remember.

"Anyway," said Alice looking at her wristwatch, "I had better make a move. Enjoy those cakes now and I'll see you later."

As she drove the Bentley away she smiled at the consummate simplicity of her plan. They had even both been stupid enough to make sure Bolton was not disturbed. The whole thing was finally coming together.

Chapter 19

Once over the river, the traffic subsided and the quiet streets of prosperity and seclusion melted away from the traffic. Some parts of Chelsea had an oldie-world air; this was an area which only those with considerable income or connection could afford. This was a territory that most Londoners did not know about. A place of plenty behind the closed doors of respectability and corruption. The drives were securely gated, the streetlamps prominent and the CCTV fully operational. There were things here worth stealing and in consequence, they were worth protecting.

Alice Parsotti parked the car under the overhanging seclusion of a large Horse Chestnut tree. A Bentley in Chelsea would not cause undue alarm and not draw attention to the driver. Had it been Brixton or Bow the wheels would probably have been removed before she had fully turned off the ignition.

The tree grew behind a tall close boarded fence which had recently been creosoted a deep and vibrant mahogany. The smell permeated the air and gave a rich and homely aroma to the vista. Alice liked the smell, it was like the smell of freshly sawn wood, it was unique, comforting. Carcinogenic or not, fashionable or not, the rich smell of creosote gave the street a sense of stability – a stability like the 1950's. A stability she could recall in a smell of childhood; a time when she had played in her grandmother's garden and watched the gardener creosote a tool shed. She had been young then and she remembered hiding in the bushes, and he, thinking there had been no one near, had openly pissed a stream into the flower bed. It was an image she could recall with absolute clarity. The large pan-handed man holding, what looked to her, as a young girl, a log, a pink fleshy log which she should never have seen. She had watched the man after that and learned much about his habits and those of the parlour maid, who he fucked deeply and frequently in that same shed. Alice remembered the whimpering scream of the girl as she reached orgasm and the pleading the man had made to her grandmother when she fired him. Alice had arranged that too, it had been her first fledgling use of power and she enjoyed it. The smell of creosote had so many memories.

When Alice Parsotti stepped out of the Bentley – there was no turning back.

She crossed the street and slipped a package into the red post-box on the corner and then stood surveying adjacent roof tops and windows for observers. She saw nothing unusual and slipped back onto the rear seats to change.

She had committed to memory the exact location of the Blondell house and was thinking about the best route for her special delivery. On her head she wore a large grey wig over the standard blue trousers and blue shirt of a postal worker. From the boot of the car she retrieved the large red delivery bag which she threw over her shoulder, and then reached inside to check for the air pistol. At the small of her back her .38 Smith and Weston snub nosed revolver nestled in the holster inside her trousers and was covered with the tail of her shirt which she wore open and not tucked in, over a lose fitting singlet blouse.

The sky was clear for a winter day and the air dry and the morning sun was warming the pavements as she walked down the first alley way. Her heart was starting to beat rapidly as she turned first left and then right. A hundred yards ahead she could see a man walking casually, he had no dog, no bag, and he was looking around as if he were a tourist, but she noted he carried no street map. She slowed her pace and watched the man pass the Blondell home and turn left at the corner. She crossed the street and noticed intense activity at the house opposite Alex Blondell's home, and then casually walked up the drive of the house next to it. Quickly she posted two letters through the door. Her mind was racing, she didn't like the look of the intense security and decided that the best thing to do would be to simply continue the postal charade, do a circle and then return to the Bentley and leave. The house was to her right now, Blondell's to her left and she could see perhaps fifteen officers moving from place to place, carrying boxes to cars and then she could see the familiar white suited forensic team moving near the front door opposite. She thumbed a pile of letters in her hand as if she were checking addresses. She dropped some on the ground and then bent to retrieve them, as she did so she studied the house. One man was smoking a cigarette outside and his head was thrown back as he laughed and exhaled a plume of rich blue smoke. She picked up the letters and moved on unnoticed, turned left at the corner and then left again and began to walk past the back of the Blondell home. In the distance perhaps eighty yards ahead she could see the walking man again, beyond that was a truck positioned next to some repair work being undertaken on the road. Two men were talking and one of them had a cigarette. She could hear a dog barking, it sounded small and then the voice of a girl calling it.

"Oh come on Noodle," the girl was saying.

The dog was barking and a woman's voice was calling, "Charlotte Blondell, come here this minute."

Parsotti's sense of alertness increased. The gate was on her left and she could see up the back driveway as she walked closer. As she stepped from behind the perimeter wall she was in full view of the security guards and the CCTV cameras. The dog began to bark at her as only dogs can at any postman who might intrude, and Charlotte Blondell was now only feet away. Angelo Massimo was close behind Charlotte, maybe three feet. Alice reached inside the post bag.

Inside his upstairs bedroom Pietro Grillva rose from his dozing and threw open the window. His senses were alerted by the cacophony of noise. Charlotte Blondell was laughing and Noodle was barking and the post woman was at the back gate handing a package to Angelo Massimo and he had flinched back his hand as if he had been stung.

Grillva scanned the street and immediately noticed on the other side a second post man walking toward the house from the opposite direction to Parsotti. His reaction was instant. Alice was stepping away now and Pietro Grillva's world was moving into slow motion.

"Angelo!" he yelled from the window.

Alice Parsotti looked up and saw him. She was taking quick backward steps from the gate; she was reaching for something in the bag; something in the bag. Grillva was shouting and then running, his Beretta out. He jumped the stairs and flew past both Blondell and Pancardi in the kitchen.

"She's here," he screamed at them both as he launched himself into the back garden.

Alex Blondell was behind him and the security men seeing the quick movement and sudden noise were up and running. They had forty yards more to cover.

Grillva could see Angelo Massimo lifting Charlotte and he had his back turned toward the gate placing his body between the child and the woman. Grillva could see something, a gun, he fired and missed and Alice Parsotti disappeared behind the perimeter wall the red post bag thrown to the ground in front of the gate.

Alice was running now, running toward the walking man. She could see him raise his hands and drop to one knee. She recognised the stance as he prepared to brace himself for the recoil while taking aim. The two workmen were also running and a second shot rang out behind her, then another, she lost count. Then came the explosion, an ear splitting roar of a boom followed by a hail of abrasive metal and glass.

She crashed through a privet hedge to her immediate left and felt the sharp point of a shard of fencing pierce her skin as she fell to the ground. Something sharper and lighter tore into her arm and she yelped like a puppy. She caught sight of the kneeling man who had been taking aim. He was running toward the truck and one man was in the road behind him motionless. The truck was moving and there were screaming voices behind her and gunfire from the Blondell house.

Now she was up, over the lawn, over a fence and into an alleyway. She took stock ran thirty feet and jumped into a second garden. She could hear more mild explosions and wondered if it might be the flat and then ran on. She turned left and sped past two naked people in a swimming pool that started shouting about private property. She was reaching for the .38 at her back as she passed and the appearance of the weapon stunned the swimmers into silence. To her they were unimportant; she tore the wig from her head and threw it to the ground. There was blood on the grey hair as it landed and her fingers were wet on the handle of the .38.

She was moving quickly making every sinuous effort to get back to the Bentley – seeking sanctuary. She could hear shouting but it seemed to be getting further away. Right into an adjacent house, through the hall, out and away, down the drive, out through the pedestrian gate, across the road, through another garden and back under the Horse Chestnut tree.

She was kneeling now, listening, panting, listening for voices behind her and in front. Just a few feet over the fence and then freedom.

Angelo Massimo released Charlotte Blondell and reached over his shoulder to try to extract the dart from his back. The fingertips on his left hand were bleeding from where the post woman had pulled against the stapled package drawing the staple tips into his flesh. Already they were numb and he couldn't find the dart. His sense of feeling was abandoning him. It was like the morphine had quadrupled in his blood stream and his head was getting light.

"Charlotte, get back to the house," he said, "run, run now."

He stumbled reaching out to steady himself as Grillva arrived.

"Hit," he asked.

"No," Massimo replied, "get after her."

Angelo Massimo watched for the split second that it took Pietro Grillva to get out onto the street. He fired once at the gate lock and then barged it open sending himself headlong onto the ground. He was rolling and firing and Massimo could see and hear other weapons. Pancardi passed him and then he fell to his knees, his breath was gone.

He fell forward onto his face and his lungs discharged a heavy froth, blood was running out of his nose and his arms were contorted and rigid.

"What can I do?" asked Magdalene as she arrived. Lifting him to ease his breathing.

Massimo was shaking his head, "Charlotte?" he quizzed frantically.

"She's in the house," she replied, "Alex is there."

She had his head cradled in her lap now as blood was appearing in his eye sockets.

"Poison," Massimo coughed, "back."

"Angelo," Pancardi was back slapping his face. "Pietro's after her and the others."

Massimo smiled and his muscles tensed as if he had cramp in his whole body. His breath was hissing, "Dart back," he said.

Pancardi reached under his companion and turning him on his side pulled the home made dart from his back. He placed the item into a handkerchief and watched as Massimo coughed an accompaniment to his own death. The mixture of venom and morphine worked at double the speed of Gerald; by the time Alex Blondell had arrived from the house Angelo Massimo had been pronounced dead.

Pietro Grillva had followed Parsotti out through the gates rolling as he fell. He had seen Kernov kneeling and fired twice, his Berretta bouncing a recoil in his grasp. On the third shot he saw the man drop to his face. A shot fired by one of the police in the surveillance car had hit and floored Petrov; he lay on the ground in a pool of blood his right arm virtually severed – a wound the size of a dinner plate pumping blood a foot into the air as he tried to stand and fire. A second shot hit him full centre in the chest and he flew back with the impact like a thrown wet rag. His head hit the kerb stone with a sickening crunch; he bounced once and then lay still.

Ulyanov had started the truck and swung the vehicle toward Kernov, who was running toward the now open door. Grillva fired at Parsotti and then the explosion ripped into the air. The manhole cover and shards of metal, nails and other debris whizzed past his ears as the police team were cut to ribbons in the shrapnel. Two men fell immediately and Grillva could see that one had lost half of his face. Parsotti dived into the bushes as he fired again and was gone. He did not know if he had hit her.

Pietro Grillva was running now, running toward the spot where Parsotti had passed through the hedge and then he lost his footing and consciousness in the second explosion.

The second explosion, a grenade thrown by Ulyanov, blew one of the parked cars to pieces as Kernov climbed onto the footplate of the truck. There was gunfire and then Kernov was stumbling into the truck and it pulled away. As it turned the corner two further grenades exploded in the path of oncoming pursuit vehicles. It had given the escapees vital seconds.

Inside the Bentley Alice Parsotti sat panting. She could feel the warmth of the blood as it ran down her sleeve. Quickly she examined it and finding a shard of glass in the wound pulled it clear and threw the offending object onto the back seat.

Her side was painful and she felt that she might have broken a rib. Her shirt was stained in blood but both wounds were superficial. She pulled a hooded jacket over her head and started the engine. She began to swing out from under the tree when the explosion in Stamford Street ripped the top of the building clear and threw it into the river below. Within seconds she could hear sirens and cars flying in all directions. It was all the hope she needed and a much greeted diversion. She drove away in the opposite direction against and away from the confusion.

"Fuck, fuck, fuck," yelled Kernov as the truck sped onto The Mall, "that bastard hit me look."

Blood was spurting from his leg hitting the inside of the windscreen.

"How bad is it Alexei?" he asked.

"Petrov is dead," he replied, "that just leaves the two of us."

"If this wound is deep, I'm fucked," Kernov said, lifting his leg high enough to bind a tourniquet around his thigh.

"Don't be ridiculous," Ulyanov snapped, "You are KGB and we were in tighter spots in Afghanistan. It's a flesh wound, a scratch." He knew he was morale boosting and that medical attention was needed. "We must dump this vehicle, and move, get you to a doctor," he concluded.

He screeched the vehicle to a sudden halt and jumping out ran to the car immediately behind the truck and forced the driver out at gunpoint. Kernov crawled onto the back seat as the car sped away through the traffic. All they now needed was a little luck and they could reach the safe house. There would be supplies there and they could get access to a doctor.

"Mikhail Kernov," shouted Ulyanov, "you will not die on me, do you understand? That is an order."

"Fuck orders," he returned as he slumped down.

Ulyanov accelerated.

Chapter 20

Pietro Grillva felt his face. Apart from the lump above his eyes there seemed to be no other damage. He tried to raise himself from the hard slabs behind his back but fell disorientated, woozy and weak. His elbows were grazed, as if he had been pumiced against the stone to remove hard skin, his trousers were torn and something was embedded in his right thigh. Though he could not see it he could feel it, there was a steady pumping of warm fluid which was gathering in his sock. He had literally been blown off his feet and had landed full on his face. On his back now he was looking at the sky above him and the slow and languid motion of the clouds. The intense blue signalled the start of a warm day, not a good day to die he thought. White cotton candy drifts passed overhead and he was not sure if, minutes, seconds or hours passed. The world had moved into the limbo of time loss, there were no references, no pegs to hang the coat of reality to. Remembering, he rolled onto his side to see if Parsotti had been blown into the hedge. Hoping to see her stretched out as he was, prostrate on the ground. Through the ripped gap where she fell he could see an empty lawn beyond and cursed in exasperation, knowing she had gone.

He rolled onto his back again, his right hand reaching for the Beretta and he felt something warm inside his ear burst and then felt the blood trickle and drip crimson onto the pavement. Above him there was a young man, a man in a green boiler suit and yellow tabard. He read the word paramedic and smiled a toothy hapless grin at the boy who was feeling his neck and shoulders.

The man was speaking, asking something. He tried to make out what was being asked and thought about Italy and the fish market; he could smell the Tuna in a Naples market all rich and red. The costermongers were yelling and he could hear the faint noise of carnival crackers popping. But the noise of the ocean and the revving delivery trucks on the quay were too loud; he could smell the carbon monoxide from the truck exhausts was too strong.

He wanted to get up, stop resting, but he could see the pavement undulating and the noise was deafening – too loud for him to make out what the man was saying.

Pancardi was there now standing on the undulating slabs, surfing the moving road surface. He was talking to a beach guard in uniform and pointing. Grillva could see a car on its side and the front end was crumpled. He tried to reason on how it had been washed up.

"Carlo, the bag, she had something in the bag," Grillva blurted.

Pancardi came over to him as a neck brace was being fitted. He was being lifted on a platform a door or something.

"There was something in her hand and Angelo drew back like he had been stung," Grillva coughed, some blood came out of his mouth, "go through the hedge, she went through the hedge." His breath was coming in monumental gasps as a needle was applied to his arm. A drip was being set up ready for transportation and he was feeling faint.

"He must have been just a few feet from the explosion," the paramedic proffered.

"Is he seriously hurt?" Pancardi asked.

"His hearing is probably the worst affected," replied the paramedic as he worked. "It could be permanent," he added. "Too early to say, the doctors will have to take a good look."

"Angelo?" asked Grillva,

"Not too good," he replied, knowing Grillva could not hear.

"He was hit!" Grillva added.

"We found a dart in his back," said Pancardi.

Grillva did not react. He could see Pancardi's mouth working but no words were coming out. The interference was too great, the feedback and the whining screech were deafening. There were planes or something like racing cars nearby and he couldn't hear him.

"Through the hedge," Grillva shouted above the noise, "she went through the hedge, I was going to follow," his voice was cracking as he tried to make himself heard above the din. The effort required was monumental as the men held him down on the stretcher and lifted him into the ambulance and his eyes began to close.

Alex Blondell arrived as the ambulance doors closed, "Is he alright?" he asked.

"Is Charlotte?"

"Fine, though she's crying, it's a bit of a trauma all this. She did see Angelo after he took that dart. Was it poisoned?"

"Probably," was Pancardi's clipped reply.

"Shit, has Pietro been poisoned too?"

"No the explosion got him."

"Oh my God this has been a disaster," Blondell's voice was subdued.

"He'll probably never be alright again," Pancardi replied. "Looks like a military grenade to me, he'll probably be stone deaf after this, poor bastard."

"A grenade, oh shit," Blondell replied, knowing only too well what such a weapon could do at close quarters. He had seen men chopped to mush when grenades had been used in confined places. "Why did she toss a grenade?" he asked. He had seen them in Cyprus in the hands of the Turks and shuddered as he asked the question.

"She didn't," Pancardi replied, "she just ran. There through the hedge," he pointed. "He," he pointed to the crumpled and bloody heap at the opposite kerb, "he threw it."

"Just who the hell is he?" Blondell asked.

"Come we will see," he said, walking across the road as Grillva's ambulance siren picked up volume and sped off down the street. Blondell could see two flak jacketed police officers laid upon the pavement, their tunics over their faces and a resident on his front door step was having glass extracted from his cheek by a Paramedic.

Everywhere armed officers were moving swiftly from house to house and into the garden where Parsotti had fled. He looked up and saw the blown windows and wondered what the man may have seen. He made a mental note to interview him once the dust had settled.

"What about Alice, shouldn't we go after her?" he asked.

"Like some wild gooses chasers?" Pancardi replied, "No, others can do that. Besides unless she has been injured she would get away. We are dealing with someone who is a fantastic professional. You above everyone else should know this now. Come let's not waste our time running around like fools."

Blondell was amazed by his matter of factness, he was cold, almost passionless, a robot and very clinical. Pancardi was suppressing his emotional reactions to the decimation of his team and that, Blondell had seen from experience, made him highly dangerous.

"Let us finally see what we are dealing with," Pancardi continued. He was striding forward now across the glass strewn street, past the dead police officers and on toward the twisted corpse.

At the heap which had once been Petrov he looked carefully. His eyes cast over the body, he noticed the virtually severed arm and the great smear of human gore spread from the impact point to the kerb. The man's head was ripped open and part of his jaw hung lose. A gross marionette with severed strings which lay crumpled, waiting for new strings and an operator

"Aren't you going to check his pockets?" Blondell asked.

"No," Pancardi replied.

"What about his weapon?"

"All of these will tell us nothing. Just like the man inside the house." Pancardi was kneeling now, "Look at the soles of these boots, the tread is exactly the same as on the other man. Same manufacturer," he dropped the man's heel to the ground. "Same tag as well. These men are Russians and I too think they are KGB. That is were the grenades came from. If they are KGB they will have gone to ground, they have refuges all over this city."

He walked out into the road, and noticed a few spots of blood next to the tyre marks on the ground. Tyres that had been burned as the truck swung around in the road.

"One of them is hit," he chirped in triumph. "See there is blood let us hope Pietro hit him hard."

"How do you know Pietro hit him?" asked Blondell.

"Because he does not miss," he laughed.

"He missed Alice."

Pancardi looked at Blondell and smiled.

"So now we have an international incident on our hands?" Blondell questioned. "Russians and guns and grenades in Chelsea. The whole thing is a monumental screw up. I expect the Home Secretary will want my resignation for this."

"Alex," Pancardi became reflective, "Charlotte is alive, Magdalene is alive, and you are alive. The rest is just a job. Jobs can be replaced, people cannot."

"But there will be questions asked nonetheless," Blondell added.

"That," replied Pancardi, "is all up to the diplomats to sort out. All I know is that we have two dead Russians, three dead police and one of my best men also."

"It's a total fucking mess," Blondell sounded exasperated. "Are we ever going to get this woman?"

Pancardi was thoughtful but silent.

"I think this whole thing is almost too absurd for words," Blondell was voicing his thoughts.

"And that is because we are not thinking straight," Pancardi mused. "Why would she come here to risk everything in such a manner? She would have known that someone was watching. What was her motive?"

"But what if she didn't know?" Blondell asked. "What if she just thought we would be here?"

Pancardi picked up the thread of thought, "She came here to give us a warning to stay away. She was just delivering a message and then Pietro saw her from the window. What precisely did he see?"

"A gun?" Blondell supplied.

"No, not a gun, this." Pancardi produced the dart. "It was in Angelo's back. But why?" He reflected on his own question, "Because he turned to protect Charlotte when Alice fired."

"So he had turned to protect her because he saw something?" Blondell was reasoning.

"No and yes. He felt something, he flinched back."

Pancardi was almost running now his cane clicking against the pavement. "The post bag, the packet, where are they?" he yelled, as Blondell followed him.

❧

The maroon car, with Ulyanov at the wheel, screeched to a halt outside the Veterinary Surgery. The car park was virtually empty. It would be perfect; it would avoid the possibility of hospital and the necessary police reports. A gun shot wound would immediately arouse suspicion and they needed space, space and time to get away. Once Kernov had been treated they would drive the car into the garage at the safe house and not be seen again for a while. Ulyanov pulled the semi-conscious Kernov to his feet and made for the door, his fingers were bloody and he realised he too might be hit.

Alexei Ulyanov held the gun firmly in his grip. The nurse was clearly distressed and her eyes widened when he placed the barrel in her mouth. Mikhail Kernov was laid out on the surgery table his teeth clenched and holding a second gun pointing at the vet's groin.

"He needs attention," Ulyanov barked.

"He needs a doctor," the young male vet squealed.

"You're the nearest we got," Ulyanov nervously replied.

"I'm a vet for goodness sake not a surgeon. He needs after care and rest and we don't have those facilities here."

"Never mind that," Ulyanov was composed now. "Stop the bleeding."

The vet was examining the leg wound and could see several veins that needed work. The flesh had been ripped apart and whilst it could be stitched he wondered how much blood the man had lost.

"We have no human transfusion services – we have no human blood." He continued to examine Kernov, "he's probably lost three pints already."

"Then we can give him some of our blood," Ulyanov quickly replied.

"But the wrong type will simply kill him," squealed the vet, "he needs a bloody doctor."

"What is your blood group?" Ulyanov asked the nurse.

She shrugged a reply indicating she did not know.

"Mine is O positive," said the vet, "before you ask."

"Mine is B positive," said Ulyanov. "In his left armpit, the tattoo, what does it say?"

The vet cut Kernov's shirt and examined his arm pit, "B positive, it says B positive."

"Looks like me then," Ulyanov shrugged. "How much do you need?"

"Two pints?"

"And this pretty little thing here," Ulyanov replied, "is your nurse, your only nurse?"

The girl, who could have been no more than 19, was silent.

The vet nodded, "We're just a small practice, and I've only been in business a year."

"Then you won't mind this extra work then," Kernov chided. "We will of course pay. US dollar, we have no wish to cheat you.

"Look," said the vet, "this man needs a doctor. It's not about money. His leg muscle is damaged and some of the veins will need to be blocked off or stripped out. Then there's the risk of infection. I don't know if I can do this. "

"What's the difference, we are all mammals here," Kernov laughed, "give me some local anaesthetic and get on with it. Get the blood out of that blonde bastard too, or I'll shoot you myself."

"You need proper medical attention," the vet was pleading, "a hospital."

"Trust me,"said Ulyanov, "where we come from the doctors are no better than vets. We're in a combat zone and we cannot go to a hospital. And besides the incentive is simple. First there's the mighty dollar, but if you do not work well this little nursey here," he cocked the hand-gun, "well she doesn't get to suck anything anymore. Except this great big gun."

"And then there's your balls," Kernov threatened through clenched teeth, nudging the vets testes with the automatic he held.

"When we have gone, both of you can laugh about this one day – tell it to your grandchildren." He paused and then considering added, "She keeps her mouth you keep your cock," said Ulyanov, "it's all very simple really." He looked at the petrified girl, "Good looking, the doctor isn't he?" he asked.

She nodded, as an injection was administered. Kernov visibly relaxed.

The young nurse still had the barrel of the gun in her mouth and looked absolutely horrified at the questioning.

"Been a nurse long?" asked Ulyanov as he studied the vet's hands.

"She's been with me since I started the practice," the vet replied, "and what you are doing to her is not fair."

The girl's eyes spoke of fear as she watched the vet. His hands were quick and nimble and already he was establishing a local reputation as both a sound practitioner and nice man. Many of the female pet owners had made eyes at him and to her surprise she had felt jealous and protective.

Ulyanov was watching her.

"She is pretty," he laughed, "have you fucked her yet?" he suddenly asked.

The girl nearly choked but was unable to speak with the gun metal in her mouth.

Ulyanov was seated now, his arm exposed and his blood pumping steadily into a vacuum sealed container which would then transfer the life giving fluid into Kernov.

The vet stopped short and wiped his hands spraying and wiping antiseptic as he went.

"He'll need antibiotics after this," he said, trying to deflect the absurd questions.

"A young woman like this and a young man like you, working together and you haven't even thought about it."

The vet was silent.

"So you have," Ulyanov laughed. "Silence can speak volumes in the right instances."

Kernov attempted a smile but the pain was sapping his consciousness.

"I'll need another shot Alexei," he added, "if you want me to move on."

"That will be impossible," said the vet. "Both of you will have to rest or he will die. Do you expect me to take this amount of blood out of your system and you not to be affected? I can't take two pints out of your system and then let you loose. You'll. ."

"You'll die?" interrupted Kernov. "Listen my friend I am already a dead man. If I stay here you will be able to see me shot. Just fix me up and I will make the decision on whether to stay."

"You'll die and he'll," he nodded at Ulyanov, "he'll collapse, pass out, or worse. You both need to rest, take lots of fluids."

The vet knew from the reply that they would leave as soon as they were able; he was thankful and looked at his young nurse whose eyes also showed relief at the thought.

Ulyanov looked at the girl, the gun barrel back in her mouth, "I bet she's thought about you, doctor." He looked into her eyes, "Thought about wrapping her pretty little mouth round something other than this gun barrel."

The girl nodded.

"There you see," chirped Ulyanov, "she'd much rather have her mouth around your cock than my gun."

The vet was stitching and holding together Kernov's wound with clamps as he worked. Ulyanov could see him, feeling the bite of the needles and the grip of the clamps, but he also knew that Kernov would not give in to the pain. In Afghanistan he had seen him inside one of the rebel's caves, seen him go down wounded and then seen him walk almost twenty miles with a wound which would have made lesser men collapse. Walk and say nothing lest the morale of the men collapse. Kernov was the real thing and Ulyanov knew that after a lay up at the safe house it would not be long before he could function again.

"After this you should take her out to dinner," Ulyanov continued with the baiting. "Give her a chance to show you how much she likes you." He turned to the girl, "You'd suck him dry wouldn't you if he asked?" he continued, "I bet you've thought about it. Hot sweaty sex with you clinging to him like ivy."

"There," said the vet "that's done most of it, but you'll have to let Vicki assist now. I can't do the next bit on my own."

The girl was nodding.

"You see Doc. I've set you up. If you don't get this young girl's pants down after we're gone, well you're a mug." He became serious, "Mikhail," he called softly and Kernov gave the thumbs up, though his head was heavy much as it had been in the car.

On hearing the name the vet tried to place the accent and knew they were Russian.

Taking the pistol from Kernov's grasp, Ulyanov kept both, one weapon in each hand, the jovial ring to his voice had gone; now he was guarding.

"I detest violence," he said, "but rest assured that if you try anything at all, I'll kill you both right here and not give it a second thought. Now finish the job, so that we can pay you and be on our way.

"Understood," the vet replied and called out instructions to his assistant.

Two hours later Kernov was prostrate on the back seat of the car, his knees bent and his eyes closed. He was lucid, determined and well bandaged. The bleeding had stopped. Ulyanov had antibiotics and several painkillers in packages in his combat jacket and the vet had $500 laid upon the table.

Ulyanov told them that if any police appeared he would kill them all, but he knew that as soon as the car left the vet would call them. He calculated ten minutes to the safe house, where they would place the car in the garage and then both of them could recover. The hunt for Alice Parsotti would have to wait a little longer, and he would have to bring in extra avenues of enquiry. At the safe house there would be a computer – that was all he needed.

"We are going to make this Mikhail," he said, as he fired the engine into life.

Kernov said nothing but gave a simple thumbs up sign of confirmation in the rear view mirror.

Chapter 21

As Alice passed Watford her anxiety was lessening but she decided the best course of action might be to abandon the Bentley early and take the train. She had researched the train routes and times, but had also opted to use the Bentley part of the way – now she was not quite so certain of her original planning. Uncharacteristically her nerve was faltering and she began to review her usual crystal clear thinking. Sitting behind the wheel, even in this most comfortable of cars, made her ache, made her uncomfortable, she needed to be able to stretch and walk to avoid any stiffness. She knew she would be bruised and also needed to rest.

The radio was playing a re-hash of golden oldies and her voice was straining to join Jim Morrison on a rendition of Light my Fire. She liked the radio stations which played the older tunes, the ones which played those named, "golden oldies;" the stations mostly played these because they attracted less in copyright dues. It was simple economics and nothing to do with nostalgia or high art. Then came the sudden news flash, the belching, high-speed interruption to her sanity. The voice was typically BBC, calm, deliberate and bland. It announced an explosion and gun fight in central London. A bomb and the subsequent street battle in Chelsea. The police had been exonerated but some of the terrorists had got away and there was now a massive police hunt on. And then Alice lost the will to listen to the strains of a concocted news story, designed to placate some and agitate others; the political debate had started and the commentators who might seek political advancement were coming forward for their turn at the microphone. The ranters and the ravers and those who seemed, oh so calm or so conciliatory, so understanding of the plight of – whomever.

"Clever bastards," she said out loud, "clever, to put the two together."

She wondered if Alex Blondell had been the mastermind behind the propaganda and then thought that he was like she was, a mere pawn in the whole political prostitution game. Someone was after the jewels, someone with connections and influence, she tried to reason who?

The radio voice continued and warned all persons to be vigilant. There was no mention of the Bentley, but she was not sure if the concierge and his half-witted assistant had eaten those cakes. If that information was being suppressed then it would give her no clues as to her plight. They might not be dead, the explosion could have gone off without them and they could have mentioned the car. She visualised them giving a detailed description of her and the car – she needed to remain vigilant. She would avoid the motorways and find a chemist where she could get bandages and then somewhere in a quiet corner where she could change her clothes.

Grace Slick was asking if she wanted somebody to love and Alice smiled when she thought of the woman who had written the song as a direct reply to Lennon and McCartney's, I wanna hold your hand. At least Slick had been truthful, she had said that he didn't want to hold her hand but for her to hold his dick. Alice was laughing out loud now, knowing full well that this small warbling powder keg had slept with most of the members of Jefferson Airplane whilst with them, before their transmogrification into Starship and the sell-out to petty jealousy. The music continued on the Marrakech Express, through All Along the Watch Tower before launching back into the tiresome pop which made her wince and reach for the mute button.

Her youth had been spent listening to old records, records which had once been the property of her mother. Records which gave a biographical tour of her mother's mind, her loves and her time on the planet. It almost felt like the only link she had to understanding what her mother felt. A tear rolled down her cheek which she wiped away with the back of her hand.

On the A41 near Aylesbury she found a chemist. There she bought bandages, some iodine and a few other essentials. Her original plan had been to head for Coventry, but she abandoned that and chose Oxford instead.

On the A418 at Thame she passed a Travelodge and then parked and booked a room. She dumped the bag from the boot at her feet as she signed in as Claudette Cicello; the doorwoman paid no attention to the clothes she wore, she was on the phone and speaking continually. She remained seated trying to continue her conversation and also trying to direct operations for the young woman at the chest high desk in front of her. Alice paid cash in advance and the woman slapped a key on the desk top and directed her to the room. She then dismissed any further thoughts of Alice as her friend was talking about the local gossip back home. Alice slipped into the corridor thankful and unheeded, she found her room, room 7 – Alice smiled.

Inside she stripped out of her clothes and throwing them onto the floor examined the extent of her wounds. She could see a gash on her side, where the fence post had grazed and torn, but the blood had dried and only the action of removing her bra had made the wound ooze a little. When the coagulated blood had been pulled clear by the dried cotton, the action tore the wound open.

The shard of glass had done nothing serious and with a little care it would soon be clean; soaking in a hot bath would relieve the tension and the bruises she had sustained when throwing herself through the hedges and over garden fences.

She examined her hair. That would be the first thing she needed to do when she got to Birmingham. She'd arrived as Claudette Cicello, but would leave early, without being noticed, as Alice Parsotti.

Emptying her bag onto the bed she took stock and then began to draw a bath. As the water began to deepen she poured in the iodine and the whole thing began to look and smell like a swamp. The water was a deep yellow in colour and the aroma stung her nostrils, but she found the dilution preferable to using the fluid neat. She had done that once before and had nearly screamed as the antiseptic bit.

She turned the television on and listened as the broadcast came over the bathroom intercom. It was mid-afternoon now and she was beginning to feel tired. She was thinking and listening and speaking to herself.

"Right," she chided, "think this through, don't be a Muppet. They don't know you have a Bentley, but in case they do, dump it. They don't have a name, and if they do dump that too." She splashed the laced water onto her wounds and they looked cleaner. "Once these are dressed you can move on. Go into Oxford get a train and then up to the flat to heal up. Shit! You had best call the bank."

She waited for the line to be opened and then dialled 9 and asked for directory enquiries. She got through to the Bank and apologised that she would not be able to get there for the morning. She made excuses about business delays and then looking at her arm said, "One week."

The manager at Lloyds was not going to argue with the woman who had all the necessary codes to withdraw such huge amounts of cash. He was used to the rich and famous doing as they pleased, one week would make absolutely no difference.

Sitting on the bed in the nude Alice Parsotti was wrapping a large bandage around her midriff. The tightness gave her ribs support and the soft lint dressing absorbed the slight ooze from the wound. She looked at her watch and placed a large sterile plaster over the small wound made by the flying glass. This she then covered with a second bandage and then resting from the exertion, sat back against the headboard. Her limbs felt stiff and she knew the price she would pay in the morning would be heavy. Her mind was formulating a plan of action.

Pulling a sweater over her head and jeans over her hips she slipped out quietly and drove the Bentley into the town, parking in a small unrestricted side street. Leaving the vehicle with the windows closed, she dropped the keys into a drain, as she crossed the street, then walked into a large supermarket, bought a fresh cheap sweater and was about to take a cab back to the Travelodge when she spotted the hairdresser.

Vidal Sassoon, the name stuck out in the small town and the place looked customer empty. As she opened the door a small girl dressed in pink and wearing heavy gold hoops in her ears smiled and asked, "Hello oo are you here to see?"

"I don't have an appointment," Alice replied.

"Well we ain't exactly busy, are we? This little town ain't ready for a good 'airdressers."

Alice played to the girl's small town prejudices, "It is a bit of a back water," she said, "not like London."

"Ain't that the truth?" the girl laughed.

Alice estimated her age at 22 at the absolute maximum. She was young and vibrant and Thame was her launching pad, rather than her landing pad. Luckily for Alice she was unafraid to voice her opinions.

"I had my hair done in London," Alice said, "but I want a really good hairdresser to give me a cut, style and colour. I don't want some country hick doing it though."

The girl visibly rose in stature, "I was trained by Sassoon's in Oxford Street," she said, "and then they send me to this place." She paused, "I can do anything those Londoner dressers do."

"Well," said Alice, "I want a bob, three-quarter length, cut, coloured and dried, raven black."

"That's a dramatic change ain't it?"

"Can you do it?"

The girl looked at the clock, "Might be a couple of hours," she said, "and it ain't gonna be cheap." The girl was testing Parsotti on her willingness to pay.

"I don't give shit about the cost," Alice replied, sensing the test, "I just want a really classy job."

Alice could almost see the girl sigh with relief; she would now get her chance to show what she could do. Alice imagined that the locals of Thame were more concerned about cost than real craftsmanship.

"I will give you the best cut and colour you've ever had." The girl replied showing Alice to a chair by a sink.

"Great, let's get to it then," she laughed.

"My name's Cheryl by the way," said the hairdresser and then she pointed to another girl in the distance, who was busy with the other solitary client's hair. "That's Marilyn."

The girl did not look up from her work and Alice sensed the introduction was her cue to respond, "Cherry," she blurted, "my name's Cherry."

"Well I never, what a coincidence," laughed the girl, "can you lean your head back please," she requested, as she launched into coincidence mode small-talk.

Alice did as she was asked and the warm fluid playing against her scalp relaxed her. She thought of the days events and began to make sense of the mess at Blondell's. She replayed the scenes in her head. The kneeling man and the shots being fired and the men in the truck. One image kept coming back to her, the man who was running after her had fired, but not at her; he had fired on the men near the truck and the kneeling man. Then it dawned on her – there had been more than one surveillance unit and better than that, they were not acting as a coherent team. She wondered who they were and how she could pit one against the other.

After two hours and forty minutes of complete fabrication Alice Parsotti left the hair salon and stepped into a taxi back to the Travelodge. Her hair was cut into a neat black bob and the effect was a complete physical transformation. The spur of the moment decision had worked and Alice knew it might buy her some vital time.

Chapter 22

A package addressed to Doctor Tropani, at the Venice institute of forensic pathology, landed on the reception desk and the postman promptly left. The receptionist had signed for the package and thought little more of it as she shoved it into one of the carriage carts, which would be the office junior's job to deliver. She was early, just has she had been for the past fifteen years, a creature of habit she knew the habits of her charges.

It was a warm winter day and the Vaporetto were already buzzing with tourists. Doctor Tropani was based in Rome and would not be in Venice until the start of the conference – but the receptionist knew her habits; she would arrive early, unlike some of the more pompous male doctors. If she had left Rome she would have arrived in Venice late at night and gone to her small apartment, in Corte Michiel off the LargoXXII Marzo. Right now she might be having her strong coffee and pastry in Benito's, before walking the alleys and bridges which linked the tightly packed activity of Venice.

The phone rang and the receptionist automatically looked at the clock which was mounted above the automated doors of the entrance foyer. In read 7.10 am; she toyed with not answering but thought better of it and returned to the desk.

"Good morning," she said, brusquely.

The voice on the end of the line was dark, confident, male and Italian.

"She has not returned for the conference yet," the receptionist continued. "I cannot say about her arrival, as you well know.

These matters are confidential." Her voice had become both protective and business-like.

"Don't be so absurd, this is ridiculous," the male voice barked in reply.

"Well I told you several times yesterday that the doctor could not be contacted. There is a possibility that she might arrive later today. More than that I cannot say."

"It is vital that I speak with her, tell her Pancardi called and it is a matter of life and death." The male voice was sharp.

The receptionist was singularly unimpressed, she had heard messages like this before. The doctor was always getting so called life and death messages.

"Inspector Pancardi, of the Questura," he continued, "and the matter of life or death could be hers."

The receptionist seemed intrigued, this one was certainly different on life and death.

"Has a package been delivered?" he questioned

"You know I cannot answer that sir," replied the receptionist.

Pancardi's patience was wearing thin, "I have tried her mobile," he said, "it is switched off, and her flat and now you will not give me further information. What do I have to do, send someone around?"

The resistance of the receptionist began to break down, "There was a package today."

"Postmark?" barked Pancardi.

The receptionist leant over the large desk to examine the package on the delivery cart.

"Are there any sharp staples, if so don't touch them or let them break your skin," barked Pancardi in exasperation.

"There is a well wrapped packet which is sealed with tape, the postmark," she turned the package to get better access to the postmark, "the postmark says London UK."

"Don't let that be opened by Doctor Tropani," Pancardi ordered. "In fact don't let her near it. It could be booby trapped."

The receptionist immediately thought bomb and gingerly let the item return gently to the carriage truck. Her hand was shaking and she began to feel her anxiety turn to the bitter taste of vomit in her mouth as the caller continued.

"Don't touch the item," Pancardi continued.

At that moment Alaina Tropani appeared at the automated door, to be greeted by an almost hysterical receptionist who had let the receiver fall from her ear. She was early and had risen after a few hours sleep to enjoy the early sun in Venice before being locked into a dull conference which would take all day. She loved Venice in the morning and had, since her brief affair with the older detective, risen dramatically in rank and importance in the world of forensic medicine. Her rich red hair was now cut shorter and strands of silver grey had begun to appear. The fresh face of youth was beginning to give way to the more mellow skinned tints of middle age but her eyes still sparkled with naked intelligence.

"Doctor," she called, "there is a man on the phone called Pancardi."

Alaina was shaking her head as if she didn't wish to speak to the caller whose dangling voice could clearly be heard from the receiver. She was shaking her head and had lifted her index finger to her mouth to imply silence on the subject.

The receptionist became animated, "But he says there's a bomb," she blurted.

"Oh Lucrezia, he always does this to get attention," Alaina replied. "I'll speak to him." She picked up the receiver, "Carlo this better not be one of your," her voice was cut short.

"There may be package addressed to you from London." Pancardi's tone was serious, "I do not joke, there may be something deadly in there. Angelo Massimo is dead he was poisoned with a dart and some staples dipped in venom. Venom from the Amazon, tree frogs." He paused, "Pietro Grillva is severely damaged and may never hear properly again, the result of a grenade, trying to protect Charlotte Blondell and I think you may be in danger too."

Pancardi had rushed the information down the line so as to avoid any notion that he might be exaggerating.

Alaina hissed under her breath, she knew he was totally serious, "What do you want me to do?" she asked.

"I want you not to open any packages until Alex and I get there. I will be on a direct flight from London City to you in less than three hours. Marco Polo by taxi direct to San Marco." Pancardi replied.

"And my conference here?"

"Just carry on until we get there."

"But you told Lucrezia it might be a bomb, she's as white as a ghost. Is there a chance it might be? "

"That was just to get her attention. She was trying to stop me getting to you."

"And why do you think that might be?" Alaina asked.

Pancardi's voice lowered, "Because you wanted her to?"

"Precisely," Alaina replied.

"Well this is important Alaina," he hesitated, "more important than anything."

"Important Carlo? My friend and her children that is important, how are they?"

"Magdalene is fine and the young ones are too," Pancardi replied. "Alex has sent them to Sicily for a while until the dust settles."

"Good, because that is really important, not your silly idea about some package for me."

"Alaina," Pancardi pleaded, "just think it through, Alice is sending warning messages to me and Alex. She is striking at the things we love the most. With Alex it is his children and wife and," he paused searching for the vocabulary, "with me it's you."

"My God," Alaina exploded, "what a cheap shot. You have done nothing but mess me about, why on earth would that crazy daughter of yours try to kill me? Grow up. You come to Venice if you like but don't expect me to play hostess to your puerile love me, love me not, games. We are both too old for that." Her voice was rising in pitch, "You open the silly package when you get here. I have a conference to run and work to do. I'm done with you Pancardi." She paused, "Completely done, do you understand," she ended. She smashed the receiver into the reception console. "Il cretino, that awful arrogant man," she said, in absolute desperation. "If he turns up here Lucrezia I do not want to see him." She picked up the package and made her way toward her office.

❧

"That went well then," remarked Alex Blondell, as he walked into his study.

"She has a package Alex," Pancardi stood looking at the Copper Beech tree from the window. "Alice actually sent something to her."

"We can't be sure of that now can we?" Blondell remarked. "It could just be something totally innocent?"

"No it is Alice," replied Pancardi. "She has vanished but she sent this before she did."

"We cannot know that."

"No, but we can be more or less accurate with our guesses no?" Pancardi's voice was loaded with disappointment. His own daughter had sent a death message to warn her own father away.

"What worries me most is those Russians, where the hell are they?" asked Blondell.

"They have gone to ground Alex, so far to ground they are like moles. They burrow and burrow."

"It's been two weeks now and nothing, everything else is coming together, and we are learning more every day. The flat in Stamford Street, the porters and the Cane Toad, even Pietro is on the mend and hearing things, but they have eluded everything."

"Patience Alex," Pancardi replied, "we must have the patience of a saint," he paused, "they will come again of that much I am certain."

"I feel like a prisoner waiting parole."

"One of them was injured, we must remember that."

"And two of God knows how many are dead." Blondell was reasoning, "Were they sent by the Russian Government? Are they in a safe house somewhere?"

Pancardi was thinking and had raised his feet onto the desk. His hands were folded behind his head and his eyes seemed glazed.

"First we need to find out who they are," the Italian said. "If they are government agents, then the Russians will disown them."

"Surely treatment by a Vet would not be enough."

"And why not Alex? You forget your training, these must be more than Russian government, I would suspect KGB."

"The KGB doesn't exist anymore," Blondell chirped.

"If you believe that then you are a Dutchman," Pancardi replied, his mind drawn into the problem. "We must think logically. These men are chasing Alice. How did they know about her? Drecht is dead so there has to be someone else giving them information."

"And it's not Alice," replied Blondell.

"Then they know about the jewels, they are KGB. Who else knew about the jewels?"

"The revolutionaries?" Blondell was piecing things together, "What if one of them is still alive and they placed the jewels in the vault?"

"Now there is a possibility," Pancardi agreed. "What if they had connections and could use a safe house in London that nobody knew about? A place where they could have food and medical supplies delivered, and rest up ready to pounce. That is likely, no?"

Alex Blondell was sifting through the shelves now, opening lever arch files and flicking through paper after paper, press clippings, post-it notes, scrawled scribblings and scattering notes onto the desk top. Pancardi was glimpsing the content of some and passing on others. Pancardi removed his feet and began to read disjointed pieces of text, some in Russian with English translations attached. Blondell was throwing them onto the desk when suddenly he let out a yelp of exclamation.

"I knew I had the bloody thing," he squealed, "let's see if that makes sense of all this nonsense."

Pancardi looked at the newspaper clipping and then caught Blondell's eye encouraging him to speak.

"Want to know more?" asked Blondell.

Pancardi nodded.

"Well I came across this when I was studying the background on the Romanovs and perhaps only now it will make sense."

"Go on explain," encouraged Pancardi, "but we must be on that flight to Venice."

Alexander Blondell looked at the large ornamental clock which sat on the ornate fireplace in the study, "The car will be here in a few minutes," he said, "why don't I explain when we are under way."

"Fine," Pancardi agreed.

Mikhail Kernov sat in a large armchair, his leg was raised and he was watching TV. The wound on his leg was healing well, aided by the high protein diet of meat, fish and eggs which Alexei Ulyanov had repeatedly prepared. The delivery of groceries had been arranged easily and neither man had even had to venture out to collect the items, as they were delivered into the porch of the house and paid for by credit card.

Ulyanov had told the store that he was disabled and bed ridden and the delivery men had dropped the items where asked, totally oblivious to the observations of them as they arrived. The groceries and medical supplies came courtesy of Tesco and left via the London sewage pipes. Bandages, lint and even dog antibiotics had worked wonders and Kernov was now mobile.

In the garage the high-jacked car still sat, the back seat covered in Kernov's, now dried, blood. The soiled clothes had been disposed of via a garden incinerator, along with false passports and all identifiable, traceable items.

"Fried chicken," said Ulyanov, as he entered with some items on a plate.

"Wonderful," replied Kernov, understanding the necessity to eat so richly, but complaining nonetheless. "I could shit through the eye of a needle, all this meat," he said. "You know what I'd like? An apple or some chocolate."

"Well," Ulyanov chastised, "this meat has given you back your strength and it may soon be time for us to move on."

Kernov nodded and smiled, pieces of chicken showing at his gum line.

"Can you walk?"

"Of course I can," Kernov replied. "You'll have to strap the leg and give me the Morphia but I am getting better by the day."

"See," laughed Ulyanov, "it's the American chicken."

Kernov nodded and taking a great bite from the leg he was holding, spoke with his mouth full. "Alexei," he said, his tone becoming serious, "we were lucky to get out of that." It had been his first acknowledgement in gratitude.

"Remember the hills of Kabul?"

Kernov nodded, "How could I forget that shambles?"

"Well now we are even, ok?"

Kernov smiled a toothy chicken grin, "But seriously," he said, "if I slow you down or we get into a corner."

"I'll do it Mikhail," he replied, "in fact if it gets that tight I'll do us both."

Kernov smiled and knew that the debt of blood between them would hold. In Chelsea his Colonel could have retreated and saved himself. Instead he had used several grenades and risked his own life for them both, much as he had done himself in Kabul, when he carried an unconscious Ulyanov back to camp. The whole platoon had been chopped to pieces by heavy 20mm cannon fire and only six of them had survived. Kernov knew he could have left him and slipped back under the cover of darkness, but had chosen not to. Ulyanov had now done the same in London. The pact was sealed as only a pact made under threat of life or death could be. Whatever the future, the rules had been set, and adhered to, by these two comrades. It was now a pact only death could break, and that was in the hands of fate. As each man ate and laughed at the TV comedy, each knew that their destinies were bound together forever.

"We've had an e mail from our source," said Ulyanov. "The Englishman and the Italian are going to Venice."

"When do we leave?" asked Kernov, "I can be ready in half an hour."

"We are not going anywhere." He waited for a reaction and then continued, "I am going to Venice and you are staying here."

"No way," Kernov squealed. He was standing now. "Look I can walk."

"So you can," Ulyanov noted, "but," and then continued, "I am going to Venice and you are staying here."

"Bollocks," Kernov squealed.

Ulyanov nodded. "You are not ready for combat."

"I am ready," Kernov confirmed.

"But I need you here to man the internet and to do some gentle investigation."

Kernov looked puzzled.

"With them out of the country it will give us access to the Blondell house and any further information they have. Also you can…"

"This is a red-herring," Kernov noted.

"Listen," added Ulyanov, "do you think Parsotti is in Venice?"

Kernov shook his head in response.

"No neither do I. But that forensic specialist is there so they have something which they wish to consult with her on. We need to know what they have. You are not fully mobile but you will be in a few days."

Kernov nodded, knowing he would be more of a hindrance in Venice than an aid.

"I'll meet with our contacts at the Foreign Office shall I?" he said.

Ulyanov nodded, "Grease their palms a little and see what they know. Also Parsotti is still here, I am sure of that. Find out what you can."

"How can you know for certain?"

"Because the grenade which killed that cop and the posse, blew her through that hedge. I didn't see her get up, but she must have or they would have her."

Kernov nodded.

"She's been hit too," Ulyanov sneered, "she's still in the UK somewhere, she's gone to ground and like us she is licking her wounds. So what do they have that makes them go to Venice, what do they know?"

"Maybe she has gone to ground there?" Kernov proffered.

"No she was injured, of that I am certain. But they know something."

"Where do I start?" Kernov asked having given way.

"See if you can find any large telegraphic transfers of cash. Get that greedy bastard at the Bank of England, or wherever he is, to earn his retainer fee. Tell him that unless he gives us the information we'll turn him in. That should make his arsehole clench."

Kernov laughed in reply, "I'd love to."

In the small six seater from London city airport, the pilot began to make contact with the authorities that were allowing air passage and doing the pre-flight checks. Alex Blondell was making enquiries on arrival times and facilities.

"First over Goodwood sir at 3000 feet and then the Channel, past the North West of Paris, turn down to the Alps and drop down to Venice," the pilot replied.

"Time?" asked Blondell.

"One hour 58 minutes airborne," the pilot replied.

"Great," Blondell affirmed and patting the pilot and his second jointly on the shoulders, retired back into the belly of the plane to join a waiting Pancardi; who had helped himself to a large glass of Valpolicella and was busy reading the snippets in Blondell's attaché case.

"Buckle up," said Pancardi, as the plane began to accelerate toward take off speed. "Where's the stewardess when you need her?" he said, raising his glass in a mock toast.

"There's no in flight service here," replied Blondell, "this is a diplomatic immunity flight, no police, no customs, and no checks, so that little persuader you are packing will not show on a scan."

"Ah this," said Pancardi, reaching into his jacket breast pocket. "This little .38 calibre is my only friend and he makes Russians allergic to me. Besides it may be that we shall need this after all."

"You could see your little protector too," Blondell laughed.

Pancardi looked confused.

"Mostro," laughed Blondell, "the best Italian detective of the lot."

Pancardi raised his glass again in a mock toast and the plane lifted into the air and turned a sharp right.

"If Mostro were here then we should already have found our woman," Pancardi laughed. "But sadly he is old and now he likes the warmth of a fire side. I expect that he has charmed Roberto's wife too. Did you know she makes the most amazing lasagne? Smooth rich and warming. Mostro he will have tried this and when this business is all over, then he will no longer wish to be with Pancardi."

"Well I kind of miss the little chap," Blondell replied, as the plane began to climb steeply.

Chapter 23

Alice Parsotti took her first walk on that December afternoon. Her breath was short and she winced as she walked down the two flights of stairs from her penthouse over looking Brindley Place. She had not wanted to leave the security of her rooftop, but knew she would have to make an appearance at her bank, to transfer money and collect a small suitcase of cash. Her ribs were strapped tight and she was bruised but she was getting better by the day.

The sky was dark and dull and the air damp and clawing, but her walk did not involve major exposure to the public. At the entrance to the building she halted briefly and then gingerly took a step out into the air. Her eyes were scanning the streets, the café tables and any eyes which might be focusing upon her. She walked to the fountain and turned left, walked through the modern boulevard of shops and over the ancient iron bridge, now restored and painted a thick globular green. At the centre she paused and allowed a stream of pedestrians to pass her, she looked at the canal below and observed the cleanliness of the breakfast bar barges, now converted into tourist traps. She watched the pedestrians who had followed her pass by and none made a sudden diversion or reached to cough a message into a handset explaining their surveillance was now blown. Satisfied with the brief check she continued into the back entrance of the newly constructed conference centre building and observed the middle aged men talking politics. There was a conference underway and she knew from their tasteless and non co-ordinated wardrobes that they were probably teachers. The women wore their hair in the lank and greasily un-dyed look of the disinterested feminist, while the men looked bloated on the gobbled lunchtime fare of flour, sugar and fat. She was walking slowly and she could hear the inane chatter about motions and immediately she smiled to herself thinking of the Life of Brian. She imagined the serious debate around the title, the peoples' popular front, or the popular front of the people. These were those people, deluded, absorbed in the system and totally happy.

They were no more revolutionary than a laboratory rat, yet they thought they were ground breakers, protectors of free speech. In reality they played the game, bolstered up the system and destroyed any individuality they came across. Her mind strayed to the laboratory rat idea and the philosophical question of whether they felt or thought. Birmingham had now become that laboratory; fresh, white, clean, rejuvenated, reinvented – a new Birmingham, a place where lesser stars names appeared among the paving stones. It truly was a long way from the yam-yam days of the industrial sixties, days of reinforced concrete and square blocks. This was a return to the boulevards and alleys ways of the nineteenth century, only the workers now lived in high rise blocks and she, like many others, had a new build on the demolished slums of the past. They were all rats programmed to run, to follow the maze. She listened as they spoke, listened to the emptiness of their words. Empty words spoken with poignant serenity, false words, shallow words; words which belonged to a bygone era. She felt she was in an alternate universe, a word apart, but it made an excellent cover for her approach to Lloyds Bank. The square at the front of the building she had already decided was the vulnerable point. She was thinking about the last afternoon in Chelsea; she had thought about it many times already. Pancardi and Blondell and the security forces had been waiting for her, but the other men, those ahead of her, those in the truck with the grenades, those were not Blondell's men. They, she reasoned, were another crew, another group with vested interest in the jewels and it was that group she now feared. Logic had told her that they might be the owners of the items and that made her wary, especially as they seemed to know who and where she was. She thought about the Lloyds cash transfer and wondered if this group had access to information other than Blondell. She concluded that this trip for the money was possibly the most dangerous or stupid thing she had ever done.

Alice stopped at a coffee shop and sat and watched as a variety of people passed. The young impressionable talkers and the cynical walkers and the only attention she got was from the men who still had a spark of sexuality about them. They looked at her legs but she felt that she was not being observed. The new dark hairstyle was perfect and her customary .38 Smith and Weston was tucked into her purse. In her boot she carried a nine inch quartered pole stiletto, a favoured weapon of assassins. She had chosen it because it had been the weapon of the Pazzi family in Florence when they murdered Guillermo Medici, as Lorenzo, the not so magnificent, had hidden in the sacristy of the Duomo. It was as she said, to the last man she stabbed with it, "A very personal weapon, historical and neat." And the hole it left was small and perfect like the puncture wound of a snake fang. The cold metal was warming against her calf, reassuring if there were a last desperate struggle. She wondered precisely who her assassin would be.

"A latte please," she said softly at the counter, as she took a Danish pastry from under the cooled glass display.

"I thought Birmingham was going to be a dreadful venue," said a calm voice behind her.

She paid for her coffee but gave no reply. It sounded as if the remark had not been directed at her. She moved to a small table near the causeway so she could observe any observers stationed and the voice reappeared, with a man attached to it.

"Do you mind if I join you?" he asked. "I saw you come out of the hall and I just had to speak to you."

No you didn't you twat, she thought, but instead she nodded as he pulled a chair out to join her.

"Birmingham, what do you think?" he asked again.

"It's alright," she replied, taking a large mouthful of pastry to avoid further conversation.

"I know everyone says seaside venues are best for conference but I kind of like it. It's fresh, new, sort of reinvented, you know like education in general. It's the face of change, the new modern place."

Oh please, she thought as she smiled, this guy is a teacher and he's coming on to me during his conference.

"The coffee's nice too," he said. "I've been coming to conference for years and I've not seen you here before?"

She moved her head from side to side in response to his words. He read the gesture as coquettish flirting, she however, was just trying to establish nervousness in his chat – up lines.

"You're a dancer," he said.

"Nope," she played along with his game, giving herself the cover of a couple, so she could check and observe the area. She knew that the next few minutes would be crucial in making sure her coast was clear. The voice on the man was droning and she could understand exactly what sort of teacher he might be. History, she plumped for history, because of his detail and lack of spark. Geography, like old Mr. Chetponi talking about Ox-bow lakes in an excited way but boring the life out of his class.

"A P.E. teacher?"

"Nope," she replied, taking another bite of pastry, totally bored now by his attempts at humour.

"Well an art teacher at least, you've got real style and your hair is lovely."

Alice looked at the man, his corduroy jacket was creased and the breast pocket held the obligatory red pen. His hair needed styling and a good cut. He wasn't ugly but his dress made him look thirty years older than he was; and he seemed jaded, out of his dimension and now, talking to her, sadly out of his depth. Satisfied that she no longer wished to talk or be talked at her rebuke was swift.

"My name," she said, "is Barbara and I'm not a teacher at all."

"A journalist then?" He interrupted quickly thinking he had made a great start.

"Wrong." She smiled at him, "I'm a prostitute and I'm trying to have a coffee in peace. I've spent all night fucking for £1,500 and I'm tired."

His jaw hung wide, "What do you get for £1500?" he asked automatically unable to think of anything else to say.

She could not believe his reply, "Everything you dream about."

Still he remained seated.

"I'm not Angelina fucking Ballerina, but I can be if you want me to be." She leaned in toward him touching his forearm across the table as she did so, “But I can pole dance and fuck like a demon, that’s why I’m so trim.”

“Erm sorry,” he said.

“I expect you are sorry you sat down now. But if you’ve got £1500 and somewhere I can shower, well we can go right now.”

“Well no, erm, I wasn’t expecting that,” he answered.

“Nope, but the truth is a bitter pill to swallow.”

“I suppose you’d like me to go wouldn’t you?” he asked.

“Guess?” she replied.

The man left with an excuse to go to the toilet. Alice left to walk to the bank. The experience confounded, confused and titillated him all afternoon. In all his years as a teacher he had never met such a profoundly open woman. By the time he left the auditorium he was completely besotted by his imaginary lover. He never saw her again.

Alice Parsotti pushed through the automated doors and stepped out into the open square, turned right and began walking toward the main entrance of the bank.

Chapter 24

"Information?" Pancardi asked, taking a mouthful of the ripe Valpolicella.

Alex Blondell reached for his briefcase, "Oh yes," he said, as Pancardi smiled toothily and took another appreciative swig on his drink. "I found this some time after the wall came down. Russian archives only became accessible after that and much of the really awful stuff which incriminated people had been removed."

Pancardi nodded, "So the communists were just like the rest?" he added.

"Worse," Blondell replied, "far far worse. Let me take you back to the time of Nicholas. The Bolsheviks had won, the liberal government had collapsed under the weight of indecision and the Mensheviks did not have the force of characters to take control," he paused, "they did not have Vladimir Ilyich Ulyanov, Lenin to you and me."

Pancardi listened patiently.

"So Nicholas and all the Romanovs were under close guard in Ekaterinberg. And this is where it gets very interesting. Ekanterinberg was under the control of the Ural Commissariat, which was in turn run by a fellow named Uroffski."

Pancardi poured them both a further drink as Blondell continued with the history lesson.

"So the Ural Commissariat had the Tsar but there was a problem, they were nearest to the White Russian Army which was advancing into Russia to return the Tsar to the throne. And don't forget this family was the wealthiest in the whole of Europe so they could still exert influence. Then the records show some confusion. Apparently, though the documents seem vague, Lenin ordered the Romanovs be returned to the capital where they would be directly under his protection. The whole family were put on a train but Uroffski intercepted it and they were returned to Ekaterinberg. Now the plot really thickens. Lenin had negotiated asylum for the Tsar in Britain and George V had agreed, but then suddenly at the eleventh hour he changes his mind." Blondell took a mouthful of wine to wet his throat. "Some said later that with the war being such a disaster and the level of dead and wounded being returned to Britain that George would have committed political suicide; after all it was the Russians and Austrians who first got the thing going proper anyway, and both of those empires fell. George was petrified that the Saxe-Coburgs might go the same way. It could have been his advisors, who knows. The result was that Nicholas and all the family were kept in the Urals. Now Lenin did not want them dead, or so they say, but one night the whole family is marched into the cellar, complete with servants, and the whole lot shot. It must have been like being in a meat grinder."

"And then came the rumours of Anastasia and Alexei buying their way out, and thc falsc claim of Anna Nielson as the Crown Princess. Swedish wasn't she?"

"There you see, even you know the story of the Grand Duchess who said she was an impostor all along."

Pancardi smiled, "That is almost a legend no?"

"And that is the problem," replied Blondell, "because this throws a whole new light on the subject." He passed Pancardi a Russian photocopy and translation document. "The handwriting is Uroffski's written in 1920 specifically for Lenin. It makes for an interesting read. First the rumours though. Some years ago several bodies were found down a mine shaft in a wooded area near Ekaterinberg. The bodies were said to be those of the whole family. Only the body of a girl and the young prince were not there. Extensive searches were made and nothing found. Rumours began to circulate that they had got away. Rumours that so many jewels were sewn into the bodices and corsets of the girls that they deflected the bullets. Even Anna Nielson said this and that she was helped away, severely injured, and that the Crown Prince died at a later date and was buried by her and the man who rescued her. So two bodies missing, rumours of jewels, Anastasia turns up and the world is divided. Those who believe in Anastasia and those who do not."

"That's not what this account says," chirped Pancardi, "who had been reading and listening intently."

"Exactly," Blondell confirmed. "Now let us suppose the clothes did have jewels in them, the captors would have found them. I mean some of these men may well have raped the girls. And even if they did not, the whole notion is absurd. So let's look at the account. Uroffski was a hardened fighter, and trying to control a virtually lawless area. His men are panicked, the White Russians are coming, and the Tsar is their prisoner. They cannot afford to let him be rescued and become the figurehead of a counter revolution; but they cannot afford to be captured themselves. The White Russians are getting closer."

"So Uroffski gives the order to execute," Pancardi confirmed. "But he has a problem where to do this act? His men might rebel and then all would be lost. Hence the cellar in the middle of the night."

"I agree," said Blondell. "Get the most trusted men and use hand guns. They even have them you know in the archives at the Kremlin. The guns that shot the Tsar."

"Really?" Pancardi enquired, "rather like the Catholics keeping holy relics and pieces of saints on display."

"But these weren't on display it's like he knew, Lenin. Knew that one day he might be made to answer for the crime. Don't forget it was touch and go for a long time that the whole revolution might not succeed. What if the Tsar's decedents had lived would they be back on the throne of Russia today?"

Pancardi considered, "That's another story though, but well worth considering, though they would have had no help from George in England, if what you have discovered is correct."

"Oh it's correct alright," Blondell confirmed, "And that's kind of strange really because George was supplying arms and aid to the White Russians but he refused asylum. That's a massive fence sitting exercise if ever I saw one. Anyhow as the White Russians got closer the Tsar lost his life. So George really did mess it up for Nicholas. They were cousins too, spent summers together one family with the other, Nicholas, George, and Wilhelm, the German leader. All bloody cousins having a family squabble over who was going to get the biggest slice of world pie now that Victoria, their grandmother, was out of the way. Awful and all those bodies and all that carnage, for money and power."

"So what do we know?" Pancardi asked snapping him back to the present.

"Uroffski right. Well so here are all these dead people what the hell does he do? Well he takes them out into the woods and decides to burn them. So they make up a fire and throw on a girl and the Crown Prince. But the bodies don't burn."

"You would need a really hot fire to do that," Pancardi stated.

"Absolutely, so they chop the two bodies up with axes. And send someone to get some acid."

Pancardi was nodding now, "And Uroffski he wrote this down?"

"Absolutely," said Blondell, "on Lenin's instructions."

"So Lenin must have known the Nielson girl was a faker?"

"Well by then Stalin had taken over," Blondell replied, "ousted Trotsky and a wall of silence was thrown up."

"So this record you think is accurate?" Pancardi asked.

"Knowing Uroffski and the way he worked, from other sources, I'd say yes he was ruthless, pitiless and dealt out justice with raw power." He paused, but Pancardi said nothing and continued to read the translation. "So Uroffski's tried to burn two bodies but they won't burn," he continued. "So they try acid and they know they have to get rid of the rest. It's getting near dawn now and the light is making them visible to the enemy who are drawing ever closer. Uroffski has to think on his feet. About two hundred yards away they spy a well. He hits on the idea of throwing the bodies in there. So that's what they do. They pour in the acid and throw the glazed containers in after them and cover the whole by throwing debris down. They put out the fire, scatter and cover what has not been burnt, get into their trucks and leave."

"And then," Pancardi picked up the account, "some die in combat, others that know the story vanish off the face of the earth, perhaps with jewels, perhaps not. Whatever jewels there were vanish too and the whole thing turns into the legend of Anastasia." He whistled once through his teeth.

"So years later when the dust settles," Blondell continued, "an investigation finds the well and the bodies. They know about the acid and the two that are missing. Even though Uncle Joe knows the truth, nothing is said, why? He could have blamed Lenin or Trotsky. Why say nothing?"

"Maybe only Lenin knew?" Pancardi reasoned.

"So Uroffski's account could be true," Blondell affirmed.

"What if Uroffski was acting under Lenin's orders?" Pancardi questioned.

"Right?"

"What if this account is part truth and part fiction?"

"Well just a few years back," Blondell was recalling from memory, "the remains of the last two royals were found in the exact spot where Uroffski's account says the burning took place. DNA has confirmed the body of a boy and a girl. They are Romanov, the only problem is that they cannot say which girl it is."

"So it might not be Anastasia at all?" Pancardi's face was stern, "the wonders of science," he continued, "so much we know and yet so little."

"But let's look at the evidence," said Blondell. "Lenin says he did not order the execution. " So why did he not go public to prove his innocence and the innocence of Communism?"

"He dies?" chirped Pancardi.

"Probably poisoned, assassinated." confirmed Blondell.

"How do you know this?" asked Pancardi, stunned now by Blondell's depth of knowledge.

"I don't," he laughed, "just call it a guess?"

Pancardi said nothing but motioned with his tumbling hands for Blondell to elaborate.

"Ok," said the Englishman. "Stalin was paranoid at the end of his life. And before you say it, just because you're paranoid doesn't mean they're not trying to get ya, I know, but he was off the wall paranoid. He never slept in the same bed two nights in a row. No one knew where he was sleeping in the Kremlin. He always carried a loaded pistol. But here's the best piece of evidence, he would not eat food. He virtually lived off raw eggs, why? Hard to poison. Perhaps he feared poison because that was how he killed Lenin. I mean his was a sudden death, and timed perfectly for him to be rid of Trotsky who Lenin felt was his successor. His baton carrier intellectually. Stalin was a Rottweiller, a fixer, a muscle man, an enforcer. So why tell him things?"

"Well then Lenin would have told Trotsky surely?" Pancardi asked.

"But he didn't."

"So no one knew about these documents until recently, and then the bodies were discovered?"

"And to make matters worse, all the assassins mysteriously died, some in combat, some just vanished presumed dead and Uroffski, shot in rather unusual circumstances."

"So much for loyalty?" Pancardi laughed.

"Precisely!" Blondell exclaimed. "They're all completely self serving bastards. But what if Lenin did order the executions? Uroffski messed up the disposal and had to give an account to Lenin personally for his cock up. Some of the killers might have got away with some jewels, but most likely they ended up with their throats cut in a ditch somewhere in Siberia. Uroffski is murdered and the legends are allowed to live on because Lenin wants them to. The jewels have vanished, the bodies have been stripped and the corsets? Well that's anyone's guess."

"Just how lawless was it at the time of Uroffski?" Pancardi asked.

"Like the wild west only colder," Blondell replied.

"So Uroffski was the law?"

Blondell nodded.

"And he answered to Lenin?"

Blondell nodded again.

Pancardi's mind was alive with possibilities, "What," he extrapolated, "what if Lenin had those jewels, kept the legends alive to cover his tracks. Stalin poisoned him without ever knowing the truth. Uroffski is silenced, Anna Nielson surfaces and the whole thing becomes a massive mess. The jewels from the family?" He was reasoning, "The legend of the deflecting jewels- someone knew they had jewels sewn into the clothes, servants maybe, the killers, someone left behind and so that is given as the saving of the missing two. So the media and the legend and truth all get mixed up like the Chinese whisper. Only Lenin knows where those jewels and the crown jewels are."

"And they vanish," Blondell was completing his reasoning, "turn up in Florence."

"Then Verechico sends in a team," Pancardi added.

"How did he know?" questioned Blondell.

"Maybe he didn't," Pancardi replied.

"Alice is out of her depth here," said Blondell.

"But we now have our answers," laughed Pancardi. "These Russians are the owners of the jewels, if owners you can call them. They have hunted Alice down through us and others." His tone became serious, "If they are in some way connected to Lenin then they will have contacts in the highest places. They will use all their influence with the church and politicians." He stopped suddenly, "Your Home or Foreign Office, this flight, us. They are all tracking us."

Blondell nodded, "We are being watched," he confirmed.

"How can these Russians know so much?" Pancardi continued. "How could they know about Alice?"

"They must have access to files," Blondell blurted, "our files."

Pancardi looked directly at Blondell but said nothing more. Instead he pulled a pen from his pocket and wrote on a pad of paper and showed it to Blondell. It read: *This compartment bugged? They have Verechico, how else?*

Blondell nodded.

Pancardi wrote again: *Do they know where Magdalene is?*

Blondell shook his head in reply.

Pancardi smiled, with genuine relief, "We must get Pietro back on the case," he said loudly. "He wants revenge for Angelo's death and his hearing. I do not fancy the chances of these Russians, whoever they are, if he catches up with them. It is lucky we have left him with that research to find."

Blondell looked perplexed and reached for the pen. He wrote: "*What research?*"

Pancardi picked up the pen and wrote: *Red-herring.*

Blondell nodded smiling.

"If anyone can find that trace Pietro can," Pancardi sniffed.

Blondell was confused and raised his hands palm up in the form of a request.

Pancardi wrote quickly: *We will send them on a wild goose chase. Pietro will be the lead – they will follow.*

"Landing in ten minutes," the pilot said.

It will give us a little space, Pancardi wrote in conclusion.

"Good!" Pancardi exclaimed. "Now we can see what Alice might do next?"

"This throws a whole different light on the thing," said Blondell, now aware that another interested party was watching their movements, and listening to their conversations. As he spoke he was writing: *Do we take the taxi?*

"Of course," replied Pancardi, "they know where we are going so there is not much point." Then he wrote: *But we must be careful what we say. Pietro – danger.*

Blondell had the pad now and was scribbling as the plane began a rapid decent: *Pietro is recovering. How will you let him know what to do?*

Pancardi took the pad and wrote: *Telegram, you keep the taxi driver distracted.*

"Old fashioned?" said Blondell.

"Very," Pancardi replied, as the plane banked and made his wine glass fall. "Now look at that," he said loudly, "on my suit too – a red wine stain on a light suit. I cannot continue without some clean trousers."

"What ?" asked Blondell. "You mean you need to buy some trousers? That's ridiculous."

"Well we have no luggage and I have the wine in the crotch. This she looks awful."

"Oh bloody hell," said Blondell with mock exasperation. "You mean we are here urgently to see Alaina, and to warn her of a bomb or something and you need to go shopping."

"I am Italian Alex," Pancardi chided, "you English may go out with the stained trousers, like you have the dribbles, but Pancardi cannot. I shall stop near the Rialto and you can admire the view with a gelato, I shall soon have new trousers for the day. Perhaps you should try our Italian beer."

On the pad Pancardi had composed a telegram to Pietro Grillva, in Italian it read: *Venice. We being tracked. Need you to fly to Geneva. Make some enquiries. Palladian Hotel. Will call you tonight. Tell no one. All being watched. Falconi case. Carlo.*

Blondell pointed at the "*Falconi case*" and raised his eyebrows in a question.

"A case we were both on," he replied.

Blondell was surprised by the vocalised reply. On the pad Pancardi wrote: *Pietro will know what I mean, we had to do this with Judge Falconi.*

The wheels of the plane touched the ground and as Pancardi left the plane he made a show of the spilt wine. The pilot apologised for the sharp turn and the trousers and Pancardi joked about liking his wine too much and walked out to the waiting car on the tarmac. The tape of the conversation in the passenger compartment was removed from the recorder, placed in a sealed envelope and as Pancardi and Blondell sped toward the water taxi point, a motorcycle dispatch ride approached; within seconds the tape was being transported toward the British Embassy.

Chapter 25

Ennio Faldoni was studying the package addressed to Alaina Tropani, he was all for opening the item before Pancardi arrived and he examined the square box carefully. It was plain corrugated card, nothing hidden in the corrugations; the item had no liquids in it and no wires, no batteries, or even a simple split strip detonator. Nothing in fact that could conduct a current or impulse; his experience told him it was harmless.

"What's the issue with it?" he asked Alaina as he placed it under the scanner. "Umm interesting," he said, as he let the x-rays do their work. "There's a note or something and no metal. No staples, no darts and no needles. It's certainly not a bomb, looks more like broken CD's or discs of some sort."

Alaina was intrigued now, "Why would anyone send me broken CD's?"

"Perhaps they got broken in transit, you know what the posties are like?" he replied.

"We had still best wait for Pancardi, where the hell is he?" She looked at her watch, "He called me nearly five hours ago, what's the delay I wonder?"

Ennio was now slipping a scalpel under the cellotape at the end of the package.

"Look no wires, nothing. I think this isn't booby trapped at all. There are certainly no explosives in here but there is a note, in an envelope, written in possibly fountain pen and as I said some broken CD's."

"Don't go any further Ennio," Alaina instructed, and then as if to placate his curiosity, "if that silly man is not here by the time the afternoon session is over we'll open the thing together – agreed?"

"Agreed," he replied.

"Now I've got to give this speech, where are my notes?"

"You left them by the door," Ennio replied.

"Right, wish me luck," she said.

"Luck?" Ennio was laughing now and walking her to the door of the laboratory. "You don't need luck, you've got the best back-up in the world, me."

"Really?" Alaina screwed her face up, "well that's alright then," she chuckled and was gone, marching down the corridor toward the most eminent group of forensic pathologists Italy could muster. She was respected in her field but the mere fact that she was a woman and strikingly attractive was still regarded as unusual.

She was thinking about Katherine Hepburn, in the African Queen as she walked; her mind drifting aimlessly; a woman who had died an intelligent spinster despite her love for Spencer Tracy. A sudden vision of a red-haired cyclist with Victor Mature blinded and pushing columns over flashed into her imagination, wrong actress – that was Heddy Lamar she thought.

At the entrance to the conference area she halted, adjusted her hair, placed spectacles on her nose, even though she rarely needed them, took a breath and passed in.

Alice Parsotti was walking briskly now and her heels clicked on the new style cobble-stones which made her gait rather noticeable. She was trying to avoid the possibility of falling, but the obvious caution and the length of her legs, combined with the cut of her dress made her hips swing. If they could speak they would scream come and get me boys. Across the square she could see the golden statue of Boulton, Watt and Murdoch. It was an impressive city monument standing at the end of Broad Street. She stopped to admire it and scanned the mass of windows which overlooked the bank. If anyone was intending to take a shot at her, here would be the best place, here out in the open. In this open area even nobility could be shot, no need for a grassy knoll. One lone nut could do the job, just like a November in Dallas. She looked up at the Hyatt causeway, a glass carriageway which separated the wealthy from the masses. It reminded her of the hidden walkway inside the Ponte Vecchio; Palazzo Vecchio to Palazzo Pitti without going outside. She imagined how the Medici could walk from one part of the city to another, crossing the river unnoticed. The Hyatt causeway crossed the road, but notables could leave the hotel and get into the conference centre and symphony hall without having to brave the public – an enclosed walkway for the stars and the wealthy. She checked once more, sweeping her eyes over all of the vantage points, and then decisively strode into the main entrance of the bank.

❧

"Just get us to the taxi point," said Blondell to the driver.

"We have a special laid on," the driver replied. "You won't have to pay the € 95," he laughed.

"How much?" Pancardi snapped.

" € 95," the driver replied.

"But that's ridiculous," Blondell added, "It's only thirty five minutes to San Marco."

"Maybe, but do you wish to use the Vaporetto, all those sweating tourists? And you will have to go to every stop on every island."

"Pirate della laguna," was Pancardi's pithy reply on the subject.

"I agree," replied the driver, "but that is what they always have been. First it was the Chinese and the millionaire Marco Polo, he made a fortune out of noodles and spices and gunpowder. I come from Bari so it was all new to me when I arrived."

"Now they have no voyages of discovery to make," Pancardi was clearly annoyed, "their victims come to them. They come for the romance and the gondola rides and the beauty and they leave with empty wallets and a sense of having… been," Pancardi added.

"But the whole place is sinking," said Blondell, "and they need to make repairs."

"The Adriatico she rises, true" said Pancardi, "and many of the houses they are unoccupied on the lower floors now. In the winter the sea she is one and a half metres up on 500 years ago. But they make the profit no? Not the repairs."

The waiting water taxi took them at full speed across the lagoon, weaving between the channel markers like a motorcyclist leaning into the bends.

As they entered the Grand Canal Pancardi tapped the driver on the shoulder, "I need to make a quick stop to get some trousers," he said. "And my friend here he needs a gelato to cool his blood. He is English and there they have the rain and the wind," he laughed, as if sharing a personal joke with the driver. "Look at these trousers, I cannot go anywhere in these."

The driver nodded and understood immediately where Pancardi would go.

As the water taxi moored near the Rialto Bridge Pancardi hopped onto the jetty and disappeared into the crowd. Alex Blondell spoke to the driver and in the distraction he created, Pancardi was gone.

At the central post office Pancardi flashed his out of date Questura warrant card and jumped the queues. He stressed the importance of the telegram and within less than a minute he was walking into the front entrance of Armani; five minutes later he was dressed in new unstained trousers, the others tucked under his arm in designer polythene.

Fifteen minutes after he had alighted from the jetty he was back at the boat ready to proceed – the other two men were nowhere to be seen. He threw the stained trousers onto the seat and clambered back onto the jetty.

Alex Blondell had finished a second beer and the driver his third despite the need to proceed back down the canal to the square of the Basilica. He was watching for the return of Pancardi and was pleasantly surprised by the speed of his return. He gesticulated and the old Italian saw him instantly. Quickly he walked over to the two men in the bar to join them

"Can you get us near Harry's Bar?" Pancardi asked as he sat. He ordered three beers.

"Sure," replied the driver, slightly surprised by the route change. He had assumed they would be going down to Arsenale and then through one of the tiny channels which lead into the back of the medical institute. "That then will give you a long walk," he concluded shrugging.

"I could do with the air," said Pancardi, "and besides I need to exercise my knee after the flight. As I get older I seem to get stiffer."

The cabbie nodded thoughtfully, well aware of the situation. "I sometimes have the same trouble," he added, in sympathy.

It was then that Blondell noticed Pancardi had no walking stick with him and he wondered if this were also a ploy. Perhaps a chance to purchase a new silver-topped cane as he meandered?

"You've left your cane?" he said, catching Pancardi's eye.

"I know Alex," he smirked, "that is foolish of me but there are plenty of places to find one here."

Blondell's mind was racing, he could think of no logical reason why they needed to walk. But he had known Pancardi long enough now, long enough to realise that he had plans and schemes of his own design.

"Harry's Bar, then?" Pancardi chirped and then rose from his seat. Tourists at the door were set to pounce on the vacant spaces the moment exit movement was spotted.

In the boat Blondell realised that the telegram still needed to be sent. Pancardi had returned to the boat too quickly, he reasoned that they would send the telegram while on foot and then make their way to Arsenale. That was the reason for the walk.

As the taxi moored near Harry's Bar Pancardi began to relax. When the taxi had pulled away he smiled wryly.

"You want to know why, no?" he asked.

Blondell's face smiled back at him, Pancardi had expected bemusement.

"First we go to Alaina's place."

"What?" asked Blondell.

"There is something she wants us to collect."

"I'm lost. I thought you didn't know where her place was and that she had blown you out of her life?" Blondell questioned.

"What the eye sees and the ear she hear, are not always true. The telegram is gone and Pietro will have it already. He will not waste time, and here out in the streets of Venice they cannot watch us. And even better they cannot hear us. Do you not think they will have boom mics on us from the trees? We are being watched and so we must break up our movements. The driver he will have reported back and they will now try to get us found but they were not expecting us to stop. They will be active at the Arsenale but they will be in the wrong place. So now we, how do you say, screw them up a little?" he was chuckling. "First the book and then Alaina."

"So all this not being together it's a ploy?"

"Well not a ploy, more of a protection scheme, insurance scheme. If they think Alaina knows nothing they will leave her alone. This is good. If they think she is in the middle of things they may go on the attack. They might think they can get to me through her."

"Who the hell is they?" asked Blondell.

"The main enemy here," Pancardi paused, "and your office is giving information and this worries me." He moved off at a tangent, "There are some very shady characters at work here. We must protect those we love. Magdalene she is safe, the children too and so is Alaina, as long as they believe the allusion that she dislikes me. And here in these alleyways we can be safe in what we say. Pietro he will be mobile now and he will follow us at a distance and maybe that way he will pick up those who follow us – a kind of double double bluff."

"So we are going to Alaina's apartment and there we are collecting a book and then we are going to walk to her laboratory?" Alex Blondell's voice trailed off, "And in all this confusion what about your daughter Alice?"

"There lies the problem," Pancardi replied. "Alice is not the problem, I wish she was. There are, how do you English say? Bastard after her."

"Bastards," Blondell corrected, "we call them bastards, and it's plural."

"Yes exactly. Alice is being hunted not only by us but by something far darker."

"Those Russians," Blondell blurted, "they found Verechico when all of us combined couldn't. That is unbelievable."

"Really?" Pancardi replied sarcastically, "you mean your people, who are employed by us, gave Verechico to the Russians and not to us? I wonder at the sheer arrogance of them," he paused and then spoke clinically, "amazing what a little money can do to grease the wheels."

"This is just absurd," Blondell replied. "Is there nobody we can trust? You are saying that everybody is against us?"

"Not everyone," Pancardi smiled, "we have each other, Pietro Grillva, our women, these people we can trust. Now let us get this book."

"What book?"

"It is a reference work on poisons," Pancardi accentuated the syllables. "Amazon tree frogs and the Cane Toad."

In the small courtyard of Corte Michiel, Pancardi moved to the right and up a small stairway. At the top of the stair he turned right again and from a small Madonna niche in the wall he retrieved a single key. Armed with the key he climbed the next flight of stairs to flat 27. Once inside, he walked quickly to the windows and opened the shutters. The bright light burst into the room and the glow made the furniture burst into dusty life. Pancardi looked out toward Dorsoduro and his mind was lost in the beauty of the view.

"Claudette Cicello," Alice said, "please tell your manager I have arrived."

The teller left the counter and spoke with the manager who immediately jumped to attention at the merest mention of the name Cicello. He came rushing over and in the manner of Uriah Heap made himself very humble. A man used to dealing with the foibles of the wealthy and the visiting stars, his sycophancy had served him well over the years. Holidays were taken at out-of-season rates but the destinations were magical. At home he drove a nice new car and lived near the Lickey Hills on the outskirts of the city. Having never married he had devoted his life to service and it had paid well. He trundled to work by train from Barnt Green, but he knew that once he had reached fifty five he could retire. His plan was simple; find himself a pretty Russian bride, the sort that could be bought on the internet with the promise of a better life; perhaps Lithuanian, Romanian or Bulgarian, he had no particular preference. The girls he had seen on his travels had been stunning and he had enjoyed a few but he wanted something more.

"Good afternoon Miss?" He offered his hand.

"Cicello," she replied.

"Oh!" he exclaimed, "we weren't expecting you today."

"I know but my schedule has dropped me here before I go on to Dubai," she replied, "I would like to sort out the paperwork, before I leave the country."

"Well what precisely would you like us to do?" asked the manager.

"The transfer of funds from both Canada and the United States, I would like the whole to be split between two sites. The monies from the United States to be placed here and the remainder, from Canada, to be transferred to Düsseldorf, Deutsche Bank."

The manager raised his eyes, "The money from the United States to be held here?" he questioned. "That is almost $ 18.5 million."

"I know," Alice replied her eyes sparkling as she spoke. "It's an obscene amount of money, and I intend to purchase an estate somewhere in your midlands. Somewhere quiet and secluded."

The manager's eyes lit up, this young woman with the black bobbed hair, emerald green eyes and light tan would be one of his wealthy clients. Her account coming fully into the bank would give him leverage, leverage to move on, maybe a promotion, he thought, as they conversed.

"I expect you have a property purchasing agent?" Alice enquired.

"We most certainly do," he replied.

For some inexplicable reason Alice was reminded of Oliver Hardy. The manager wasn't large or bungling but he had that air of a small boy wrapped in the clumsiness of a buffoon and her nearest comparison was Hardy.

"We can offer services on stocks and bonds and a whole variety of investments," the man continued.

"But to start with," said Alice, "I need £100,000 in small notes, perhaps tens and fives. Could you arrange that for me?" she asked.

"With us it's more usual to book such large sums for collection," he replied. "You see we often don't have that much on the floor, that's in the vault." He was trying to make excuses now.

Alice touched his forearm and made eye contact, "Oh be a sweetie," she said, "just this once, just for me."

Twenty minutes later she had once again passed the golden monument to the age of industrialisation and this time was crossing the Hyatt causeway back toward her flat. She carried a bag containing £100,000 in small untraceable, used notes. Any money lodged at Lloyds Bank could be transferred to anywhere in the world at anytime.

She was smiling and noted the way the manager had pandered to her ministrations and fluttering eyelids – she was home and dry: Home and dry.

Chapter 26

Jeremy Stapleford was a tall thin man with greying hair and wire rimmed spectacles, which perched on his nose like a crow on a gate. An aquiline face showed deep lines, lines borne out of his attempt to keep fit by lack of food and excessive exercise. This was a man who would end up with the complexion of a leathery prune and deep gorges, like the fissures in water eroded rock, on his face. He was a man who was not going to embrace the aging process gracefully, a man for whom youth was all. His face was neither handsome nor ugly, like so many men in middle age he was just average. His life was average; his career average; his home average; his unlucky gift, was to be motivated by greed and he lacked the raw intelligence to control the sin.

His suit was dark blue with a fine pin stripe and the small hand stitching showed clearly at the lapels; he looked neat, and took time over his appearance, he was well presented and his perfect teeth, which were false, shone as the walking man approached him.

The walking man walked purposefully and for the first time of the many times they had met, was using a cane. He was solid, broad shouldered and with his trousers cut in the continental fashion, it was apparent that he was not English.

Stapleford threw some stale bread to the ducks which had been feeding and which made their easy living in St. James' Park. It was crisp but the sun had made Stapleford sweat a little. He could feel the damp growing at the base of his spine and he wondered if the coat or his apprehension were the cause – he began to wish he had left his overcoat at the office. To the casual observer he was just amusing himself, taking a quiet lunch break in the park. To the surveillance team he appeared jittery.

"Glad to see you could make it," said Kernov, in a rather matter of fact manner as he approached. "No one about I see?"

"No problem," Stapleford replied, as the two shook hands. "I'm not being followed and this is a perfect place to meet."

A woman with a push chair and small child were approaching from the grass. The child was carrying a plastic bag – the obvious intention being to fatten the ducks.

"How's that nubile little blonde?" Kernov asked, his tone friendly.

"Fine," Stapleford affirmed his tone apprehensive.

"Fine? I'd say she is," Kernov laughed. "That little cousin of mine was always too hot to handle."

"The leg?"

"Just a scratch," he smiled, "a little love bite, more than an injury."

The small child was throwing bread to the birds now only feet away and the mother was encouraging the small boy to break the bread into pieces. She spotted the men but took no notice of them and smiling ushered the child to place the empty poly bag in the litter bin next to the men. Then she and the child began the long walk around the lake to find an elusive underfed duck.

"Listen Mikhail," said Stapleford, lowering his voice, "if you are mixed up in this terrorism business I can't help you."

"Jeremy," he clapped a hand upon the Englishman's shoulder, and laughing said loudly, "you enjoy her don't you? How many years younger is she?"

The woman with the child looked up at the sound, and quickly ushered the small boy along and out of earshot.

"Twenty three," Stapleford replied.

"So young and so athletic. That little cousin of mine she loves to spend your money and she loves the good life." He caught the other man's eye, "And you, you like to see her in her little lace panties, or out of them should I say. I bet she looks good naked; I bet she's soft and smooth and tight." He spoke thoughtfully, "We are friends, after all I introduced you, I ought to get some thanks for that."

The woman heard the words, "lace panties" and "naked" and decided distance the best policy and placing the child in the pushchair began to walk away briskly. In less than a minute she had reached the avenue of trees and slowed her pace to speak to another familiar young mother in the park.

The Englishman knew what was coming. True the young girl had proved to be a wonderful possession. She dressed to please him and he had walked her around like a trophy and in turn the subsequent ego boost for him had been enormous. To his surprise she had been totally loyal and had not strayed with other, better looking, or younger, men. She had proved to be seductive, sexual and totally devoted to servicing his needs, but the cost had been the occasional demands from Kernov. Demands for information, demands which he had to acquiesce to because of the simple fabrication. Fabrication of passports to get her into the UK. She had been fifteen when he first met her and sixteen when she arrived to be his wife, though the Russian passport had said nineteen. A passport which in fact belonged to an older sister. It had been Mikhail Kernov who had arranged the subtle alterations with the Russian officials. At the time the marriage had been frowned upon by his colleagues at the Home Office, but times were changing and that had been over fourteen years ago. Now many of the men who had made so many of the derogatory comments were divorced and miserable and wishing they too had had the foresight to seek out a more feminine partner. It could have been Stapleford's turn to deride their choices, get back at them, score points, but instead he talked of the demasculation of men and how feminism should have been about equality of choice and not absurd discrimination. Like all things the pendulum had swung from the sublime to the ridiculous; but his young blonde had developed into a full breasted and round hipped woman and her devotion to him had not diminished as she grew up, in fact it had increased.

"I just need a little information?" Kernov continued.

Stapleford knew the quiet request. A request based upon his knowledge of the deceit. He wondered how many further times this request would be made, how many favours he would need to fulfil before he could be rid of the Russian. He considered the facts: He had not bought her; there had been no dark monetary exchange; no trading; he had met and fallen in love with her. Then he considered what others would make of a thirty nine year old man falling in love with a fifteen year old girl. His deliberations did not take him long – his conclusion was even more swift.

He threw a last handful of bread to the ducks and moved to sit on the vacant bench. He wanted to have the whole affair out in the open, but knew Patricia would be deported, there would also be a threat to his career and no doubt somebody would scream paedophile, citing him as a monster. The repercussions of that would be too great – it would be financial suicide. He was stuck in his own web of deceit unable to sever the ties which bound him. All he and Patricia wanted now was a white-washed villa on the shores of the Mediterranean, somewhere to swim , eat and make love as he slipped into late middle age. If he could ride out this latest storm he could make retirement – he decided to co-operate once again.

Mikhail Kernov sat next to him on the bench and stretched out his leg as if he had cramp, massaging the thigh.

"I need to know about money moving transactions in England. I am looking for that person that we spoke about before," he said. His voice was calm, cold, and remote.

"The woman?" asked Stapleford.

Kernov nodded, "I need you to trace every large entry of cash over the last two months."

"That would be impossible," Stapleford blurted in sudden reply.

"Not companies, no males, just females."

"But I don't have access to that kind of information in my department, and," he was searching for excuses, "it would take too long to trawl the data. We would need at least half a day."

"But I need it done," Kernov continued, "by Friday."

"That's insane," replied Stapleford. "Even if I could get that raw data I would have to analyse it and that could take hours."

"Well there are thirty six before Friday," Kernov mocked.

"Yes," said Stapleford, "but I'd need to get access to another department and then download or copy the data, then I would have to programme a run with a specific data sift – I can't do that."

"But my little cousin that you can do? Her little arse you can fuck? What tricks have you taught her to perform for your pleasure?"

Stapleford's face reddened.

"Patricia she is yours now think of that Jeremy and all I ask in return is this little favour – I thought we were friends."

"But this is too much," blurted Stapleford, "I'll get found out."

"But you owe me," Kernov's tone was becoming harsh.

"But, I'll have to involve others and they'll know."

"So involve others," replied Kernov.

"But, but, they could report me or blow the whole thing to pieces."

"So offer them money," Kernov coerced.

"But, they might be the wrong type to ask?"

"Listen Jeremy, every man has his price, or every woman for that matter."

"But you don't understand," Stapleford was becoming agitated, "this is far too risky. I mean we would need to access the whole system and then cover our tracks. Do you really think the Bank of England is some sort of amateur?"

"So many buts," Kernov was sensing a real task ahead. His previous requests had been small, pale imitations of the task he now wanted. "Find someone who wants a bride like yours."

"What?" he was totally astounded.

"Find another man like yourself." He paused, "And I will find this man another cousin."

"It's not that easy," Stapleford replied, almost pleading like a schoolboy to be excused.

"Really?" Kernov continued, "have you not seen them, the others in your office. The ones that look at you with envy. Those that fantasize – the ones that wished they had Patricia in their bed. What about those that gamble, those that have nasty little habits, those that are saving to leave their wives when the time is right. Offer money, offer anything just get me the information I seek. What about those that would like a tight young cunt to fuck? I can arrange it. Anything they want I can get, blonde, brunette, even a red head, perhaps even black."

Stapleford was shaken by the gritty obscene language.

"We were friends enough when Patricia offered her young cunt to you. How old was she? This is the last thing I will ask of you," Kernov was continuing.

Jeremy Stapleford was shaking his head, "I can't do it," he

said. "It can't be done. I mean I'd have to fabricate some serious issues to work on the computers at night. I can't, I won't do it," he said, and he rose from the bench.

Mikhail Kernov grasped his forearm with a grip that made him wince. "Then consider this my friend, when next your young plaything is kneeling before you and performing acts of penitent devotion;" he smiled a wicked smile. "How pretty and loving her eyes are when they stare into yours. That stare, at your point of climax, that encouraging stare which simply says – yes I will."

Stapleford tried to pull his arm away.

"I'll send you those eyes in a jar," Kernov threatened.

Stapleford froze.

"So you can look into those eyes whenever you want." He was laughing now, "She won't be looking over her shoulder at you any more. You'll have to fuck her in the dark. I'll make sure her face is so scarred no man, including you, will ever want to look at her again."

The shocked Englishman knew that he was in too deep, and the Russian knew his trump card had now been played and the hand won.

"You people are monsters," Stapleford hissed, "total monsters."

"Oh, please," Kernov replied, his tone of threat now gone, "we don't want you to get the wrong idea."

"Wrong idea, wrong idea?" Stapleford was almost squealing now.

"This will be the last thing that we ever ask of you Jeremy."

Stapleford knew that was a lie.

"We will then leave you to enjoy..."

"Enjoy what a prison sentence?" he interrupted.

"You are far too intelligent a man to get caught," Kernov replied, pulling himself to his feet. His leg was stiff but workable. He reached into his breast pocket and produced an envelope. "£25,000 and of course I can get a woman if that is the bargain you have to strike." He handed the envelope to Stapleford, "The details are in there and," he paused, "Friday, same time here?"

Jeremy Stapleford watched as the Russian began to walk away. He wanted to scream at the man, rush behind him and throttle the life out of him; drag him to the water and hold his head under until his kicking and life ceased. Instead he just sat as if stunned. He thought about the beautiful girl who had come into his life. To others it might seem like a crude transaction, but he knew that whatever and however their life had started together, he had never been happier. She was everything he had ever desired and he was not going to have her disfigured, maimed, or driven from his life. His first marriage had been a disaster, a marriage made in haste, for which he had repented at leisure.

Kernov was moving away slowly and he wondered if the man was being honest in his threat. Stapleford watched his gait, his slow methodical response to pain and he knew that the man would remove Patricia's eyes as easily as he could a splinter in his thumb. He shuddered, stood up and began a slow walk back to the office. He needed to work out a process, an excuse.

As Kernov left the park by one entrance the women with the children in push chairs followed at a discreet distance. When Stapleford left by another entrance a small man in a jogging suit came to the litter bin to recover the short range radio transmitter which had been deposited by the child.

He lifted the lid of the bin and removed a poly bag. Giving quick thumbs up sign to the watchers on an adjacent roof, he began to jog out of the park following the route which Stapleford had used.

Jeremy Stapleford began to churn over in his mind a set of excuses that he could use to remain at the office, after hours. He would also need some help, someone bright, bright and willing to take risks. His mind trawled the personnel files; men who gambled; men who had casual affairs; men who liked to use prostitutes; men who hated their wives. Finally he settled on a woman – Marjory Humboldt. A woman who had taken him into a store cupboard at a drunken Christmas party and allowed him to fuck her. Perfect, he thought, an absolutely perfect cover.

Chapter 27

Ennio Faldoni was sitting across the laboratory table from the package. He had scanned it, examined it, x-rayed it and he was itching to start. It had been his natural curiosity which made him such a superb scientist at Rome University; curiosity which drove him into forensic medicine and the same curiosity which was egging him on right now.

He looked at the clock – the conference was over-running and clearly Alaina had been way-laid by a series of questions. Pancardi and Blondell, for some inexplicable reason, had also been delayed. Curiosity was making him turn the package in his hands. He was certain that the items inside were plastic and broken. The more he guessed the more he wanted to examine the contents.

Faldoni made himself a coffee and looked out across the lagoon toward the island cemetery. It seemed a quiet and calm place, a place where the private boats and taxis would go for peace and harmony. His mind was drawn to the beauty of the Islands but also by the cruelty which had perpetuated the wealth of the ancient families still in Venice. Death he reasoned was a final release from the anguish of life and curiosity, but he was not going to go there just yet.

"Right," he said aloud, as if answering an inner debate, "this package needs to be opened and any tests completed quickly." He set the coffee cup down and began to wash his hands in the anti-microbial wash. His movements were methodical, precise and very effective. He had not once in his whole career contaminated a crime scene, and he had no intention of doing anything to corrupt this package. Once the surgical gloves were in place he lifted a scalpel from the sterilizer and taking the package to a central dissection table allowed the overhead light to aid his first incision.

The cellotape hissed as it came apart and the outer transit package was slid away from the gaily coloured inner box. Faldoni quickly examined the corrugated outer and satisfied that there was nothing concealed he turned his attention to the inner box.

The box was approximately nine inches in depth and a foot square. It sat with a lid fastened once with pink ribbon and tied in a double bow as if it were a birthday gift. Tucked under the ribbon was an envelope. There was no name on the card or the box, but the pink, pale-blue and violet stripes encouraged, or rather enticed the recipient to open the item swiftly; rather like a child opens brightly coloured presents at Christmas or Birthdays: Ennio Faldoni was more cautious.

He checked once again for wires and connectors as he drew the envelope free of the package. Once free he placed the item on a light box and illuminated the inside. The contents were shown as a small square of card with a design on it and a small hand written note. The scalpel separated the flap of the envelope and the two items inside were examined. The first seemed to be a business card. It was printed on hand made paper and the note simply read:-

"Apothecary – a friendly drop to help you after."

It was signed *"J."* He wondered who J was and why the note had been written inside inverted commas. It must be some sort of joke, he deduced, but then why would Alaina be so careful about a booby trap? His reason was counterbalancing his first thoughts- this was not a note that had been scribbled in haste. The business card simply showed a traditional jack-in-the-box, grinning, as a logo, with the inscription: *"Total – Toys,*

For good girls & bad boys.

The Fetish House, Kensington, London."

Ennio examined the items and apart from a water mark in the paper he could find nothing. Nothing which would help decipher the message which he believed to be a code. He wondered if there were a second note inside the package, quickly he lifted it onto the x ray plate. There appeared to be nothing inside and he resorted to the scientific method of curiosity appeasement, and shook the item whilst lifting it to his ear. The sound which greeted his curiosity was as cornflakes being shaken in a box.

"This is ridiculous," he said, and laying his palm flat upon the lid sliced the ribbon free. When he removed his palm the effect was simple, sudden and dramatic. Like a silent firework, a stream of broken and sharpened plastic Compact Disc sections were projected into the air. He turned his head to protect his eyes and as he did so a point of one CD struck the top of his head before it returned to earth. Another had caught his lip and he involuntarily placed his teeth and gums over the slight wound, sucking as he did so. His gum line turned red as the warm sweet fluid of his own blood coursed into his mouth. One shard had narrowly missed his eye and had embedded itself in his right eyelid, just under the eyebrow. He pulled it clear and examined the depth of the wound in a mirror. It was then in the reflection that he noticed the strange picture drawn on the inner base of the box and an even stranger array of elastic bands and plastic springs which had propelled the sharpened plastic weaponry into the air. This had been a mock bomb, one designed to frighten, one designed to instil fear – a joke. He saw a drop of blood appear at his nostril and using the back of his hand he casually wiped it away. His pupils were dilating and his heart rate had increased; small beads of sweat had appeared on his forehead and looking into the box he saw the picture of a clown and written beneath that a short inscription which read:-

"I hooked a berry on a thread,
And now wonder girl – is dead."

The face of the clown seemed to be laughing at him like the raucous "ha ha" of ducks on a pond. Seagulls were screaming and all of his senses were heightened as he stepped back from the bench and his right knee gave way almost instantly. Legs buckled, crumpled and he stumbled; when reaching out to steady himself he fell, his jaw hitting the bench edge before he landed for a second blow to his head, as he hit the floor.

When he came to he had no idea whether he had lain there for hours or minutes. His breath came in short gasps and try as he might he could not lift himself, turn or stand. His limbs were becoming rigid and his muscles tense, he contorted into weird shapes as spasms hit him – he tried to reason himself out of his predicament. Broken neck was his first guess but that made no sense of the nausea and the heavy fluid which was gathering at the back of his throat. He tried to cough to spit, but his jaw and chest were locking. On his back and becoming more rigid by the second, he tried to push his hands against the floor but knew his arms were not working and he reasoned a broken back – the fall had broken his back.

Curious to the last Ennio Faldoni tried to reason the cause of his demise as he drowned, choking in his own vomit unable to move or clear his throat.

Pietro Grillva received the telegram and without any notice simply left the hospital. His ears had been ringing but they were getting better and the Voltarol prescribed for the headaches eased the pain but also made him drowsy. He was fed up with the constant checks to his ears and the tests and bleeps – high or low pitched sounds.

In the taxi back to the Blondell's home he tried to evaluate the damage to his hearing. His head felt like it was inside a goldfish bowl and the dried blood would have to be washed away again before he made any trip.

At the house, he checked the street for movement – there was none. He did not notice the dark red car and the man chewing gum, watching the darkened building. The watcher was very careful and did not move; but he observed Grillva scan the parked vehicles; he had parked beyond the illumination of the overhead street lighting and even his silhouette could not be seen. Satisfied he was alone, Grillva slid his key into the lock and entered with the stealth of a cat. The surveillance team had been drawn off and the house shut down. He walked to the alarm system and punched in the six digit code, at least his brain was working, he thought. Blondell had told him that all of his personal affects would still be in the guest room he had occupied; and true to his word they were still there. His passport and the nine inch flick-knife, the sort Blondell had told him were banned in Britain, both were still there. The knife was a weapon he had seen the gangs use in Rome after the war – a silent weapon and so deadly in the right hands. What he really needed was Angelo Massimo's "specials." The morphine, that would be his life line against the pain and the weaponry that Massimo carried would be of extra significance, as his own Berretta had been held by the police for forensics.

At the kitchen table he loaded Massimo's personal favourite for high tension situations. It had been designed by his brother-in-law, a gunsmith in Milan. Loosely based on a Russian design he had adapted it for close quarter fighting. It was not a gentleman's weapon; this was designed for close combat and house to house warfare. Massimo had called it the meat-mincer and it could do just that when fired at any opponents. The cartridges were designed to deliver high impact .45mm shells into the victim at close range. The shells themselves were soft cased with a liquid core, the result was total disintegration upon impact, internal shrapnel Massimo had called it. Once hit, the impact and spinning of metal was designed to stop an elephant in its tracks. It was a dirty weapon – a weapon designed to maim. Auto clip-loaded it delivered 22 shells in 6.4 seconds, with the single shell option being increased in accuracy by the lengthening of a screw on barrel and a support shoulder stock. Massimo had used it no more than five times, but Grillva had seen the devastation it could deliver and now he sat casually loading it in readiness for Pancardi's opponents. If the men he faced were using grenades he knew that this item of Angelo's could even the balance of power.

Propped before him lay the report of the Stamford Street terrorists. He was reading slowly, taking in the fine detail. Next to him sat a mug of strong coffee and a handful of chocolate biscuits.

"Life is short Alex," said Pancardi wistfully, "and we are just passengers in it."

He seemed in no particular hurry to move and sat casually watching the ebb and flow of the boats as they moved along the length of the Grand Canal. "I would have liked to settle in a place like this," he continued. "A place with water and some…"

"That's the problem," Blondell interrupted, "everyone wants to settle in a romantic place, but it's all an illusion, a fantasy, and

I thought you above everyone else would have realised that it was nothing more than that – a fantasy. You should know better."

"What is your problem Alex?"

"The same old problem everyone has about Venice. The romantic problem. Why don't you see things as they actually are?"

"Have we made you cynical Alex?"

"I just get fed up with it. Venice is a working city. The tourists come here and then they go with their camera full of pictures. Where are the young people who do not want to ride gondolas and wear the striped shirts? They're off to other cities to get excitement and real romance not this false..."

"Sit down Alex," Pancardi motioned to a chair, "and enjoy the view."

"But I thought we were in a hurry and we..."

"What we need to do," said Pancardi with deliberate slowness, "is wait."

"Wait?"

"Si."

"Wait for what, for hell to freeze over?"

"For Pietro to phone." Pancardi was smiling, "He should be at your house about now and I expect him to call once he has read the detail on the Stamford Street explosion. He is old and clever and thorough, and that is what makes him dangerous no?"

Blondell seemed confused, "The terrorists ?"

"Both you and I know they were not terrorists. They were Russians and damn clever ones at that. Pietro, his ears may be ringing but he will be our back-up. From your home he can use his mobile phone and we can learn much from the file. There is a problem with your Home and Foreign Offices," he paused and looked across the Grand Canal. "Palazzo Dario, we had the strangest case there you know," he digressed. "Bizarre, ghostly, as if something unworldly was there, a real sense of malice and foreboding – it's hard to explain. I investigated with Pietro but we never really got to the bottom of it. The place has changed hands now, but those walls are steeped in blood," he paused, as if in recalled thought, "blood money."

"Can we get to the point?" snapped Blondell.

"And what is that Alex?" Pancardi replied. "We must trust in instinct no?" He paused and then lowered his voice an octave,

"Like that palazzo there is something dark and malevolent at work. We are not receiving information. Are you telling me with all the powers both of these offices have they cannot find out about money transactions?"

"Maybe Alice is far more clever than all of them?"

"How so?"

Blondell shrugged.

"Precisely," hissed Pancardi. "She is clever, she is cunning, but she will and does make mistakes. We know of the poison from the autopsy on Angelo. We know that Stamford Street had a dog with the same poison and we know that the place was blown to pieces. Then the concierge and his young assistant are found dead too, presumed blown up or crushed in the rubble, but we find yet another poison – in them."

"The Russians?" Blondell affirmed.

"No, why would they kill her? They need to have her alive. Alive to torture her and to find out where those jewels and where the money are. Someone else set the explosion of the gas."

"It could have been Alice," Blondell offered.

"True!" Pancardi was thinking now, "But those offices in your London they have crooks too. We are being kept in the dark and someone is finding out things which we can only guess at. I do not like this, this hiding in the dark from our own people." He was deep in thought, "Alex we are very much on our own. Trust we must have if we are to find Alice."

"So until then we just sit and watch the world go by?" Blondell was being sarcastic now.

"Why not? It is beautiful here, the package is warned about and all our loved ones are safe, what else could we need? Plus, and here is a big plus, no one knows about this place. Here we can talk-privately."

"Then why the hell are we rushing all over the place yet again, if as you say there is no hurry?" asked Blondell. "Is this your little love nest? You and Alaina."

"Because," Pancardi paused, "look there is a carnival barge. Come look?" He pointed out of the window, "We Alex are like them in their Casanova masks. We make them think they are safe and all the while their chances hang in the balance. At last we have an advantage."

Blondell was bemused and raised his eyebrows to communicate his confusion.

"Let me explain," Pancardi continued, "everyone wants Alice and why?"

"Well that's obvious, so don't patronise me," he paused, "please."

"But we both know that no one cares about Alice except us. The Russians, they are after the jewels," he paused again, "after all they stole them first." He laughed, "And then there are those in your government. This will be your greatest chance for advancement. If we are subtle," he smiled, "and if we do not get killed first, you Alexander Blondell will be able to bring these people down. These nameless people who have the control. Together we can split them like a nut. So the fewer people know of our actions the better."

Blondell was nodding now.

"And on top of that," Pancardi continued, "we, we the investigators are expected to believe that at the same time, by sheer coincidence, there was a terrorist attack. These people are fools if they think that Pancardi is such a fool. This is one elaboration too many, and why because it is not true? There are many dark forces at work here and all of our paths must diverge. Like petrol and matches meeting there will be trouble. We must not be standing in the petrol when the matches are dropped."

Blondell sat down heavily and looked out of the window, "And everyone wants a piece of the action," he said. "They all want to find Alice, and we, we just sit here while the carnival rushes past. Mardi Gras for Italians, and we just sit. It's crazy, bloody ridiculous in fact."

"If we wait Alex," Pancardi replied, "we will find out who are our friends and who our enemies. All the woodlice will crawl out once we kick the log over. Alaina she is to be trusted, Pietro too and Alice."

"Alice?" Blondell's face gave a contorted twist of misunderstanding.

Pancardi laughed. "She is only trying to get away. So she will always do the one thing."

"Then why all these letters and packages and the visit to my family and Massimo and Grillva?"

"You dear boy," Pancardi paused, "you."

"I don't get it?"

"You are hunting her." Pancardi was making eye contact, "You think that by catching her your career will be safe. And that if she gets away then you will be side-lined. You will be side-lined anyway, as soon as you no longer remain useful. These people are like the Alsetti, they come in waves like the sea. Ever they come, first one wave, then another, then a storm until the land she is eroded to nothing. You are that land. No we are the land, both."

Blondell sensed that Pancardi was drifting into the realms of poetic romance and he tired to snap the conversation back.

"Strange isn't it" he mused, "how people all clamour when there is a little money involved? Like rats they come running."

"More like sharks," said Pancardi stoically. He paused and then thought of the situation, "Pietro is central for us, he is our fail safe; how do you say our ace-in-the-hole. Here, in this flat, we can speak, we can talk, but once we get to the laboratory we will be under surveillance, there will be eyes everywhere so we must make no mistakes. Give away no clues."

"Christ is there nobody to be trusted?"

"No, it is far worse, every body wants..." The Phone rang and he stopped mid sentence.

"Well," said Pietro Grillva, "Stamford Street is not terrorists."

"So who?" Pancardi quizzed.

There was silence on the end on the phone.

"He can't hear you," said Blondell. "This is hopeless, a deaf man following someone who we have no idea about; and all we know is he is following us. It's bloody absurd."

"Not that absurd," Pancardi replied, "after all he saw him. The Russian behind the wheel as they drove away, Pietro saw him."

"Well by the same token the Russian saw Grillva," Blondell retorted. "So that makes it evens. In fact," there was a pregnant pause, "if the Russians are as good as you think then Grillva might be in danger, more danger than you think."

"Alice!" Grillva suddenly exclaimed. "I cannot hear too well Carlo, but I can think. And I think it was a diversion. It was too well planned and it happened at precisely the right time. I think that Alice was responsible and not terrorists."

"Me too," Pancardi replied.

To Pietro Grillva it sounded like, "Meeeoooow."

"Angelo he is killed," Grillva continued, "as a warning to Alex, but it all goes badly wrong." Grillva was reasoning aloud, "The package goes to the girl, your girl, and then as a postman she walks away. The fear is there and then she goes to ground. But it goes horribly wrong when the other postman he turns up and then the Russians they try to get her and….."

Pancardi switched the phone to loudspeaker mode.

"I think," Grillva continued, "that she was in hiding and maybe someone discovered her so she blew the place to pieces. She must have been there because of the poison. Maybe the Russians were on to her and someone else was on to them?"

"So where is she?" asked Pancardi.

Grillva heard, "Swear she." He responded after a pause to evaluate the question, "She is still in London, or Britain."

"Why?" Pancardi asked.

"Because she cannot get out and I think she was injured at Chelsea. But you want me to get behind the scenes and give you information? So I will fly out to Italy."

"Try to pick up who is tailing us," Pancardi replied. "Stay back and don't be seen."

There was no reply on the end of the line and it was clear that Grillva had not heard the instructions.

"Bloody ridiculous," Blondell interceded.

"I'll text you," Pancardi chirped and hung up.

Within seconds he had sent a text to Pietro Grillva. Giving him their location for the next few hours.

"So what happens now?" asked Blondell.

"We play for time," Pancardi replied. "We visit Alaina, we make sure that everyone gets to know where we are."

"But I thought you said we couldn't trust anyone so what's the bloody point of that?"

"The point is that Pietro will pick us up and he will not be followed, he will pick up who is following us."

"This is going to turn into some trouser-less farce." Blondell squirmed in his seat, but threw a knowing look at Pancardi's recent purchase. "We won't even know if he has found someone. Or even if there is someone. Brian Rix couldn't have written a better piece of nonsense. Don't expect me to run around without my strides on."

"Pietro is the best in the business." Pancardi was standing now. "You won't even see him. But he will be there, far in the background. We have done this before, in the days when there were no cell, or as you say mobile, phones. We managed then, we shall manage it now. Have faith in the old methods. Those Russians will not be expecting this approach. It is low tech and foot slogging – but it works."

"Low tech I should say so," Blondell said.

"Some times the old ways are better, no?" Pancardi was laughing again.

"I sometimes feel like a blundering novice," Blondell replied.

"But blundering novices they do well." Pancardi was doing his best to sound confident. "We once flushed a serial killer out, because he always came to the crime scene after the event, just happened to be in the area time and time again. Foolish no? It was Pietro who followed him, found out all about him and although he looked totally unconnected to the crimes he made his simple mistake. "

"Ok, I can accept that," Blondell was back tracking, "but there are so many people in the mix here."

"But what if Pietro does find something out?"

Blondell was nodding.

"What if we over complicate the matter."

"Ockhams?" Blondell questioned.

"Precisely!" Pancardi was becoming philosophical again, "What if the simple answer is," he paused for effect, "the correct one. What if a few corrupt individuals are at the heart of this? Russians and English together or separately."

"The simple answer need not be over complicated?" Blondell replied agreeing, and Pancardi was encouraged. "But," he paused, "what if this goes right up to the highest levels. What if the centre of government is the problem?"

Pancardi shook his head in a thoughtful manner.

"It could be?" Blondell added. "And if that is the case this little band of dwindling musketeers is in trouble."

"But sometimes..."

Blondell interrupted the older Italian, "What? Right wins over might? Crap and you know it. If you are wrong we might end up dead."

"Let us hope then," Pancardi replied, "that we are not. We must now go to the institute and find Alaina." He paused and looked Blondell in the eye and for the first time, a seed of doubt was apparent. "If I am wrong they will kill us all," he whispered.

Chapter 28

Alexei Ulyanov walked out of Marco Polo airport in jeans and a casual shirt. The small rucksack he carried held a passport and a spare change of underwear. There were no weapons and no luggage, he was after information. Whatever the Italian and the Englishman knew, he wanted. Everything he could possibly need would be stored in one of the Italian safe houses; in his wallet he had the number of a post office box which would have the address and key for the house in Venice.

He had taken a connecting flight via Rome and although it was late, he had managed to get a water taxi to take him to Antica Locanda Montin on Dorsoduro. He had wanted to stay at Des Bains on Lido but he thought the irony rather too strong.

As a boy he had loved Venice, especially Lido, with the sand bars which ran down to the warm Adriatic. Swimming had been a pleasure and something which he had enjoyed.

The water taxi had gathered speed and the thirty minute run gave him time to reflect on his childhood. He had been lucky to be born into such a family, a family made famous by his grandfather; but his father had no political ambitions, in fact he had been lazy. He had much preferred to live life away from the turmoil of Moscow and the wrath of Stalin and in consequence, Alexei had survived and made a name for himself in the KGB. By the time he had grown into adulthood the legacy of his grandfather had been forgotten and he was nothing more than a Colonel with a similar name. Vlessivich Ulyanov had always gone on about, "the family secret," and how if everything went wrong they would all be safe, financially. Alexei had as a boy often wondered what the family secret might be, but not until the death of his father had he finally found out. Then came the political turmoil, the wall coming down and Gorbachev and eyes turned on him and questions being asked about the Romanovs. When at last the dust had settled again and everyone was convinced that the insane rumours of the last days of the Tsar were nothing more than rumour, he had slipped out of the country to make arrangements. Arrangements to move and sell on some of the jewels. Then to his horror the bank, his bank, had been robbed and his legacy taken.

The water taxi moved up the Grand Canal and then turned sharp left, passed the Guggenheim museum and he thought of the mounted rider with an erection which stood like a bronze sentinel at the estate entrance. He wondered how many dignitaries the old Peggy had shocked when the removable cock had finally been welded into place. He kind of admired her for that – for sticking two fingers up at the establishment, but he wondered if she would have been so eager if she hadn't been so obscenely wealthy. She had been lucky, to be the daughter of wealth; even if her father had gone down with the Titanic the wealth continued. She was now buried in the garden and the home had become a museum, but despite the wealth she had not been happy. Failed marriages and the death of a daughter, the money hadn't been much use to her in those departments. Money hadn't saved the Romanovs either.

It was a place which attracted the strange, that white bungalow. Marchesa Luisa Casati had thrown wild parties there, futurist parties in the Palazzo Nonfinito. They had been an excuse to indulge herself by having naked servants wandering the grounds and no doubt being fucked by the guests at will. Orgies of the rich and famous and the pretty girls of Venice being paid to take off their clothes and ride the wealthy or be ridden by them. The jewels were his and with them they could expunge the obscenities which now made Russia weak and a laughing stock. There were some locals who told him as a boy that the crazy old Marchesa had all the plants in her garden sprayed lilac, and monkeys had been let loose.

He remembered as a boy going to the zoo and there all the monkeys seemed to do was eat and screw. He had a sudden amusing recollection of the teacher, he couldn't remember her name, going red when the Moscow monkeys started copulating and the kids started asking what they were doing. He couldn't have been more than seven himself.

Ulyanov wondered about art and life and luck; the luck which had made Pegeen Vail the daughter of wealth, an artist, but the fate that had given her absolutely no talent to paint, just a wealthy mother. Her pictures seemed to wobble in the space which was tucked away in an anti-room far from Picasso and Margrite. There seemed to him to be an irony there. And then there was the Olive tree, in the garden, planted as a piece of living art. He began to laugh out loud; performance art in a black sack on stage, as John Lennon's wife; Jack the Dripper, it was all there to see in pretentious hyped glory.

The taxi halted and tied up and Ulyanov leapt onto the jetty. Paying his Euros he looked over his shoulder at the night sky of San Marco toward the distant poverty of the fake designer bag sellers who gathered their wares on a sheet and ran, whenever the police appeared. He knew he had to find the woman, and if the jewels had been sold, the cash.

As he stepped into the hotel lobby he knew that all of this could depend upon what Kernov's contact had been able to find out. If the Old Italian knew anything it would not take long to find that out by following them. They after all would not be expecting him in Venice.

❦

Alaina Tropani had pushed open the door to the laboratory, she had been delayed by the banal questions of colleagues and was about to apologise to Ennio when she saw him. He lay perfectly still on his back his arms outstretched at his side. His eyes were open and his mouth, chin and neck covered in vomit. Tears began to roll down her cheeks and she knew that the fate that had befallen him had been the one which should have been hers. Alice Parsotti had used the same poison she had used on Angelo Massimo and perhaps she had more of the same for the rest. Pancardi was at their flat collecting a reference work on poisons – sadly it was now too late.

When Pancardi and Blondell had arrived it was already evening, with the sun falling into the ocean and the coroner in the business of collecting Ennio's body. The Questura had examined the package and Alaina had explained how the jack-in-the-box mechanism had been designed, either to frighten or kill her. They had questioned Pancardi and, retired or not from the Questura, they were less than pleased with what appeared to be a murder.

It was dark now and Pancardi was snoring lightly next to her. Alexander Blondell was in the spare room but she couldn't sleep. Their little flat was supposed to be a place of sanctuary, a place to hide, but the cover was now blown. She marvelled at Pancardi's ability to sleep with a clear conscience no matter what the issue. He gathered himself in and let the world pass by.

She got up, went to the toilet – flushed and moved into the kitchen. Alexander Blondell sat at the table in the dark blinking like a mole when she turned on the light. Immediately she dimmed it.

"I can't sleep," she said.

"Snap!" he replied. "I made myself some tea," he continued, "coffee might just make things worse. Hope you don't mind?"

She was shaking her head, "He wasn't just a colleague," she said, "he was a friend as well."

"I know," Blondell replied, staring into the cup he was holding. "So many dead already, when is this madness going to end?"

"Those jewels have brought everybody bad luck; it's like they are cursed. First the Romanovs and then the assassins, and now us. One by one we all seem to die, or everybody around us seems to," Alaina reflected. "And Carlo he sleeps like a baby, does he not have any idea what would happen to his daughter?"

Blondell looked up, "They'll kill her as soon as wink."

"Exactly, exactly," she repeated the word as if it were a revelation of Archimedes. "If you get in the way, God help you."

"That's why we need to get to Alice, before the Russians, her life depends upon it."

Alaina was re-filling the kettle, "What about the bambini?" she asked.

"They are very safe," Blondell replied, "her family will take care of that. She is more scared for me."

"Let's go onto the balcony," she cajoled, "the air is fresh and we can see the canal from there."

"I know," Blondell replied.

"Of course you do, you were here earlier today – sorry I forgot."

The two of them sat looking across at Dorsoduro, in the distance Santa Maria della Salute was lit like a Christmas tree, giving a clearly defined entrance to the mouth of the Grand Canal.

"Like all things this city will fade you know?" Alaina said. "The whole of the water level has risen at least one metre in the last thousand years, and it's still rising."

"I know the square floods in the winter and the buildings are often flooded on the lower floors. I think I'd rather live in Florence, at least it's dry there," he chuckled.

"I like Florence too," Alaina agreed, "but I chose here to be romantic."

"I have some wonderful memories of Florence," Blondell replied, lowering his voice, "W.H.Auden, stop all the clocks," he said.

Alaina looked at him as if he were speaking in code. She tried to understand the drive which pushed him on, without giving any quarter. Tried to fathom the reason he had to continue. When his family were under threat, what drove him? At times it was bordering on obsession.

"Pietro Grillva is probably in Venice right now," Blondell blurted. "He might even be watching us. Pancardi has said that we must pad about for a couple of days so that someone can pick up our trail and Grillva can then pick them up. It's like a giant game of cat and mouse."

"Why will you never, give up on this?" Alaina suddenly asked. "What drives you?"

Blondell shrugged.

"Don't pester him," Pancardi's voice came from the dark behind them. "Whatever the reason, whatever the cause, we are hunting Alice. It started as one thing and it has turned into another."

"It has turned into a nightmare," said Blondell.

"Well if everything goes to plan ..."

"One plan after another gets shot out of the water," Blondell interrupted. "I hope your man is as good as you say, because if he isn't we will all end up dead."

"He is better than that, and tomorrow we shall give him a chance to find us." Pancardi smiled at Alaina, "We need to go over the laboratory inch by inch."

"And what do you expect to find?" she asked.

"A mistake," replied Pancardi.

"What like leaving her forwarding address on the parcel?" Blondell was mocking now. "Perhaps she left us a telephone number so we can have a quick chat."

Pancardi had his head turned to one side, "Alex, even a small clue would help no?"

Blondell nodded.

"Well as we are all up shall I make us some coffee?" asked Alaina.

Both men nodded.

When she had left the balcony Pancardi spoke quietly to Blondell. "Now is the time to finally tell me about your scars and your role, when you got them. I would like to hear the truth and not some wild story about Northern Ireland. There is someone in one of these departments who is making life difficult for us and when we get back to England we shall lead the Russians to them. Let us see how careful they are then no? We will set the cats on the pigeons."

Alexander Blondell thought about spinning a line but thought better of it, "I had a short spell in MI6," he said. "I was assigned to an investigation, the Brinks Matt robbery. There was a lot of office talk about insider knowledge and the Home Office and that it went all the way to the top of the service. "

Pancardi nodded in a way which meant give more detail.

"My superior and I were on to it and then we got caught in the line of fire. To cut a long story short he died and I, well, I was injured and the investigation stalled and then when I recovered I was moved to another sector – desk job. They never did find the leak. The whole thing sort of vanished into the back rooms of Whitehall. My boss just died and then there was someone else and it was almost as if he had never existed. It's a bit like that there. One minute it's God save the King and two minutes later, it's God save the King all over again. Only it's not the same king anymore. No bugger really gave a damn as long as I vanished too. Then I dug up the stuff about the Romanov fortune and the same things and faces came up."

"Corruption?"

"Totally," Blondell replied. "And I sort of kept on looking whilst I was doing other things. They tried to freeze me out, keep me tucked away. But I found out too much and then they thought that you might be a burnt out old ..."

"Enough," snapped Pancardi, "we will expose these people, destroy them. And they will see what a man without a spleen and broken down has-been can do." His voice became steely and harsh, "Roberto and Angelo will not be forgotten, give me a name," he barked.

"But I have no idea who might be controlling this."

"Yes you do," replied Pancardi.

"I have no evidence."

"Evidence, smevidence," he paused, "take a guess. Use your intuition. Let the Russians do their job. Let them cut our opposition down to size. We can see how they like it and just pick up the pieces. The more mayhem is caused the more chance we have of finding Alice before they do."

"What get them fighting among themselves, rather than always watching us?"

"Pietro he is watching our backs and there could be no better man for the job. Silent but deadly."

"Like a fart in a lift then?" Blondell added flippantly.

"Si, Si," Pancardi snorted, as he choked back the laughter. "A name?"

"I have a sneaking suspicion that the central figure is Michael Cleverly," Blondell replied. "The Right Honourable Michael Cleverly MP."

"Well that would follow wouldn't it?" Pancardi laughed. "Wealthy, worldly and part of the establishment. The English equivalent of an Alsetti. This man we must destroy. Do you have files, information, detail?" he asked.

"I have everything stacked away in my study but those berks are too thick to know where to look. I wanted to keep it for a rainy day."

"This I like," Pancardi laughed, "and I forgive you for the lie in the past."

Blondell looked sheepish, "I do want to take this bugger out," he said.

"Well is he as you say, a bugger?"

Blondell began to laugh, "What like public school bugger?"

Pancardi began to snort and chortle, "Well I think there is a storm coming," he laughed, "and how do you English say, it is going to piss down?"

Both men laughed more as a tension release to sleeplessness, rather than any meaningful future plan of vengeance.

"So what's all the hilarity?" Alaina asked, as she arrived with a pot of freshly brewed coffee. "I've hunted out some after dinner mints too," she laughed. "We might as well get fat, as well as sleepless and bleary eyed."

"We shall keep to our beds in the morning," Pancardi snorted eating a mint as he did so. "They can wait and we can sleep. Pietro he could do with the sleep too. I will text him to say when we shall start."

"So tomorrow is all for show?" asked Alaina.

"At first yes." Pancardi was thinking as he spoke. "Then you will go to Rome and make a great fuss. There will be a show of forensic evidence. Alex and I will go back to London, but not together. We will make them dance a while."

"And what's the point of that?" asked Blondell.

"Confusion," Pancardi laughed, "confusion and mis-direction."

"Do you know it's nearly four in the morning?" said Alaina.

"So we go back to bed," said Pancardi, "for this last night we are safe, and then we set our traps to catch our rats. I will send a text to Pietro that we shall not be on the move before eleven. This is good no?" And he gulped a large mouthful of coffee.

Pietro Grillva's phone vibrated in his pocket as lay sleeping on the British Diplomatic flight which was close to landing in Venice. Angelo Massimo's meat-mincer lay in the overhead locker, the bag unopened and unchecked at customs. A couple of phone calls needed to be made but he felt they had been worth it. Pancardi had wanted the cover blown so that their adversaries came into the light. That, he thought, might help and having the weapon made him feel more comfortable if they did get into another fire-fight like Chelsea. If someone did follow him, he knew that he would spot them quickly, and better still lose them quickly. So the gain was all on their part.

His ears were aching and sleeping on a flight had not improved his mood. He had been unable to get an earlier departure and for hotels he could only find a Travel Lodge near the airport. He read Pancardi's text and his mood improved dramatically. He calculated bed at five and then up at eleven. He knew where his people would be and by twelve he would be in place to scan for the other surveillance team. He punched the smiling symbol in reply.

As he left the airport he noticed the crowds as they swarmed around the exit points and baggage carousels, there seemed to be other people interested in getting some sleep. Some lay in sleeping bags under seats or had tucked themselves into corners behind stacks of luggage – it was a typical late night airport vista. Most people looked bleary eyed and were irritable.

At the airport entrance he turned toward the Travel Lodge and glancing behind him noticed one other traveller in the distance who seemed to be moving toward the same hotel.

His eyes were not focussing well and he knew he needed to sleep – urgently.

Chapter 29

Mikhail Kernov woke suddenly and reached for the mobile flip-phone which was buzzing and jumping on the bedside table. His leg was stiff and as he reached to be woken from his afternoon refresher he dropped the item and it snapped shut. Retrieving it from the floor he looked at the missed calls log and noted the number had been withheld – he had been expecting Ulyanov to phone with either instructions, or a set of further requests.

He cursed his own clumsiness but as the phone rang again, he knew it had to be important.

"It's Jeremy," a feeble voice offered.

"What have you found out?" Kernov barked.

"I can't talk, it's not safe for me," he whispered in reply. "Can we meet?"

"Where then?" Kernov's tone was terse.

"Trafalgar Square?"

"Ok. Where in there?"

"Outside the National Gallery, the entrance that faces down toward the cenotaph. In about an hour?" Stapleford was almost hissing now in an attempt to cover his words, "I think they are on to me. It's not safe. Not sa..." He suddenly slammed the receiver into the cradle and the line went dead.

Kernov looked at the clock next to the bed it read 2.30pm. Quickly he dialled for a taxi hoping he could get to Trafalgar square before Stapleford and those who now had him under surveillance. His intention was to move swiftly, try to be one step ahead of the pursuers; he paused to reason. If they had a tap on

Stapleford's phone they could trace him, but he had not been on long enough for them to locate the safe house, unless they could pin-point the satellite location.

His mind reverted to his KGB training, as he spoke aloud, "They will try but they will fail to beacon, as there is now no signal." He switched off the phone. "That's fucked them," he laughed. "But Mikhail you must be there ahead of them," he was using the third person as if conversing with Ulyanov. "They will not be able to get anyone there faster, that gives you the advantage. They will follow the fool, and well..." He started whistling – a tune by the Beatles and in between the broken musical phrases of Day Tripper, he chuckled and moved into Get Back.

Standing on his feet he quickly pulled his trousers over his freshly bandaged wounds. He had inspected and cleaned them when bathing earlier in the morning, they were healing well and though the muscle tissue was still weak, the seeping and weeping had completely stopped. There would be scars, but they too would fade with time. Kernov snapped the head off a glass vial of morphine and drew a small amount into a hypodermic; with one deft movement he stabbed the needle into his bare upper left arm, before pulling a shirt from the wardrobe. The dose would be enough, he calculated, to stop the pain, but not enough to cloud his judgement or perceptions once in the field.

As he dressed the morphine allowed a greater mobility of his leg. The stiffness subsided; in consequence, he decided not to take a walking stick. Firstly it would draw attention to him by any observers and secondly it could serve no strategic protective purpose. Drawing a shoulder holster over his shirt he stuffed a 9mm Polyenkoff automatic into the leather pouch and a spare clip into his jacket. This was the standard issue at safe houses, though he wondered why the weapons had to be Russian. It would be so obvious to any ballistics expert that the weapons were KGB issue.

A knock came at the door, and he quickly slipped a pair of loafers onto his feet and a wallet into his pocket – he did not bother with socks. Twenty minutes later he was stepping out of a black cab in front of St. Martin's College dressed in combat trousers, a lose jacket and a woollen hat. To any passer-by he could have been a foreign art student, or a tourist to the National Gallery.

He scanned the skyline for the barrels of snipers and watched cars disgorging groups of men. Noticing a group he studied three men who jumped quickly from a black Ford Focus and moved smartly toward the National Gallery. Kernov knew from their movements and the precision they used when they separated, that they were a surveillance team. Smiling he walked into a coffee shop and then took the beverage toward the fountain area; his intention being to intercept Stapleford before he started up the steps. Knowing he would be followed Kernov wanted to be able to extricate himself quickly if the situation turned into a fire-fight; wanted to be among a crowd of innocents so that when the firing started confusion would reign.

Placing the drink on a stone parapet he studied the many entrances and exits to the open square, it was a good choice by Stapleford. Too many tourists for a boom mic to be effective, too many bodies for gun fire – it would be a place where panic would work in their favour. Kernov fingered one of the two C2 grenades which he had in his pocket and a smile crept across his face. If all else failed he would simply drop one of these into the mix to end any surveillance in the instant.

He checked his watch and then studied the crowd for Stapleford, first toward Big Ben and then toward Buckingham Palace – he was late.

"Distretto, un aqua minerale?"

"Prego?" the waiter asked.

Alexei Ulyanov reverted to English, "Strong coffee and water please."

"Sparkling or still?" the waiter asked.

"Still."

Alexei Ulyanov had placed himself some distance from the National Medical Institute. He had been up early and found the most strategic viewpoint by scouting the area and was satisfied that from this café he could watch the arrival of his quarry.

The early morning walk had cleared his head and now he was on full alert scanning as he sat obscured behind a newspaper.

At 10.30 am Ulyanov ordered a second coffee, while across the canal a smaller lithe man sat reading the Nationale. As Giancarlo

Pancardi and Alexander Blondell passed the smaller man he did not look up. Merely lifted the paper higher to turn the page and then nonchalantly folded the item again to make it more readable. The two men were joined by a red-haired woman in high heels who was dressed in a formal suit, and as a trio they began the walk up to the main entrance of the Forensic Medicine Institute.

It was 11.00 am and the sun was already high in the sky. The winter day was warming and Pietro Grillva raised his eyes from behind his newspaper, he was scanning for movement. Alexei Ulyanov saw the trio enter the Forensic Medicine building and rose quickly, took a mouthful of water and walked to the front of the building. For one moment Pietro Grillva thought he was going to enter behind Pancardi, Tropani and Blondell, but at the doorway Ulyanov checked his step and then walked out into the park which lay to the front and right of the building. He then sat himself in the shade.

Pietro Grillva opened his phone and sent a simple text: *He's here, got him marked.*

In the coffee shop which Ulyanov had just vacated a large good looking man in a soft green shirt appeared and ordered a hot chocolate and a pastry. He spoke in a low voice with a pronounced accent and laughed, a deep throaty laugh, flirting with the waitress. At the corners of his mouth a flirtatious smile appeared; his physique was taut, firm, muscular and he clearly kept himself at a physical peak. The waitress had noticed that fact and seemed to be responding positively to his flirtations; Grillva noticed the girl's face redden and he too smiled at her embarrassment. He wondered what the man was saying as they were beyond earshot, but clearly the man had found a reason to stay longer than perhaps he should. The waitress in turn was leaning into the man and giggling, so whatever was being said was striking a chord with her and Grillva wondered if they would end up in bed before the end of the day. At that point he suddenly realised that the Russian was no longer there, and he cursed his own stupidity under his breath.

"Let us examine all of the items," chirped Pancardi.

"I've had some of my men in this department check on one or

two things already," said Alaina. "The C. D.'s in the box. Those were just standard Toshiba recordable discs. They could be bought anywhere."

The door to the laboratory opened and a small athletic man who could have passed for a younger version of Pietro Grillva walked in. His face was lined and Pancardi tried to estimate his age – he settled on twenty eight.

"Have you checked the watermark like I requested?" Alaina asked.

The man nodded in reply.

"Oh," she continued, turning to Blondell and Pancardi, "this is Sandro Bichere, and before you ask he is absolutely trustworthy. He and Ennio used to work together and I am certain that if he had not been on leave when that damn packet arrived Ennio would still be alive today."

Pancardi greeted the man with a warm smile and a rapid gabbling in Italian, while Blondell merely nodded and offered his hand in a handshake.

Pancardi's phone buzzed, it was Grillva, "He's got him," laughed the Italian, "see I told you Pietro was good." He seemed ecstatically happy with the news.

"But I saw him," said Blondell.

"Only because you were looking for him, how else would you have known?"

"Where was he?" asked Alaina.

"The man behind the newspaper," Blondell replied.

"What man? What newspaper?" Alaina looked stumped.

"You see," Pancardi laughed, "not everyone knows where to look. My plan she is working and we have one of the followers in Pietro's sight. This is good, this is very good. " He was clapping his hands now , "Ha they all think that we are the fools that will lead everyone to the jewels and to Alice and so they leave us in peace but they do not know the guile we have. We shall beat them all one by one."

"But our man is KGB he is no fool and what's more he will be highly dangerous." Blondell seemed uneasy, more cautious and less optimistic, "The KGB are professionals they…"

"So too are we Alex, so too are we no?" Pancardi interrupted. "Who can we trust but ourselves?"

"The poison is as you suspected Dendrobatti," Sandro began.

"That's Amazonian tree frog, sweat from the mucus glands," Alaina added. "Certain tribes of the Amazon use it to hunt with, and before you ask, when the meat is cooked the venom becomes harmless. It is almost the perfect poison; perfected over the Millennia by the finest laboratory," she paused, "evolution."

"The tape wrapper and all of the packaging can be bought in any department store," the young Pietro continued. "No skin, hair, no blood, no sweat, no finger prints, nothing. Even the seal on the envelope was just water. It's like it was prepared in a vaccum. Whoever prepared this parcel did not want to get caught; they were so very careful – forensically careful."

"Or prepared by someone who knew exactly what they were doing. Knew what we would be looking for," Blondell dejectedly interceded.

"But," Sandro continued, "the letter is another matter." He paused for effect, "This is hand made, in Birmingham in the UK."

"How hand made?" Blondell asked. "Birmingham?"

"Well they distribute to some very wealthy places; Turin, Milan, Genoa, Venice."

"Christ she's here," Blondell almost whooped in triumph.

"It was posted in England," Sandro continued, "in London. And there are only three outlets which supply this in the UK. Two are in London and one is in Birmingham."

"How the hell do we trace sales of bespoke paper, it could be everywhere?" Blondell slipped back toward despondency. "And anyway it could be something Alice got from somebody else. A gift or anything?"

"Can I say something?" asked Alaina. "What if it gives you a general area. I know London is a big place and so is Birmingham," she paused; all eyes were focussed on her. "What if she is near where she bought the paper, what if she doesn't know it is that rare. What if she just likes it?"

"What if she has made her first real error?" asked Pancardi.

"What if we are all running before we can walk?" snubbed Blondell. "Shouldn't we be a little more clear headed? This is a very narrow lead and we have to work virtually in isolation. Besides she has given us red herrings in the past."

"But," Alaina replied, voicing what she was thinking, "your

department has access to all large transfers of money in and out of the UK."

"We don't have access to them, just have information about where they took place; but we can't be certain even that will find her," Blondell answered. "And then the entire world and his wife will know we are on to something. Others will start checking and maybe they will find the link to Alice before we do? "

"Can we access that computer data base from here?" asked Pancardi.

Sandro Bichere nodded, "Interpol links but they are not fast," he said.

"They'll know it's me though," said Blondell, "codes are entry listed."

"Yes agreed," said Pancardi, "but we shall take all of the raw data. How will they know what we are looking for? By the time they discover what we are doing they will…"

"Guess?" Blondell interrupted. "They'll guess, and besides there is the issue of that bloody Russian KGB man outside."

"So we give him a herring?" Pancardi smirked.

"Why a fish?" Sandro Bichere seemed confused.

"It's a figure of speech," Blondell tried to explain. " Like the metaphor when we are all in the same boat, but we're not really in a boat at all." Sandro looked confused. "Well it's like that and anyway it's a, red herring," he corrected Pancardi.

Sandra Bichere was now approaching apoplexy mentally but his exterior veneer was in tact. Boats and red herrings which had nothing to do with the case merely made the whole line of enquiry more absurd. But try as he might to understand the situation the madness continued.

" So who's the bait, or should I say what's the bait?" asked Blondell.

"Alaina," Pancardi replied, "and Sandro here."

"Hold on a minute," Blondell was now as confused as Sandro.

"Look," Pancardi had slowed his pace. "First we get the data, then we investigate here. We choose the most likely location. A place where Alice she might be?" He looked at the other three, " Then Alaina and Sandro they go to one or two places and they draw off these watchers and you and I Alex we vanish suddenly in the confusion." He was grinning broadly as he spoke, "We have sown doubt and we find Alice before they find us. Simple no?"

"No," snapped Blondell, "what if we're wrong what if," he paused thinking, "in fact there are so many variables that it's mad."

"So we take a guess? Work on instinct, take a gamble."

"And the Russians?"

"Sheep, they will follow us no?"

" They might decide to kill us?"

"No this they will not do." Pancardi continued to evaluate, "And why because they want us to get the answers? Once they have these, then they will kill us."

"I don't like this," Blondell looked at Alaina and Sandro. "It's too dangerous for others."

"For who?" asked Sandro.

"For you," Blondell barked.

Pancardi had decided and the others knew that one way or another he would get his way. Either by charm or by sheer bloody minded doggedness. Blondell looked at the man who clearly believed that despite the internal betrayals at Interpol, the obvious lack of support which was happening at both the Home and Foreign Offices, it was still possible.

"So let's get the information downloaded," Pancardi was enthused now. "We need a programmer who will know what to sift for."

"We will have to get Dante back then," Alaina said to Sandro.

"He's still here," he replied. "Well at least he was before I came down."

"Well give him a buzz," she instructed. "He needs to get on to this right now."

Blondell walked to the window, "So none of us can leave here until we have the information. What do we do about Pietro?"

"Go for a walk," Pancardi quipped. "A guided tour of Venice. Give them something to follow, then we come back and then..."

"We lead them away?" Alaina added. "I see what Carlo wants to do he wants to create some space in which to work. We find out the names of those accounts and we piece the puzzle to make it fit."

"Not to make it fit," Pancardi cackled, "much better than that we actually put the jigsaw together. Anywhere there are large gaps we fill in the blanks."

"I still say it's risky," Blondell added.

"But," Pancardi had become serious now. "We must not make wild assumptions, we are so close that I can smell them."

Suddenly the phone vibrated in his pocket. He read: – *Russian gone. May be more than one, though not able to locate 2nd. Need movement to flush.*

"Come Sandro," said Pancardi, ending the discussion. "Our services are needed. We shall take a walk. Alaina you must tell Dante what to do."

The clear instructions on the processing of the raw data were being relayed to Dante Pollonari as Pancardi and Sandro Bichere left by the front entrance. Pancardi made much of tying his shoe on the front step and Sandro lit a cigarette with the languid air of someone who had come out for a smoke to clear his head. They wanted to be seen, wanted to be spotted – and it was working.

In the café the man in the green shirt instantly came alive, though no one but the waitress spotted it. He studied the pair intently and noticed their lack of hurry. Both he and his brother had seen this over casualness before, and although his brother was no longer alive, as the younger sibling he had learned by observation. James had told him to be aware of the over elaborate lie, to read their eyes, study their movements and never to trust more than two men in ten thousand. Jimmy had been his Frank and he had been Jesse, and the only other man who might have been worth a spit had been bled like a sacrificial lamb on a mountain altar. There were times when he missed his brother's logic, missed the cold calm which had made him the best in the business. He didn't want revenge he wanted the perpetrator, rough justice he had called it. Cancer had been Jimmy's rough justice and that could never be avenged, but this, this was the right and proper thing to do.

His wife hadn't agreed, she was for him laying low, after all he was the sole survivor and that would be the smart option, but something drove him on, something dark and pitiless, anger in his soul. Like the scales of justice he hung in the balance; the last of the horsemen, the last and most deadly of them all; not death, death was a relief from the pain of life, that he had seen with Jimmy. He was the cancer, the pestilence, the plague – that was the real enemy, hunger, doubt and greed, and this time he was going to destroy her utterly.

Beverly had almost begged him not to go and little Claire had picked up on it – there had been tears and wailing but in the end he had gone. He knew when he returned they would love him all the more.

From behind a set of bushes in the park Ulyanov also studied the pair at the entrance and as they moved off he began to follow at a discreet distance. The man in green turned his observation onto Grillva who he realised had not moved. Rapidly he scanned for the second pick-up thinking there was a team working the surveillance, that worried him as he had not found the link.

Pancardi punched a number into his phone as they set off at a leisurely pace. The message was a simple one to Pietro Grillva, *don't follow*, it said, they would be back within the hour. He had told Blondell and Alaina they had one hour and then they would have to break up and return to the flat.

Pietro Grillva vanished from sight.

As the Italians passed the coffee bar, the observer had no trouble in understanding what was being said, and reassured, he remained at the table as the two passed him completely oblivious of who he was. His knowledge of Italian had been honed during the past two years and he knew that debts, however bizarre they might seem at first, would be honoured. He was the last man standing. Watching the old Italian as he strode past; his hair seemed greyer and his gait a little stiffer than he remembered it. Pancardi was walking with a cane; a steady clicking accompaniment to his animated loud discussion. A Venetian cane of ebony and silver and new; he pondered on the fact that an injury had been sustained here, but then evaluated the time lapse between now and Florence and deduced that age had been the main culprit.

After a few minutes the blonde Ulyanov also passed him and he studied the man's face, committing it to memory.

"More coffee?" the waitress asked.

The man shook his head, but also realised he needed to change his vantage point or he would be spotted on their return. His mind was working like a steel trap and having watched the little chap vanish after Pancardi's text, he knew they were simply giving the watchers a run around. He rose and walked in the opposite direction from the Italians.

The disgruntled waitress watched him leave and imagined what his buttocks looked like outside his trousers. The muscles were taut and she imagined his sheer raw power as he...

"Gina?" called the owner, snapping her out of her fantasy.

"Si," she replied, and then swiftly went on to the next set of tourists who had come in for an afternoon snack. She looked at the clock and calculated forty minutes to the end of her shift.

Forty minutes later she was walking across the park to see Mr. Greenshirt. She had seen him sitting and watching, studying, and she had misconstrued it as him watching her. If he would not broach the subject she would; she imagined that he might not have the nerve to ask her; it was clear to her that the man wanted her and she knew she wanted him. She could feel the tightness in her stomach and as she sat she could sense the moistness of her sex.

"Well?" she asked.

"Well what?" came his reply.

"You've been watching me all afternoon."

He smiled like a child who had been caught with their hand in the cookie jar, a nervous smile she thought. A sexy, nervous smile, which she needed to see over her flat stomach as she watched him, eating her.

"Would you like to come to my place?" she asked. "I will be having a nap. I have to come back for the evening shift, though." All the senses in her body were on high alert now and she could feel her nipples pushing against the material which cupped her breasts like a baker's hand kneading dough.

"Where do you live?" he asked.

"What's your name?" she replied, pointing to a window which overlooked the park and gave a clear view of the Institute entrance. "That's my place, there. The third window from the right, no balcony though just.... "

"John," he replied interrupting. He knew that luck always played its part in any situation and this was his. "Shall we go there then?"

She nodded an affirmative reply.

From the coffee shop, the owner watched the two of them leave the park. He had tried on several occasions to entice the girl into his bed. In fact that was why he still tolerated her. Not for her waitressing skills, but for the vague notion that one day she might bend herself over in front of him with her back arched and her knickers tied around her wrists. His anger rose, and now she was off to fuck this man with a beard. For a brief second he imagined her flat on her back with her head falling back over the edge of a bed while he stood above her. He could almost hear her choking remonstrations as he held her ears and pushed ever deeper. He would have forced her, forced her to swallow, made her drink his juice; become a water fountain from which she could gulp over and over again. This girl would do things only the very best porn stars and whores could manage. And now she was walking away, away to a strange hairy bed.

Greenshirt had his arm around her narrow waist, he could not believe his luck. He wondered how flexible she was, whether she could arch her back when she had sex. Wondered whether she'd giggle or object when placed on all fours. He wondered whether she would talk dirty, encourage him to outrage and finally what his wife, the only woman he had ever loved, would do if she found out.

"It's a small place," she said apologetically.

"Good," he replied smirking, "a small place for a big man. I like small places."

"And I like big men," she laughed.

She could feel the dampness, flooding her underwear and her ever more exposed clitoris was being rubbed into arousal by the cotton thong which she was wearing.

Inside the entrance to her flat, he kicked the door closed and lunged forward pining both of her arms behind her back. He could smell her sweet perfume as he lifted her tabard and tore her knickers clear. She was moist and her sex engorged as he lifted her. She clung to his neck and lifted her buttocks, the backs of her knees supported in the crooks of his elbows. Then she was pushing with her pelvis, thrusting, biting his ear lobe, urging him, with repeated, "Fuck me, fuck me," calls, to take her there and then. Her hands were released and instantly she was undoing his belt and his trousers fell to the floor. He stepped out of them and as she clung to him he lifted her toward the couch. He wore no underwear and her hands had fastened around him as she tried to make him hard and place him inside her. Pulling away he slid down between her thighs allowing his tongue to drive her to virtual insanity, she in turn spun and contorted her body and reached for the growing manhood she still held and slipped him into her hungry mouth . Her excitement was at fever pitch now and as the head of his erect penis touched her tongue, he lapped and flicked a few rapid movements with his – the effect was almost magical as her whole body went into spasm. Then he entered her while simultaneously reaching into his jacket pocket. Her whole body was contracting around him and her eyes rolled in their sockets; the grip on his loins was tight and coming in shuddering waves of pulsation, as the needle bit into her flesh. Her mouth opened in a gasp and her head tilted back in a gurgling crescendo of lust and then she subsided.

Less than thirty seconds later she was nothing more than a crumpled heap on the floor and he was withdrawing the needle which had administered the knock out punch to her orgasm. At one point he thought he might have had to continue, because he could not get a hand free to find the syringe in his pocket.

"Sorry," he said to the now unconscious girl, who he carefully lifted into the bedroom. "Maybe twenty five years ago we could have, but you're too young and I'm too late." He was still erect and he could have entered her again to take his pleasure, but it was Beverly who stopped him. There had been many women before her, more than he could remember, but none after, and this he reasoned did not count – this was business. And he loved her more than anything in the world, with perhaps the exception of his daughter. If Jimmy saw him betray her he would never forgive him, but worse he would have lost his own self-respect. He looked at the girl, she was young and her body was lithe, her legs were smooth and the pubic hair was shaped to arouse. At the point where she had him in her mouth, he thought his willpower might explode away from him, he thought perhaps he had made a mistake, and then he smiled as his arousal began to subside. Placing her in the recovery position he stroked the line of her hips and admired the narrowness of her waist. She was not going to make her shift for that evening but she would remember the orgasm and passing out. Perhaps she had not even felt the needle penetrate. It would be a tale to tell her friends, who would never believe such heights could be achieved during sex.

Pulling on his trousers he went to the window, drew back the shutters, squatted on a chair and began to continue his vigil. He wondered if the girl had any decent coffee in the place.

Pancardi and Bichere walked to the Rialto bridge, went to the post office and then dodged into a small alley way and out through a shop front. Ulyanov had to close in to find them and as intended they led him on a merry dance through the streets.

"Make things easy," Pancardi said, as if giving advice to a junior. "Most people like to see and make things far more complicated than they either are or need to be. Just make it natural."

"But what if we lose him?" asked Bichere.

"We won't," was Pancardi's reply. "And if we do, well, we'll give him time to catch up. We are playing for time. We know more about everything than they do, but we may be being watched by others. Come we shall have a coffee here."

"Right out in the open?"

"Si, out in the open with the vultures and the buzzards. For then they will see us, but we shall also see them. It is better that we see our enemy no?"

Sandro Bichere merely nodded and doing as Pancardi instructed, noticed the visibly flustered Ulyanov as he sped around a corner his eyes on full alert.

Pancardi smiled showing his teeth in a broad grin of success.

Chapter 30

Jeremy Stapleford came into Trafalgar Square at break-neck speed, his tie was loose and perspiration had stained his shirt. He was visibly nervous and his brow was running with sweat, sweat which only men who are out of condition can produce. His jacket was casually draped over his arm and his breath was coming in short gasps as if he had been running. His eyes twitched and he was nervously checking behind him to see if he was being followed.

Kernov gave a high–pitched whistle to attract his attention as he approached, "Here," Kernov shouted and turning sharply Stapleford joined him.

"I think they are on to me," he said, "so we will have to make this quick, where can we go?"

"You are being followed?" Kernov announced innocently, knowing full well that the group were already in place at the National Gallery.

"Are you mad, I lost him but we can't stay here?" Stapleford looked over his shoulder as Kernov grabbed his arm and ushered him toward The Strand.

"Over the river then," he said, leading his informant.

The two men moved at a quick pace weaving through the crowds, bobbing in and out of the tourists like corks on a tempest. Stapleford wanted to run but Kernov counselled against it, holding him back from his flight mode.

"You have to blend into the crowd, not carve a trail through it," Kernov advised. "Be cool and don't draw attention to either yourself or me. We're just a couple of silly foreign tourists bumbling along, seeing the sights. Two old bitching queers on an ice-cream day out." He grabbed Stapleford's arm and drew him closer, "We get to the tube and vanish, make sure that no one knows where we are, give the bastards a run for their money." Stapleford was shaking and Kernov could feel the anxiety in his arm. "Listen they are not going to take a shot at us here, so just walk steadily," he continued, "relax, you'll be fine. You must have some good information? "

"It's alright for you," he replied, "but they're on to me." Stapleford was almost squealing now, "Its' all buggered up. My whole career down the toilet."

A passing woman heard the expletive and shot him a look like thunder.

"That's it, all down the toilet," he continued. "All gone, all gone now," he repeated.

Quickly the two men crossed the river on foot, heading toward Waterloo station. The commuters were passing them but they had a clear view of all the people that might be following. Kernov knew the area well; the many exits and entrances, the train and tube lines – this was a good place for him to vanish. As the two men approached from the north Kernov suddenly pulled Stapleford into one of the archways; on through a small walkway and toward a lock-up storage point tucked into one of the myriad of smaller arches, under the multitude of London rail lines. Checking to see that they had not been followed, and that they were not being observed he produced a key to open a heavy pad-lock. Flicking a switch the small vacant storage facility was bathed in light.

The room had a vaulted ceiling like some Old Saxon church. Interlocking flint and bricks, which had been loosened by the vibration of trains and blackened by the smog and soot, were hanging poised to fall from their lime mortar. The place smelt damp and the flagstone floor oozed with the grime of past generations. At the far end of the building sat a few empty crates; stained crates made to haul old engine parts. A single light bulb encrusted with thick dust gave the only light which was yellow and pale, and without it the area could have passed for a dungeon. The air was thick and spore filled with the scent of moulding leaves as the undercurrent. Stapleford wondered how Kernov knew the place, but decided not to ask.

"Right," Kernov said, turning to the now almost wet Stapleford, "we don't have long. They have men at the National Gallery, I spotted a surveillance team so your phone will be tapped, but we can both get out of this alive. If we are quick. You were probably followed but I think we have lost them. Speak."

"I want £150,000 extra," the Englishman blurted. "I can't go back to my place and I need to have some extras."

"But you have been getting a retainer for years old boy." Kernov smiled a toothy grin as he spoke, "What? Spent it all on old whores?" he paused, "or rent boys?" He made a tut tut sound, "My we have been careless and carefree." Kernov was very calm, there was no threat in his voice, "You already have many payments from us," he then stated blandly.

"But everything has gone tits up and I don't think that I will be able to continue. I need to get out."

"Ok," replied Kernov, "they will be after you and I hope for your sake that you have been prudent. You want get away money?"

Stapleford nodded.

"Telegraphed to your Swiss account?"

Stapleford nodded again.

Kernov relaxed and tilted his head to one side and then a broad smile broke upon his face, "Ok," he said, "but first I need to see what you've got."

Stapleford considered his options, to talk or to trust the Russian. He opted for the latter trusting they would do, as they had always done – honour their pledges

"Well we did a trawl of all the withdrawals," he blurted at high speed, "and we found two that might fit the profile. One in London at the Bank of Scotland, Bow and another at Lloyds in Broad Street Birmingham. Both were large sums and both withdrawn in cash and both by women." He smiled at broadly at Kernov, "That's got to be worth the extra, and that will be us done, finished."

"There have been no other deposits?" Kernov continued.

"I thought you said withdrawals?" Stapleford looked worried. "We found all we could on the mainland UK, some further deposits may have been made but I couldn't find any other cash withdrawals. There have also been some other transfers of money, stocks and bonds but you said not to bother with those."

"That is fantastic work comrade," Kernov mocked him with the use of the word, knowing full well that he was no more a Communist than Mickey Mouse. "So now all we have to do is get out of this alive."

Stapleford nodded. "The money?" he asked.

"By transfer in the usual way. Even I cannot get that amount of cash quickly."

Stapleford nodded again. "I can't go back you know that, they'll arrest me," he said.

"I know," Kernov replied. "So we leave now, together and you come with me. That way you have some chance of survival. Agreed?"

Stapleford eagerly nodded in agreement.

"Right I leave first," Kernov barked.

"What and I stay?"

"I check to see if there is anyone outside, and then I come back."

Kernov left quickly and Stapleford stood behind the door listening. The seconds turned into minutes and his heart began to pound. Kernov had not returned and he wondered what would happen when they eventually found him. He toyed with the idea of rushing out and then pondered on waiting for dark. Finally he settled on the rush hour as his best option. He looked at his watch; Kernov had at least given him that blending advice.

There was a quick tap at the door – Kernov had returned.

"Where the hell have you been?" Stapleford asked.

"Sneaking," Kernov replied, smirking.

"What?"

"Checking to see where they have men posted and that takes time. They don't know me but they know you and we have to have some route to get away. That is unless you want to disappear and rot in some secure MI5 house."

"I'll end up dead first," Stapleford replied.

"Don't wish too hard for that one," Kernov snapped, "your wish might just come true and then where would you be?"

Stapleford was shaking hard now and Kernov knew that he would collapse or run under the stress of gun fire. He looked to see if a puddle of urine was appearing at his feet.

"You go first. Then I lock this and follow," Kernov ordered.

Stapleford gingerly looked out into the empty courtyard and saw nothing, not even the heavy barrel of Kernov's pistol which struck him from behind at the nape of the neck. His knees buckled and he began to fall as a second and then a third blow cracked his skull open like a walnut. Kernov then slammed the door into his head and wrenched Stapleford back out of sight. Blood began to run into Stapleford's eyes and his mouth whimpered and then he attempted a scream. Kernov finally delivered a series of frenzied kicks to his jaw which snapped like a piece kindling, the removal of it finally silenced him. One eye fell from the socket as his cheek bone disintegrated.

Quickly he rolled Stapleford's jacket around the pistol and dragged the prostrate being to the rear of the cavern by one ankle. Stuffing the barrel into the floundering man's mouth he pulled the trigger. Even with the padding there was a resounding boom as Stapleford's head exploded into a soggy pulp. It would not be easy to identify him now; half his head had been torn away and the other smashed under a heavy boot heel.

Kernov was kneeling, poised, waiting, listening carefully for the sound of approaching feet and hearing nothing dialled Ulyanov in Venice. The signal was poor, but strong enough, for long enough, to impart all the salient information. He gave him the names of the Banks and told him that Stapleford had been discovered and that he had to kill the man somewhere near Waterloo. Ulyanov in turn told him to destroy the evidence and get back to the safe house. He would meet him there as soon as he got back.

Mikhail Kernov was thankful for his KGB training as he made an improvised booby trap from a C2 explosive grenade. This would allow him to leave by the route he had come, but blow the next person who opened the door to hell and back. Satisfied with his work he propped Stapleford's body against the door to ensure there was sufficient weight to force a hard push and thereby trigger the explosive charge. Then stepping into the walkway he moved with precision toward Waterloo – once there he would get a tube to Holborn and then a cab back. He could rest up; his leg was aching and he needed pain relief.

Stopping he popped two painkillers from their foil wrappers and working saliva into his cheeks he swallowed the two bitter tasting items with that fluid. The foul taste woke his senses. On red alert, he studied the people on their way toward the London eye, the slow moving ferris wheel with futuristic pods. Across the river he could see St.Paul's Cathedral and the barges converted into passenger ferries which would run back and forth to the Thames barrier flood gates.

As he stepped across a corner he noticed a man in a wheel chair opposite, an old man being pushed by a woman, a woman in her fifties who looked worn with caring. The couple were moving slowly toward him and he could see that the woman was labouring under the burden of responsibility. Checking behind and to both sides he could see nothing.

He did not see but felt the blow which destroyed his knee. The silencer shot passed through his right knee cap and bounced across the pavement shattering the windscreen of an oncoming car. Kernov could feel himself falling and was reaching for the pistol with which he had killed Stapleford. He was scanning and looking to aim, checking the car windows, the roofs and vantage points as he fell. Looking at his leg, a second shot tore off his forearm sending his lower arm, hand and the gun into the air. Blood spurted onto the pavement and he tried to move, to get his other good hand to the back-up weapon in his boot. The middle-aged women chair pusher stopped him with a well aimed kick and then something black was being pulled over his head. He was being moved, bundled into something. Then he was being bounced around inside something metal – a van and his blood was soaking into his shirt. He was kicking now, howling and kicking. A heavy punch landed in his solar plexus, and his wind left him.

Finally something sharp – a needle, bit into his buttock and the darkness engulfed him.

Chapter 31

"Now that was fun and Sandro here he had a laugh or two no?" Pancardi said to all, as he burst back into the laboratory. "So Alex where are we going to find this money?"

"Jeremy Stapleford was one of our best computer operatives," he replied. "I hope this man of yours is as good?"

Pancardi nodded in a way which invited continuation without a verbal request.

"Apparently he said he wasn't feeling well and needed some fresh air. He went out for a walk and has not been seen since. I have made a few covert phone calls while you've been out and about, sight-seeing."

Pancardi said nothing but Blondell could read his thoughts.

"They are trusties," he blurted, "I would trust them with my life."

"Let us hope that we do not have to?" Pancardi hissed almost inaudibly.

Blondell continued unperturbed. "After his lunch, when he failed to return, someone, and before you ask, I don't know who, went to his home and it looked like he had packed and left in a hurry. Stuff scattered but not in a burglary kind of way more in," he paused, searching for a phrase, "a on the run kind of way."

"Do you know this man at all?" Pancardi asked.

Blondell shook his head, "He just vanished from his flat without so much as a by your leave."

Pancardi knew they had stumbled onto something by chance, but his reaction was interrupted by his new young accomplice.

"Coffee?" asked Sandro, filling a kettle from the curved tap which ran from the autopsy table head to the sink. The water sounded harsh and hollow as it bounced into the chrome kettle with the surplus spilling onto the blood draining grooves and running freely back to the sink.

"Tea, I wouldn't mind some tea," Blondell replied. "I haven't had a tea for ages and my head feels a little thick from all the coffee."

"You English and your Boston tea," Pancardi remarked.

"Americans," Blondell informed, "The Boston Tea Party, that's American."

Pancardi grinned, knowing full well that he had tried to goad a response. "Where's Alaina?" he asked suddenly, changing the subject.

"Went back to her flat about half an hour ago, something to do with getting things together," Blondell casually replied.

"Are you insane?" Pancardi yelled. "There may be agents crawling all over this city now and she could be danger."

Blondell's face went white.

"Would you let your pretty wife be alone at such times, or Charlotte?" Pancardi hissed. "I will go now and bring her back."

"But you'll be followed."

"Then you must send someone from here."

"I'll go," said Sandro. "No one will follow me it is you they are after."

"It is dangerous," Pancardi smiled.

"I have seen him now," Sandro smirked as he talked, "and he has seen me, but I do not think he will recognise me in a crowd." He began laughing, "And besides if he did I could just run away. It's not like he can fly or anything – he is just a man." He extended his arms into wings and then into the one-armed superman comic stance.

"This is no laughing matter," Pancardi scowled, "there is more than one of them I am sure and now Alex has a man missing in London. This Staplewood what does he really do?"

"I'll go then?" Sandro said, his eyes questioning for a response.

"Go where?" asked Alaina as she opened the door and dragged in a small suitcase on wheels. "I thought I'd go to the flat Carlo. Lock it up and get what I needed. That way while they were busy watching you lot, I would get some peace and they wouldn't know where it is either. I don't fancy clearing up after a mock burglary. And," she added, "that nice young boy on the second floor he is keeping an eye on the place for me. I gave him €100 for…"

"€ 100 to observe nothing?" Pancardi interrupted.

"Yes you old skinflint," Alaina snapped "and we owe him € 200 more when we get back. Oh and I gave him your mobile phone number and mine just in case."

"€ 300 for nothing?" Pancardi's face scowled. "What a waste of our money."

"It's not a waste of money," Alaina smirked. "And it's not my money, it's yours," she paused, "so technically it's a waste of your money not mine. You don't think I'd give him so much do you?"

Blondell was laughing now as he watched Pancardi be boxed and gift wrapped before his very eyes. Alaina Tropani knew her man well and she had taken a huge risk, but she had calculated that the odds were in her favour. He liked that and he understood why she and his wife got on so well – each reminded him of the other.

Sensing he had lost any argument Pancardi turned to Blondell, and in an attempt to change the subject asked, "This Stablewood?" he said, "what else do we know?"

"CCTV camera footage shows him talking to someone in Trafalgar Square."

"And?" Pancardi was now listening intently.

"And? That's it. They went off toward The Strand and then they vanished into the crowds. Perhaps they went across the river on the bridge, or took a tube at Charing Cross. Either way they vanished. No other CCTV has picked them up yet."

"Then they must be in that area no?" Pancardi asked.

"Maybe, maybe not."

"Do you take sugar Mr. Blondell?" asked Sandro interrupting. He had returned to his tea-boy duties once the doctor had reappeared.

"One," Blondell curtly replied as an aside. "The most important thing is the information he found and that we could retrieve from his machines."

Pancardi nodded. "What did he find?" he asked.

"He had been searching for large cash withdrawals."

Pancardi nodded again.

"He started searching in Britain. I suppose he had figured that he ought to start somewhere?" Blondell continued.

Pancardi stopped him, his coffee cup raised to his lower lip, "So you did not instruct him to search?" he enquired. "The enquiry was on his own?"

"No," Blondell replied, obviously eager to continue. "He started the search and then suddenly he goes ill. Coincidence?"

"Bah !" Pancardi snorted and took a mouthful of coffee.

"I suppose he started a trawl and then was going to move on to other European countries later. Perhaps he found something?" Blondell was hopeful.

Pancardi looked unhappy, "Why start with the UK?"

"No idea," Blondell replied, "he was a bit of a maverick. Did his own thing."

"I'll tell you why," Pancardi snorted, "because someone told him to, that's why."

The room went silent.

"There is your informant. And now he has given some information to someone which is vital and run. What did he find that made him run for cover? That we must find out. How do we do this?"

"We go back to London?" Blondell replied, "after accessing the information more fully from the files here in Italy. We find Stapleford?"

"No!" Pancardi exclaimed, slamming his cup down hard. His hands were clapping like a trained seal in a circus – he was elated. "If we can find the information here in Italy then the contacts at your MI5 they cannot know, especially if we block the trace. So we must find what we need here."

"How precisely do we do, the blocking?" asked Blondell.

"By pulling in a few favours," Pancardi replied. "And that way the tail we have following us is none the wiser. We can keep him guessing and when we are ready we can all break and run in different directions." He smiled a broad smile, "Like the cat he cannot have all the mouses, no? So he must choose."

"It's mice, the plural is mice," Blondell corrected.

"And so the mouse runs and the cat he chases and the rest get away."

"Carlo you can't be serious?" Alaina squealed, "this man is

very dangerous and who ever he follows will be in terrific danger."

"Si," he added, "but it will only be me or Alex and either way we can set a trap for him."

"Well I don't like it," she snorted, "it's all rather hap-hazard."

"Like a good blues song no?" The old Italian added, "kind of loose like a noose."

Dante Pollonari entered the laboratory silently through a small, single, side door. He was used to being quiet, used to being ignored or unnoticed; his role demanded quiet stealth and subservience. His hair was dark, greasy and badly styled and his skin extremely swarthy, his colouring Asian, but his eyes surprisingly light and clear. When he smiled all of his teeth stood as individuals with clear gaps between them, small white solitary pegs set in a field of pink gum. Under his right arm he carried a file full of data print outs and in his left two single sheets of paper. His spectacles were thick and his eyesight poor and the black frames which held the heavy lenses were sliding down his nose. He coughed as he sheepishly entered.

"Dante!" Sandro Bichere exclaimed. "This is Dante Pollonari," he introduced the rather shy and shabbily dressed man to the others.

In reply Pollonari grinned and placed the papers on a desk and nervously pushed his spectacles back toward to the bridge of his nose.

"You have found something?" Pancardi asked.

"Dante Pollonari spoke with a nervous stammer, but it was obvious that his mind was as sharp as a razor. "I, s, s, started to m, m, m, make a trawl." Beads of sweat appeared on his brow.

"They tell me you are the best in Venice," Pancardi chirped. "There is no need to give us, how do the English say? Verse."

"It's chapter and verse," Blondell interceded.

"Si" Pancardi laughed. "You see how they treat me?"

It was clear that Pancardi was attempting to put the man at ease to enable some of his nerves, which caused his stammer, to be dispelled. Pancardi was acknowledging his skill, and encouraging his participation. Pancardi could wait, listen and then strike, rather than impetuously lash out and miss his mark. At that moment Blondell understood once again why those who worked alongside Pancardi or under his guidance came to respect him. He watched as the old Italian skilfully listened and then asked in humility for an opinion. Not once did he try to hurry the man and not once try to put words into his mouth, or complete his sentences out of frustration and impatience.

"This is most interesting Dante," he concluded. "Don't mind if I call you Dante?"

"N, n, no."

"Good then this," he began to summarise and Pollonari, nodded or shook his head at the appropriate points, "is what we know. Two large withdrawals one in Birmingham one in London."

Pollonari said, "Yes," clearly.

"So there were no others?" asked Pancardi. "Are you absolutely certain?"

Pollonari shook his head and Pancardi deduced the "n" as his personal stumbling block.

Pancardi continued, "Then one of these must be Alice? She has money transferred to an account and then she takes a large sum out of the system in cash. Who else does that?"

Blondell was out of the blocks, "Well someone else did, so there must be something else going on."

"But that Alex could be totally legal, could it not?" Pancardi replied.

"Rather a large amount to have kicking about in your wallet though, for a shopping trip," Blondell added.

"Oh my God," squealed Alaina after seeing the data, "it's London, she's still in London."

"And how do we know?" Pancardi reflected.

"The package was posted from London," Alaina answered.

Dante Pollonari was tapping the table with a ball point pen and struggling to be heard, "There w, w, were some other d, d, deposits made," he said.

"And these were made from the Broad Street bank no?" Pancardi smiled.

"I c, c, c, cross referenced the d, deposits with the w, w, ith d, d, drawals."

"And only one came up didn't it?" Pancardi asked.

Pollonari nodded.

"That ties in nicely." Blondell confirmed. "She's laying low in a hotel. I'll get my contacts to check every hotel in the centre. If she's there we'll find her."

"But you won't," Pancardi stated.

"And why not?" Blondell seemed peeved.

"Because she's not in a hotel, it would be too obvious," Pancardi reflected. "All that cash, the transfer, the safety, her safety. She is in her own place. Another bolt hole, and what is more, it is close to the bank." He began to unpack the information for the others to follow. "First she posts the package to here and then at the same time she makes the attack on you." He looked at Blondell, "The package takes time to get here, things go wrong, she has not a hiding place in London and so she runs. She must go somewhere to be lost in a crowd – a city. That is why the Stamford Street flat was blown up and the concierge killed. She was covering her tracks."

"I c, c, can say that the b, b, bank in B, B ,B , Broad, S, Street," Pollonari was becoming excited and in consequence his stammer more pronounced, "d, d, d, did have some uh, uh, other transfers on that d, d, d, day."

"Where to?"

"There were t, t, t, two," he paused to regain his composure and as he did so his eyelids fluttered and his tongue moved across his lips with the nervousness of a startled animal. "One to Zurich."

"And the other?" Blondell asked, adopting Pancardi's patience.

"Well that, c, c, c, concerned me, at f, f, first, b, b, because of the location." Dante Pollonari was struggling with both his own excitement and the way in which his audience were willing him toward a conclusion. "One of the d, d, deposits went to the B, B, B, Banko, R, R, R, Rolo in …"

"Not in Florence?" Blondell interrupted.

Pancardi was laughing and clapping again, "Clever girl," was all he was saying repeatedly.

"Bloody hell, cover me in sugar, flour and eggs!" Blondell exclaimed.

"You are then a pancake, or is it a doughnut?" Pancardi asked.

"She's going back to Florence." Blondell was thinking logically now, "Unless she wants us to think she is going back to Florence as a bluff. So why the money in Zurich?"

Dante Pollonari was tapping the pen again trying to attract attention, "The money in Florence will only be there in transit," he said in perfectly clear Italian. "After that it will be transferred to another location, but she has to do this transfer in person. It cannot be done in any other format. The money in Zurich can be transferred electronically."

"A mistake," Blondell whooped, "she's made a mistake, finally."

"Either that or she has some other plan organised," Alaina added.

"B, B, B, but this new rule she c, c, c, can not know about, b, b, because the regulation only c, c, came into f, f, force in Italy after the new E.U. law, ch, ch, changes."

"And these changes when did they come into force?" asked Pancardi.

"The f, f, f, fir, s, s, s, t," Pollonari was finding it hard to continue. He had not spoken this much in months.

"The first of this month," Bichere concluded for his friend.

Blondell immediately looked at his watch, "It's the 13th today, we've got her. It's our lucky day. She'll have to go to the bank in Florence and when she does..."

"And when she does," Alaina piped in, "this time you had better get it right."

Pancardi stood silently.

"What's the problem?" Blondell asked. "She's made the mistake you wanted?"

"If we can find this out so can others. We must be careful for both the sake of Alice and ourselves," he said, catching Alaina's eye.

Chapter 32

Mikhail Kernov came to in a warehouse, he was naked and his wounds had been crudely attended to. Strapped to an iron-framed bedstead his arm had a tourniquet around it and a pressure bandage had been applied to his knee. That had stemmed the flow of the blood, but the pain of the shattered knee cap was intense and he needed to relieve himself.

He started to urinate and the sound of his fountain stream resonated around the empty space. He realised in his disorientation that the frame he was strapped to was upright and that his feet were slightly off the ground. There was a heavy pain in his shoulders as they bore the brunt of his weight.

His eyes rolled as he struggled to see across the open space, he imagined it to be a hanger of some sort or a disused bondage warehouse; he could see nothing except his nakedness and missing arm and a severe chill made him shudder. Blood had been wiped from his torso and he wondered how long he had been there. The building appeared to jut out over a river or the ocean and he could hear the lapping of the tide below. The place seemed morbidly quiet and seeing his arm stump he knew that he had made a fatal mistake.

"Ah," the voice came from behind him, "awake then are we?" it asked. It was female and gentle and simultaneously a hand stroked his backside which he involuntarily clenched. The taut muscles in his body reacted to the female touch, and goose bumps began to appear on the flesh of his back.

"You are very fit," the voice continued, "beautiful almost." A warm hand was sliding between his buttocks as she spoke. "I bet you could crack walnuts between these," she mocked.

Her finger was making a circular motion around his anus now and he could feel the edge of a finger nail as she entered him. He winced and gave a sharp intake of breath.

"Hurts doesn't it?" she asked, "and yet men want to do that to us all the time. Bend us over and slide like baboons from one hole to the other – pure pigs, that's," she paused, as if remembering some ancient learning, "that's what you are, all of you, fuck-pigs, monsters. Only now it's your turn," she paused again, "and it won't be pleasant."

"What the fuck are you? Some woman with attitude? Piss off!" was his cracked, dry lipped reply. "What are you then a Lesbian? Do you get your kicks from munching the carpet? Licking the bean?" His voice was harsh and challenging and clearly designed to enrage his captors. "You're no better than a man," he paused, "worse in fact – you got no dick and however hard you try you'll never grow one." He let loose a scornful laugh which descended into a coughing fit of blood stained phlegm, which he spat out in defiance.

She forced a second finger inside his opening and he gave a sharper intake of breath in response.

"I'll ask the questions, if you don't mind," the woman continued, trying to force a third finger into him. "Now, you met one of our men in Trafalgar Square, Stapleford, the computer geek," she pinched hard internally, "and then low and behold you are nearly at Waterloo and he is not. I'd like to know where he is." She twisted her hand.

"Piss off Dyke," he screamed, as she ripped his rectum.

Her intrusion was becoming painful and he attempted to push his hips forward to avoid the pain, "Go eat shit," Kernov yelled.

"Oh dear, we're not very sociable today are we?"

The woman's hand had travelled now and she toyed with his testicles as she spoke. It was as if she were weighing apples in a street market, gauging the sweetness of the juice as she rolled them across her palm.

"Oh we could arrange for someone to make you do that, if you'd like," she was whispering into his ear. "We could get a nice big black boy to show you a good time."

Her breath was hot on his ear and her hand was pulling on his penis now masturbating him gently.

"Big aren't you?" she added. "I bet you'd like a tight little girl to fuck? " Rather than me letting some greasy old perverts fuck your arse until their balls were empty and your arsehole bleeding?" Her hand stopped moving, "Besides it's a waste, a lovely big hard thing like this." She squeezed his cock until the glans turned deep purple. "We could play hide the salami if you like?" Her hand movements doubled their pace, "All you have to tell me is your name."

Kernov shook his head.

The woman released his now hard penis and then did the same to the tourniquet on his arm. His blood started to pump out, a rhythmical squirting in time with his heart beat.

"If I left you here like this you'd bleed to death," she said, "and what a waste that would be." She retightened the tourniquet and he felt a sharp jab into his upper arm. "Novacaine," she said, as he felt the sudden stab of a needle.

A second woman was administering pain relief to his leg; she was dark haired, young and dressed in a white medical coat. She knelt before him, her eyes level with his erection as a second shot was administered to his knee. The relief was immediate and he felt his sweat drying on his skin as the pain subsided.

"So easy," the woman behind him cajoled, "life is full of choices. Sometimes they are easy and sometimes they're not." Her hand was rapidly stroking his erection again and he could feel his fluids begin to rise at her command. "The difference between pleasure and pain can be so simple. Take Corrina here," the sultry voice behind him continued, "she could slip her mouth over you and suck on you until your knees buckled."

Kernov felt the warmth of the girl's mouth as his erection was being stroked, pushed toward a conclusion by the voice. "Come on," it said, "she's hungry for you. She wants to drink you, taste you, suck on you and give you more pleasure than you could ever imagine."

Kernov felt a tongue tip searching to get inside him and the insistent hand of the speaker was now moving faster and faster and then his buttocks clenched and he gave a series of involuntary thrusts as he ejaculated.

The voice said, "So easy and so pleasurable."

The kneeling girl in the white medical coat now stood up, she was taller than he had expected; dark eyed, not pretty and yet not ugly either, the sort of non descript city girl one might pass everyday on the tube. And making eye contact with Kernov, he noticed sharp, cold, wolf grey orbs staring back at him. She opened her mouth and using her tongue moved his fluids around her teeth. She did not say a word; her actions said it all as she appeared to be savouring his full taste before she swallowed.

Instead, with lightening speed, she had forced her mouth on to his and was spitting his semen into his own throat. He attempted to turn his head but she had hold of his ears and his resistance was futile; something sharp was penetrating his ear and warm blood was flowing down his shoulder. Disengaging she opened her mouth again to show him it was empty and winking she walked out of sight behind the iron frame.

Kernov was spitting now.

"Not so nice either?" the questioner laughed. "Don't worry it's an acquired taste and maybe we'll get someone else to give you some." Her face was close to his ear, "You know, someone who wants to make you their bitch."

Kernov smiled and spat, "Capitalist scum," was all he said.

"So easy," said the voice. She had released his penis as his power subsided. "You see, we can give pleasure or we can give pain. But you know what that feels like don't you?" Kernov wondered if he were hallucinating as the voice continued, "In about 3 hours the painkillers will have worn off and then we'll be back to talk again." Her hand had moved to his backside once again, "And we can do things to you," she paused, "that you can't even imagine. The pain will be so intense that you will beg us to kill you. But we won't; so the choice is yours, pleasure or pain. Perhaps you'd like to think about that one."

She had stepped back and was no longer touching him as the heavy electrical current shot through his body.

Mikhail Kernov screamed, "Fuuuuuck youuuuuu," as his whole being tensed, as if he had multiple cramps; his body going into preservation mode, his eyes rolled and he stopped breathing. It was then that he knew the reason for his nudity and the iron frame to which he was strapped.

Suddenly the current stopped and his heart pounded to recover equilibrium.

"Hurts don't it honey?" the sultry voice began again. "Pleasure or pain; pleasure or pain, the choice is yours."

The current was applied again.

"You chicken shit. You fucking piece of slime," Kernov was panting, as the pain died away. "I'll rip off your head and shit down your neck. I'll tear you apart like a fucking roast chicken."

"Oh dear, see me quake, Mr. Whatever your name is," the woman replied. "You are just another one of the Russians we have dealt with in the past. You are not even that good. And besides, if I wanted to I could gut you like a pig and spread your entrails all over this floor. You are worthless. Worse than worthless, useless." She whispered into his ear, her breath hot and sultry, "I can kill you whenever I please, because I enjoy it," she paused again, "and you will answer all of my questions – eventually."

The current was applied again and Kernov's body went tense and then suddenly relaxed as he passed out.

"Right?" asked Blondell, "how do you want to play this?"

"Play Alex?" Pancardi replied. "We shall not play, we shall draw our quarry into the chase, we shall be the mices that catches the cat."

"It's mouse," singular, scoffed Blondell.

"Mice, mouse," Pancardi laughed, "then there is the house and the hices, no?"

"No houses," Blondell corrected.

"So," Pancardi was toying now, "mice and not mouses, but houses not hices? Only the English can make the language so complex."

Blondell nodded.

"And you think Italians are mad?" Pancardi laughed.

Blondell smiled back at the idiosyncratic ways of the man; at the way he often shifted from the sublime to the ridiculous when tension became too great. He had spotted the obvious anxiety in the younger Sandro Bichere and recognised the sheer terror in Alaina's eyes and had then moved to the word play.

"Well at least we don't stand on street corners gesticulating like we are conducting an orchestra. If one gets too close to you lot one could lose an eye," was all Blondell could muster to reply with.

"Does one ?" Pancardi mocked, using the affected English tone.

"Bloody right," Blondell said in response slipping into the vernacular.

"It is language which makes us more than the animals," Pancardi snorted.

"So who goes first?" asked Alaina with sudden clarity.

"We do," Pancardi replied.

She moved toward her bag.

"No not that we," Pancardi was now moving his hand so rapidly between Blondell and himself and repeating, "we, we," that all began to laugh. "Laughter is good no?"

"Case proved." Blondell mimicked the rapid hand action of Pancardi.

Pancardi's face suddenly darkened, "We go first and he will then be drawn off. Sandro he stays here and Alaina you go ahead to the Questura building and get some further access to the Interpol files; make some excuses for access; try and get them to believe we are still hunting. We will run him around for a while and then..."

"And then what?" asked Blondell. "They might not take your red herring."

"But they might think we have nothing and they will not know what we have found." He paused, "Then we go after Alice and your man Staple, what is it? Ford? And we find him too in the process."

"You have this all worked out don't you?" replied Alex Blondell.

Pancardi shook his head.

"What if this guy who is tailing us has no further need for us? What if Grillva misses him or loses him? What then oh wise one? What if his aim is true and his sight not jaundiced?"

Pancardi's voice dropped an octave, "Then he will kill us," he said.

"Well that is reassuring," Alex Blondell replied as he pushed open the laboratory door.

Mikhail Kernov coughed as a warm hand gripped his penis and shook him awake. The tourniquet on his arm was released once again and the build up of blood exploded like an ejaculation over the floor. The pain was intense but the release of tension a relief. Trying to estimate the amount blood, he wondered how long it would be before he went into a coma; he was beginning to accept that the last stage of his KGB training might need to be applied.

"Pleasure or pain?" the voice behind him asked.

"Arseholes," was his single word reply, as the tourniquet was retightened. "You think you are so clever. You fucking piece of slime. What are you going to do? Torture me until I talk? Well I'm talking now. Dyke! You can do what you like but you'll never be able to grow a dick." He spat blood defiantly across the floor. "Never know what it's really like to go balls deep in a woman. Look at you, you're pathetic. A piece of fucking scum."

"Right so you are awake then?" a female voice replied.

"Yeah I'm not so fucking easy to kill, you sack of shit, you fanny liking piece of scum." He spat again, "Go fuck yourself or your little friend, go pretend that you're a man. You're a chicken shit, an arse-wipe, a waste of a perfectly good skin. The best thing you could be is a bar of soap."

"Well what a temper you have?" The voice was calm, "For a man who we could slice up like a pizza and deliver where we want."

"Fuck off you little tart," he replied, "we had ways of dealing with your kind in the Motherland. I'd have had you dragging a fucking cart. You're not even worth fucking. You smell like shit, look like shit and that is a good clue, that you are shit."

"I like to hear defiance," the woman said softly into his ear, "it makes me wet."

"Well get your kicks honey because that's all there is for you," he paused as she bit his ear lobe. "Dyyyyke," he yelled as he tried to wrench his head away.

"Oh dear a little feisty aren't we, for an unarmed man? Or should I say a one armed man?" the voice cajoled, backed by a bitter ringing laughter. The woman hit the end of the exposed wound and a pain like Kernov had never experienced shot up his arm. "Wow, sensitive isn't it, and then there's infection. I think that without proper medical attention you could die. I can make sure you get that attention. All I need are a few little answers. We know you're Russian, and thank you for that little confirmation. You see you may have one of these," she held his penis, "but you are rather stupid. Perhaps we'll cut it off and make you eat it." She released her grip.

Kernov could just see her now near his severed arm; she was examining the wound as if it were a piece of porcelain in a show. Blonde hair with greying roots and a face stretched by Botox perched on a turkey neck; the nose was sharp, angular but he could not see the eyes. Focussing on her he spat out a challenge yet again, a challenge based on what he had seen.

"How many more years of pearl diving you got left, you mangled old hag. Taken a look at yourself in the mirror lately? More wrinkles than a tortoise, facc like a bag of spanners. Age, you can't stop that."

The woman said nothing.

"Go eat shit," Kernov spat the words out.

There was a sudden jolt of pain as his body went into spasm again and he thought he could smell the fine hair inside his nostrils disintegrate in the electric current.

"Not a good day Mr. KGB man," the voice continued, "not a good day at all. You are KGB aren't you?" it questioned.

"Go to hell," Kernov snapped.

"I think we'll all be going there," the woman laughed and turned up the voltage.

"Arseholes, you fucking slut keeper," Kernov spat and then gritted his teeth as he convulsed. There was more blood in his mouth from where he had bitten his lip.

"Oh what a difficult man you are," the woman was behind him now and squeezed hard on his semi-erect penis as the current was turned off. "Funny isn't it," his tormentor continued, "I once saw a man who had been struck by lightening. He had a perfect little hole in his head and another in the sole of his foot. It was as if someone had fired a spit right through him." She paused as if in thought and then her hands started moving. "I believe, though I cannot be certain, that his bollocks had simply exploded. Can you imagine that, a voltage of such magnitude that his testicles exploded? Now that would have been a sight."

Kernov could feel some form of cream or paste being applied to the gap between his buttocks. There were two hands now, pulling, poking, searching to get inside his rear opening. Something else was being pushed into him, something cold, something made of metal. His immediate reaction was to struggle against it, to fight the intrusion, but the more he resisted the more the item was pushed. He could feel his flesh ripping.

"This is going to hurt you far more than me," said another female voice. "The pain will become far more intense than you can possibly imagine. If we begin to heat this you'll cook from the inside."

"Fuck you," Kernov replied.

There was a sudden jolt of electricity which shot into his anus and Kernov's knees buckled in response.

"Your prostate, you should take care of that," the woman's voice continued. "Once this starts to heat that will be the first thing to explode. Like a pudding in a pan, only yours will still be inside you. That is soooo," she drooled the word, "going to hurt."

He could smell cigarettes now, he wondered if there were a third person behind him. The smoke was sweet and yet also stale and he could taste the comforting almonds on his tongue.

"Where did Stapleford go?" came the question.

"Up my arse," was Kernov's reply.

"If you carry on," the voice said, "we'll pull your teeth out one by one, and then shove them up that arse of yours."

"Ooo yoooo scary bitch," was Kernov's swift reply.

"Oh dear," said the voice. "Turn up the voltage," she ordered.

"Don't fucking think you can scare me with this shit."

Kernov laughed and tried to turn his head to see his tormentors. A cigarette tip burnt into the centre of his vision as his left eye went out. Suddenly his jaw was being forced open and some sort of rubber bung was placed between his teeth. Then came the pliers, gripping his front teeth and they wrenched at one of them. Blood started to pour from his gums and the pain became so intense he could hardly contain his mind. He saw the tooth held by the pliers, the root covered in the bloody residue of his gum and bone.

"Pain? A bad choice," said the voice, as the voltage bit into Kernov's limbs yet again. His body convulsed and he urinated on the floor.

His torturer stepped back to stay dry and slapped his face, "You filthy little pig," she said, "look at you pissing yourself."

As the current stopped the voice asked again, "What did Stapleford know?"

A second tooth was torn from its mounting and his mouth was turning to mush. He spluttered blood. The pliers had removed both central front teeth, ripping a gaping hole into the face of the Russian. His pain was excruciating, but he chuckled loudly as blood spurted from his nostrils, his blood vessels bursting in the further electrical current. His whole being contorted, twisted grotesquely, convulsed and then hung like a damp dish cloth on a washing line.

"For the last time," the voice repeated, "where is Stapleford?"

Kernov remained silent.

"What did Stapleford find?" the voice repeated.

Kernov did not move. The woman behind him pulled on his testicles and then punched him hard in the kidneys. His body did not react, it hung like a butchered carcass. Then the woman in the white coat appeared in front of the Russian and tugged at his hair, lifting his face from the slumped position of chin on chest to examine him – there was no resistance; his eyeballs rolled white in their sockets.

"He's dead," she said calmly, "looks like poison to me. Did you check his teeth?"

"I thought that went out with the Nazis," the gleeful torturer replied. "That is so..."

"Archaic?"

"Absolutely," she confirmed and lit a cigarette.

"What a fucking waste," said the coat. "What a waste of a man?"

"It's more important than that," came the terse reply. She spoke through the cigarette smoke which she pouted leisurely into the room around Kernov's dead head.

The woman in the coat turned and raised her eyebrows as if to question the remark.

"Wasted my time, wasted time, my time," the interrogator replied, as she inhaled deeply.

"Such a lovely body and a cock to die for. What a fucking waste," the white coat replied. "You know these Russians are hard as nails. Not like the Whitehall wonder boys, all public school and shagging and fagging. These guys are seriously dangerous."

"Well Russian or not we'll have to explain how this worthless shit died on us."

"But he didn't, he poisoned himself. We could just dump the body then and say nothing?"

The interrogator smiled, "Thames fish food?"

"Oh Christ do we have to dismember again? I hate that, it takes so long to chop it up. Can't we weight it down in the mud?" And then she laughed, a deep guttural laugh which carried the edge of pure sadism in it. "Well at least his bollocks didn't explode this time, that would have been really messy. Last time I had to get all of my clothes dry cleaned, and the guy at the counter gave me a look like you wouldn't believe. Thank God for lab coats that's what I say. I mean how many times do you take clothes in that are splashed in blood and spunk? "

"Walk slowly," Pancardi ordered, "we need the cat to follow the mouse. We must be the mices that catch the cat."

Alex Blondell thought about correcting the language and then thought better of it. Instinctively he knew the Italian was winding him up; he had seen it before and he was beginning to understand how the older man broke the severe tension with jibes. His mind played back the Dalvin room, in which Pancardi and Roberto Calvetti had made him the butt of their joke and he smiled learnedly, but said nothing.

"Let us hope," Pancardi said, as they had made their first four hundred yards, "that they do not find your man, before us."

Alaina Tropani saw them go, watched as Ulyanov followed, saw Pietro Grillva in pursuit, but missed the bearded shadowy figure which slipped into the chain with such subtlety as to be totally unnoticed by all.

"We go to the Questura slowly," Pancardi continued, "and then when we leave there, we go at high speed to the airport and head for England. That will make him follow because he will think we are on to something."

"You know you seem so certain that Alice is there, what makes you so certain?" asked Blondell, as they strolled through the park and across the bridges.

"I am never certain; just call it an educated hunch." Pancardi nonchalantly looked over his shoulder; he could not see the Russian. "Our quarry is very clever, no?"

Blondell remained silent.

"So clever that she thinks she can outsmart us. She will stay in Birmingham until the day she goes to Florence. She will arrange to transfer the money and then she will vanish."

"So she will stay put, because we expect her to run?" Blondell asked.

"Reverse psychology?" Pancardi was opening out now, "And what better place to run to than the last place we would think to go. Think how you would evade pursuers? Britain she is an island and you have all the ports and airports covered. If you set up surveillance for the beginning it is fine. Then nothing happens, people they become lazy, guards grow fat, and sleepy." His head tilted as they walked, "Then finally they become bored; so bored that they miss their quarry and she will go then. Alice knows this."

"How the hell can she know this?" Blondell questioned, guessing that the Italian's logic was probably correct.

"No man can know this Alex, but they can think. Think like the terrorist. We the guards must be alert all the time. We must never cease to observe, to watch. Alice she is like the terrorist, she can wait, and rest and strike only when she is ready. She only has to get it right once, with us it is all the time."

"But what if she has gone already?"

"Then we will have lost."

"And because she is your daughter you think you can read her thoughts?" Blondell was becoming cynical. "There are limits."

"Yes and no," Pancardi replied. He slowed his speech, "She is a hunted animal no? What would you do?"

Blondell coughed but said nothing.

"She will go to ground, lick her wounds, recover, set up a way to escape and then poof," he gesticulated a towering smoke cloud to illustrate his theory; " to her final hiding place and that we will never find. She thinks she has a safe lair in which to temporarily hide and lick her wounds, and that is Birmingham. Her final rest will come in the last place we would expect her to be. It is almost perfect, and then there is the making of the joke – of using the same bank that was robbed."

"We have to find her now or once she has gone she'll be gone for good?"

"So she will wait," Pancardi paused, purposely repeating the word wait, "wait and lay low until the time for excitement has passed. Wait for her pursuers to become sloppy with boredom. And then like a cunning fox she will slip through our net and be gone."

"You seem to have this all worked out?" Blondell replied.

"But this is just a guess."

"And you know that you are probably right, that's what's so infuriating," Blondell agreed. "Don't you ever get it wrong?"

"But don't you see?" Pancardi replied. "Alice has made one crucial mistake. She has to go to Florence; she must appear in person to move the money. She has tied herself down. She may not go tomorrow, she may not go next week, in fact she will wait. In Birmingham she will lay low and though we shall try to find her there, she can rest, revive and prepare and then one day, one hour in Florence and vanish."

Blondell was smiling, "So all we have to do is wait for her in Florence," he said.

"But you forget," Pancardi corrected, "your Stapleford man has vanished. If we have worked this out so has he. He has told someone, he was working for someone; and something has scared him so much he has run. And we are now in a race, the winner he gets the prize."

"So what do you suggest?" Blondell asked.

"If we go to Florence then we will be seen. We are being followed, no?"

Blondell nodded, but looked quizzical.

"So if we were to go on a stakeout then we might miss her and we will also draw all our enemies to that one spot. So let us go to Birmingham and find her first." The phone in his pocket buzzed, "Si, Si," Pancardi snapped and shut the phone. "That was Pietro. We have lost our tail."

"What?"

"We have lost our tail Alex, but Pietro he has decided to stick with him to see where he goes. We don't need to continue this silly charade anymore. I think we are no longer being watched."

As the two began to walk back toward the laboratory, a large bearded man crossed their path and then disappeared into an alley unnoticed by either. When they had passed he turned, reappeared and resumed his stealthy vigil behind them.

Chapter 33

"Soft shelled crab, cooked whole is one of our Cajun specialities," the waiter said.

"And this is absolutely delicious," Alice replied, when he asked her if she were happy with her meal.

It was going to be time to leave soon but she just wanted to taste this once again, and Clearwater Cajun Joe's, was the only place to get this, even if the waiter was obviously black country and about as true Cajun as she was. She had no idea when she would be back, or even if she would be back and this was her last chance to eat Cajun. Her celebratory meal for freedom.

She assessed the situation and wondered if now that some of Blondell's men had died, whether he would understand her threats against his family. She took a small mouthful of light batter which crunched as the soft fluid of the crab played upon her tongue; she savoured the rich complexion of the dish. The spices were aromatic and danced in her nostrils, while the sound of accordion and guitar, played at low volume, added to the wholesome back-woods swamp atmosphere. She knew that the Bayou might be a place to visit in future years, a place to explore as a simple obscure tourist.

Her wounds and bruises had completely healed now and her hair re-cut and styled by a visiting home hairdresser. The quality was not as good as the little roadside rescue she had stumbled upon that afternoon when she dumped the Bentley and the conversation not as interesting, but at least it had been anonymous. She had told the hairdresser that she wanted an expert cut and dye

– one that no one would be able to spot. And the young mother of two was only too pleased to take her time and get paid twice the rate. She had two small kids to feed. This was her little cash sideline she had told Alice. Her husband had a job at Staples making furniture, and it didn't pay that well, so she had a few clients who paid cash and what the taxman didn't know wouldn't harm him. Alice had agreed and gave the woman a £ 10 bonus.

Every morning at five she had gone for a run along the edges of the canals, carefully avoiding the emerging early morning shift workers who were too bleary eyed and engrossed in the daily toil of survival to notice her. She had varied her route and explored, avoiding the major thoroughfares. At times she had amazed herself at the massive clean up which the city had undergone. The concrete cubes of the 1960's had been replaced by modern chic, and the roads which characterised the industrial past, broken up or pedestrianised. The early mornings smelt of flowers and grass, and the air was clean: It was a new city, a modern city.

Usually back at her hideaway by six, she took a shower, had coffee and read for a while. Then she slept again until early afternoon. In truth she was finding the pattern of her life a little dull, she longed to be able to stroll around the shops, visit a coffee house and just watch the day drift past. She had contemplated whether she might actually be in a prison of her own design. A modern landscape of loneliness and fear, a panoramic panoply of isolation, the only advantage being she could move outside into the fresh air if she so chose. Knowing that if she did move too openly then she might be seen.

The television news of bomb attacks in London had dried up and only the turgid political programmes of the late night continued to examine the alternatives. None of them considered a solitary person setting off an explosion – the lone nut theory. Often she found herself laughing out loud as these nonsensical commentators belched forth some new theorem which gave them air time and public exposure. Her explosion had been discussed, dissected, theories advanced and rejected and yet she knew the matter was nothing more than a ruse. A simple diversion which any basic military strategist could have spotted. What made the whole even more absurd was the way in which the TV channels perpetuated the possible doom and gloom scenario, based upon nothing more than rumour. They dissected, endlessly, the possible political factions responsible – but all of them were wrong.

Alice Parsotti took a mouthful of wine, rich red and warming and followed that with a chocolate and orange tower dressed in cream and laced with Cointreau. Life was good – but now it was time to disappear.

⁂

Neither Alex Blondell nor Giancarlo Pancardi spotted the man. He was careful, thoughtful, well trained and he had watched them since Venice. He was big and powerful but the darkness of his visage had been reduced by the removal of his full beard in favour of the Van Dyke. If the surveillance continued for much longer he would have to shave his face clean. He had already changed from the jeans and plaid shirts into a more sophisticated style of suits and ties, with the ever attached brief case. He studied the pair from a distance as they entered the Broad Street branch of Lloyds Bank. His careful eyes scanned the building tops and doorways for back-up teams – there were none. He had watched them go in and then minutes later leave. The two had taken less than a few moments to decide upon their next move and he had seen them talking and laughing outside, in full view, and he wondered if that were for show, for an observers benefit – his. Blondell and Pancardi had not been followed and he wondered where the blonde man and his endless little companion were now. He had taken a gamble and he could wait; his logic told him that if anyone could find the woman, Pancardi could. Slowly his thoughts drifted toward his dead brother and what he would make of vengeance – fool hardy he would have reasoned, just like his wife, with whom he spoke regularly by telephone; at least he was thankful that she understood, or tolerated his reasoning.

⁂

At New Street Station Alice Parsotti stood in line on the platform; she had been there many times before and today she easily blended into the commuters, becoming liquid like them. A small number of personal effects were stashed in two pieces of luggage, one a guitar case and the other a knapsack. In the safe at her Brindley Place flat there was over £50,000 stacked in neat little piles. Next to it lay two clean passports, one British the other Hungarian; these were her escape documents should she need them in the distant future. The various taxes and charges had been paid for the forthcoming year and the next would be dealt with via an agent in Rome. It was to be her little English hobbit hole. In her knapsack she carried her travelling cash £30,000 and change in large notes, to reduce the bulk.

As she waited for the train she thought about Christmas. She had spent it watching television and eating and drinking wine. She loved the traditional Christmas cake with the smells of Brandy and Pine predominating; she had put up a tree, a real tree, which lost needles and was now long bare in some council dump. Lights in the city were gone, the madhouse of the sales had passed and the long dreary run up to spring had started. Her body was healed and rested, her mind sharp and her plans well made. No one had seen her, she had been to the bank and gone with such speed that even she could not believe her luck. She had been certain that she would have to kill again, she thought of the street CCTV, the police, and sheer difficulty of finding one person.

She wanted to get out of England now and longed to walk the quiet streets around the Duomo. She thought of attending mass in Santa Maria Novella and smelling the roasting chestnuts which the street vendors sold on frosty February nights. Once there, back at the house with Laurel and Rhododendron bushes and the seclusion up behind Belvedere she would be safe. There she could melt into the background and wait, wait until the time was right for her to transfer the money. Then a long bit of travelling; lock the place up for a year, see a few places, perhaps the States before finally returning when all the dust had settled. She thought about Duane Rightman and his drawl and wondered if others from the south were like him. She smiled thinking how easy it had been to dispose of such an irksome character.

Christmas in England had been nice, drinking too much, sleeping in the afternoons, but now as February drew to a close it was time to move on. Spring, with the wisteria in bloom was calling her back to Italy. April would bring the cart of fireworks and the medieval pageants to life and the Florentines would once again lift her spirits with their mad-cap markets.

On the train into London she watched as one woman opposite transformed before her eyes. The woman, who was travelling backwards, an action which always made Alice queasy, looked frumpy, unkempt and lacklustre. Alice wondered that she had not been sick travelling backward, but to her credit the woman applied her makeup which gave her face both depth and tone. Her oily skin grew paler, her lips brighter and her cheeks more well defined, finally she put two contact lenses into her eyes; an action which made Alice wince and then finally she licked the residual lipstick from her teeth as the transformation became complete. Alice looked at her hands but could see no wedding ring and wondered why the nameless woman put herself through the public humiliation of paint and paste every morning; wondered what man might approach her to try out his smile. She looked at the fellow travellers, men with their heads propped against the glass, mouths open like lizards in the sun. Others assiduously studying the mindless pap of daily journalese in their assorted future chip wrappers. The faces in the carriage looked from person to person but noticed nothing, the daily grind for cash had driven them into the stoic silence so much part of the British stereotype. Try as she might she saw no light behind their eyes; these were the people who just continued, slaved and saved, heading for their shallow graves – she was thankful it was not her plastering on her make-up so publicly.

In the window glass of the carriage she saw her reflection staring back at her. The thick spectacles, with plain glass, and the worn and tired sweater which had holes at the elbow. She looked neither young nor old, instead she had gone for a dowdy, ageless non-descript look. A look which spoke of disinterest – disinterest in men and disinterest in herself. The clothes came from a charity shop, Help the Aged, or Cancer Research, she could not remember which, but she remembered the face of the old woman who served her. The woman had smelt of sandalwood soap, and there had been the slight undercurrent of milky vomit, as if grandchildren had impregnated her skin with the smell of their belched greetings. Alice had wondered how many grandchildren the woman boastfully bragged to friends over; how many times photographs had been plied. She looked at Alice as if she were something odorous which had crawled in under her nose. It was as if she knew of Alice's plan, knew of her unwillingness to breed, and her false teeth had given a mock smile when Alice had paid for the items she now wore.

"Oh fuck off," she had wanted to scream as she grabbed the woman by the scruff of the neck. "Take a fucking look at your meaningless life. Breeding, working behind a counter and the endless homely get togethers where son-in-laws commented on the succulence of a Sunday joint or the content of a sherry trifle. Alice had wanted to yell but instead had simply smiled back; a knowing smile which extended the gulf between them.

Alice flipped her left wrist over to examine the Omega wristwatch. It was perfect a piece of precision wrapped in gold and held in place by the finest soft leather – she was glad of her wealth. It was 8.13 am and by 11 am she would have dropped her bags, checked in and be melting into the crowds at Gatwick. Her mind began to recall the smell of the leather bags in Georgio Chiari's shop on Via della Scala.

She was going home.

Chapter 34

Pietro Grillva urinated into the screw top bottle which he then placed in the milk crate with the others – there were eighteen and this new one made nineteen. Mentally he calculated the amount of time he could remain without moving. There were five empty bottles left – he would have to cut down his fluid consumption. Each vessel held a full litre and he marvelled at the level of fluid excreted from a single human in the space of four days. The van was beginning to stink too, stink of sweat, and the chemical bucket in the corner was growing riper by the minute; he had thought about emptying the contents down a nearby drain, but realised that he could not make one single mistake. So he sat in a smelly van with the reek of his own faeces clinging to the air like a fart in a lift. One trip to the drain he had already done, a second might be his undoing. He had gone to the drain at 4 am, the darkest hour before dawn; the time of the dawn raids; experience and training had conditioned him into believing that was the best time. He was certain that the Russian was alone in the house and that he would not see him. Even they had to sleep he reasoned, KGB or not he too needed to recharge his batteries. The second visit to the drain would have to wait. If his cover were blown then the blonde man would run and there would be no hope of tracing him. He knew he needed a shower too, he could smell himself.

His eyes had begun to bulge like onions on a stick from the constant peering through smoked glass; he needed a clean shirt and a decent meal, but this had been the best cover he could devise at short notice. The first week he had spent in a variety of cars and small vans, and now he had graduated to a full size wagon in which he could stand, stretch and sleep. The mattress, now scattered with empty sandwich packets, gave him a chance to bed down. It left him vulnerable but he knew that his quarry also needed to sleep. He had spoken with Pancardi at the beginning of the month and true to form the old Italian sleuth had managed to get a second surveillance team in place to give him some respite. They were totally clean and beyond corruption, mostly due to the loyalty which Pancardi had inspired whilst being in the Questura.

Christmas had been miserable, cold and rather dreary. He had watched as the Russian walked; on one occasion he had followed at a discreet distance and nearly blown his cover when the Russian had entered a corner paper-shop, and as he passed, unaware that he was inside, came out. They bumped into one another and Grillva had apologised, using English and the Russian had shown no reaction beyond an acknowledged smile. Nevertheless Grillva had been careful not to let that happen again. In fact he had been so rattled by his sudden folly on that day, that he returned to the van to ensconce himself more quickly.

Grillva had called in for back-up immediately, just in case, and was then driven past the Russian as he walked back to the house. He was certain that the Russian had not spotted him and breathed a sigh of relief as the incident passed, unnoticed, forgotten. Another team took over for a few days and then Grillva returned for a further stint. These were younger men, stone hard, and beyond reproach, the kind of impressionable youngsters that would die rather than give way – Pancardi's SS he called them.

It had given him nearly a week to sleep and recover and get into deep discussion with Pancardi. This however, had always been done by telephone, so that Grillva was not noticed or recognised by anyone.

Blondell had gone to spend time with his family, who had now returned from enforced exile and Pietro Grillva had joined them for a few days – Pancardi had disappeared, though he could be contacted by telephone. Pietro liked that about the detective; he took care of his men and put himself in the firing line rather than them.

January had dragged on and February looked no better. Pancardi had both banks staked out. They had missed the woman in Birmingham, and she had gone to ground, vanished like mist, but they had Florence covered.

Since Venice Grillva had tracked his man, shadowed his every move; even though the quarry was rarely on the move. At times he even wondered if the man might have slipped away unnoticed and days passed, but just as he thought about investigating the house the man would suddenly appear. Show himself at a window, or receive shopping deliveries from dull vans brightly decorated with company logos.

Today was just like every other day – Pietro Grillva was bored to death; surveillance bored; end of a long day bored. Bored to the point where he had to do something, anything to stay alert.

The razor rasped across his face as he wondered how long the man would lie low.

How long he would rest on his laurels and where and how he received communications, the phone was line was tapped and yet remained silent. At night curtains were drawn and lights went on and during the late morning curtains were drawn back and windows opened, presumably to allow fresh air to circulate. Apart from that the place looked empty or perhaps occupied by a pensioner.

That morning, as Grillva shaved, a house-to-house salesman was working the street, clipboard in hand and Grillva had studied him moving from home to home like a resigned religious evangelist. Blue jeans were covered by a shabby jacket which had seen better days; his shoes were worn and he looked like the type of man who had fallen upon hard times. Shoulders slumped he moved from door to door smiling and grimacing in equal measure. He called, was rejected and stoically moved on to the next door; when he called at the Grillva house the blonde man under surveillance answered the door. Grillva wondered if he had gone or was going stir crazy too, when he invited the shabby seller in.

They were two men locked into an unknown and ridiculous charade of cat and mouse. Grillva wondered if the blonde man might kill his visitor, take his clothes and attempt to leave in disguise. Then he reasoned that there would be no point unless he had somewhere to go, he, Grillva, would stay put, wait for the call to arms.

When the salesman left the house, he seemed to be glowing with expectation, if not slightly disorientated. Then disregarding the next few houses he walked straight past Grillva's van. At the side of the vehicle, and unseen by Grillva he suddenly stopped, listening intensely.

Inside the van Grillva foolishly nicked his chin and as he reached down to grab a piece of tissue to staunch the flow of blood, knocked an empty Coke can onto the floor. The resonance of the falling can had the clarity of a ringing bell and was enough to tell the listener outside that there might be someone inside. Quickly he walked away and disappeared into an adjacent street and then entering a phone box dialled the number he had written on the back of his hand. The mobile phone rang three times before it was answered. The caller had seen a land line in the house and wondered why the foreign guy had given him a mobile number.

"Mr. Uls?" he asked.

"Yes," Ulyanov replied.

"You are right, there is something strange about that van. I think there's someone in it," he said. "I heard something, well I think I heard something but I couldn't really be sure. It sounded liked a can being dropped or someone kicking a bucket." He snorted gleefully at his own sense of humour.

"On a scale of one to ten how certain are you?" Ulyanov asked casually.

"Eight," came the ginger reply.

"Right," Ulyanov paused, "well if you walk back to the house, quickly, like you've forgotten your clipboard, I'll give you the money."

"OK," replied the man, "but are you sure it's safe. You said the guy was a bit of a nutter."

"Look," Ulyanov laughed, "if you'd fucked his wife he might come after you. But you didn't I did." He was coughing with laughter now, "The shit can sit there for days and rot as far as I'm concerned. We said £500 didn't we?"

"You did," the salesman replied, thinking he was about to be paid money for old rope.

"Then come and collect." Ulyanov slammed the receiver down and drew the automatic from behind his back and fitted a silencer to the barrel. His suitcase was packed and the house was ready to be left. It was time to go if they were on to him. Kernov had been taken, that was obvious by his failure to return, but Ulyanov knew he would rather take the cyanide capsule lodged in his rear molar than give the game away. Kernov had given him the information he needed, but he could have done with the man now more than ever. If his information was sound then he needed to go anyway, perhaps providence had smiled on him and a little bit of luck had finally fallen his way.

A few moments later Pietro Grillva watched the salesman return to the house and collect his clipboard and also a small plastic carrier bag. Then the man turned and disappeared in the direction from which he had originally come; his pace was quick and his step urgent. Around the corner, out of sight from the house and where Grillva could not see them, two men stepped from a car and man-handled the salesman and his clipboard onto the back seat and then drove away. The plastic bag of money lay discarded in the gutter, its open mouth, fluttering an invitation to any person that passed.

It was a fourteen year old paperboy, with a thirst for stardom and fame that found the item; being a dutiful citizen he took it to the police and reported it lost. Some weeks later he lay claim to the unclaimed sum and bought a Mexican 1960's Stratocaster copy and a Fender Amp for the band which rehearsed in his parent's garage. Years later, after his band The Hump Monkeys third successful album, he would claim that fate had given him the cash, almost as if it had been his destiny to become a guitar god.

Less than half an hour later Alexei Ulyanov appeared at the door with a suitcase.

Pietro Grillva reached for his mobile phone and sent a short text to Pancardi, simply stating that the blonde man was finally on the move.

Alexei Ulyanov left his front door and with a few strides was out into the street and walking toward the van on the pavement. Once he reached the side of the van, he placed the suitcase on the ground. He drew the silenced pistol from the small of his back and emptied the whole clip into the vehicle, spreading the pattern across the vast expanse of metal. With a swift flick of his left index finger he released the empty cartridge carriage and as it clattered to the ground rapidly replaced it with another drawn from his back pocket. Keeping low and on high alert he was using all of his KGB training and instinct.

Fumbling, Grillva attempted to punch a second text into his mobile pad, but his fingers were slipping in the blood which was running down to his fingertips from the wound at his neck. Survival instinct began to kick in and he drew out his automatic with his free hand and fired at where logic and clattering sound told him the gunfire had come from – but his target had gone. He could see his own blood pumping and knew he would pass out in less than a minute. Returning fire through the body of the vehicle he dropped the phone and steadied his pistol in two slippery hands.

At the back doors Ulyanov dropped to floor level and emptied a second clip.

Pietro Grillva was hurled forward against the metal mid-screen by the impact of the bullets. As the front windscreen shattered his arms and legs took on a marionette like quality. Flailing as if he were swimming in air, his abdomen opened like a Halloween pumpkin and his liver and spleen fell onto the harsh metal with a resounding slap.

Ulyanov was at the front of the vehicle now and fired once through the shattered glass. One clean clinical shot which passed through the top of Grillva's cranium and lodged itself in his lower back region, having exploded several lumber on the way down. Then with a swift motion he replaced the gun to the small of his back and retrieved his case from the roadside, cursed the hole which Grillva had made in the item in his frantic effort to return the unwanted fire, and walked casually around the nearest corner.

As he passed the telephone box he started to whistle a cheerily tune. The strains of Whistle While You Work lifted his spirits and let him know that he was back. His information was good and the foolish man in the van had so easily fallen into the trap. He thought he had seen the man before, but the escapade outside the shop had sealed it. It had been the same man who had fallen onto one knee to take a shot at Parsotti in Chelsea; the same man who had screamed a warning from the upper window in Blondell's house and the same man who had shot at them as he tossed a grenade from the repair truck. This time he had made sure – this time he was dead.

"But I have never done anything like this before," said Sandro Bichere.

"Well I can't do it can I, she knows me," Alaina replied. "But I can spot her and point her out to you when she comes in."

Bichere seemed unconvinced.

"And there is not likely to be a fire fight," Alaina reassured. "Look you wear this earpiece and that keeps us in constant contact. If you think there is a problem then you sing out and..."

"But I'm not a field agent," the young man interrupted, "and I don't think I can pretend to be a teller or a manager wandering around in a bank," Sandro replied.

"Neither was Ennio," Alaina grimaced, "and he didn't deserve to die."

"The grace of the holy virgin, I don't wish to die either," Sandro's voice lifted an octave. "This is more than I bargained for."

"You've seen the Russian too, so we have an advantage," Alaina was trying to be convincing. "If the thing gets sticky then you just back off."

"But he's seen me," Bichere squealed.

"Then you are even."

"I don't call that very even. That's like putting a beaver up against a bear," he paused nervously, "and I feel like the buck toothed beaver here. Besides this guy is a mean killer, Pancardi said he was a KGB man. He's not going to be an amateur like me."

"Well I think you're a pussy not a beaver," Alaina laughed, "think about how easy it will be. And besides you have a bullet proof vest on. How dangerous can it be?"

Sandro Bichere was not convinced.

"That's bloody terrible, you're so dodgy," Blondell blurted indignantly. "You would risk her life, the woman you are supposed to love, to a catch a criminal?"

"Not just any criminal – my daughter," Pancardi snapped in reply. "And who said that I loved her? If we cannot get there or Alice gets to Florence before us then we have a fall back plan.

Alaina is a clever thinking woman she will not jeopardize the apprehension possibilities."

"But they are both unused to being in the field and those others that are after Alice are KGB. Last time they used explosives. This is so dangerous, it's almost ridiculous. If the Russians get cornered this could turn into an absolute blood bath."

"Listen Alex," Pancardi's voice lowered in genuine concern, "I would rather use someone that we can trust, but we have run out of people, we have no one else we can really trust. Look at Stapleford, my officers, your people." He stopped suddenly. "We are on our own, there is no one we can really have faith in." And then as if to qualify his reasoning he said, "Besides Pietro will be behind the Russian. He is one of the best. He will cover their backs if we are not there."

"But what if he fails?" asked Blondell.

"Then we shall be like Laurel and Hardy. It will be another fine mess, no?"

"This is no joke!" Blondell exclaimed.

"I know, but what else would you have us do?"

Blondell looked directly into the older man's eyes, "What if it all goes wrong?"

"Then I will take the blame."

"It's not a question of blame," Blondell replied, "I don't want anyone hurt."

Pancardi shook his head, "Neither do I."

"But if they use grenades like the last time – there will be a mess. A real mess, with body parts everywhere. I've seen it and it isn't pretty."

"Now you are coming clean," Pancardi smiled.

"Look," Blondell replied flatly, "I've seen the results of a grenade attack. There wasn't much left when the dust settled. They had to wash him out with a hose – then bury him in a large polythene bag. Blood and bits everywhere."

His face lengthened and he looked as if he were stepping back inside his memory. Re-living the pain and shock of something which he had witnessed first hand, but would rather forget.

"Pietro Grillva had best be alert and keep the Russian under close surveillance then," Blondell continued. "Not just watching, but watching like a hawk."

"He will," Pancardi smiled. "He is the best man; he will not let the Russian get past him."

"I just hope he is as good as you say." Blondell licked his lips which the nervousness of the situation had dried.

"Better," Pancardi confirmed, "the Russian will be no match for Pietro of that I am certain. Look, we know things are happening and Pietro has sent a text to tell us that the Russian is on the move. He will stay silent until he has something to tell us. Have some faith Alex – have some faith."

Chapter 35

"And therefore, members of The House, I commend this Bill to you in the understanding that this government's legislation will have a profound effect and impact for the next forty years. We," he paused to stress the we, "we cannot rely upon the MOD for this," he paused again for effect, "our great country..."

There were jeers from the opposition benches and shouts of, "Sham, shame, lies and shameful."

"We the government of this great nation," he continued, "must act now, to stop the endless march of terrorism. The time has come to act and the public must know that this elected house intends to do all within its power to safeguard our citizens. If this means that we must take the fight against terrorism to the terrorist, then this we must do." His voice was raised and the body language became confrontational. The index finger of his left hand was poking accusingly into the air, as if admonishing a wayward child. "They can never be allowed to win; must never be allowed to win and we," he was almost shouting now, as fine spittle was showered before him. "We will not continue to turn the other cheek and watch our innocent citizens massacred in the streets – we will act. And you members of the opposition must work with the government to combat this scourge of the twenty first century. Terror can never win; must not be allowed to win; the 9/11 style attack must never happen again and this legislation will go a great way toward achieving this. "

There were further cries of, "Shambles, and traitor." Accompanied by the Speaker of The House shouting, "Order, order."

When the division bell sounded, the chamber quickly cleared and the Right Honourable Michael Cleverly MP left his colleagues on the Conservative benches and walked quickly to his consultation room. He shared the room with a member for a backwater, whose primary involvement in politics was the Commons Catering Committee and trying to get his hand up the skirt of any young secretary that was employed by the Conservative Party. Usually he was either half drunk, and sleeping during debate, or late. Cleverly had encouraged him to abscond, especially as the recent addition of televised debate did the man, and the party, no favours.

"Better to not be there at all, than to be asleep, that way your constituents might believe you were actually doing something," Cleverly had advised.

His colleague had accepted the advice eagerly.

When Cleverly entered his consultation office he loosened his tie and took his jacket off. His trousers were held in place by a pair of braces which crossed behind his shoulders and he was dressed in a two tone shirt of fine pale blue pinstripe with a non matching white collar. He was in his early forties, clean shaven, an open Christian and church goer with a squeaky clean reputation. There had been some public discussion about his involvement with a weird religious sect but he had weathered the storm by talking about religious values in general, rather than citing his own Church of the Temple Brethren; a branch of the Catholic Church which had connexions to both the Knights of the Temple and the later transmogrification – the Jesuits.

At election time Cleverly always appeared at hospitals and old peoples' homes; talked with pensioners in the street; walked and knocked his constituency doorways; kissed babies in front of the local press and showed his mock-turtle caring side and crocodile tears of concern. His hair was neat and well groomed, though on top he appeared to be thinning. In general he portrayed the open approachable man, so smooth he was able to slide right under a door without ever opening it. When crisis hit the party, he had been lucky to be in the right places to avoid it. Choices he made had come good and as a result he had risen; and now as member of the cabinet he was doubly careful about who he slept with and what he said.

His marriage was a sham, sexless, abortive and dull. His children were much the same and his wife a rather timid and nondescript woman, who enjoyed the cash and country home, while her husband languished in London or was touring the country. She had no interest in sex, or who he slept with, as long as she did not have to. The thought of him approaching her with a view to copulation sickened her now; it was a political marriage.

"Who the hell let you in?" Cleverly asked, as he heard a noise.

"That girlie of a secretary or is it a PA now?" the woman replied. "You see we're women, and nobody thinks women are dangerous do they?"

She was tall, well dressed with blonde hair which was turning grey at the roots. Her facial skin was taut – the result of surgery, he deduced. She spoke softly but both her voice and her mouth seemed cruel. She had the look of a woman who could use people and then casually toss them aside. He wondered if she might be a lesbian, but then reasoned that she probably wasn't. That was often the issue he had discovered with men and women and their assessment of each other. Men had to like cars and football, whilst women capable of intense acts of cruelty, had to be lesbians. Likewise, the thought of an eighteen stone, rugby playing macho-man, being queer, was incomprehensible to some. In the time he had spent at college he had seen it all and after years in the commons nothing shocked him anymore.

"He died," she said, "didn't say a damn thing."

"I thought we told you not to kill him?"

A second voice pierced the room from the darkness of a dimly lit corner, "He poisoned himself – cyanide probably. Hidden in his tooth, like the old Nazis. Was he a fascist?"

"I told you never to contact me here," Cleverly barked.

"We thought that you would like to know," said the dyed blonde, "what we did with the body."

"I don't give a flying fuck about it." Cleverly snapped. "I just want you out of this office. You've been paid so what the hell are you doing here?"

"Oh my God I can't believe it, what a potty mouth you have. Did you learn that in school? Wykehamist language? Did some of the older boys teach you that dirty word before they made you their fag? What other dirty little tricks did you learn to perform?"

Cleverly went red, "What the fuck do you want?" he asked.

"That Michael," said the voice from the dark, "must be apparent. We being the gooood," she drawled the word, "girls, that we are, are ready to sell you some information."

Cleverly swallowed loudly, "Go on," he said.

"We dumped the body, that was rather messy but he'll not be pieced together easily."

The blonde woman lit a cigarette.

"You can't smoke in here," Cleverly barked.

"Oh do fuck off dear heart," she casually replied, with affectation, "we can smoke in here, piss in here, do what we want in here. In parliament no one can hear you scream."

The second woman in the dark also lit a cigarette and Cleverly could see the darker complexion and the wolf like eyes which were illuminated briefly and then were gone.

"Look," he repeated.

Both continued to smoke unperturbed.

"No you look," the blonde woman added. "You may be used to getting your way with your minions but we're professionals and we could drown you in the toilet right now and make it look like some choking, wanking fantasy."

Cleverly's temper was rising at the threat.

"We can give you the name of the bank that your little Italian slut will be at. We know that much."

Cleverly's temper was smothered with politicians calm and the silence he had learned at school. These women would be dealt with later, he concluded after silent consideration.

"If you want to know then it's going to cost you a little more," the dark woman said, as she puffed smoke into the air. "£50,000 more in fact."

"I don't have that here," Cleverly quickly confirmed.

"We know that," she replied. "And we expect you'll have to talk to your paymasters whomever they are?" she chuckled. "Then if you're a good boy for them, well I expect they'll give you the cash," she paused, "and it has to be cash."

"And what the fuck do we get for this?"

"You get the bank, the country, but unfortunately not the date, but I'm sure that won't worry little old you will it?"

"How much more will that date cost?"

"That I'm afraid is not for sale. Our insurance old boy, don't ya know? Oh and this is a one time non-negotiable offer. Mess up and we simply vanish."

"I could have you," he slowed his speech, "disposed of?" Cleverly threatened.

Both women laughed in unison.

The blonde woman looked at Cleverly and with quiet calm repeated, "The country, town and bank, yours for £50,000. Your Russian is gone." She made eye contact with him, "But if you try to cheat us," she smiled, "we will expose a sex scandal involving you and little boys."

"No one will believe you," Cleverly replied.

"Really? What even with a real live witness and your suicide. Think of the scandal, and all for £50,000. Don't ever threaten us, others have tried but failed. You may think you are clever, Cleverly, but we are pure bitches and with us it's full fucking time."

Cleverly was thinking rapidly about the virtue of involving yet another party in the hunt for the Romanov jewels. He wondered how The Elders would react to further requests for cash. Clearly these two had no idea of the value of the robbery or the content itself and they could be bought off. Later they could meet with an accident; simply be bodies in a house fire or something like that.

"St. James' Park?" he offered, "At two?"

"Where precisely?" the woman asked.

"The curved bay by the duck feeding area. There's a bench there. I'll be there at two."

"Fine," said the woman from the dark. "One of us will be there."

"Not both?"

"The other will have a high powered weapon on you and if there is any monkey business she'll blow you in half."

As the door closed behind them Cleverly cursed both and picked up the phone,

"I'm going to need another £50,000 Roland," he said. "They have the bank and the country, I think they...."

"Do you believe them?" the man named Roland asked.

"I do."

"Fine. I'll send a man to your office at what time?"

"One at the latest."

The voice on the phone continued, "If however you are wrong Michael, there are going to be very many people who are likely to be very very upset. The Brethren do not take kindly to being swindled. Especially by one of their ..."

"I understand completely," Cleverly interrupted.

"Good, then let us hope the information we are about to buy is worth the cost."

Alice had spent the morning clearing the fallen leaves from under the old sycamore tree where the motorcycle had remained parked up under the tarpaulin. The light green of the mildew had settled on the dark green of the cloth and the wind had gathered leaves into neat little piles, which had been driven under the edges of the covering. As she worked she expected to see families of hedgehogs ensconced for the winter, their tight faces rolled up against their vulnerable bellies. She loved the way animals seemed to be more honest; their cruelty was borne out of necessity and not out of the calculation for a percentage. She reasoned that she was like every other predator.

The house was set back from the road and had served as the base for her life in Florence, such as it had been over the past two years. She had been there twice and each time she had made a show of having lights on and activity happening. She had had the place renovated from top to bottom, as at one time it had been a holiday let; it was neither grandiose nor plush. Like her place in the Maldives it was homely and though it held no memories in the way of photographs and family heirlooms, it was home. The really important parts of her life were now firmly deposited in a bank vault in Zurich. She smiled as she wondered what any would-be thief might make of a haul containing old photographs, some soft toys and a few pieces of cheap jewellery. These things however, were Alice's life history, wrapped gently in tissue and laid in a shoe box.

She lifted the leaves into the cart she had been trundling around, but no wildlife appeared as she raked. It was now April the 14th and the warm weather had started, though there were days when the wind was still keen. The day the Titanic went down, she suddenly recalled, and on the 20th Bram Stoker died in obscurity; one event so big and so powerful that it overshadowed everything else. One boat and so many dead and the death of Mr. Vampire himself, now almost completely forgotten; one event overshadowing another. She pondered on luck and chance and how things sometimes just happened. Then it came to her in an inspirational flash, like a bolt of lightening it came and her mind raced through an idea. It was as if she had been waiting, waiting, biding her time for the final piece of the puzzle to slot into place, and now while she was relaxed and carefree, doing gardening of all things – it had suddenly arrived. In two days the mediaeval pageant for Easter would be in full swing, she could drop down into the centre, walk past the Duomo and check to see if she was being followed. A quick series of double backs through the crowd and then into the bank, sign the transfers and be away into the crowds again.

She tried to start the motorbike and the flat battery made an electronic start impossible. She forced her whole weight onto the kick start, once, twice and on the third time the bike roared into life. A Norton 750, black and red, old fashioned, stylish and fast – her final escape through the alleyways and back streets should she need it.

Carrying the battery to an old shed she placed it on charge and deciding she needed a coffee break, went into the house. As she entered the back door she casually lifted the phone from the cradle against the wall and removing her earring punched in a number with her thumb.

"Could I speak to the manager?" she asked, almost casually.

There was a pause and some music was piped down the line – Vivaldi. Eventually a voice appeared at the other end. A deep voice of a man annoyed by the obvious intrusion.

"Si Doletti," he said.

"Good morning," Alice cheerily replied, and then gave her name and account details.

On hearing her name, the response of the man was instant, but guarded, and Alice immediately picked up on his reaction. She wondered if he had a notion of who she really was and whether the bank had been staked out in readiness for her arrival.

"We've been waiting for your call," he replied, now overly eager. "You wish to make a withdrawal?"

"No just a straight transfer."

"Good, good," the manager chirped.

He made no attempt to dissuade her, no attempt to engage her in investment opportunity discussions; no attempt even to set up a formal meeting to try, as any decent manager would, to persuade her to leave the money with them. There were no questions as to why the contact had taken so long – nothing in the way of business niceties. Something was wrong. He was almost like a man who was talking to an unwanted lover in the presence of his wife. Alice could feel his tension.

"I wish to come into the bank on Friday?" Alice requested.

"But the bank is closed on that day," the manager replied. "Closed for Easter."

"I know," said Alice.

The man became flustered and Alice sensed, more that knew, that another person was listening on the line – a person to whom the manager was deferring for advice. The pauses in his speech were too long and his hesitant replies lacked the confidence of leadership. She could visualise him as he spoke, shrugging and accepting the hand signals of instruction.

"I won't be flying in until Friday morning," she said, "so should we say about 1pm?" She in contrast exuded confidence. There was no acceptance of the closure, no doubt in her mind that the bank would open for her to make the transfer.

"Fine, fine, absolutely fine, 1 pm fine, fine," the manager replied. He was eager to get off the phone – that much was blatantly obvious.

Alice could almost hear his sweat dripping into the receiver. "What ID do I need?" she asked.

"Passport, just a passport," he replied nervously, "just a passport," he repeated.

"And just in case I'm a little late, what time does the bank usually close?"

"Five," Doletti almost squealed, "Five at the latest."

"Lovely," said Alice, "Bye, bye for now then."

Costa Coffee, sat like a secure mooring buoy in the busy Oxford Street human tempest; two women sat drinking hot-chocolate in a window seat, as the full pace of London life rushed past them. One, a young woman, slightly plump, was sitting nervously as if on interview for a precious, much needed job; the other, an older woman, was relaxed, smiling, and almost casual.

"If you are telling me porkies Marjory?" said the older woman.

"No, this is Gospel," Marjory Humboldt replied, "I saw him write it down. I helped to do the computer work."

The older blonde woman smiled at her drinking companion. She clasped both of her hands around the cup as if it was mid-winter and the heat of the beverage was warming them. Her eyes were stone-cold and her parchment skin was older than her face. The backs of her hands had wrinkles and the skin had lost elasticity; the bright nail polish served only to underline the disparity between both hands and face. Her dyed hair needed doing again at the roots and Marjory wondered why she had not bothered with that detail, when she so obviously had had surgery.

"So we have a deal then?" Marjory Humboldt asked. "£15,000 I think we agreed?"

The older woman smiled as a dark haired woman drew up a chair to join them.

"She's alone," she said to the greying blonde.

"In this handbag," the older woman said, as she placed a brown leather satchel style bag on the table, "is the cash. Now just for the record? " she asked, "Stapleford has vanished you say."

Humboldt nodded as she spoke, "He's not been seen for days, but the bank and the city of Florence are confirmed. I helped him to find them. I didn't know what he was looking for." She looked from woman to woman, "There's been people all over the offices and one of the men said that there might be something in it for me, if I knew anything? He said I should talk to you."

"That's very sensible of you," the dark haired woman replied, smiling. "Clever girl and pretty too."

Marjory Humboldt let out a nervous chuckle in response.

"When we leave," the blonde woman continued, "you take your bag and go and buy yourself some nice frocks. Perhaps something to sparkle and delight, a jewel or two; some of those lovely Italian knickers, all lace and thongs and frilly edges." She licked her lips and paused, "You never met us, you don't know us, got it?"

Marjory nodded, "But I don't, I genuinely don't."

"And that's the way we want it to stay."

"But," the dark haired woman interceded, "if you are telling us lies, I will come back to visit. I'll pour drain cleaner down your throat and slice you up like a turkey. In fact when I've finished with you, you won't even be able to look at yourself in the mirror without being sick. Do you understand me?"

Marjory Humboldt nodded. Now she looked petrified; this was not what she had expected at all; all she wanted was to get the money and leave.

"You have a nice day now," the women laughed in unison, as they stood up, pulled on coats and made for the door. The dark haired woman winked at Marjory, through the glass of the front window, as they passed outside. It made her shudder, repulsed her, but did what it was intended to do – frighten her.

Marjory Humboldt sat staring at the bag on the table, almost too scared to touch it. She wondered if there was anything inside it. Anything more than a few bits of newspaper? Then suddenly she grabbed it and opened it, half expecting it to be empty. Inside there were crisp neat piles of twenty pound notes, with bank bands around them; she noted fifteen in batches of £1000 and quickly closed the bag. Suddenly she felt scared that someone might have overheard the conversation and try to steal her money from her as she left the café. She looked at the adjacent tables and noticed nothing but courting couples and tourists and breathed a sigh of relief. Nevertheless she wanted to get away now – her senses pushing her adrenaline levels to panic flight mode.

A large smile of success appeared on Marjory's face as she left the building. Simultaneously the two women vanished into the tide of inhumanity; washed aimlessly from shop to shop and on toward oblivion.

Chapter 36

Marco Doletti was the last person to leave the bank. His keys had locked all of the inner doors and the consultation and teller areas were now sealed and the alarms set for the night. He had spoken briefly with the security guards and now he was talking to a young man and a woman with striking red hair. They seemed to be laughing and joking almost as if in relief.

Outside in the cold night air the three people quickly split up. Doletti walked slowly, ambling almost, along the gravel path which ran beside the road, while the other two crossed through the stationary traffic and wove between the whirl and thrash of humanity. Neither of them noticed the old beggar who was sitting on the ground observing them. There was a cup and a sign which read: Old and poor spare a few Euros.

The beggar sat, eyes down cast, observing the red-hair and the long legs which belonged to the forensic scientist that had been engaged on the robbery. Her face had been emblazoned in the papers at the time, and the beggar remembered clearly – but she was easy to remember. Both passed the crouched figure without a second thought though Sandro Bichere had dropped 50 cents into the paper cup as he passed. Once the pair were out of sight the beggar rose and walked quickly through the crowds to follow Doletti.

Marco Doletti was a man of simple habits. He and his wife had a small house on Don-e-Scula. A small select development tucked neatly behind the Boboli Gardens. Houses were walled and gated and the drives lay in red paving like the lolling tongues of giants lapping an empty hillside. It was modern, wealthy and soulless. They kept a dog, went for walks, ate out in cafes and generally enjoyed a comfortable life in preparation for retirement. They were a safe couple who had inherited a little wealth from previous generations and had been posted to Florence after the public relations disaster; the robbery which made all the major tabloids in Italy. Doletti had been appointed as a lacklustre, but safe pair of hands. Someone quietly steadfast, someone without imagination and someone without flair. A perfect replacement for his predecessor. In short – he was a boring man.

At Mario Juno's restaurant he sat and ate a bread stick in preparation for the arrival of his plump wife; who appeared in a fur coat with a small black poodle under her arm. The watching beggar sat down on the bare flags opposite, back against the wall, which rose to stop the invading Arno from storming into the city once again and rattled a cup as tourists passed. The ground was cold and the bare cardboard served to provide some insulation but the wind was bitter and droplets of moisture were forming on the beggar's small nose. It was hard to say what gender the beggar was and even less easy to establish what it saw or noticed.

Throughout the meal the woman kept up a constant flow of tit bits for the animal that took the morsels one by one and then hid behind the woman's copious coat as customers came and went.

Finally the middle-aged couple rose and placing the dog on the ground began the slow amble home. Twice the woman bent to pick up the residue from the squatting animal and placed it, like a precious gift, into the dog bins which lined the pavements.

The beggar rose and followed, stretching as it did so, rubbing to restore the circulation.

"Friday 1pm," said Alaina as Pancardi began to eat. "I can't believe it. You are finally going to get her." She placed a forkful of food into her own mouth.

"We must not count our chickens must we Alex?" was Pancardi's smiling reply.

"But we have to be there," Blondell added.

"And what if she sees us, what then?" Pancardi asked.

"She'll be gone and you'll never see her again?" Sandro Bichere offered.

"See," said Pancardi, pointing gently with his fork, "even the boy has more sense than you. We have waited this long, we can wait a little longer."

"So what are you actually going to do then?" Alaina asked.

"Nothing," Pancardi replied. "Absolutely nothing. Alex and I will not be far away, but we will be far enough away not to be seen."

"Why won't you say where you are?" asked Alaina.

"If you don't know, then you can't say or give us away can you?"

The man sitting at the table next to them coughed and Sandro noticed his Van Dyke beard which looked grey and old. His hair too was grey and Sandro observed he dined alone; briefly he wondered what had happened to his wife. The man smiled politely and tapped his chest repeatedly as he took a drink of water – the implication being that he had inhaled rather than swallowed something. His eyes were watering and Sandro wondered if someone might need to perform the Heimlich manoeuvre, but just as quickly the man regained his composure and the incident was forgotten.

"Look," said Pancardi, "she is due to come to the Banko Rolo after 1pm. We shall be near the bank and then after she comes out we can take her. No fuss just a quick lifting job. That way no one inside the bank is involved and no one outside gets hurt."

"But Friday is the day after tomorrow," said Alaina. "She definitely said Friday?"

"Good," said Pancardi, "only this time we will be ready. We will all be there before her."

"Do you really think she has no idea we are on to her?" Alaina asked.

"How could she?" Blondell asked.

"She could guess," Bichere added, "like Jesse James she could always be one jump ahead.

"She does not know," Pancardi concluded, "we are finally one jump ahead."

Alexei Ulyanov was smoking a cigarette looking at the Bank Rolo building across the river. He could see a group of bins at the front entrance leading to a driveway. He planned his extraction method as he observed. That was where he'd leave the car. As they came out he would...

"Pretty isn't it?" the woman asked.

Ulyanov nodded.

"Lots of the tourist come over here," she smiled, "if you know what I mean? This district is interesting and fun to come in."

That was all he needed, a tart trying to pick him up for a few Euros.

"Do you like what you see?" the woman continued, opening her coat to let him see her fully.

She was dressed in stockings and suspenders, a bra which accentuated her cleavage and a throng which gripped her sex like the fingers of a grasping hand, and nothing else. Her flat stomach was toned and her legs shaved and smooth and Ulyanov knew she would sport a Hollywood in her profession.

"Fifty for a blow," she said refastening the coat. "And we could do that right now if you want. A hundred for a half and half, and if you want extras we can talk."

"What do I get for a thousand?" Ulyanov asked.

"As long as you're not into some real painful kinky shit, anything you want, at least twice, or as many times as you can manage." She thought he was joking.

"Ok," he said, "deal, shall we go?"

"Money first."

Ulyanov had been formulating his plan to extract Parsotti outside the bank. Trying to find a way to get up close without drawing attention. He needed an angle, something to give him cover, and then suddenly providence had smiled down and the whore appeared. It was perfect.

Alice Parsotti had watched the Dolettis and their little black poodle enter the small house. And as they switched the lights on and began drawing the curtains she entered the garden over the wall. She dropped to the ground in total silence but the dog noticed her and jumped forward with a bark. The barking dog was silenced with a simple application of fuss – it did not seem to mind the smell of the intruder and eagerly accepted the morsels of biscuit which she had in her pocket.

Dressed as a beggar she could smell herself, and knew that the simple disguise had everyone fooled. Nobody seemed to want to stay too long near an acrid individual, including the forensic scientist who had been so unobservant, and whose name she could not recall. Like one of those facts buried deep in the sub-conscious she knew that when she no longer required it, it would suddenly jump into the fore-front of her mind. She had not seen Pancardi or Blondell but she knew they would not be far away. She hoped they would not be too close but she also knew she had to take the risk.

Doletti's wife came to the back door calling for her dog and Alice seized the opportunity promptly marching her back into the building with the loaded .38 calibre pointed at the back of the woman's head.

Marco Doletti was watching television as the pair entered with Alice holding the poodle and the gun.

"Mr. Doletti?" she asked almost casually, "my name is Cicello, Claudette Cicello, we spoke earlier today." She thought that he might suffer from angina by the ruddiness of his complexion. And as she spoke she could see he was a man who was easy to scare. "What a lovely, little place," she continued, as she motioned for the woman to sit. "I expect you know all about me though, don't you?"

The man began to shake his head rapidly.

"Everything they told you is absolutely true." She smiled broadly, and placed the poodle on the ground. He promptly jumped up into the lap of Doletti's wife. "I am your worst nightmare," she paused, "but I'm glad I found you in."

"What do you want with us?" Doletti asked meekly.

"Nothing really," Alice answered, "just the transfer of the money and then I'll be on my way."

Doletti looked at his wife for a solution.

"No help there, I'm afraid," Alice smiled, "you see these two are my collateral. If anything goes wrong I'll kill them both and leave you some polythene bags to clear up the mess. I might even send their eyes back together in a jar – pickled."

Doletti said nothing, but his hands trembled.

"Tomorrow morning," Alice continued, you are going to go to work as usual, and then you are going to make an excuse and come home, because your wife is not very well. When you come home you are going to bring the transference documents and all details to me. You will transfer the money to a special numbered account in Zurich. Do you understand so far?"

Doletti nodded.

"Then when the transaction has been completed you will come back, give me the security codes and then I will tell you where your lovely wife is?" Alice waited until the man nodded, "Then everybody gets to live happily ever after. Rather simple really. Nod if you understand."

"How do I contact you? They'll be watching." Doletti asked.

"You don't contact me," Alice replied, "I contact you."

"Sometimes the transfer has to be verified by computer and they might suspect?"

"That is your problem. Get it wrong and bang, bang your wife's dead. One clean bullet to the head." Alice smiled, "Would you just listen to that," she said. "I'm the poet that doesn't know it."

Doletti was nervous and his hands were fumbling one thumb over the other in a nervous rolling motion.

"Is that your car on the drive?" Alice asked.

"Yes," Doletti replied.

"Good," said Alice. "Keys? A nice big car the BMW plenty of boot space."

Mrs. Doletti looked from Alice to her husband and back again, her face contorted into sheer horror- she feared what was coming.

Doletti passed the keys and Alice stood by the door, "The dog can stay here," she ordered. "You come with me."

Outside Alice opened the boot and made the woman climb in.

"I can't," the woman wailed, "I'm claustrophobic,"

"Get in, you do as I say," Alice replied, "I don't care what you are. You make a sound and I'll kill you right now." And with that she drove the car up to the electronic gates flicked a button and was gone. As she drove away she could hear the woman whimpering in the back. At one stage she thought Mrs.

Doletti might have been sick, but she didn't care enough to look.

Once back at her house she backed the car into the garage and left the woman in the boot.

Chapter 37

When morning dawned Marco Doletti walked to the bank at full speed, he wanted to arrive early and get things underway before anyone would suspect a problem: Suspect anything come to that. He needed a little space and then with a bit of luck he could get the transfer done during the morning rush.

In the house at home the poodle was becoming distressed because it had not had either a morning constitutional or food. The whole routine was upset and in consequence, the animal defecated on the kitchen floor and then crept under the sofa to sleep, knowing a punishment would come later. It hated the man when he became agitated and angry because he simply forgot about her. It was the woman who really cared and she had not been there that night.

Doletti was already inside and scuttling about, moving from teller to teller like a giant terrapin turtle, when Alaina Tropani arrived accompanied by Sandro Bichere.

"Good morning," she said cheerily. "It's colder out there today; you wouldn't think that spring was well under way. How are you?" she asked innocently, as she removed her coat.

"Fine, fine, really fine," he nervously replied, anxious to elaborate.

"Did you sleep well?" Bichere asked.

And again the man replied uncharacteristically, "Why wouldn't I sleep well?" he asked. "Sleep well, of course I sleep well; I'm not the kind that doesn't sleep, I don't suffer from stress. I like the job! " he exclaimed, before walking off.

Bichere assumed that the man had had an argument with his wife, or that some other issue had made him tense. Perhaps the idea of opening tomorrow, on Good Friday, when the pageant was on upset him. Perhaps he was a devout Catholic and deciding not to pursue the matter further he walked to the teller's desk, where once again he would take up his position behind the closed sign.

His role was to observe, look for the Russian and the woman and anyone who seemed, "Out of sorts," Pancardi had said, "someone shifty." Bichere had joked that if he saw anyone in a mask and a striped shirt with a black bag he would immediately alert him.

Pancardi and Blondell were ambling along a small lane which ran up to San Miniato al Monte, the same lane which Paul West and his crew had used all those years before. The lane ran beside some dry stone walls through which gates passed into the homes of the wealthy. Tuscany at its best; landscaped gardens with large expansive swimming pools hidden behind wrought iron gates which stank of plenty.

When Blondell spotted Ulyanov he grabbed Pancardi's arm and pulled him into the shadow of an awning which overlooked one of the antique shop windows. La Bella Mori Antiques spoke of money and pulled in tourist after tourist to collect items which were salvaged from the deceased rich and famous; those once treasured possessions, the spoils, which greedy vulturous relatives had cawed and fought over.

"Down there," he hissed, "the Russian, that bloody Russian is here. Shit he's here, now we are in really big trouble. The bloody game's up if that's the case. Look," he pointed, "down there next to that woman. I'm sure it's him." He was straining to see, "It is him," he continued.

"Not possible," Pancardi replied, "you're seeing things. How could he know where to come?"

"Hells teeth," Blondell replied. "Look, he's walking past the bank with a woman. Oh my God he's scoping it out. He knows, Jesus Christ how the hell does he know she is coming here?"

Pancardi's eyes strained into the distance and try as he might he could not make out a familiar face. All he could see was a couple walking hand in hand as they passed in and out of vision behind trees and bushes.

"Why are we walking up here?" Blondell asked, "we should be down there."

"Because we know she will not be here until Friday?" Pancardi replied. "And I want to have everything covered, escape routes and everything. This time there must be no mistakes. If she does run this will be our very last chance. All these years Alex we have been so close and each time she has…"

"So why is the Russian here?"

"The same reason we are? If it was him."

"So who tipped off the Russian?" Blondell asked.

Pancardi shrugged.

"That bloody manager that's who. Christ almighty is there no one alive that we can trust? He must have told someone – that's the only thing that can explain it." He was becoming excited, "Hell!" he exclaimed, "this is all going to turn to shit. I wanted to lift her quietly, just the two of us, get her under arrest and be out of the country before anyone knew. Now it will all go crazy. If he knows who the hell else knows? The next thing will be the paparazzi again and then you and I will be seen and the whole thing will be a mess – another Amsterdam."

"We must stay calm," Pancardi replied. "There may be someone, or is it your Foreign Office?"

"I think I know who is behind all of this," said Blondell, "I know the leak comes from the Foreign Office, and I think our man is right up at the top. I have a file and when this is over," he paused thinking carefully. "Under secretary or junior minister maybe, something right up there. It has to be someone at that sort of level. Someone who has clout, and influence."

"Do you have any real proof in this file of yours?" asked Pancardi.

"Some," Blondell replied, "but I need more detail. That Russian could probably give it to us."

"Enough? Are you are sure?" Pancardi asked again.

Blondell studied the couple who now had their backs to him and he began to doubt his sanity. Perhaps he was seeing things, becoming paranoid, and the man below was nothing more than a humble tourist. Then suddenly he couldn't see the couple anymore.

"We could get a little closer?" Blondell requested.

"If we get closer Alex, and it is the Russian," Pancardi hissed, "and he sees us then our cover is totally blown. The whole thing will turn to mush and somebody might get killed. Last time they threw grenades and ..."

Alice Parsotti had spent a very quiet night tucked up in her warm bed. The Doletti woman she had left in the boot of the car, inside the garage. Even if she had screamed, from in there no one would have heard her. Alice toyed with the idea of killing both her and her husband and wondered whether both would fit into the boot. If they did she'd shoot them and leave the vehicle in the drive. Eventually the smell would give the crime away, but by then she would be long gone and the flies would have done their work.

She drank a coffee, flicked on the TV and then ate some cereal. Twenty minutes later she was in the garage with the Doletti woman.

"Please don't make me go back in there," the woman pleaded. "I need to go to the toilet and I won't say a word I promise. I won't scream."

"There is a toilet through that door," Alice ordered. "It's a utility room. I will wait here and if I even think there is a problem I'll shoot you. Make no mistake about that.

Gina Doletti sat relieving herself, and wondered whether she should text someone on her mobile phone and reasoned against it. She had no idea where she was, so what was the point? Unless they could use satellite tracking and then the woman might find it. It was too risky and she wanted to live; let her have the money it wasn't their money and the bank was insured. She needed to stay calm and she knew she could not go back into the boot of that car again.

John McDermott sat checking the vista from his window. He had washed the grey dye from his hair and shaved away the Van Dyke beard. As he studied his face in the mirror he wondered at how easily he had managed to track Pancardi and Blondell. They had not even been looking for him, despite his links to the robbery; he had managed to evade them with ease and here he was now, ready to act. His reflection stared back at him, his beard gone; he could see the resemblance to his deceased brother. If Jimmy had been there he would have counselled against his present action; but he knew it was the right thing to do – for his own conscience.

Below him the river flowed easily and the balcony gave him a perfect view of the entrance to the bank and all of the major entry and exit points. He sat quietly studying the distance; less than half a mile he made it through the sight scope. This was the perfect spot – so serene so neat and so unknown. He was far enough away not to be seen and yet close enough to be effective. On the small coffee table in front of him lay the clip of ammunition; all hollow tip copper inner and all coated in Teflon for high velocity accuracy – flying grenades he called them. Jimmy had shown him how to use them once; back in Scotland they had tried the shells on a wild stag. The single body shot had made a complete mess of the internal organs. The stag had run on for a further twenty odd yards before the legs buckled and the lower jaw slid into the highland turf like a ploughshare. He had been pleased with what he had seen.

Already he had spoken to his wife and told her that he would be home soon. His daughter had clapped in her excitement, when he had a few brief words with her on the telephone. He just needed the one chance, a tiny bit of luck, and then he would simply disappear.

On the bed lay the case with the weapon assembled; in the morning he would set up slowly and be ready for Parsotti. He thought about his brother again, who would have told him he was an absolute idiot, and then while drinking a second coffee he noticed familiar faces in the scope. Pancardi and Blondell had led him to the right place, of that he was now absolutely certain.

The red-haired scientist Tropani was inside with a young man, that much he had established, while Pancardi and Blondell were somewhere near the rear of the building. Much as he would have done – covering a possible escape route. And then suddenly there he was again, the blonde man from Venice; briefly he looked for the smaller lithe follower but he was nowhere to be seen. Twice he checked and double checked – the woman with the blonde man was walking hand in hand and he wondered who she was. No matter he thought, I just need one opportunity.

Slowly assembling the tripod he clipped the sight scope into place on the rifle. Might as well give it a whirl he thought, in readiness for Friday. He balanced his body weight behind the weapon, lowered the tripod to adjust and the barrel now rested on the balcony balustrade – it was rock-steady. He was seated, comfortable and ready. As he studied Ulyanov across the river a small red dot appeared on the image in the lens. A dot so fine and so light that it was hardly noticeable. It marked the spot below Ulyanov's left eye where the bullet would enter, guided by the laser sighting – were he to pull the trigger right now. McDermott imagined the Russian's head exploding like a pumpkin blown apart by fire crackers. There would be shards of bone and pieces of face scattered across the road and the lovely companion would be screaming as her decapitated lover crumpled in a bloody heap. It would be impossible for him to fail now. He smiled and then fitted the silencer to the weapon and took careful aim.

❧

"I told you it would be easy money," said Ulyanov. "The easiest money you'll ever make and all you have to do is pretend. You do that all the time," he added, "fake orgasms to keep the customers happy. Just a bit of acting really; and you don't even have to take your panties off and let some middle-aged loser fumble around and slide all over you."

"You mean, I don't even have to screw for it?" the whore asked.

"Nope," Ulyanov replied. "Later we'll get some lunch and then we'll walk along this bit again and at about five or so we'll go back to your place."

"And then I suppose you'll want me to do something really kinky?" she asked.

"Nope."

"Not even a blow job?" she asked, almost disappointed. "I'll give you something special," she added.

But his face was cold, dead eyes, lacking in any imagination. "Nope. I'll just stay the night; you'll get the rest of the money in the morning and then you can do as you like," Ulyanov concluded, as he drew her into him and kissed her for effect.

The action served to cover the surveillance should anyone be observing, though he had not seen the old Italian and his sidekick yet. He was certain they would be somewhere close, but not too close. That would give him the advantage, he reasoned, just long enough to get the red-head into the car and away. By the time everyone got active he would have her out of Florence. Then into a safe hideaway to get his questions answered. He wondered how long she would last under torture. Whether she would scream when he dug one of her eyes out with a spoon and showed it to her, or dripped sulphuric acid onto her finger nails until they began to dissolve.

Doletti was beginning to sweat and Sandro Bichere noticed that his movements had become staccato and rather uncoordinated. He was constantly looking at the clock and he had already visited the central computer desk seven times; on each occasion he had entered something; the final time he seemed to be punching in something which he had written on a scrap of paper.

"Alright?" asked Bichere, nonchalantly as he drifted toward the man out of sheer boredom.

As he approached Doletti became visibly agitated, and started to shift uncomfortably in his chair. It seemed to the younger man that he was trying to complete something, something he did not want seen.

"Done," he suddenly said, and smiled at the young man. It was as if he had completed some urgent task and then relief hit him. The screen in front of him went dark. "Done and dusted."

"What's done?" asked Bichere.

"Oh nothing really, just a little thing I had to do for a special customer. E mails and some other little things. I wanted to get it all done before Easter and especially Good Friday. But it's all done now, thank goodness, that's been worrying me all morning, and I think in about half an hour I am going to go for some lunch."

Doletti's mood had lightened considerably and Bichere sensed, rather than knew, felt rather than deduced, that something was not quite right. The man was now too light, too relieved, too everything in fact, especially for a man about to come face to face with a woman as cold blooded as Parsotti. In truth he should fear her, not gaily skip about like he was off to some summer fair.

"In that case I'm going to have a coffee," Sandro lied, and walked toward the rear of the bank where staff went to relax a little, and take their breaks. Doletti watched him out all the way and then turned back to the computer screen; once illuminated he copied something onto a small note pad. Bichere was watching from the doorway now. Watching the man throw a second piece of paper into the bin and shut down again. He wished he were closer.

John McDermott sat watching the Russian and the woman through the telescopic sight. He tried to reason what she was, a plant, a decoy, an accomplice. Either way it would make little difference – if she got in the way on Friday he would have to be swift and decisive.

On the bedside table lay his passport and an open-ended plane ticket from Rome to Edinburgh. One simple hit, maybe two at the most and he had five opportunities in the clip. Then gone, vanish into the unknown. They would not even know it had been him – it was perfect. He'd take the train from Florence central; no one would suspect that he would head further into Italy. They'd all be looking at Pisa and an early exit. Planning and precision as Jimmy had always said, "Don't be a hot-head, don't do anything without planning it and never over- reach, if you over – reach you'll fall, so don't." He could hear his brother's voice now and saw the smiling face nodding at him. Suddenly from nowhere, into his imagination, came the face of Paul West the friend he missed.

"There's something wrong," Sandro said. "With the bank manager."

"What do you mean?" Alaina asked.

Sandro looked rather sheepish. "Well he's very nervous almost jittery and he has been shifty. Like he's been doing things he shouldn't have."

"That's called a job Sandro," Alaina laughed.

Sandro did not rise to the bait. "Ha, Ha" he replied, "but I'm serious he did something at the computer there and then wrote something down on a scrap of paper which he shoved into his top pocket."

"What was it ?"

"That's just it, I don't know. But why did he get nervous when I got near him and why a scrap of paper? People don't normally do that."

"Unless they don't want someone to see something. Maybe he's got a mistress tucked away in some little corner."

"Well if he has, he's going to see her at lunchtime today. He told me," Sandro added.

"Told you he had a mistress?"

"Told me he was going out to lunch."

"That is strange."

"And he threw something in that bin, but if I go to look he'll know that I'm checking."

"When is he going to lunch?" Alaina asked.

"I'd say about now," Sandro replied, as he watched the man push his arms into his coat. "Quick get on the phone to Pancardi, I'll check the bin."

Parked in the Doletti's car Alice Parsotti watched, as the blonde Russian passed her with his arm around a woman. Her instincts told her to abort and leave the woman next to her sitting there. Her mind was racing now and she knew the man she had just seen had been in Chelsea; the man with the grenade was the same man walking along the edge of the Arno. Simultaneously Marco Doletti stepped into the street and started to walk toward where Alice and his wife were parked – there were only split seconds to decide. Alice decided to stay.

Sandro Bichere had emptied the contents of the bin onto the desk, and was fumbling through the scrunched up scraps. "It says Zur...

6789-5678-3456-," he said, as he unravelled the smallest scrap.

"It's an account number, he's done the transfer." Alaina said, as she rushed to the main entrance and pulled her mobile phone from her pocket. She was looking up the street but Doletti was no where to be seen, he had already passed the slight curve in the road and was gone. In the distance, however, she spotted Ulyanov and the woman.

Alice Parsotti got out of the car and intercepted Doletti – the exchange was swift.

"I've done it, just like you asked," Doletti said, passing her the scrap of paper from his top pocket. "They all think you will be here tomorrow, so they were not expecting this."

"The early bird catches the worm. Your wi…" Her reply was cut short.

Ulyanov saw her and instantly recognised her – his reaction was to draw a weapon. His companion screamed and Doletti heard her and immediately broke into a panic run. A heavy footed run, such as only over-weight middle-aged men can do. A pantomime run which consisted of sweat and virtual heart failure. A run toward his wife and his car and safety.

"Doletti has done the transfer for her," Alaina squealed into the hand set. "He's left the bank and he's on his way toward you and the Russian is there."

Pancardi's reaction was instant and he was running, hobbling, and shouting to Blondell, "She's here now, she's ahead of us again. The manager," he panted, as they appeared from an alleyway. Instantly they saw the Russian and he saw them. Alice saw all three and the world slowed to a tenth of normal speed.

Blondell was firing and the Russian was firing and Pancardi was running, running toward his daughter. Doletti was at the car with his wife and as he opened the door an explosion ripped into the serenity of the Florentine air and bits of car and the couple flew past those on the street. A human hand hit a bystander as he crouched to avoid the gun fire and the result was instantaneous apoplexy. Alice's booby trap had worked and vital seconds been gained in the shock; the pursuers covered their eyes to avoid the flying debris and glass. Alice stepped back, jumped a low wall and turning was running now, running hard up toward the old church of San Miniato. Ulyanov was firing and another woman in a parked car was screaming – pandemonium had taken hold.

Pancardi turned and fired at Ulyanov and then he too vaulted the wall and was after Alice. Blondell was less than a second behind him.

❧

On the hotel balcony across the river, John McDermott was taking stock when the sudden sound of gunfire and yelling punctuated the still spring air. Luck had been on his side today and by the time the explosion ripped into the air he was fully prepared and loaded. It had taken seconds.

The bodies were moving through the rising smoke, but he could see two men and ahead his target Alice Parsotti. Behind that came a third man and some distance away the woman from the bank. He fired and the first man fell- hit.

Alice Parsotti had turned and was stationary, firing behind her now, and that split second of stillness gave him his chance.

❧

Pancardi felt a bullet smash through his collar-bone and as he fell his weapon was thrown from his hand. Alex Blondell was passing him now and he could see Alice ahead, she was still and taking aim; then suddenly she fell backward to the ground and blood exploded from her chest. The air was suddenly silent and all Pancardi could see were puffs of smoke as the weapons around him discharged. He could see cartridge cases eject and land on the stone – but the world was silent. Silent like a snowy morning in an ancient landscape. Everything was going slowly, his blood was pumping and all he could hear was his own heart beat and the crackle of his breath in the chill air. His hand was fumbling for the back up weapon and Ulyanov was firing behind him. Firing at Alice, at Blondell, at him; he could sense the bullets whizzing by in all directions.

Alex Blondell was there now, between Alice and the Russian. Pancardi saw him defend her as he regained his own balance. Ulyanov was hit and reaching for something, another clip – firing at Alex repeatedly.

Blondell was hit once, twice, three times, before Pancardi

could fire on the Russian. Alice was scrambling backward up stone steps like an inverted crab, firing, desperate to keep moving. Pancardi had his support .22 and was firing; he counted four, five and Ulyanov fell, the top of his head opening like a soft boiled breakfast egg. An unprimed grenade rolled from the Russian's hand and then both he and it became still.

Alice stumbled to her feet. Blood was pouring from her chest wound and she was looking at her father in disbelief. In the split second it took Pancardi to reach her, McDermott touched the trigger once again and the high velocity shot passed through Pancardi's hip shattering his pelvis; and he fell into the marble steps as shards of the same bullet passed through Alice. Her eyes opened wide and her mouth made to make a word which he could not discern.

To give a warning to anyone that might hear he yelled, "Sniper."

The third and final shot hit Alice as she lay on the ground. Her body bounced, thrashed and then...

~

As father and daughter collapsed in a crumpled heap together, John McDermott was already dismantling the weapon and placing the silencer, stock and barrel into the carrying case. He was smiling at his good fortune; he had been preparing for Good Friday but by chance he had been in the right place at the right time.

When Alaina Tropani arrived McDermott watched her confusion through the high powered telescopic sight. He could see blood and a chest wound in Parsotti as she rolled the old man off his daughter; and he watched the moment of death; the moment when the blood ceased to pump and the eyes ceased to see. Then quickly he placed the sight into his pocket and began his exit.

It was a ten minute walk to the main train station, and as he strolled he wondered how long it would be before they would work out where he had fired from. It did not matter he would be long gone.

Police cars buzzed and the mournful wail of ambulances stung his ears, but a smile grew on his face. Revenge had been delivered, cold and hard, and the scales of pitiless justice had finally tipped against Alice Parsotti – her luck had run out. The measure of wheat had been purchased, consumed, and now the cup was empty.

The bag containing the rifle would later be found abandoned on a train in Rome, and after a controlled explosion the contents discovered. Not a single mark or any forensic evidence would be present, John McDermott had seen to that.

Sandro Bichere tested every millimetre of the case and the item itself but nothing was discovered. It was his first and only taste of failure.

Alaina Tropani was turning Pancardi over, pulling him from on top of his daughter as Sandro Bichere arrived. Blood was bubbling from Pancardi's mouth and he was gasping for breath, arching his back as if he were stretching after a good nights sleep. His eyes were glazing and his hand gripped hers tightly.

"Don't you die on me," Alaina was screaming. "Giancarlo Pancardi don't you dare die on me."

Sandro Bichere was next to them pushing his jacket under the older man's head and simultaneously checking Alice Parsotti's pulse and shaking his head.

"Alice?" Pancardi blurted, followed by a deep cough of blood.

Alaina wondered if his lung was punctured, whether she should sit him up; cradle him to stop him drowning.

She was sitting behind him now, lifting his head to her chest, supporting him. Her arms were around him, under his armpits and across his chest and the dress she wore was sticking to her as his life oozed away. Tears were running down her face and she replayed the final seconds of what she saw like the final bars of a song.

"You have to stay alive," she whimpered into his ear, "I'm pregnant," she added, "I'm having your child. Don't you dare die on me."

"Alex?" Pancardi asked again, as his eyes closed and large gouts of blood appeared at his nostrils and his head slumped to the side. He was fighting to stay alive and losing.

Sandro Bichere was lower down the steps now, beside Blondell. He was feeling – feeling for a pulse as the paramedic teams arrived.

Armed Questura were on the steps checking the bushes.

Pancardi's eyes opened and he registered her presence. Looking at her, a smile broke across his lips as the medics arrived; a needle went into his arm and then his hand went limp and Alaina began to sob.

Chapter 38

The injured man sat by the window, his face was white and his eyes looked older, more sallow. His skin had lost some of the tautness of youth and the chin was beginning the slow descent into older age. There was a slump to his shoulders and the old fire in his personality had been staunched, as if he had been doused in pain and smothered with anguish. On his lap in the wheelchair lay The Times newspaper praising him as a hero and leading on the triumph of the new English Foreign Minister in Europe. The great Italian detective who had finally solved the case of the Romanov jewels on one hand, and the corrupt politician who was the toast of high society and a new thinking woman's pin-up, on the other. Underneath the newspaper was the thin file on Michael Cleverly, the file provided by Alexander Blondell's wife. Silently a tear fell onto the crisp paper as Pancardi's mind was thrown back to – what if?

Magdalene had sent the file to him when she had gone through his office. Alex had finally pieced the thing together. The links, the sub-plots, the internecine warfare which characterised the aristocracy of Europe and the sheer greed of those that wanted to depose them, sprang from the pages of Blondell's research. The whole thing stank and made Pancardi sick. Like some foul disease the pestilence ran through everything and everyone – the pestilence that was greed.

He could see it all clearly now, Angelo Massimo's grasping hand reaching for the dart. Pietro Grillva's mashed corpse which looked as if he had been thrown around inside a blender. He could see Roberto Calvetti in his imagination, the vivid red of his blood pumping from his chest as his legs thrashed in their dance of death; and finally the young Englishman who had been so courageous and yet so stupid in the same instant.

❧

At the doorway stood a red-haired woman with green eyes. She was in a dressing gown – her face was fresh and smiling, "How long are you going to sit there?" she asked.

"I was thinking," he replied.

"What about?"

"About Charlotte and Magdalene, more about Alex really. Why did the young fool have to do that? Look where it got him. It was all an awful foul mess and I created it. All those people dead, all that anguish and Charlotte, all alone without a father. I keep thinking it should have been me. Look at me. It's been over six months and I can hardly walk. In and out of hospital – worthless. What am I going to do?"

"Well the first thing I thought we could do is find a new place to live. I don't think I want to go back to Venice. Magdalene she says the hills above Palermo are nice, warm in the summer and a good place to recover and make a home. Somewhere near where they got married, somewhere you and I can heal. Somewhere you can be a father to Charlotte; you owe him that much."

"I still think you're mad." Pancardi smiled. "I'm a broken down cripple now – look at me."

"Please don't Carlo; I don't want her to hear." Then turning behind her she produced a squawking bundle wrapped in white linen; walking toward Pancardi she placed the baby in his arms. "I'd like to call her Alexandra," Alaina said, "Alexandra Alice Pancardi."

Pancardi pulled the covers back from the tiny face of a three day old infant and looked into her striking green eyes, "She's beautiful," he said, "like her mother. Absolutely beautiful. Look I think she's going to have red-hair too."

Alaina leant over her man and placed her left hand gently on his left shoulder. "I know you'll miss him," she said quietly, "but you have to move on. I want you out of that wheelchair. You need to take this little monster swimming and playing. She has to have a better start than Alice and she has to be the one decent thing we leave behind – our greatest achievement."

Another tear rolled down Pancardi's nose, "Your daughter is beautiful," he said.

"No," Alaina corrected, "our daughter is beautiful."

Suddenly there was a loud announcing bark, and in walked a small white dog. His movement was stiff and his eyes had the slightly glazed look of old age and some teeth had gone, but the feisty alpha male character was still there.

"Mostro!" Pancardi yelled, as the little white Bichon Frise jumped up at him. "Where did he come from?"

"He's telling you it's time," Alaina laughed. "Time to start again. We have all been damaged, him included, but look he is still fighting back. It is time for you too. Carlo you are the strongest man I have ever known; never have you taken the line of least resistance just for the sake of expediency," she paused, "don't start now." She took the infant and sat on the bed.

"She's absolutely right," said a voice from the doorway. It was Magdalene Blondell.

Pancardi became apologetic almost immediately, "I am so sorry," he said.

"It is my time to talk," she replied, "and your time to listen old man."

"I did everything I could," Pancardi continued undeterred, "but he just flung himself between and ..."

"I don't want to hear that," Magdalene snapped. "Alex did what he had to. Now you need to do what you have to. You know what to do, you have read the files. That man is an animal and there is no one left to take him down except you. If you fall down now at the last hurdle, I will never forgive you. Charlotte will never forgive you. When she is grown you can explain how finally they beat you down, crushed your spirit and let the murderers of her beautiful father get away."

Pancardi attempted to speak.

"Listen to me Giancarlo Pancardi," she barked, "while you sit here and wallow in self-pity and self-doubt that piece of slime is making a name for himself. That man had people killed. My husband was on to him – is now dead because of him. Are you prepared to let this go? If you do I shall kill him myself."

Alaina Pancardi cradled her infant in her arms, and placed her nipple to the child's mouth.

"Do you want those people to win?" Magdalene demanded. "Stand up and fight back."

"She's absolutely right," Alaina interjected.

"Mostro is old, he has lost his teeth, but he would continue to fight for you to his last breath," Magdalene said. "With Calvetti's wife, he grew soft and rested but he was not ready to die by the fire and neither are you. When I went there he jumped up and was ready. Ready to go to work again." Her voice was shaky, emotional, "Look at Angelo he was dying and he came, and Pietro too. You owe it to them; you owe them your loyalty and if you do not step on that worm who will? He must be destroyed utterly and discredited."

Mostro was now on the floor barking and Pancardi was standing. His face grimaced with pain but his feet were on the ground and the once shattered pelvis held him upright.

"Walk," Magdalene Blondell ordered. "Walk over to me and collect this." She produced an envelope and held it toward the detective in one hand; in the other she held the antique cane he had left behind in their Chelsea house, when the pair had rushed off to Venice.

"I don't think I can," Pancardi replied, and began to move as if he was going to sit again.

In a flash Mostro jumped into the seat of the wheelchair behind Pancardi and was barking loudly announcing to everyone that he was back, and that Pancardi was about to sit on him. It was as if he understood what the women were doing and was adding his persuasion to the chaotic mix.

"Fight back Carlo," Alaina added.

Pancardi took a step forward and reached for the bed frame. Then once steadied he took another and then another.

Magdalene gave him the cane to steady himself as she stepped to greet him with the open envelope. The message inside consisted of two pieces of card, between which was taped a needle bound with twine and faded purple flights. Next to it was a small photograph of a young Michael Cleverly; he was on a bed with an unknown nude woman. Written below the item in the familiar hand of Alex Blondell was one word – *Murderer,* and a date *25th April 1976.*

"You have to complete this puzzle," Magdalene Blondell pleaded. "You simply have to."